D0013061

B.J.
NEW YORK TIMES BESTSELLING AUTHOR
DANIELS

Under a
KILLER MOON

HQN

ISBN-13: 978-1-335-63989-9

Recycling programs
for this product may
not exist in your area.

Under a Killer Moon
Copyright © 2022 by Barbara Heinlein

Before Memories Fade
Copyright © 2022 by Barbara Heinlein

For questions and comments about the quality of this book,
please contact us at CustomerService@Harlequin.com.

HQN
22 Adelaide St. West, 41st Floor
Toronto, Ontario M5H 4E3, Canada
www.Harlequin.com

Printed and bound in Barcelona, Spain by CPI Black Print

CONTENTS

Many thanks to my longtime editor Denise Zaza
who is always there when I need her.

UNDER A KILLER MOON

PROLOGUE

JENNIFER "JEN" MULLEN used the dull children's scissors to cut out the article from the *Billings Gazette* about the 125th birthday celebration of her hometown. She'd started keeping a scrapbook of articles about Buckhorn after being committed to the state psych ward for the criminally insane.

She was told that she'd killed at least three men. If that were true, then the men had it coming. Her doctor said that wasn't a good excuse. She told him that she figured there were more men just asking for it as well. He told her they would discuss that during her next session.

Jennifer had smiled and thanked him. Dr. Moss was another reason she needed to get out of this place. He thought he could "fix" her like she was a broken doll. Even if she did need fixing, she didn't think it was possible. But thanks anyway, Doc.

The main reason she had to get out of here was that she'd left a few things undone in Buckhorn. People back there may have forgotten about her, but she hadn't forgotten about them.

Like her aunt Vivian Mullen. Was she worried about her favorite niece being in a place like this? There was no reason for concern. Most everyone here left her alone, which made her laugh. They all seemed a little afraid of her.

Using the glue with the attendant watching to make sure she didn't eat it, she pasted the article in her scrapbook. It gave her a sense of pride to see that her aunt was the organizer of the celebration, according to the article. That was so like Vi.

She tried not to let it bother her that her aunt hadn't come to visit. It wasn't like she wanted anyone from Buckhorn to see her here. A place like this would scare them.

She did, however, miss her best friend Shirley Langer and her cousin Tina Mullen, now Olson after marrying Lars. Tina always had such nice clothes and had been a good sport about letting her borrow them. The last time she saw her cousin, Tina had been so pregnant that she'd looked like she might pop. But that had been more than three years ago now.

For the first six months of her incarceration, Jen hadn't been allowed to have any phone calls from even a relative. That was so no one upset her, apparently. After the six months were over, the only person who'd taken her collect calls was Shirley. Her friend had left Buckhorn after getting her heart broken and was now working at a motel in Billings.

"Didn't I tell you to dump Lars Olson a long time ago?" Jen had said. "I always knew you could do better."

Shirley was the one who'd told her that her cousin Tina had given birth to a baby girl she'd named Chloe. Just recently, Shirley had told her, "Lars and Tina got married. They're expecting another baby."

"What is it with my cousin and babies," Jen had said, unable to hide her jealousy. She was missing so much here. She might have wanted a baby someday. But she'd never had any luck with men—unlike Tina. Maybe if she'd been born a redhead like her cousin... "Are you still blonde?" Shirley had told her that she'd gotten her hair cut short and gone blonde. "Do you have more fun?"

"You're not missing anything, trust me," her friend had said. They'd run out of things to say even before their time on the phone was up.

Jen finished gluing the last of the articles about Buckhorn's birthday into her scrapbook. The attendant took the scissors and paste, probably afraid of what she'd do with them if left to her own devices.

She reread the celebration article before the attendant remembered to come back to take her scrapbook for safekeeping. Jen figured Buckhorn's birthday party would draw a lot of people she knew with the carnival and the dance. There were some men she wouldn't mind seeing again. She thought of Marshal Leroy Baggins, the man who'd arrested her for the murders. Good-looking, but a little uptight. Not really her type. Still, she wouldn't mind seeing him again as long as he wasn't thinking he was going to haul her back here.

No, once she escaped from this place she wouldn't be returning, one way or the other. As she pretended to read the article yet again, she watched the comings and goings in the large communal room. She'd been so well-behaved that they let her hang out in the main lounge without an attendant standing over her. She'd been watching the way things worked around here for months as she'd planned her escape. Until now, she hadn't had a definite plan.

But thanks to her aunt Vi, she had a date and a destination. The 125th birthday celebration in Buckhorn was the perfect time to make her break and return home. She smiled as she thought of how people in her hometown would react if they knew that she'd be attending without guards or a straightjacket. There would be so much going on, she figured they wouldn't see her unless she wanted them to.

The attendant glanced in her direction, then came back

to take her scrapbook. A moment later, a guard stuck his head in and motioned that it was time to return to her cell. In the shatterproof mirror on the wall, she caught her reflection as she rose and headed for the door. She'd changed during her time in here thanks to the drugs they'd been giving her and the hours she'd had for reflection—at least that's what she let the doctor think. Dr. Moss liked the idea that he had been doing something to rehabilitate her.

"You're so young," he'd said. "This isn't the end of your story. We just need to get to the source of why you've done the things you have."

"Maybe I'm just evil."

He'd put on his serious face. "No. That's not true. Something triggered this behavior. I suspect it's something in your past. Once we know what that was…" He'd smiled and she'd smiled back at him, thinking he had no idea what he was talking about. "You're doing so well. So we'll keep digging, yes?" She'd nodded her agreement, even as she thought the man was a quack. But she liked making him happy because then he gave her more freedom.

With the Buckhorn celebration coming up, Jen thought of her image she'd seen reflected in the mirror. The hair that she'd sawed off with the dull children's scissors when she'd first arrived here had grown out. But it wouldn't hurt to change her appearance even more after she left here. She wanted to look her best when she went home.

It was all she could do not to break into a little dance. Look out Buckhorn. Surprise! *I'm coming home.*

CHAPTER ONE

IT WAS LATE by the time Marshal Leroy Baggins reached Buckhorn's new fairgrounds. Parking his patrol SUV in the lot, he stepped out and stood for a moment enjoying the quiet darkness. The air smelled of pine and the nearby creek and campfires. The scents marked the end of summer and the end to the busiest time of year for a lawman in Montana. Things would have been winding down—if not for Buckhorn's 125th birthday celebration.

He cursed softly under his breath and tried to enjoy this moment of peace and quiet before the festivities began tomorrow. The mountains all around town rose to meet the clouds that moved restlessly past on the breeze. Buckhorn was already filling up for the celebration. By tomorrow night, there would be nothing peaceful about this once large stretch of pasture on the edge of town.

The air would be heavy with the scents of cotton candy and corn dogs. Tinny carnival music would compete with the sounds of vendors hawking their wares and the shrieks of young and old on the noisy rides. The place was already busting at the seams. By tomorrow, traffic and parking would be a nightmare if even half the people Vi Mullen expected were to show up.

With the tourist season almost over, Vi would have single-handedly turned this quiet, small town in the middle of nowhere into a circus.

As he made a loop through the property, he could hear the murmur of voices and the crackle of campfires by the creek where the carnival crew and some of the vendors were camped. Deeper into the darkness, he passed still empty rows of temporary stalls constructed for retailers to sell everything from jewelry to homemade jams and jellies, wooden signs to antler lamps and paintings to pottery. Food trucks would soon be parked around the outside edge of the fairgrounds with the carnival rides and more booths in the middle. A bandstand and wooden floor had been erected at the back near the creek for nightly dances next to the beer garden. During the day, the raised dance floor would act as a stage, since he was sure Vi Mullen planned to make numerous appearances. The thought of her with a microphone made him shudder.

Leroy shook his head, reminding himself that the celebration was only for four days. Four very long days that would stretch his small force to breaking. That was one reason he'd wanted to stop by tonight, to walk around the fairgrounds before the crowds and noise and trouble got there. Law enforcement could always expect some trouble at crowded events. Pickpockets, con artists and crooks. There would be fistfights, rambunctious teenaged boys doing reckless things, and wailing lost little kids who'd been separated from their parents. On top of that, there would be a full moon by the last night of the event.

"It will be mayhem," the marshal had told Vi, pleading with her to keep the event small. When he'd realized she had no intention of doing that, he'd told her she would have to hire some private security to assist his force, which was too small and already stretched too thin with so much county to cover as it was.

"You worry too much, Marshal," Vi had said, after she'd

agreed to employ a private security team. "Everyone is going to have fun and talk about this for years to come."

"Fun," he'd said under his breath. She had no idea what she could be getting the town in for.

She'd tilted her head to eye him. Fifty-something with a cap of dark hair that could only come from a box, she was the matriarch of the town and she let everyone know it. "Don't be such a stick-in-the-mud. You make me wonder if you were ever young."

Leroy had looked down at his boots, knowing he should be insulted since he was still young—not even forty yet. "I just know what goes on at these types of events and the kind of law enforcement it takes to keep everyone safe. Traffic and parking alone will be a nightmare, not to mention housing all these people you think are going to come. I've already alerted the state highway patrol and county game wardens that they might be needed if things get out of hand."

Vi had laughed, shaking her head as she did. "It's no wonder you're still single."

He'd wanted to argue, but what would have been the point. She was right. He was all work and no play. It's how he'd become the marshal of this large county at such a young age. That, and, he suspected, no one else had wanted the job.

Breathing in the crisp night air, he shoved back his Stetson and tried to put Vi Mullen out of his mind as he walked. Buckhorn was already filling up fast. Trailers and campers and vendors' rigs were parked along the outside of the edge of the fairgrounds. Every accommodation in town was full including the makeshift campgrounds in ranchers' pastures and the new hotel on the east end of town. Leroy wasn't sure how Vi had gotten Casey Crenshaw James and her husband, Finnegan, to build the hotel—let alone to get it up and operating so quickly.

A sharp clang echoed in the air making him freeze. He could see nothing but shadowy darkness among the rides, but he sensed he wasn't alone. The extra security Vi had hired wouldn't be starting until tomorrow. It was one reason he'd wanted to check things out himself tonight.

Metal clanged again and a moment later he heard the rough grinding sound of an engine cranking up. He followed the noise toward the center of the fairgrounds and the skeletal black outline of the carnival rides etched against the dark sky. All the rides sat silent, unoccupied—except one. As he watched, the Ferris wheel began to turn to the shriek of tinny music.

For a moment, he thought the wheel had started up on its own since he hadn't seen another soul on the grounds. He'd read enough Stephen King books that it gave him a start—until he saw the man operating the ride in the darkness.

While the front gates were all locked and a chain-link fence surrounded the fairgrounds property, there were several large gates along the back and sides that might have been left open after some of the vendors had driven in earlier.

"What's going on?" he asked as he approached. The darkness around him felt complete since the waxing gibbous moon hadn't risen from behind the mountains yet. It seemed a strange time to be testing the equipment.

The operator, he saw on closer inspection, was somewhere in his teens and appeared embarrassed as if caught in the act of doing something he shouldn't have been. Seeing Leroy's uniform, he hurriedly stopped the Ferris wheel. The chairs rocked and creaked above them.

Leroy repeated his question.

Ducking his head, the teen shrugged and mumbled, "She wanted a ride."

She wanted a ride?

Leroy pulled his flashlight off his belt, snapped it on and shone the strong beam upward past all the empty chairs to the one still rocking at the very top and the figure now silhouetted against the dark sky.

As his light illuminated the figure wearing a dark hoodie, she ducked her head. He turned to the operator. "Get her down."

The teen quickly restarted the motor and the Ferris wheel began to move. Leroy stood waiting impatiently as the chair came slowly downward. The moment it reached the bottom, the teen shut down the engine.

The marshal had expected both the ride operator and the girl to take off at a run once she was on the ground. But it was only the teen operator who mumbled sorry as he hurried toward the carny camp on the river, leaving Leroy and the girl.

"The fun's over. Come on off there," he ordered in the ambient glow of his flashlight pointed downward so as not to blind her. He'd caught only a glimpse of her face under the hoodie.

"Killjoy," she said under her breath as she lazily pushed aside the barrier and stepped out of the chair to come down the short ramp toward him.

As if on cue, the nearly full moon peeked over the rim of the mountains, and he got his first real look at her—and his second shock of the night. Stopping a few feet from him, she threw back her hoodie and shook out a mass of dark curls that cascaded down around her shoulders. With a swiftness born of practice, she scooped up the long mane to pull it into a ponytail before she turned her attention to him.

He'd been expecting a teenager. Having worked one summer on the road with a carnival when he was young, Leroy remembered the young local girls flirting with him, trying to get free rides. He'd assumed that is what had happened here tonight.

But the woman standing before him in the moonlight appeared to be closer to his own age—mid to late thirties. She was slim, wore cutoff jean shorts below her sweatshirt, her long legs nicely muscled and tanned all the way down to the biker boots. No wonder he'd thought she was a teenager.

She was striking, from her wide green eyes to her high cheekbones and full lips, but what threw him off balance was the unflappable confidence she radiated. She'd just been caught by the local law and yet she didn't seem in the least bit concerned. Who was this woman and what was she doing here riding the Ferris wheel?

His shock must have shown on his face because she laughed, clearly finding his discomfort and confusion more amusing than he did.

"Marshal Baggins." She spoke the words with authority, her voice slightly husky, almost sexy. She didn't really think she could charm him, did she? Maybe she'd beguiled the Ferris wheel operator but he was just a teen. This wasn't Leroy's first rodeo. He wouldn't prove to be such a pushover.

Moonlight danced across her face as she closed the distance between them. "Everything I've heard about you is apparently true." She held out her hand. "TJ Walker, hired gun."

There was now a teasing sparkle in those eyes that said she was enjoying his discomfort. Not only had she caught him by surprise, he realized that she'd been watching him from her perch on the Ferris wheel.

Everything she'd heard about him? He took her hand

automatically. Her grip was strong, the skin cool even on this warm end-of-summer night, but not as cool as her demeanor. She seemed to know who he was, but he had no clue as to her. Frowning and caught even more off guard, he had only a moment to wonder how she knew anything about him since she clearly wasn't from around here.

"Hired gun?" he repeated with growing exasperation. Who was this cocky woman who'd probably only had to flash that smile of hers at that teenaged carnival operator to get him to start up the Ferris wheel for her?

"I'm here with my security team," she said. "We were hired by Vi Mullen on behalf of the town to make sure this event goes off without a hitch. I can assure you—"

"You're security?" He couldn't keep the astonishment out of his voice. "And you think this—" he waved his arm to take in the carnival ride "—is the best way to keep everyone safe?"

She chuckled. "I'm a sucker for a Ferris wheel, but I also like to check things out before everyone arrives. I like getting a feel for where I am, and it was a nice view from up there—until you shined your flashlight in my face and blinded me. It's a wonder I didn't fall."

She touched his bare arm with just the tips of her fingertips, but it was enough to make him react as if touched by a live current. She quickly drew her hand back, grinning as she said, "I'm kidding, Marshal. I was fine up there. You don't have to worry about me. I'm here to make your job easier."

He had his doubts about that, which must have been written all over his face.

"I've seen enough for tonight though. How about you?" she said and motioned toward the exit as a semi geared down at the edge of town. The two-lane strip of blacktop cut right through the heart of the small town, traveling past the new fairgrounds. The highway was the only way in—or out—of Buckhorn.

She removed her sweatshirt, exposing a pale green short-sleeved T-shirt beneath and a holstered weapon snug against her side.

"You have a permit to carry that?"

"Of course." She casually slung the sweatshirt over one shoulder. He could feel her gaze on him as they began to walk toward the exit. "I can see that you're not convinced about me and my team. Maybe if you meet us, discuss any reservations you have, we can convince you that we know what we're doing."

She didn't give him a chance to answer. "How about tomorrow morning?" she continued. "Breakfast at the café? I heard a woman named Bessie makes the best cinnamon rolls in this part of Montana."

Leroy felt as if he was on one of the wilder carnival rides. This woman threw him off-kilter in so many ways. He wasn't at all sure that she and her team could do the job. Which meant they would have to be replaced. He groaned inwardly. The celebration started tomorrow. How long would it take to get another security team—even if one could be found?

"Seven good for you, Marshal? You look like a man who likes to start the day early."

"Seven." He told himself that if her "team" was anything like her, he would be having a serious talk with Vi Mullen. Where had Vi found this woman? When he'd told Vi she'd have to provide private security, TJ Walker was definitely not what he had in mind. He hated to think what her crew was like.

As they reached the parking lot, he watched her head

for a large motorcycle sitting off to the side in shadow. He hadn't noticed it when he'd parked his patrol SUV earlier.

"See you in the morning, Marshal," she said over her shoulder. She was smiling as she stuffed the sweatshirt into a bag on the bike, pulled on a helmet and leather jacket and swung onto the seat. He couldn't help noticing her shapely, muscled, bronzed arms and long legs again as the engine rumbled to life and she took off in a cloud of dust, leaving him standing in the lot shaking his head.

He'd had more than misgivings when Vi Mullen had told him about her plans for Buckhorn's birthday. Now he felt as if the whole event was already out of control and it hadn't even officially started yet.

TJ ROARED DOWN the main drag of Buckhorn, Montana. She thought of the marshal, the man so full of indignation and authority in his Stetson and boots, and couldn't help smiling. The cowboy cop was just as uptight as she'd been told. A by the book lawman. What she hadn't realized was how young he would be or how attractive.

She could appreciate both—from a distance.

TJ had barely gotten her speed up on her bike when she had to shut it down again. The town ended at the new hotel out past the old-timey gas station. Buckhorn was the kind of town that had she blinked, she would have missed it. She was amazed that the burg had survived for a hundred and twenty-five years and even more astonished that it seemed to be growing. While in a beautiful setting in a narrow valley between two mountain ranges, the town was so far from anything, she wondered how people survived here.

She breathed in the sweet night air scented with pine. Buckhorn had its appeal, she had to admit. She liked being in the middle of nowhere with more cows than people. She liked that the town was tucked into the mountains, secluded and small enough that everyone knew their neighbors. It was a nice change from the big cities where they usually worked.

She'd done some checking on Leroy Baggins, whose nickname was, according to one of the other deputies, By the Book Baggins, no doubt for a good reason. She'd been anxious to meet him. Now that she had, she thought he fit right into this country. A born and raised Montanan, he knew his way around a gun and a horse. But when it came to women?

From what she'd heard no woman had ever put her brand on him. A few had tried to hog-tie him, but he'd slipped the loop. Was he just skittish when it came to women? Or had he never met anyone who could get past that stuffy reserve of his?

She smiled to herself remembering his surprise when he'd met her. She definitely hadn't been what he'd expected. She and the team would have to prove to him tomorrow that they were up for the job. She wasn't worried.

TJ was always curious about the law enforcement she'd be working with. Marshal Leroy Baggins intrigued her. She couldn't imagine how he could be any more fusty. She wondered what it would take to get him to loosen up. Not that she planned to find out.

As she swung into the parking lot of the recently completed Buckhorn Hotel, she told herself it was only for four days and then she'd be on to another job, another state, another hotel room. The nomadic life had chosen her almost four years ago, filling her with a restlessness, making her feel that she had something to prove to herself.

Her earlier adrenaline rush from the Ferris wheel ride—and the new job—was waning even with the fun of meeting the inscrutable marshal. She realized she was tired after a long drive across the state. Sometimes she wished that she took more time between jobs. As it was, she hated to fly, preferring to hop on her bike to the next job whenever she could. She liked the open road, that feeling of freedom—something else that had changed in her life not quite four years ago, she thought as she parked.

Yawning, she stretched and looked up at the amazing night sky overhead. So many stars against that midnight blue canvas. She hoped she didn't regret taking this gig. Only hours ago, she and her team had provided security at a private party of celebs at Big Sky. Just like the jobs, the two communities couldn't have been more different. Big Sky was more of an enclave for the wealthy while Buckhorn... It was as rural, isolated and antiquated as a place could get.

When the Buckhorn birthday party job had come up, she'd jumped at the opportunity since the team would already be in Montana and had the time. The celebration at the fairgrounds would definitely be a change of pace and who knew if they would ever get back to Montana again.

As she started through the hotel lobby, she caught the sound of laughter coming from the lounge and glanced in that direction. It was a typical hotel lounge, though smaller than most, with stools at the bar and a few booths off to the side.

But what caught her eye was the television screen at the end of the bar. The image of a man had appeared and disappeared so quickly that she wasn't even sure of what she'd seen. Just a flash of a man's face in profile.

Instantly, her stomach dropped, her pulse spiking, heart hammering. She felt that old sickening feeling before she reminded herself that she'd put the fear and shame and humiliation behind her. She wasn't that innocent young woman anymore. She was strong and capable, a woman to be reckoned with. Her life had completely changed after her encounter with him. Because of him. And she hadn't even gotten his name—something she later realized was the way he'd planned their meeting. He'd never wanted her to be able to find him.

He'd called himself Worth, but that had turned out either to be a lie or only part of his real name. He had definitely not been registered at the hotel under the last name Worth. It had been four years, but she hadn't forgotten the night she'd lost more than her innocence—or the man who'd taken it from her. She'd often wondered what she would do if she ever saw him again.

Walking into the hotel lounge, she saw that there were only two couples in a booth and one man on a barstool talking to the male bartender. "That man who was just on the TV," she asked the patron at the bar and the bartender. "Did you catch his name?"

The bartender looked startled. "Sorry, I wasn't paying any attention."

He glanced at the man he'd been visiting with, who said, "It was the local news, if that helps."

She nodded. "Thanks." As she walked away, she questioned whether it had been him. But a glimpse of the man's profile had brought back the trauma.

You're just tired, she told herself as she moved through the lobby, but she knew better. It had been him. She was sure of it. But if she was right, what was she going to do about it?

A part of her wanted to track him down. And do what? Just tell him off? No, she thought, she needed to concentrate on this job. Better if it wasn't him. Hadn't she been trying to put that night behind her for years now?

She texted her team to meet her in the conference room downstairs. They'd all opted to stay here in town at the hotel so they could be near the action and close to the job. TJ knew she would get plenty of "action" on the double shifts she planned to work during the four-day event. She didn't sleep that well anyway. Because of the long workdays she was glad to have a room so close by so she could at least try to grab a few hours' sleep.

By the time one woman and two men entered the room a few minutes later, TJ was back in full control, the glimpse of the man on the television forgotten. She'd hand-chosen her team for this because they were good at their jobs.

Lane came in behind the other two, closing the door behind him. Ash and Zinnia had already pulled up chairs on either side of her at the table. Lane joined them, all of them looking expectant since they hadn't planned to meet again until morning.

Lane and Ash were both surfer blond and scary strong. They were the muscle, but they were also supersmart. Zinnia, or Z as they called her, was deceptively sweet looking so more dangerous than a person suspected. She could open any locked door or device faster than anyone TJ had ever seen. She also didn't mind small spaces and, being petite in stature, could crawl through narrow openings when needed.

TJ had worked closely with all three of them and trusted them. That's why she'd chosen them for these particular jobs in Montana. They were in Buckhorn to protect not only people and property at the event, but also to see that the proceeds from admission were secure each day after the celebration closed down for the night.

"I met the marshal earlier," TJ said as they were all seated. "We're having breakfast with him in the morning at seven at the café downtown. He's a little concerned about whether or not we can handle security on this job."

Zinnia chuckled. "You want us to demonstrate?"

"I doubt it will come to that." She looked at each of them in turn, knowing each of their strengths. She'd worked with all of them, but this was the first time the four of them had worked together.

After this event, they would all be working other jobs for Walker Security Inc., across the country, each going his or her own way. TJ had her reasons for mixing it up. She didn't like any of them to get too comfortable with each other.

"This is an easy gig," she told them now. "Almost like the end of summer vacation." At least she hoped that was the case as she wished them all a good night.

Once in her room, she turned on the television, but the local news was over. If that had been the man she recognized earlier, she'd missed it. What would he have been doing on the local news anyway? She was in Buckhorn, Montana. It wasn't the end of the earth, but it felt that way.

She turned off the television and moved to the window, opened it and breathed in the cool night air. She could see the black outline of the mountains that bordered the town on two sides.

For some reason, as she looked out at the night, she thought about the marshal and wondered how deep his roots went in this county. She'd heard he was all lawman, a confirmed bachelor and an unflappable marshal. From what she'd seen, she could attest to that. It was that strong, stubborn jaw of his, she thought and smiled.

But what kept him here? The land, the lifestyle, the job? He was ambitious, the fact that he'd made marshal at such a young age proved that. It had to be more than the land and the job. Not a woman apparently.

Yawning, she closed the window and the curtains and got ready for bed. Tomorrow would be a big day. If she couldn't convince the marshal that she and her team knew what they were doing, they could be hitting the road.

While she didn't think that would happen, she had a feeling that she and Baggins had entirely different approaches to security—and life.

CHAPTER TWO

DAY ONE

VIVIAN "VI" MULLEN stood in the predawn dark of her general store simply reveling in what she'd accomplished. Today was the first day of Buckhorn's birthday celebration! She couldn't have been more excited. She just hoped that everyone who'd promised to attend would.

Taking deep breaths, she tried to relax. She loved this time of the morning before the town had yet to come alive. Well, as much as Buckhorn could come alive. She felt such a sense of ownership and not just because her family had helped found the town.

She'd put her heart and soul into Buckhorn over the years, but no more than she had recently by planning its one hundred and twenty-fifth birthday celebration. It was her baby, both the town and the event. And damned if she would let anything—or anyone—spoil it, especially her ex-husband.

Axel had sent a text that he would be attending the celebration and that they needed to talk. She'd signed the divorce papers he'd sent her and returned them to him, so what else was there to say? Since getting the text, she'd had a bad feeling she couldn't shake and realized she hadn't had confirmation that the papers had ever been filed.

She'd been surprised when Axel had agreed to walk

away with what he'd brought into the marriage—little more than the clothes on his back and what she considered severance pay. This store, the antique barn, the property, all of it had been in her family when he'd come into her life with his big talk and disarming smile.

Had he changed his mind and now he wanted more of a payoff?

That would be a mistake on his part, she thought as she clenched her fists at her sides. If he knew her at all, he should be smarter than that.

Her cell phone rang, making her start. Because she'd been thinking about him, she thought it would be him. Axel hadn't said when he would be arriving. With the celebration starting today, she assumed it would be soon.

But as she checked her phone, she saw with relief that it wasn't him. What had she been thinking? He never rose this early in the morning unless forced to.

Her relief was short-lived as she saw though that the call was from the mental facility where her niece Jennifer was being held. "Now what?" she said under her breath and quickly declined the call. Whatever trouble Jen was in would have to wait. Vi couldn't deal with it right now. She had a birthday celebration to worry about. Everything had to go just as she'd planned it. Her reputation was at stake.

Her thoughts returned to Axel against her will—and that first day he'd hit town. Cocky and cool, he'd walked into the store and flashed that smile at her. She'd been easy prey—a plain Jane who'd never been more than a hundred miles from Buckhorn her whole life, all eighteen years of it.

Behind the counter, she hadn't been able to take her eyes off him. He carried a backpack plastered with patches from all the places he'd visited. She'd been transfixed by this older, worldly man who'd made her heart pound when he told her she was sexy.

Vi shook her head at the memory, thinking no one could have been as gullible as she had. She'd fallen for his adventure stories hook, line and sinker, as her father used to say. The next thing she knew she was pregnant and getting married before the justice of the peace over in Lewistown after her father threatened to kill Axel if he even thought about hitchhiking out of town.

And now he was coming back to Buckhorn to see her after he'd run out on her when she'd needed him the most— and after more than thirty years of marriage. Hadn't she always known what kind of man he was? So why had signing the divorce papers been so hard? Why was the thought of seeing him again making her stomach fill with butterflies and her heart ache?

Her cell phone rang again dragging her out of her thoughts. She wiped her eyes of tears she hadn't realized she'd shed and checked the screen. Whatever Jennifer had done this time, it must be worse than the other times when she'd chopped off her hair with a pair of kiddie scissors or attacked one of the other patients for looking sideways at her.

Vi sighed and again declined the call, ignoring the earlier voicemail. If they called again before the celebration was over, she would block the number, she told herself as she pocketed her phone.

Nothing was going to spoil this momentous event for her. Not Axel, not her murdering niece. Not even her own vengeful nature, since last night she'd dreamed that she pushed her longtime archenemy, Karla Parson, off the Ferris wheel. Vi couldn't help but smile at the memory.

She checked her watch. She needed to get things squared

away at her store so she could be on hand when the event started. She wasn't about to miss this, her crowning glory—if nothing spoiled it, she reminded herself.

THE MARSHAL HAD no idea what to expect as he pushed open the door to the café at six forty-five that morning. After meeting TJ Walker, he was expecting the worst. The café was busy already this morning with the extra visitors in town. He'd wondered how Vi planned to get all these people housed and fed and how he had any hope of keeping the peace.

So far, Vi seemed to have pulled off a miracle. She'd gotten Casey Crenshaw's husband, Finn, to not only build a hotel in record time but also offer a breakfast buffet. She'd also helped Dave Tanner and his fiancée, Melissa Herbert, to add a steak house behind the bar. She'd even talked area ranchers into offering pasture for campers and gotten vendors from all over the northwest to bring in a wide assortment of "fair food" and products to sell.

He had to hand it to Vi, it appeared that she was going to pull this off. But he couldn't imagine how he and his deputies would be able to handle the traffic. Buckhorn had one main highway—right through the center of the small town. Parking would also be a nightmare even with a large open field for the overflow. All that aside, he and his deputies would also need to make sure no one got robbed, assaulted or, worse, killed. With his limited officers, he had all trained law enforcement from game wardens to state highway patrol officers ready should there be any major problems. Not that it relieved his mind, since if needed, it would take time to reach Buckhorn because of its isolated location and Leroy knew that just about anything could happen in the next four days.

To his surprise, TJ and her team were already sitting at one of the large circular booths. Punctual, well, that was something anyway. She grinned and motioned him over as if reading his mind and finding his thoughts amusing.

If anything, TJ Walker looked even more striking in daylight. She also looked as relaxed as she had when she'd stepped off that Ferris wheel last night.

Taking a breath, he told himself to be diplomatic. He would meet the rest of the team, then he'd go see Vi and tell her to hire some real security.

But as he neared the table, he took in the two young men sitting there. Both appeared clean-cut and in obvious good shape. TJ did the introductions, going around the table. Lane Frederickson, Ashley Connors and Zinnia "Z" Southwick. Each had a strong handshake, each looked him in the eye and had a professional air about them. Like their apparent leader, they exuded confidence.

After he took a seat, the waitress came to take their orders. He opted for his usual, chicken-fried steak and eggs, and listened as each offered their background in the security business. He was impressed since they weren't as young or as inexperienced as he'd expected—TJ included. Leroy found himself changing his opinion.

He could tell that TJ didn't like having her team or herself doubted. He felt her watching him. No, that wasn't exactly right. Not watching, studying him, appraising him. He'd thought he was evaluating the team except as they began to question him about his career while they waited for their meals, he realized he had always been the one under interrogation.

"Aren't you young to be a marshal?" Z asked. She was pretty with wide brown eyes. While small in stature, she came off as highly competent.

"I was just in the right place at the right time when the former marshal retired," he said. "Thirty-eight isn't that young for a marshal around these parts."

Their breakfasts came and they ate, talking and laughing as they questioned him about his job and Buckhorn. He was happy to answer their questions since most dealt with the security job they would be doing over the next four days.

They discussed traffic and parking problems, emergencies that might come up. He explained that they had an ambulance and EMTs on scene. As for law officials, he would have several deputies on hand. He explained that being an hour away from the nearest other towns—and none of them large—would mean calling on the state highway patrol and even game wardens if there was any real trouble.

"So do we meet your expectations?" TJ asked after they'd finished breakfast and the others had gone back to their hotel rooms to get ready for their shifts at the fairgrounds.

He realized that she'd known how he'd felt about her and her team before breakfast. Now he wanted to ask her if he'd measured up as well. Not that he still didn't want to know more about TJ and her team. "They seem like a good group, although Zinnia…" He wasn't sure how to put it.

"Z can hold her own. She looks meek and mild enough, but that's part of her strength. People tend to underestimate her."

He met TJ's direct emerald gaze and realized people probably made the same mistake with her as he had when they first met. Last night in the moonlight, her eyes had been dark as a bottomless sea. This morning they were luminous. There was intelligence there. But also challenge. He had the feeling that she'd fought her way back from something. She didn't exactly have a chip on her shoulder, but there was something unresolved there.

"How did you get into this business?" he asked, more curious about her than he wanted to admit. There was more to this woman than any he'd encountered in a long time.

She smiled at that, cocking her head as she met his gaze. "I like a challenge and I don't mind the risk."

He'd already figured that out. He thought about her rocking up on the top of the Ferris wheel last night. "You like danger and defying the odds. That sounds…reckless."

"You think I got into this for the thrills and chills?" She shook her head. "I don't have a death wish, Marshal. I'm just confident that I can do my job and so can my team. You have nothing to worry about."

He huffed at that. "There is always something to worry about." But his words held no sting. They both knew that she and her team had passed the test if for no other reason than it would be next to impossible to get in another team at this late date.

But as he dragged his gaze away from hers, his instincts told him that he'd be smart to keep a close eye on her. He lived by his instincts.

"I appreciate you trusting me and my team," she said as they were leaving the café. While her tone betrayed nothing of her thoughts, the questioning look he caught in her eyes did.

He felt a start. Was she really wondering if she could trust him? As disturbing as the thought was, TJ would be keeping a close eye on him as well. That alone should have warned him that he was in for the wildest and most dangerous four days of his life.

CHAPTER THREE

ONCE OUT IN his patrol SUV, Leroy ran the names of the security team. No red flags came up. He'd run a search on TJ Walker's name last night. Real name Terrapin Juniper Walker had him curious about the parents who'd named her. He could understand why she'd decided to go by TJ.

She'd started Walker Security Inc. only three and a half years ago, but had built a reputation for herself quickly. Before that... He frowned. She'd been an elementary school teacher. Really? Four years ago—after receiving some kind of Teacher of the Year award—she'd quit. A few months later she attended the police academy before starting her security business.

That seemed like an odd trajectory, one he questioned. What did it really matter though? It didn't worry him like the fact that he could find out little else about her. No personal social media. No photos of her anywhere he could discover. He found that even more unusual in this day and age, and then reminded himself that he wasn't really out there either. But there were photographs of him on the internet because of his job. How had TJ Walker managed to avoid that, he wondered.

While he could find nothing objectionable, what he did find did little to relieve his concern—or interest. There was just something about her... He tried to tell himself that it was this celebration and TJ and her security team that had him on edge as he walked down to the general store.

Still closed, he went around to the alley entrance, knowing Vi always came in early and usually left the door unlocked. Just as he suspected, he found Vi behind the counter giving orders to two young workers.

"Could I have a word in private?" he asked Vi.

She ordered the teenaged clerks to get everything ready because it was almost time to open the front door. From her pained expression he could tell that she resented the interruption as she led him back to her office. She'd been busy planning this event for months and hadn't wanted or seemed to need any input from anyone. This had a lot of the locals' feathers ruffled. Leroy knew his inquiry wasn't going to go over well either.

"Just a quick question—how did you find the security team you hired?" he asked.

Vi frowned for a moment looking confused. This was clearly not what she'd been expecting. "I used my browser and did a search. They came highly recommended. Also they were going to be in Montana at Big Sky covering some exclusive celebrity function before this." She shrugged. "Why?"

"Just curious how you found them."

Irritation showed in her frown and rock-hard glare. "Just *curious*? You do realize that I'm extremely busy and anxious to get to the fairgrounds before the gates open for the celebration and with—"

"I won't keep you then," he interrupted and started to leave.

"Wait. Is something wrong with the security team I hired on behalf of the town?"

He turned to look at Vi. "You've met them, right?" Immediately, he saw that she hadn't.

Her chin went up in defiance, lips pursed, eyes hardening. "They come *highly* recommended. I'm sure they're fine and you're just being you, Leroy Baggins."

Leroy nodded, hoping she was right as he returned to the fairgrounds.

THE FAIRGROUNDS HAD become a beehive of activity by the time TJ arrived. Vendors were preparing to open at ten as planned. Others were setting up, still others were busy bringing in equipment and supplies for the throngs of people expected to attend.

She found herself taking in the sights and smells as she moved through the growing groups of people already milling around even though the gates wouldn't open for another hour. This morning she'd caught the news once again, but there had been no sighting of the man she'd thought she'd seen the day before. She seldom second-guessed herself anymore and refused to now.

TJ found each member of her team to discuss how best to patrol the fairgrounds. Z pointed out some problems she saw with the spaces between the vendors—especially at night because of the lack of lighting. Ash was more worried about the open area behind the temporary stage and dance floor with all the pine trees and the creek. Lane thought most of their problems would be near the beer garden and carnival rides and one of the deputies had assured him that they would be patrolling that area. They discussed the best way to provide security in those areas and then split up.

She'd seen the marshal only in passing. He'd tipped his Stetson to her, his blue eyes hooded as he'd kept walking. He was so darned handsome she'd seen the way women did a double take when he passed. He seemed to take the attention in his stride, ignoring it.

She thought about the way he was around her and smiled to herself. She couldn't help finding it humorous that she made him uncomfortable. He was just so damned uptight. Was there a passionate cowboy under that Stetson? She liked to think there was.

Or maybe with Leroy Baggins, he was as stoic as he appeared in all aspects of his life. She recalled Vi Mullen had told her on the phone, when asked about law enforcement in the area, that the marshal was dull as dirt.

Still, TJ couldn't help being curious about him. She knew there had to have been women in his life—at least temporarily. Hadn't at least one of them lit that fire in him—if there was anything smoldering in him? If there was, he kept it well contained.

She knew that she was probably focusing on the marshal rather than worrying about the man she'd thought she'd seen on the local news last night. Four years ago she'd been so traumatized that she'd never wanted to see him again.

But that was before she took control of her life, before she'd changed from that woman to the one she was now. Since then, she'd told herself that if their paths ever crossed again, she would confront him. It wouldn't be justice, but it would be closure to call him out on what he'd done to her.

She shoved that thought off, remembering how the man had lied about everything, including his name—which had made it impossible to find him and in hindsight, she now knew why. He'd had her at a disadvantage in more than one way. He'd already known her name because it was printed on the award she'd won the night they met.

He'd introduced himself as Worth. "First name or last?" she'd asked.

Flashing her that perfectly straight-toothed broad white smile, he'd said, "Just Worth."

LEROY RECEIVED THE call about Jennifer Mullen forty-eight hours after she'd gone missing. He'd missed the call on his radio because he'd been canvasing the fairgrounds. Now he wondered if her aunt Vi had been notified and if so, why Vi hadn't mentioned something that important when he'd seen her this morning.

He swore, knowing he would have to stop by and find out. Vi needed to know—if she didn't already. Hell, the whole town needed to know. Jennifer was dangerous and he suspected that having escaped, she might be headed this way—probably for this darned celebration.

Leroy had met Jennifer years ago now when he'd arrested her for three murders and suspicion of a fourth. He thought of that moment when he'd begun to read her rights. "You have the right to remain silent—"

"That's hilarious, Marshal," she'd interrupted. "I've never been silent in my life."

He recalled the look in her eyes that had haunted him since that day. After he'd finished reading her rights, she'd simply looked at him as if waiting for him to tell her she could go. Her eyes were wide and bottomless, wounded and painfully trusting. Even as he'd cuffed her, he'd had trouble believing—against overwhelming evidence—that she'd done these crimes. She just didn't look like a woman who'd murdered anyone.

He'd had little experience when it came to murder although he'd been with the former marshal when he'd responded to the first murder at the Crenshaw Hotel back when he was still wet behind the ears. That murder hadn't been solved—until the day he'd arrested Jennifer.

Now she was on the loose. He had no illusions. She would kill again. She'd felt justified in what she'd done. He doubted that she felt any guilt and if headed for Buckhorn, he figured she had enough grudges built up over the years here that half the townspeople should be worried.

The problem was how to find her and stop her before she got the opportunity to kill again. He wondered if her victims had looked into those eyes, seen all that innocence, and that's why they were now dead. He figured it was how she'd gotten close enough to kill grown men twice her size.

Her victims didn't see what was behind that wounded innocent look—until it was too late. That's why he had to alert his men and the private security team. Something told him that TJ, in particular, wouldn't be fooled by Jennifer.

But first, he had to warn Jennifer's aunt and cousin. He hoped he was wrong, but Vi and Tina could be the most vulnerable if Jennifer was on her way to Buckhorn.

TINA MULLEN OLSON finished brushing her daughter's hair before she looked past Chloe into the vanity mirror where the little girl sat. "She has your beautiful red hair," people always said. "She's just the spitting image of you."

No one mentioned that neither of Tina's parents, Axel and Vi, had red hair. Nor did they question her husband Lars's contribution to their daughter's genes. Buckhorn was a small enough town so anyone who cared already knew Lars wasn't Chloe's biological father. There was no sign of the man who'd impregnated her—not in Chloe, not on the horizon, and Tina was glad of that. It had been a one-night stand that she'd regretted and had put behind her. In the past more than three years, she'd quit looking over her shoulder. Chloe was all hers—and Lars's. He was born to be a father. Chloe adored him and so did Tina.

Her cell phone rang.

"Mommy?" Her daughter met her blue eyes in the mirror and smiled as her phone rang again. She saw it was the marshal and probably something to do with her mother. She swiped left letting the call go to voicemail.

"What is it, sweetheart," she said to her daughter.

"Make me pretty too," Chloe said and pointed to Tina's makeup.

Tina felt that rush of emotion, love so strong it made her chest ache. She put down the brush and hugged the toddler, hiding the tears that blurred her vision. They were tears of happiness, of love, of an almost unbearable gratitude that things had turned out so well. They were also from the pregnancy hormones.

Lars was now her husband and they were expecting a child of their own. Not that Lars had ever thought of Chloe as anything other than his daughter. Tina often wondered how she'd gotten so lucky.

Yet there was always that worry that something or someone would destroy it. That the man she'd had the one-night stand with would find her and demand his daughter. Or that Lars's old flame Shirley would come back and steal him away. She was most afraid she'd lose this baby she was carrying because she didn't deserve to be this happy.

"That is the most ridiculous thing I've ever heard," Vi told her when Tina had confessed how she felt to her mother. "I don't want to hear that kind of foolishness ever again. Can't you just be happy?" Vi had stormed off tsking over her shoulder.

Her friend Amelia had been more understanding. "It just seems too good to be true, right?" Nodding, she continued, "I feel the same way sometimes. Like I'm waiting for the other shoe to drop."

That was exactly it.

So when Earl Ray Caulfield had called to invite her and Chloe to breakfast this morning at the café, Tina had heard something in his voice that both scared—and worried—her.

"Maybe just a little blush," she said to her daughter, putting on just enough to make Chloe smile.

"Ready to go eat?" she asked. Her daughter loved going to the café where Earl Ray's wife, Bessie, gushed over her, bringing her special pancakes that looked like some of her favorite animals.

Chloe raced to the door, more anxious than Tina.

"I NEED YOU to handle this Buckhorn problem," Governor Jamie Jacobsen said from his desk in the state capital in Helena, Montana. "Worth? Stop looking for a hookup and pay attention."

From the chair across the desk, Prescott Rutherford Hollingsworth III, or Worth as his friends called him, looked up in surprise. Jamie knew him too well since they'd met as boys at boarding school.

Now, as the governor's aide, his advisor, his right-hand man and old friend, he was at Jamie's beck and call. Most of the time, that was great since he thought Jamie Jacobsen was headed for the White House and Worth was more than ready to make that trip with him.

He set his phone aside. "Buckhorn?" That's all he'd caught of the conversation.

"I need you to deal with this woman who keeps calling determined that I make an appearance at her town's birthday celebration this weekend. I've put her off as long as I can. I need to give her an answer."

"Where is this place?"

"East some distance from the middle of the state," Jamie said as he concentrated on the pile of mail spread on his huge desk.

"Sounds like the middle of nowhere," he commented.

"Admittedly, it's part of the state that I've pretty much ignored, which is reason enough to go. I don't have anything conflicting on the calendar. Could be good PR."

"Sounds like a waste of your time," Worth said.

But the governor continued as if he hadn't heard him. "Drive down there tomorrow and check it out."

"Seriously?" Worth echoed. "How far is it?"

"Three or four hours one way." The state was so large and had so few highways crisscrossing it, that driving distance was figured in hours rather than miles. "You can always go today, spend the night, have a look around."

Worth looked at the time. He had a date tonight he'd been looking forward to. "I kind of have plans tonight and tomorrow."

The governor pulled a folded piece of paper from an envelope. He glanced at it before saying, "Reschedule your date. I think the woman ramrodding this celebration told me that there's a new hotel in town. If it hasn't opened yet, there's a motel."

"I can't reschedule the date. Her husband's coming home tomorrow night."

Jamie finally looked up at him. "I need you to do this. Sorry about your *romantic* plans, but there will be other women. There always are." The governor began searching his desk. "Where in the hell's my phone?"

Worth spotted a corner of the phone peeking out from under the papers piled on Jamie's desk and reached over to pull it free. He laid it down a little too hard in front of the governor.

"I really think you should rethink Buckhorn," Worth said. "I mean, there can't be that many votes to worry about in that whole area. I can send this woman a signed photo of you and maybe a couple of our campaign flags."

The governor looked up again. "You know I can't ignore these small rural areas. These people put me in this office. I'm not any more excited about it than you are, but this woman who set it all up, well, she is apparently one of my big supporters." He rubbed two fingers together to indicate money. "So take care of it. If it's a go, I'll even keep my speech short at the closing ceremony and we'll call it good."

Worth swore under his breath as he glanced at the state map on the wall and saw where he was headed. Seriously, it really was the middle of nowhere.

Jamie, he noticed, had picked up an envelope in a plastic bag from his desk. "Another death threat," his friend said quickly dismissing it. He had a stack of them from some disgruntled voter.

The door opened and the governor's secretary announced that Jamie was going to be late for his meeting. She gave Worth one of her side-eyes as if he didn't do anything around here to help.

Worth ignored her since he was no fan of hers either. Trying one more time to get Jamie to change his mind, he said, "So if I go to Buckhorn tomorrow and I still think this is a bad idea, we'll come up with an excuse to cancel your speech there, agreed?"

"You got it," Jamie said with a playful slap on his friend's shoulder as he handed him a sticky note. "But you'll have to convince me with more than you might miss a...*date*."

After Jamie left, Worth stood in the man's office dreading a trip across the state. It would be a long, boring drive, he thought looking down at the sticky note in his hand. Vi Mullen. There was a number written after her name in Phyllis-precise handwriting.

He sighed. No matter how long it took, he wasn't spending the night in Buckhorn. He'd drive down in the morning and back tomorrow. Maybe the husband's flight would get delayed. Even if it was late, he could wake her up. Maybe he'd surprise her if her husband's car wasn't in the drive. He smiled to himself liking that idea of finding her half asleep and half naked.

That thought cheered him. Also, he knew he couldn't say no to Jamie. He had to do whatever the governor asked. It was his job, although there were times he resented it given the way they'd met in boarding school. There'd been an incident. Worth had covered for Jamie, saved his ass actually, and he'd never let Jamie forget it. Which is why Jamie had offered him the job when Worth had seen that his old friend had gotten into politics. "Dirty business," Worth had said. "You'll need me to keep you out of trouble."

Worth did his best. A married man, Jamie was a serial cheater. Worth covered for him and was good at keeping secrets. Also he was smart enough to know that the luckiest thing that had ever happened to him, other than being born into a wealthy, privileged family, was meeting Jamie Jacobsen. Worth was protected in a way that other people couldn't even imagine, and his future was gold.

CHAPTER FOUR

TINA WAS EVEN more worried about this breakfast when she found Earl Ray waiting for her and Chloe as she walked into the café. He looked nervous as he got to his feet, always the gentleman. His hair was more salt than pepper and the lines on his face deeper, especially the laugh lines around his blue eyes. Tina knew, like everyone else in town, that Earl Ray was a war hero, but he meant much more than that to the community. He was the person everyone in Buckhorn depended on. He was the man you called when you needed help.

His wife, Bessie, greeted them from the kitchen in the back. Tina put down Chloe, who ran back to see Bessie, leaving Tina to make her way alone to the booth where Earl Ray waited.

Earl Ray had never invited her to breakfast before, but over the past year she'd often caught him watching her. He'd made a point of encouraging her to continue pursuing a career in photography after she'd shot her first wedding for local couple Jasper and Darby Cole.

"You have talent," Earl Ray had said, and a week later, he'd sent her a telephoto lens that he'd said he never used. It had looked brand-new. She'd later taken photos of him and Bessie as a thank-you. He'd had the print framed and hung it on their living room wall.

She'd told herself that Earl Ray took an interest in all

Buckhorn residents and that she shouldn't read anything into it. Just like this breakfast. But still she was having trouble catching her breath right now. She could hear Chloe's excited voice coming from the kitchen as she sat down in the booth across from Earl Ray and tried to convince herself everything was fine.

"How are you this beautiful morning?" the older man asked pleasantly.

Tina couldn't bear sitting here talking about the weather. "Tell me what I'm doing here," she said, her voice breaking.

He looked surprised, but only for a moment before he cleared his voice. His eyes seemed to mist over for a moment. "You're right, there's something I need to tell you." He stopped and cleared his voice again. "It's about your mother."

Her thoughts were racing wildly around in circles. She'd been right. Something was wrong. But it involved her *mother*? For a moment, she was relieved. This was about Vi and probably Buckhorn's birthday celebration. Her mother had been so anxious about everything being perfect that most people in town were afraid to offer an option or even ask a question about the celebration—let alone complain. Some had come to Tina to ask her to talk to Vi on their behalf because they didn't feel their voices were being heard.

But she hadn't expected Earl Ray to be one of them. He wasn't afraid of her mother. He...

"I'm your father."

She realized he'd just said… What? It took her a moment to make sense of his words since what he'd spoken was the last thing she'd expected.

"There is no easy way to say this." His expression was

so worried, his gaze so searching, she felt her heart drop. And then he repeated his statement again. "I'm your father."

The sounds of the busy café became a roar in her ears. Tina felt light-headed. It was as if he'd kicked her feet out from under her. She gripped the edge of the table, turning to look toward the kitchen, suddenly worried about Chloe. She started at the warm touch of Earl Ray's hand on hers.

He reached across the table and covered her other hand as if he knew how she was feeling. His hands were large, slightly callused and yet his touch soothing. "I know this comes as a shock. I've debated for months how to tell you."

Months? She stared at him. She'd known this man her entire life. She trusted him with her life. Most everyone did. She pulled her hands back, shaking her head, unable to imagine him with her mother. It couldn't be true. She saw the hurt in his expression, but she couldn't stop herself.

"You and Vi?" The words came out sounding as disbelieving as she felt.

"No," he said quickly, drawing his hands back. "It wasn't like that." He must have seen how betrayed she felt, for herself, for her father. Or at least Axel, the man she'd always believed to be her father. Earl Ray leaned forward and dropped his voice. "Please, let me explain. Your mother gave birth the same night as my late wife, Tory."

"Tory?" Tina knew that Earl Ray and his wife, Victoria, had never had children. She'd never heard anyone mention that Tory had been pregnant.

"It's an involved story, but your mother's infant didn't survive. Tory's did. The babies were switched by the county nurse without your mother knowing it. I only found out when the former county nurse's journal surfaced." Earl Ray paused as if waiting for her to say something.

Tina opened her mouth, but no words came out. She closed it and pressed her lips together tight.

"I've tried so many times to tell you but…" He looked lost.

She'd never seen him like this. Nervous, worried, upset that he'd troubled her. She'd seen him worried a few times when problems had come to town, and maybe even scared, but not like this. "Victoria? Tory, your wife, had a baby?"

He nodded, sadness and an even deeper darkness in his eyes. "She didn't want children. I did. Apparently, that's why I never knew she was pregnant until I read about it in the county nurse's journal that only recently turned up."

The realization hit her hard. How many times had she seen her mother staring at her in the same mirror she'd stared at Chloe in only this morning with that question in her eyes? Where had that red hair come from? No one in Vi's family or Axel's had red hair like hers. "My red hair." Chloe's red hair. The two of them had gotten it from Tory, who had the most beautiful red hair, according to people who had known her.

"I didn't mean to upset you," Earl Ray said, sounding so regretful that Tina came out of her thoughts and reached over to take one of his hands in both of hers.

"I'm not upset." It wasn't exactly a lie. "I'm just…" *Shocked, overwhelmed, shaken to my core.* "I never suspected." She shook her head because she had wondered, maybe even suspected. "You've answered a lot of questions I've had for a very long time." She met his gaze. "But I couldn't possibly be upset to know that you're my biological father." She took a breath. Her whole body seemed to be trembling. "Does Bessie know?" she asked of his wife visiting with Chloe in the kitchen. He nodded. Her voice broke when she voiced her worst fear. "The rest of the town too?"

He hurriedly shook his head. "Only a handful of people know. I gave you the abbreviated version of what happened. You're welcome to read the whole story about that night in the journal Thelma Rose left. I have it at the house."

She nodded, still in shock, but slowly coming out of it. As impossible as it sounded, she knew Earl Ray would never lie about something like this. She knew it was true because she and Vi had often wondered why they were so different, not even to mention that they looked nothing alike. Vi wasn't her mother. All the times an angry Vi had said, "I can hardly believe we're mother and daughter," it had been true. They were different for a good reason.

"You're sure?" she asked.

He nodded. "I had to verify it first through DNA tests before I said anything to you. It's true."

"Everything okay?"

Leroy disconnected from his call about Jennifer's escape and turned to find TJ standing beside him. He hadn't heard her approach. He'd been too lost in his thoughts. "Just thinking about what a victim saw in his killer's eyes before he died."

"Pleasant thought."

He mentally shook himself. "Sorry, I was going to come find you. Jennifer Mullen. She's a local woman, early thirties. She's escaped from the mental institution where she was being held for the criminally insane. If she's heard about Buckhorn's birthday celebration, then I suspect she's headed this way. She's already killed three men and is suspected of murdering another. I wouldn't be surprised if she had a few more scores she'll want to settle while in town."

TJ raised a brow. "Anyone special?"

"I was just going to warn her family before I looked for you."

"Her family?" TJ asked.

"Vi Mullen is her aunt. Tina Mullen Olson is her cousin. I figure she'll contact them. We just have to find her before she gets into trouble."

"I suppose if she's determined to come back to Buckhorn, during the birthday celebration is the best time," TJ said. "The crowds will give her good cover."

"Plus it will bring back former residents, many Jennifer would know. Apparently, she holds grudges."

"Don't we all," TJ said.

"Not the way Jennifer does," he said and sighed as he watched carload after carload arriving in Buckhorn. All morning, vendors had been pulling in and setting up. The air was already ripe with the scent of hot grease when he pulled into the parking area designated for security and saw TJ's motorcycle already there.

He glanced over at her again. He hated the thought of Jennifer Mullen on the loose. Worse, she'd be a wild card in the middle of all the people attending the celebration just as TJ had said. Given the timing, he suspected it was no coincidence that she'd escaped now. Obviously, those in charge of keeping her locked up had underestimated her determination. Leroy had no intention of doing the same. He knew how smart Jennifer was—and how deadly.

"I'll get a photo of Jennifer that you can distribute among your team. Please warn them that Jennifer is a violent woman who looks just the opposite. I want her taken into custody as quietly and carefully as possible. There's a good chance that she could be armed by now. Either way, she is definitely dangerous."

"Just text it to me." She'd given him her phone number

as well as contact information for everyone on her team this morning at breakfast. He noticed the small grease-stained bag she was holding at her side. It had a donut logo on it. She saw him looking and laughed as she raised it. "It's a weakness," she said guiltily and licked sugar and cinnamon off her fingers. She flashed another heart-thudding smile as she held out the bag. "Can I tempt you, Marshal?"

He had the feeling that she wasn't talking about donuts. As tempted as he was in ways that surprised him, he shook his head.

She pulled a cruller from the bag. It smelled as if it was still warm. He'd seen a donut truck and now he realized why the scent of grease and dough and sugar and cinnamon was so strong.

From the expression on her face as she took a bite, the confection must be delicious. She grinned as she finished eating it, crumpled the bag and lobbed it into the nearest trash container.

He wondered if donuts were her only weakness. He still worried about TJ Walker and her team as he watched her dust off the last of the sugar and cinnamon from her fingers before brushing crumbs off her jeans. No cutoff shorts today. The jeans looked worn with the holes in the denim exposing those tanned, muscled legs.

She wore a snug white T-shirt with the word *SECURITY* printed across the back. Her long dark hair was tucked up under a baseball cap. Long silver earrings dangled from both ears. Her sunglasses were mirrored where he couldn't see her eyes, but he could feel them on him.

She looked young and eager. She didn't look like the leader of a security team. She would have blended in well with this crowd except for the word *SECURITY* on her T-shirt. He figured the others would be dressed much the same and again found himself wondering if Vi was right. He was old for his age, a no-fun stick-in-the-mud just as he'd been told.

Was that how TJ saw him? And he wondered if that's what she'd meant last night when they'd first met. What had she heard about him and from whom?

She exuded both confidence and a young rebelliousness. He wondered what she'd been like as a teenager and had been surprised to find out that she hadn't had any run-ins with the law in the past. At least nothing had come up when he'd run her name.

He shook off thoughts about the woman, even though there was a granule of sugar at the corner of her mouth he itched to brush away. It was time to get back to business. "I'll have flyers printed up with her photo and relevant information, with updates posted on our website."

TJ nodded as she slipped her tongue from her mouth to capture the errant grain of sugar. "Goes without saying that Jennifer is smart and crafty if she's escaped from that kind of facility."

"Very," he said. "She's the kind that attracts trouble." Leroy saw TJ almost wince at his words and wondered what he'd said to cause it. He almost asked but stopped himself. "You'll have a photo soon, but we have no idea what she might be wearing or what she might have done to disguise herself."

She nodded. "We'll watch for her."

"Don't approach her on your own," Leroy warned. "Tell your team the same thing. Even if you aren't sure it's her, notify me and let me handle it. You have my number."

"Yes, I do have your number, Marshal." The way she said it made him smile. "But I doubt I'll need you. If I do, then I'm in more trouble than even you can get me out of." She winked as if it were a joke as she turned and, pulling out her phone, walked away. "Don't worry, you'll be hearing from me the moment I see anything suspicious."

He watched her go, hoping it was a joke. He didn't want anything to happen to her or her team. She thought she could handle Jennifer. Probably the men Jennifer had killed had felt the same way. With TJ, he didn't want to find out if it was true.

The grounds were coming alive with an air of excitement. He questioned whether or not TJ was taking this event seriously enough. The news of Jennifer's escape had filled him with dread. He felt the weight of his position more than ever right now. Had he ever been carefree? He didn't think so.

Vi was right. He wasn't fun. But as he watched TJ walk away he felt envious. She seemed to shed worries about trouble like water off a duck. He wanted to be more like her. But that would mean being someone entirely different. That, he thought, would be okay sometimes.

But not even TJ could change By the Book Baggins into the kind of man a woman like her would look at twice. Where the hell had that thought come from? This birthday celebration and everything that came with it was getting to him. The thoughts he'd been having were so out of character that he barely recognized himself.

DOWN AT THE CAFÉ, Tina didn't ask how Earl Ray had gotten her DNA or how many months he'd known she was his daughter. She might have, but Bessie came out of the kitchen with Chloe and their breakfasts. The older woman eyed Tina as she put down the full plates and helped Chloe into a high chair. Bessie was a large woman so full of life that it spilled over in her smile, in her laugh, in the way she showed her love with food. For years everyone in town knew that Bessie was in love with widower Earl Ray. Only recently had the two finally found each other and gotten married.

"You okay?" Bessie asked quietly, compassion in her gaze.

Tina could actually smile this time when she nodded. She was okay. For years, she'd wondered about a lot of things when it came to Vi and herself. Now she finally knew.

She shifted the smile from Bessie to Earl Ray. "It's a shock, but a nice one." She saw him relax, tears welling in his eyes. She squeezed his hand and let go to help her daughter with her pancakes.

"You ready for that cinnamon roll I promised you?" Bessie asked her husband as if to fill in the emotional tension at the table.

"I am," he said, cleared his voice and took a sip of his coffee.

Bessie laughed. "Center cut lots of icing coming right up." She looked to Tina, who shook her head. The pancakes and bacon she always had were plenty. Chloe was already digging into her cakes that Bessie had shaped into bunnies with slices of banana for feet.

For a moment, it felt like any other morning in Buckhorn, Montana. But then Earl Ray reached over to help his granddaughter with the small fork that Bessie kept especially for kids and it hit Tina all over again. He was Chloe's *grandfather*. So different from the man Tina had thought of as her father all these years. Axel had left town before Chloe was born. He'd never seen the child because he'd never come back.

"My mother…" Tina swallowed as she realized what Earl Ray hadn't told her. "Vi. She doesn't know?"

"I wanted to tell you first," Earl Ray said.

Neither of them said it, but Tina knew they were both thinking that Vi was going to lose her mind over this.

"Maybe we should wait until after the town's birthday celebration is over," she suggested. The truth was that her mother was on edge even more than normal. Something like this…

Earl Ray looked regretful. "I wish we could." She watched him swallow before he spoke again. He started to say "your father" but caught himself. "Axel contacted me recently about some DNA tests he'd had run involving you."

She frowned and then felt her eyes widen with comprehension. "About my paternity?" The red hair. Axel had known she wasn't his daughter. Or at least suspected it.

Earl Ray nodded. "He is contesting the divorce settlement apparently, his focus on proving that your mother had an affair, got pregnant with another man's child and lied about the paternity of the child so he'd marry her and help raise you. Apparently, he's coming to town for the town's birthday celebration."

Tina closed her eyes for a moment. She wondered how long the man she'd known as her father had felt this way. Was that why he had left Buckhorn and hadn't looked back? Not a phone call. Not even a text. When he'd left Vivian, he'd left her and Chloe as well. She hadn't understood his lack of interest in meeting his first and only grandchild. Until how. He'd known that she wasn't his blood and neither would any child of hers be either.

Still, he'd been the only father she'd known. Knowing the truth didn't diminish the hurt she still felt, but it did explain it. In fact, it explained so much. She understood why Earl Ray was telling her this now. "He knows I'm not his biological daughter and he plans to use it against my… Vi." She shook her head. It was just like Axel to pick now to drop the bomb on Vi since he knew this celebration meant so much to her.

"That's why Vi has to be told before she finds out from him," Earl Ray said. "I thought we should tell her together."

CHAPTER FIVE

THE MARSHAL'S WORDS still rang in her ears. "She's the kind that attracts trouble." TJ had thought that was her. How else could she explain what had happened to her? She must have done something to attract a man like Worth. Must have a certain look. Or done something that signaled to him that she was an easy mark.

Those thoughts had haunted her for a while after it had happened. She had attracted trouble. She must be that kind of woman. She'd heard too many people say those words about other women as if whatever happened to them were their own fault.

It had taken a while to realize it hadn't been her and not to take the blame for what happened. Over time, she'd changed. She was no longer the naive, trusting, vulnerable woman she'd been. She'd armed herself with both weapons and defensive training. She never wanted to end up in the clutches of a rapist again.

After notifying her team about Jennifer Mullen, she sent the photo from the marshal with his instructions. They had a killer probably headed this way. She recalled the way Leroy spoke about Jennifer. The woman had apparently unnerved him. She found that interesting because it seemed out of character. She wondered if, like her, he'd built walls to protect himself. It made her wonder why.

She'd felt him studying her earlier as if trying to figure

her out. Good luck with that. She had no intention of letting down her defenses, especially for a too-good-looking cowboy marshal in the middle of Montana. As uptight as he was, she wondered what it would take to disarm the man emotionally.

She had to admit, she was tempted to find out.

Her team promised to keep an eye out for Jennifer Mullen, leaving TJ to patrol the crowds already filling the fairgrounds. The pine-covered mountains gleamed in the morning sun. She caught the scent of the creek on the light breeze and listened to the rustle of the leaves as they shifted in a grove of nearby aspens.

She stopped to take in all this beauty in this town so different from the large metropolitan cities where she usually worked. What it must be like to live here and see this every day, she thought. She tried to imagine Buckhorn after the celebration was over and this small, isolated place went back to being itself. It must be so peaceful.

It made her think of the marshal again. Montana suited him, she thought and found herself smiling as she went back to work.

When Vi heard someone come in the back of the store, she'd turned, afraid it would be her ex-husband, Axel. She'd heard he was in town, though she couldn't imagine that he'd come for the celebration. When he'd left her, he'd left Buckhorn behind him. The last thing she needed was him around.

She was trying to get to the fairgrounds, but one thing after another had kept her busy and away from the celebration she'd planned, and she was getting damned irritated by it. She would be giving a speech later at the bandstand on the history of Buckhorn and her family's part in it. At some point she hoped to announce her surprise guest, who would be at the closing ceremony.

The problem was that the governor's office kept putting her off. Having the governor speak before the crowd the last night would be the perfect end to the event. He couldn't be that busy. She was still waiting to hear if he was going to show up or not.

In the meantime, she had no time for Axel or anyone else with problems today. But it wasn't Axel coming through the back door of the store. To her delight, it was Tina and Chloe heading toward her. This, she realized, might be her only chance to see them before she got too busy.

She frowned though as she saw Earl Ray bringing up the rear.

Her lips pursed before settling into a thin, tight line of irritation as she realized this wasn't simply a quick visit. She knew that look on her daughter's face. When people didn't have the courage to come to her, they often went through Tina—or Earl Ray. Both appeared to have something unpleasant on their minds. Vi told herself that she didn't care what it was. She didn't have the time nor the patience for this.

"Whatever it is, the answer is no…" she began, but Tina cut her off.

"Let's step into your office," her daughter said in that no-nonsense tone of hers when she climbed up on her high horse. "Please," she added. "It's important."

"I really don't have—" She was going to say "time," but Earl Ray spoke up.

"You need to take time for this," he said in a conciliatory tone. They filed into her office and Earl Ray closed the door.

"Well, spit it out," Vi snapped as she went around to

stand behind her desk. "In case you haven't heard, I have a birthday celebration to—"

"I'm not your biological daughter," Tina said.

The words were so unexpected and so far out of left field that it took her a moment to react. Tina used to get mad at her when she was little and tell everyone she was adopted. That wasn't as bad as when she told people that Vi had stolen her from her real mother. Tina held so little resemblance to her that Vi felt lucky that no one had believed the child.

She took a breath and let it out. "I beg your pardon?"

"Your daughter died at birth," Earl Ray said. "That night when the county nurses were aiding in your difficult delivery, one of them switched a live baby with your stillborn one."

This was the most unbelievable thing she'd ever heard and she said as much.

"It's true," Earl Ray said somberly. "It's a long story, but my wife, Tory, became pregnant when I was home on leave. She hid her pregnancy—even from me, especially from me. When the baby was born…" It was clear he found it hard to admit. "She never wanted children, wanted nothing to do with the infant and demanded that the county nurse get rid of it. When your baby was stillborn, the county nurse switched them, giving the precious infant a mother. Tina is my biological daughter. I've run the DNA tests. It's true."

Vi's legs felt as if they might give out under her. She stumbled and dropped into her chair. "Even if I believed any of this, why on earth would you chose now to tell me?"

"Axel knows that Tina isn't his biological daughter," Earl Ray said. "He had a DNA test done, possibly with some of Tina's hair from her brush or with saliva from a toothbrush, I don't know. But he plans to use it against you, contesting the divorce settlement. I believe it's why he's coming back to Buckhorn now. I didn't want him to be the one to tell you that Tina isn't his biological daughter—or yours either. You needed to know the truth. I apologize for the timing."

Vi had always prided herself on her strength even during horrendous times. But right now she didn't feel strong. She felt gutted. She looked at her daughter. Tina, not her daughter. That head of red hair so like Tory's. Her gaze fell to her granddaughter on Tina's lap and that same hair color, that same face as Tina.

She wanted to scream and yell and break something. She wanted to rail against the gods. Her baby dead? Her daughter and granddaughter not hers? Worse, her husband on his way to claim that she'd had an affair and lied about the paternity of the child she'd carried more than thirty years ago?

"It was all in a journal written by the county nurse," Earl Ray said. "I would be happy to make you a copy if you still don't believe me."

That was the problem. Vi *did* believe him and she could tell that her daughter did too. Just look at Tina. Of course she wasn't her child. The red hair aside, they were nothing alike.

She dropped her face into her hands and began to sob. Tina put down Chloe to come to her. She knelt to hug her. Vi heard her whisper words of comfort, but it wasn't until Chloe climbed up on her lap that she choked back the last sob, lifted her face from her hands and wiped her eyes.

"Nothing has changed, Mom," Tina said. "You're still my mother. You're still Chloe's grandmother."

Vi smiled up at her through her tears as she hugged Chloe to her. *Everything* had changed. Suddenly her losses seemed to close in on her along with this world she'd built for herself. Buckhorn felt too small and confined. She tried to breathe as if even the air had changed.

Only sheer willpower pulled her together. With each ragged breath, she knew she would survive this too because she was Vi Mullen and this town needed her—and she needed it.

TJ STARTED AT the sound of a bloodcurdling scream coming from the direction of the carnival rides. She knew the difference between a scream of excitement and that of terror and took off at a run.

The moment she turned the corner, she spotted the crowd that had gathered around the Ferris wheel. She followed their gazes skyward. A boy hung from the front of one of the chairs. His friend was trying without success to pull him back up to the safety of the seat. The boy's jacket appeared to have gotten caught on the edge of the chair—the only thing that had saved him.

TJ pushed through the crowd to find the ride's operator bent over the motor trying to get it started again without any apparent luck. The boy's chair was two from the top. It appeared that it had been on the way down when something had made it stop abruptly, throwing the boy out.

Not hesitating, she quickly began to climb up the Ferris wheel. She tried to ignore the boy's screams, the crowd's gasps and her own pounding heart. From above, she heard the boy's jacket tear as he struggled, feet kicking.

"Don't move," she called up to him. "I'm coming to get you. Just stay still. I'm almost there." She was close enough now that if he fell, he'd take her down with him, but she didn't think about that. Her only thought was getting to him before it was too late.

She was within inches of him when she heard the jacket's fabric rend and the boy let out a scream of terror. Dangling by one hand, she grabbed for him, caught hold of his ankle as he began to fall. Below her, a roar rose from the crowd as the two of them hung from the gridwork precariously.

TJ knew she wouldn't be able to hold on with one hand long. She saw that her only hope of saving the boy was to swing him out and drop him in the lower chair on the wheel. Two teenaged boys in that chair had been watching wide-eyed.

"You're going to have to catch him," she said to the teens. Both turned in their chair and held out their hands as TJ began to swing her and the boy back and forth. She could feel her hand slipping on the bar. She had to drop the boy now.

Heart in her throat, she swung him out toward the chair and let go of his leg. A cacophony of screams filled the air as she grabbed hold of the bar with both hands to keep from falling. It wasn't until then that she was able to look down.

The teenagers had caught the boy and pulled him into their chair. The crowd below let out a cheer as TJ began to climb down. She heard the ride operator get the motor going. She was shaking hard and fighting tears of relief as she finally touched down on the ground and signaled for him to start the ride and get the other passengers off.

People were coming up to her, congratulating her. She was too shaken to speak even when the marshal pushed through the gathered throng. He looked as shaken as she felt, but he must have seen that she was in no shape to deal with the crowd. He took her arm and led her back through the vendors to the open field, where she stopped, bent over and vomited. That had been too close.

Being Marshal Leroy Baggins, when she finished throwing up, he handed her his handkerchief. It was a folded square of white fabric. She looked from it to him and had to smile as she wiped her mouth.

"Nice work," he said and his gaze filled with a warmth that seemed to wash over her. "I'd tell you not to ever do anything like that again, but I know it wouldn't do any good." His voice softened. "You scared me."

She chuckled, still shaken. "I scared myself."

"Why don't you take the rest of the day off," he suggested.

TJ shook her head. "The best thing I can do right now is work." She met his gaze. "I suspect you know that feeling."

He nodded. "Again, nice job." He glanced down at his boots, then straightened his Stetson and cleared his voice. "I suppose we should get back to it then."

CHAPTER SIX

LEROY HAD BEEN on his way to talk to Vi when he'd heard the screams and roar of the crowd. He'd turned around and gone back to see what was going on to find TJ dangling from the Ferris wheel by one hand, her other hand wrapped around a small boy's ankle.

He tried to banish that image as he walked down the main drag of Buckhorn to the general store. He still couldn't believe what TJ Walker had done, the risk she had taken and how shaken she'd been. She'd taken a terrible chance with her life and the boy's, but she'd saved him. The woman was now a hero. That could have been a disaster at the fairgrounds if TJ hadn't acted as quickly as she had.

By the time he reached the store, he'd calmed down some. Vi wasn't inside. He was directed to the alley, where to his surprise he found her smoking next to a large trash container. In all the time he'd known her, he'd never known her to smoke.

She hadn't heard him approach. She had her face turned up to the sun, smoke haloing around her. He cleared his throat. She turned, clearly startled. Seeing him, she hurriedly dropped the cigarette and ground it into the dirt. Blowing out the last of the smoke, she finally faced him.

Her look said, "You really don't want to mess with me right now."

He wished he didn't have to. "Jennifer escaped from the

mental facility forty-eight hours ago." He wasn't sure what he'd expected but it certainly wasn't the reaction he got.

Vi stared at him for a moment before bursting into laughter. It was a full-throated belly laugh that had her bending over and holding her stomach. When she looked at him again, tears were running down her face, but she didn't try to wipe them away. Instead, she continued to laugh as if overwrought.

He didn't know what to do or say. Fortunately, she eventually hiccupped and stopped laughing. She wiped her eyes and then, shaking her head, said, "This town is just full of good news this morning."

"I have a BOLO out on your niece," Leroy said, getting down to business. "I have also alerted your security team at the event site. My deputies and the security personnel all now have her mug shot and have been told to treat her with caution."

"Caution?" Vi guffawed. "She's a *killer*. I should hope everyone treats her with caution." Her eyes narrowed. "You're assuming she'll come back to Buckhorn. Why would she?"

"I suspect the birthday celebration played a role in her escape," he said.

She nodded, her smile tainted with bitterness. He hadn't meant to make it sound as if he blamed Vi for this too. "You really aren't a lot of fun, are you, Marshal?" She waved a hand through the air. "You don't have to answer. It's pretty obvious." She eyed him, clearly finding him lacking. "You're not going to be partaking in any of the festivities, are you. No carnival rides. No cotton candy. No corn dogs. Do you even dance?"

He wasn't sure what any of that had to do with the problem at hand, Vi's niece Jennifer, and this event that would have his department scrambling to keep everyone safe. "I'm just doing my job."

"Well, you best get on with it then," she said, sounding sad, as if she held no hope for him.

He might have responded, but the back door of the store opened and slammed shut again loudly. He heard someone approaching and turned to see Axel Mullen, Vi's estranged husband, heading toward them like a heat-seeking missile.

"Great," Vi said.

His cell phone rang. Stepping away, Leroy took the call. It was Darby Cole, the editor and owner of the local online newspaper, the *Buckhorn Independent Press*. "I was at the fairgrounds and took a great photograph of the woman saving that little boy on the Ferris wheel. But you got her out of there before I could find out who she was."

He hesitated only for a moment, happy to tell Darby with a sense of pride about TJ Walker as he walked down the alley, leaving Axel and Vi alone to sort out their differences. TJ deserved a hell of a lot of credit for her heroics even if it did scare him. He could see why her business had such a good reputation. It had one amazing leader.

Vi CLOSED HER eyes and breathed deeply as she heard Axel approach. "At least I'm getting all the bad news over quickly," she said under her breath as she slowly opened her eyes.

"Vivian?" He stopped directly in front of her and frowned as if not sure what he was seeing. "Are you all right?"

She hated what she heard in her soon-to-be ex-husband's voice. It didn't feel like concern in his tone. He'd always sounded as if he were talking down to her. Now his look was smug. She could tell that he couldn't wait to drop his bombshell on her. He thought she was in trouble. He thought he had her back against the wall. Axel should have been here earlier when she couldn't quit laughing, she thought. He would have thought her mad.

Taking a deep breath, she let it out, lifted her chin and faced the man she'd married all those years ago when she was young and naive and quite frankly foolish. She blamed love, because she *had* loved him. "Axel," she said and waited.

"I was hoping we could talk." He glanced pointedly at the trash container and the alley before returning his gaze to her. "Maybe somewhere more appropriate?"

"What could be more appropriate than next to a dumpster?" she asked. "It's maybe even poetic."

He frowned again and sniffed. "Were you back here smoking?"

She sighed, just wanting this over. "What is it you want, Axel?"

"I'd hoped we could do this in a civil manner, but I should have known better."

"Oh, please, you've come here wanting to change the conditions of our divorce and take what I've worked my whole life for—after you walked out on me when I needed you most. You forfeited any right to the life I've made here."

He looked away, a muscle in his jaw tensing. "Have you forgotten that I worked for years in this general store right beside you?" His gaze returned to her. "Shouldn't I get something for that?"

She wondered how long it would take him to mention her alleged affair and Tina's parentage. "I gave you a cash settlement that covered your…contribution."

His gaze hardened, his hands going to his hips as he

leaned toward her threateningly. "My *contribution*? While we're on that subject, let's discuss Tina."

She smiled. It hadn't taken him long at all. "She's not yours."

He reared back, clearly surprised. He hadn't expected her to admit it. "Finally, the truth."

"The truth is, she's not mine either," Vi said, hating how much that hurt to admit. He blinked, clearly confused. "You should take it up with Earl Ray," she said and started past him. "I really don't have time for this."

"Wait." He grabbed her arm, but she jerked it free and gave him a look that warned him never to touch her again. He dropped his hand to his side. "What does Earl Ray have to do with—"

"He'll explain it," she said, suddenly tired even though her day was only beginning. "Oh, and by the way, Jennifer has escaped and is probably headed to Buckhorn." She cocked her head at him. "She never liked you for some reason, did she? Hmm. You might want to stay out of her crosshairs since she's probably come back to settle some old scores. I know that's what I would do if I was in her situation. I'd suggest you cut your losses and get out of Buckhorn as fast as you can, because I'm not giving you anything more."

With that she went back into the store, leaving him standing alone in the alley looking nothing like the man who'd once stolen her heart and then broken it.

With the morning she'd had, she quickly forgot all about her niece Jennifer. Nothing was going to rain on her damned parade, she thought with her usual determination.

JENNIFER MULLEN HAD been convinced her escape plan would work due to befriending one of the guards. He would accidentally leave her cell door open so she could slip through.

The hard part would be walking out, so she'd chosen a time when she knew exactly where everyone would be. All those hours she'd spent gluing clippings in her scrapbook hadn't been wasted. She'd been watching the comings and goings. People had routines, especially late at night. All she'd had to do was wait until the gatekeeper went into the kitchen to get her nightly snack, go to the main desk, shut off the alarm and out the door she would go.

And it had gone pretty much the way she'd thought it would go. There had been one small problem she hadn't anticipated. Actually, a rather large one, she thought looking over at him now. She'd been forced to bring Kyle Robert Archer along.

K. Bob as he was known had been locked up for so long that she doubted he remembered why he was still behind bars. He was a good twenty years older than her, somewhere in his fifties. She hadn't wanted him to come with her, convinced he would only mess things up and get her caught. But he'd made it clear that either he came along or he'd squeal on her. She had to remind him that she had been locked up for multiple murders of men who'd pissed her off.

"You don't scare me," he'd said stubbornly.

"Then you're a fool."

He'd smiled at that, making him look goofier than usual as he added, "Right about that, but I can help you."

She'd realized that he might come in handy to get over the wall, but after that they would be parting company. Once she'd scaled the enclosure fence with his help, crossed numerous pastures and finally hit a two-lane paved road, she'd been the one to flag down a rancher with a load of hay while K. Bob hid in the ditch.

Jen had climbed into the cab to ride shotgun. From her side mirror, she'd seen K. Bob leap from the ditch as the truck began to move. She distracted the driver while her accomplice climbed into the back, disappearing into the load of hay.

The rancher dropped her off at the edge of a small Montana town. If K. Bob was still somewhere in the back, she didn't see him. Relieved to be rid of him, she found a drugstore and bought a few things with money she'd stolen over the past few months from visitors who didn't watch their purses closely.

In the bathroom, she changed her hair color, going red like her cousin Tina. With a pair of decent scissors, she gave herself a haircut as well. Once she put on the cheap pair of clear-lens glasses with the animal print frames, she didn't even recognize herself.

At a used clothing store, she bought worn jeans and a T-shirt with a logo of a band she'd never heard of, along with a baseball cap. To finish her look, she made several "tattoos" on her arms and neck with a marker. Anyone who picked her up would remember the tattoos. It might make finding Jennifer Mullen a little more difficult.

She studied the young woman in the mirror. Not even Aunt Vi would recognize her.

Buckhorn's first day of the town's birthday party was coming to a close by the time Jen jumped down from the semi that let her off at the edge of town. She waved thanks to the driver and looked down the main drag of her hometown and grinned. She was home! She couldn't wait to see everyone, especially her best friend, Shirley, who'd promised that she'd be here. It was just a matter of tracking her down, something Jen had always been good at.

It was late enough that she could see people leaving the

new fairgrounds she'd heard about. She stood at the edge in the darkness. She could hear music still playing from somewhere on the grounds, but clearly, she'd missed most of the first day of the event. She told herself that was okay. The celebration wouldn't be over for three more days.

She would find the people she'd come home to see—but they wouldn't see her. Not until she wanted them to.

CHAPTER SEVEN

THE MOON RISING, TJ followed the sound of the music as she walked past closed booths and a dwindling crowd. She felt a strange kind of exhaustion and knew it was from what had happened earlier. She'd taken risks before since going into this business, but that one had been too close for comfort. The only thing left was the exhaustion and the gut-wrenching relief that the boy had reached the ground safely.

She recalled seeing the boy's mother drop to her knees in tears as she took the boy in her arms. TJ couldn't have handled talking to anyone right then, especially the mother. Fortunately, the marshal had gotten her out of there. He had somehow known that she couldn't handle it.

All around her now, tired kids and adults found their way to the exit. The band at the back of the fairgrounds broke into a boot-stomping song. TJ checked the time. Everything was about to shut down, including the band. She could see a half dozen couples still dancing. She'd already heard the last call for alcohol from the beer garden. Soon the band would be playing its last song of the night.

Throughout the fairgrounds, lights were blinking off. Most of the booths had already closed. Only a few carnival rides were still going. It gave her a melancholy feeling, a reminder that all of this would be over in a matter of days, vanishing and leaving only memories.

She moved toward the dance floor. In the growing darkness at the back of the fairgrounds, the hanging lights circling the floor seemed almost intimate. She watched the couples, some moving so gracefully that she knew they'd been dancing together for years.

TJ felt wistful longing tug at her heartstrings. She wanted that kind of relationship, a love that never tired of slow dancing together. For so long, she'd felt as if a love like that was out of her reach. As if she'd felt so betrayed by what had happened to her that she no longer believed there was a man for her out there.

Out of the corner of her eye, she saw the marshal standing in the shadows also watching. Had something happened to him to make him as closed off as she'd been? She tried to read his expression as he watched the dancers, wondering if he'd been thinking the same thing she had, but it was too dark. All she could see was the shine of those blue eyes under the brim of his Stetson.

The warm last-of-summer night, the aching music and a need she didn't dare put a name to had her in this mood. She blamed the day she'd had. She knew she should just be glad to be alive after what had happened. But right then, she yearned to slow dance. She wanted to be in strong arms, needed to be held.

"First day almost down," TJ said when she walked over to him and the song ended and the band announced the next one would be the last of the night. They began to play a slow tune. "I think that calls for a dance." Before he could decline, she reached for his hand. It was large and dry, warm and slightly callused.

"I really don't think—"

"There is nothing to think about," she said. "Last dance. You do know how to dance, don't you?"

He glanced toward the dance floor and back at her. She

had his hand and was drawing him up the steps to join the few couples determined to dance right until the last note. "You'll probably regret this," he said, but he grinned.

She stepped into his arms, shaking her head as she met his gaze. "Just hold me." Her voice cracked and his grin faded. Eyes locked with hers, he pulled her closer as if he knew exactly what she needed tonight.

TJ swallowed, surprised how close she was to tears. That had been such a close call earlier, closer than even she had wanted to admit. She'd been so afraid she would drop that boy. She blinked back the tears as the marshal wrapped his arms around her and she leaned her cheek against his warm shoulder.

Leroy smelled of the great outdoors and a male scent that was both reassuring and alluring. She relaxed into the cowboy cop's strong arms, feeling his strength and his compassion. She'd made a point of not getting too close to any man in the past four years. As trained as she was, she knew she was still vulnerable when it came to her heart and trust. She warned herself not to get too close to this lawman.

To her surprise, the two of them moved as if they'd been doing this for years. She lost herself in the music, the movement, the feel of being safe—at least for the moment—in his arms. She could feel his lips against her hair as he quietly hummed along with the music. She couldn't remember being this content and yet there was an electrical current that seemed to purr just under her skin. The marshal was a sexy man and when he let his hair down…he was almost irresistible. The cool night air felt like a caress. She closed her eyes.

When the song ended, she didn't want to open her eyes. She didn't want to move, let alone let this moment end. Leroy still had her in his arms, making her feel as if he wanted to continue holding her as much as she wanted it. As much as she needed it.

Recognizing that need, she drew back and they awkwardly stepped apart. Other couples began leaving the dance floor as the band said good-night and began to break down their equipment.

She felt even more vulnerable than she had earlier. Being in his arms had made her realize how much she'd missed intimacy, how much she wanted it and needed it. That she'd let down her defenses with the marshal though was something she'd never expected. By the Book Baggins. Could they have been any more different? She blamed it on the not quite warm late summer night, the growing full moon, yes, this handsome lawman. It had all been too appealing and still was.

"Thank you, Marshal," she said feeling self-conscious as she took a step back.

"It's Leroy."

She swallowed at the look in his blue eyes. Was that desire she saw mirrored there? Had he felt it? Because she thought she glimpsed a wistfulness in his gaze as well. "Leroy," she repeated, actually feeling shy. Shifting on her feet under that gaze, she looked away and stuffed her hands into the back pockets of her jeans.

Still standing in the middle of the dance floor, TJ was the first to break the heavy silence that fell between them. "I'm glad to see that I was wrong about you."

"Is that right?" His voice sounded husky. He cleared his throat.

"By the Book Baggins can let his hair down," she said and smiled at him. For a moment, she felt back on solid ground. Until her gaze locked with his. She saw the same aching need in his eyes and something more. He was looking at her with something like awe. She felt a knot form in her chest.

Don't fall for me, Marshal. Her voice dropped a little as she said, "Thank you again for the dance, Marshal."

"My pleasure," he said a few beats before breaking eye contact to look away. His expression was one of surprise as if he'd just noticed that they were alone in the middle of the dance floor. He looked uncomfortable and suddenly as uncertain as she was. "I suppose…"

She nodded. "Best see to my team." Lane would be staying until morning, and then Ash would take over from there, but the marshal already knew that. She knew that one of the seasoned, older deputies, Deputy Kenneth Yarrow, would keep an eye on things as well. "Day one down," she said, reminding herself that in a few more days, she would be going on to the next job.

"Three to go," Leroy said.

He looked thoughtful, almost sad as if he would miss her as they said their good-nights and went their separate ways.

Or maybe she was the one who was sad about it. She was growing fond of the marshal. Too fond.

THE FAIRGROUNDS TOOK on an almost eerie feel as Leroy walked toward the exit. The moonlight cast long shadows along the sides of the booths. All around him the night grew quieter—unlike his thoughts—as he walked.

He felt like he had the first time he'd danced with a girl. He'd been clumsy and self-conscious. He'd gotten better since then.

But having TJ in his arms tonight, he'd felt thirteen again, hoping not to embarrass himself. He'd forgotten how much he liked to slow dance. TJ, no surprise, was a good dancer. She had moved effortlessly. He thought about the first time he'd seen her—high in the night sky on the Ferris wheel.

He shook his head, feeling as if he'd been intrigued with her from the moment the moonlight had shone on her face, and she'd looked at him with those big green eyes. Leroy quickly reminded himself that, intrigued and admittedly captivated by the woman, she wasn't his type.

The thought almost made him laugh. Did he even have a type?

But the point was, TJ Walker felt dangerous. She took too many risks. Earlier today, she'd terrified him. He would always see her dangling from the metal frame of the Ferris wheel as she reached to save that little boy. His heart began to race all over again at the memory.

He'd felt so helpless, knowing anything he did might only make things end in tragedy. Instead, he'd had to watch like everyone else as TJ risked her life to save the boy's. That the woman kept surprising him at every turn was putting it mildly. But she was also scaring him too—maybe especially when he was holding her in his arms like he'd done only minutes ago on the dance floor.

His heart had been pounding like never before. He'd forgotten what it felt like to want a woman as intensely as he'd wanted TJ tonight. She'd broken down his reserve and made him feel more than he'd ever felt for another woman.

And it scared the hell out of him on so many levels.

Even if she wasn't leaving in a few days, even if she felt the same way, she was all wrong for him. While it was exciting to feel this intensely, he couldn't imagine it lasting—and if it did… He shook his head, telling himself it was just a dance in the moonlight at the end of summer that had made him feel like this…sentimental.

Yet he found himself smiling as he headed for his patrol SUV. He couldn't remember the last time he'd danced or enjoyed it so much. Nor could he remember a woman he'd dated in recent memory who made him excited to see her again.

Not that he dated much. He took his job seriously and being the marshal of such a large county with such a small force, he had little to no time for dating.

But dancing with TJ had felt good. Maybe too good. This woman had a way of getting to him. Did she realize the effect she had on him? He smiled to himself, figuring she probably did.

At the fairgrounds lot, he saw her standing beside her motorcycle. Was she waiting for him? He hesitated, still feeling the thrill of her like a slow-simmering fire moving through his veins.

"That was fun tonight," he called to her as he unlocked his patrol SUV. He realized there was a quick way to nip this attraction in the bud, as his grandmother would have said. He walked over to her and voiced the thought that had been nagging at the back of his mind since their dance. "What will you do after this job is over?"

She didn't seem surprised by the question, as if she'd been thinking the same thing. "Another security gig, another town. Where exactly will depend on how things go here."

He laughed. "I hope your future isn't contingent on four days in Buckhorn."

She shrugged. "You're only as good as your last job. It's the nature of the business."

Leroy told himself to step away, to say good-night, to put the dance and the desire she seemed to stoke in him away for the night. "You must like what you do."

Again, she seemed to give it some thought before answering. "I'm good at what I do, but there are other things I'd like to do with my life someday."

"I'd love to hear what those are sometime," he said and took a step back, telling himself that it was late and they both had to work tomorrow. Still he was curious about her, curious as to why she quit teaching elementary school to do this line of work. Maybe he would have asked her, but her cell phone rang. "Good night, then."

"Good night." She turned her back to take the call as Leroy headed for his patrol SUV.

He wondered who was calling her this late and mentally kicked himself. Of course she would have a man in her life. Who else would call at this hour to see how her day had gone, to tell her that he loved her and missed her?

TJ ANSWERED THE CALL, wondering herself who could be ringing this late. She just assumed it would be a member of her team checking in.

"TJ Walker? This is Darby Cole. I'm the editor of the *Buckhorn Independent Press*. I know it's late, but I would love to do an article on you for my online newspaper after that amazing rescue you pulled off earlier today. Everyone's talking about it."

"I appreciate your interest, but I was just doing my job," she said. "Good night." She disconnected. She didn't need the publicity, preferring she and her crew kept out of the spotlight because of the nature of their jobs. Often, like with the Big Sky VIP job, they'd been hired to be almost invisible, blending in, making everyone safe without calling attention to the need for security. It was a strange business, but because she and her teams could adapt, she'd been successful at it.

She also didn't like or need the attention, she thought

as she disconnected before climbing onto her motorcycle and heading for the hotel. Being in the spotlight made her nervous since attention was what had gotten her into trouble four years ago.

CHAPTER EIGHT

DAY TWO

When TJ came down to the hotel's complimentary continental breakfast the next morning, she found Z eating alone, her cell phone propped up in front of her.

"I'm guessing you haven't seen it," Z said as TJ slid into the booth. At her confused look, Z said, "Sorry, I know how you feel about any of us being singled out publicly." She slid her phone across the table. "The story's gone viral. Like it or not, you're a hero."

TJ stared down at the photo of her and the boy dangling from the Ferris wheel. She'd been identified as TJ Walker, owner of Walker Security Inc. There was a quote from the marshal. "Oh, Leroy," she groaned under her breath as she read, *"She's the most amazing woman I've ever met. She gave no thought to her own safety to save that boy."* TJ quickly scrolled down to see that the photographer had taken another shot, this one closer, as she had come off the Ferris wheel. Her face was easily recognizable.

She pushed the phone back at Z and shook her head. It was unfortunate, but not the end of the world, she told herself. And yet she'd lost her appetite. "I have to go."

"Wait, aren't you going to have something to eat?" Z called after her, but she didn't answer as she left the hotel for the fairgrounds.

WORTH KNEW HE couldn't get out of going to Buckhorn today the moment he walked into the governor's office that morning.

"Have you seen the news?" Jamie was all smiles. "Talk about luck. The story went *viral*. Buckhorn made national news and put the place on the map. I couldn't have calculated this better. Like I said, it's all about optics. I'd actually been planning to cancel. I could tell yesterday that you weren't wild about the idea of going down there today. But this cinches it. Check this out." He turned his computer screen where Worth could see. As if he gave a shit. "Isn't this amazing?"

Worth glanced at the story about some woman who owned a security company saving a little boy who'd almost fallen to his death on a Ferris wheel at the Buckhorn Birthday Celebration. He could see the silhouette of a woman and boy dangling from one of the supports.

"Wow," he said, not all that impressed, and started to push the computer screen back around when he saw the second photograph that accompanied the story. It was a shot of the woman after she'd saved the boy and reached the ground. She was nice-looking, really nice-looking, but other than that…

Jamie pulled his computer back over in front of him. "Isn't this the best luck ever? Make sure I get my photo taken with this woman. She's hot, huh." Jamie gave him a knowing nod. "So I need you to get down there today and set everything up. I thought we should hold a press conference to congratulate the young heroic woman. Maybe get the kid and the mother there. You can make all the arrangements. Coordinate with the woman, the organizer. I gave you the number yesterday."

Worth groaned inwardly, seeing that there was no way

out of this. He was going to Buckhorn today. "I'll get right on that," he told him as he looked on Jamie's desk for the sticky note his boss had tossed to him and he recalled putting down somewhere. "Who did you say you talked to about the speaking event?"

"Vivian Something. I think she owns most of the town. Maybe she's the mayor. She's definitely in charge. If she wants me there, then she'll help you set this all up including finding us a place to stay since I'd like to take advantage of the opportunity to be away from home… You know what I mean, Worth. We'll go the day before."

As soon as he reached his office, he found the sticky note and put in the call to the Mullen woman. Just as he'd hoped, she was able to give him all the information he needed on TJ Walker and the mother and her son. "The governor would like them to be there for the press conference." He collected their phone numbers even though Vi Mullen said she would set it up.

He confirmed that he and the governor would be attending the event a day early and asked if she could help them out with a place to stay. The woman said she'd get back to him.

Worth quickly disconnected and left his office. He was going to Buckhorn and not looking forward to it in the least, but he had to think about his long-range destination. As impatient as he was, he knew that Jamie could take him clear to the White House. All he had to do was keep his friend happy and out of trouble. He'd seen the gleam in the governor's eye. He'd make sure that Jamie got to meet this TJ Walker woman. He'd just have to make sure whatever happened after that never went public.

While he and Jamie weren't that different when it

came to the temptation of a pretty face, his job was to protect the governor from himself.

Vi COULDN'T HAVE been more excited about the article Darby Cole had written in her online newspaper and the exposure it gave Buckhorn as well as the birthday event. She felt such a sense of pride and couldn't wait to boast about her choice of security to the marshal.

She'd been busy all day with one thing or another, so she hadn't seen him. Nor did she find him in the crowd that had gathered that evening at the fairgrounds. She was beaming as she took the stage and gave her speech on the history of Buckhorn. A small group of people gathered at the foot of the stage to listen, and she was gratified that at least some folks cared about Buckhorn's history. Others just wandered past.

She realized that she wasn't just looking for the marshal in the crowd as she finished her presentation. For a while, she'd forgotten about her murdering niece, Jennifer. The marshal seemed to think she would come to the celebration. Vi just hoped she got caught and locked up again before that happened.

As she walked off the stage into the cool darkness of the structure, a figure stepped out, startling her. For a moment, she thought it was her niece and had to stifle a scream. It would have been just like Jennifer to want to surprise her.

To her short-lived relief, it wasn't Jennifer. Almost as bad though, it was Axel. He'd apparently been waiting for her in the shadows. He looked anxious and irritated. He'd never made a secret of the fact that he found Buckhorn history boring. Actually, he'd found Buckhorn—and her—boring.

"What's the point in putting me off?" he snapped. "Let's get this settled and then you'll be shed of me for good."

"And you of me," she said as she put a little distance between them, stepping back behind the stage. She turned to look at him. A shaft of light from the stage bore down on his face and she was startled by what she saw. Axel had aged. Or maybe he'd done that before he'd left her and she just hadn't noticed.

How had she not realized how haggard he appeared yesterday in the bright daylight of the alley? Funny how people saw what they wanted. He'd never cared much about how he'd dressed, but now he seemed more ragged than usual. He stood, hands deep in the pockets of his worn jeans, looking both anxious—and desperate.

That realization made her hesitate, but only for a moment. "Let's take a walk away from all this racket." She started off, knowing he would follow. The moon had only barely crested the mountains, the sky to the east ablaze with it.

Leaving behind the noise and crowds, they walked to the far edge of the fairgrounds. Vi stopped and looked over at him. His shoulders were slumped, his head down as if careful to watch each step he took. When had he gotten so elderly? She almost felt sorry for him.

"I deserve better," he used to say so she wasn't surprised when he said it now without looking at her.

"Better than me, you mean." She wanted to argue that she'd given him a life, a family, a place to grow roots. But admittedly, those weren't things he'd actually wanted. They'd started their marriage on the wrong foot, so to speak. Her pregnant and him still filled with wanderlust. She knew that he'd felt like she'd trapped him. Had she? Had she wanted a man in her life so badly that she would have done anything to make him stay in Buckhorn?

The irony of it struck her at heart level. Their baby had

died, freeing Axel. He could have walked away and not looked back—if that was really what he'd wanted. If the county nurse hadn't switched the babies, he would have been free years ago. It had been just his bad luck that had kept him in Buckhorn. And her good luck?

"I'm sorry," she said surprising them both. His head lifted, his eyes somber as he looked at her. She realized that she might have ruined his life. When her marriage hadn't been as fulfilling as she'd hoped, she'd still had her daughter, Tina. She'd had her place in this town. She was... somebody to envy.

But she could see that Axel had never fit in here—as hard as she had tried to make him grow into the husband she wanted and needed.

JENNIFER LOVED CROWDS. She moved through this one, keeping her head down, her face mostly hidden by the baseball cap, feeling invisible. It felt strange to be back here like this. Hiding under a disguise afraid to see someone who knew her. Buckhorn was a small town. Everyone had known her—or known of her.

Tonight, the town felt strangely alien. She saw a few people she knew and quickly avoided them, but mostly the faces she passed were those of strangers. The noise, the congestion, the throngs surrounded her and offered cover to her.

She had heard her aunt's voice amplified drifting over the fairgrounds. Vi had a microphone and was going on about how she'd pulled this event together almost single-handedly. So like her Aunt Vi. It had made her laugh. She wished she could share this with her cousin since Tina would appreciate the horror of Vi with a microphone and no one to stop her from talking.

As if on cue, Jen heard someone interrupt her aunt. Tina? She felt a tug at her heart. She and Tina had always been close. Not Tina, just someone reminding Vi that her time was up.

Jennifer's smile turned to tears as she stepped into the darkness behind one of the carnival trailers. This wasn't the way she'd wanted to come back to town. She should have been up on that stage with her aunt and her cousin. She was family. She shouldn't be an outcast.

Maybe you shouldn't have killed three people, she reminded herself, tears burning her eyes. She wiped at them. Vi was no longer talking. Music began to play. The song made her feel even more melancholy.

Suddenly, she wasn't sure why she'd come back here and just wanted to leave. But when she started to step out of the shadows, she saw a woman approaching. She was crossing the open field, coming from a nearby dirt road. Jen recognized Karla Parson, a former childhood friend of her aunt Vi's. They'd had a falling-out years ago over a broken vase.

Jen could see Karla's old car parked carelessly in a shallow ditch back on the dirt road. What were the chances that Karla had left the keys in the ignition? Otherwise, Jen figured it would be easy enough to take the keys from the woman—and any money she might have.

But before she could act, someone called to Karla. "Great parking job!" a man mocked from somewhere overhead. Until that moment, Jen had overlooked the view from the Ferris wheel and what those at the top might be able to see.

"I ran out of gas!" Karla yelled back and shrugged as if to say "Silly me." Jen stayed where she was, letting the woman pass within feet of her. She had to be more careful, she thought, and spotted her aunt talking to her uncle Axel.

Vi WANTED TO walk away but when she turned back to Axel, she was surprised to see tears in his eyes. "I never wanted this," he said.

She felt herself bristle. "It wasn't like there was a gun to your head. You could have walked away years ago."

He frowned and shook his head. "I'm not talking about us, our life. I never wanted it to end like this."

For a moment, she thought he was going to ask if he could come back. A bubble of joy began to rise in her chest, but was quickly pricked and deflated with his next words.

"I deserve more money."

More money or anything else of hers wasn't what he deserved. She stared at him, wondering how he'd gone through the settlement money so quickly, but at the same time, not caring. What he did no longer mattered. She'd found a kind of peace after he'd been gone, and the heartache had subsided some. She'd learned that she could live without him.

"How much more do you think is fair?" she asked, but only out of curiosity. However much he thought he was worth would be amusing, she told herself, remembering the humiliation, the hurt of the abandonment by him when she'd needed him so much more than she ever had.

Relief made his eyes widen a little. She could see him considering how much to ask for. In truth, under Montana law, he could have taken half of everything except that her father had made sure that the general store, antique barn and the land would always remain safe and not get divided in a divorce. Her father hadn't liked Axel and would have been shocked that he'd stayed with his daughter as long as he had. Axel had known that going into their marriage and had reluctantly agreed to forgo the bulk of her family's estate early on.

"I'll tell you what, Axel," she said because watching him calculate what he could get out of her was annoying and she wanted it over with. "I will write you a check in the amount I am willing to add to what I have already given you. You can pick it up when the celebration is over—and sign a legal document that you get no more, that you will ask for no more and that I will never see you again."

"How much are you talking?" he asked, sounding excited about the prospect but at the same time worried that it wouldn't be enough.

Out of the corner of her eye, she caught motion behind one of the food trucks at the back edge of the fairgrounds. She felt her eyes widen in alarm, her pulse jumped with both fear and surprise as she focused on the figure hiding there.

Jennifer, her murderous, criminally insane niece, stood watching them argue. Vi wondered how much she had overheard. That question was quickly answered when her niece gave her a little wave, then made the sign of a gun with her hand, forefinger extended, and pointed it toward Axel before she disappeared around the end of the truck and back into the crowd.

"How much, Vi?" Axel demanded.

She turned her attention back to him as she tried to still her racing heart. She had to tell the marshal that he was right. Jennifer was here. She had to warn him, warn everyone—maybe especially Axel. She hadn't been joking earlier about Jennifer seeming to dislike her uncle. Or was it not trust him? Either way, the two had always seemed wary of each other.

But even as she thought about what to do, she knew she couldn't tell the marshal and panic the crowd. She'd put too much work into this celebration. She wouldn't let Jennifer spoil it.

"If you're still around Tuesday morning, Axel," she said and cleared her throat, "stop by the store and I'll have a check waiting for you. Hopefully you'll go away satisfied." Because you'll be alive—that's if you haven't crossed paths with your niece, she thought.

Leaving him, she didn't look back even though she knew if she had that she would have found him standing at the edge of the fairgrounds looking after her. He'd thought she would put up more of a fight and it had thrown him off guard. If Axel was still around Tuesday morning, she'd have a check waiting for him. Enough to get him out of town.

But knowing her niece, Vi didn't see him living long enough to ever cash the check. Axel should have been nicer to Jennifer, she thought. But she didn't have time to dwell in the past. She could hear laughter, screams and music as she headed back downtown to the store, taking pride in the fact that her celebration was a success. Buckhorn was filled to overflowing with people having a good time. Nothing was going to ruin what she'd accomplished single-handedly. Buckhorn was her town, she thought as she spotted the marshal coming toward her.

Leroy noticed how pleased Vi looked with herself. The article about TJ and the boy she'd saved had everyone talking about the rescue. TJ had been incredible. He'd felt a sense of pride in her, so he was sure Vi was busting her buttons over it since she was the one who'd hired the independent security team.

"Evening, Vi," he said. He could see that there was something she was dying to tell him.

"I just heard from the governor's office," she said excitedly. "They saw the news about the rescue. We're setting up a news conference that morning and then the governor will speak that evening at the closing ceremonies. Now I just have to find a place for them to stay." She had that I-told-you-so look on her face. "TJ Walker turned out to be a good choice, don't you think?"

He couldn't help but smile. "Great choice. Everything all right with you and Axel?" he asked, having spotted the two of them having what looked like a heated discussion at the edge of the fairgrounds.

"All taken care of," she said looking her usual confident self.

"That's good to hear."

"Oh," she said as if remembering something. "The governor's assistant, a man named…" She pulled out a small notebook from her jacket pocket and thumbed through it until she found what she was looking for. "Prescott Rutherford Hollingsworth the third." She looked up as she snapped the notebook closed. "He said he goes by Worth. Anyway, he wanted to hear all about TJ. I wouldn't be surprised if she gets a commendation from the governor. He said he would be working closely with TJ for the governor's security. He'll be in town today to make all the arrangements."

Do governors give commendations? Leroy wondered, then caught the last thing she said. "Vi, don't you think you should have mentioned that it might be dangerous for the governor to come? For all we know, Jennifer could already be in town. You know your niece. If she wants to make a point, she might use the governor's speech to do it."

"That's ridiculous," Vi snapped. "Have you seen her?" She rushed on. "You don't even know for certain that she's headed this way. And what point would she be interested in making? I'll be the first to admit that Jennifer has her…

problems, but they aren't with the governor. She probably doesn't even know who the governor is." Vi shook her head. "Don't make trouble where there isn't any, Leroy. Why can't you just try to enjoy the celebration instead?" With that she turned and stormed away, leaving him shaking his head.

THAT'S HOW TJ found him. "Something wrong?" she asked, then spotted Vi lumbering away. "Oh," she said in understanding.

He turned to face her. "Vi just informed me that the governor isn't just coming for his closing ceremony speech at the end of the celebration and then returning to Helena. Apparently, he will be doing a press conference that morning before speaking that night at the closing ceremonies. Vi is trying to find them a place to stay. I'm sure she'll kick people out of the hotel if it comes down to it."

TJ laughed. "The governor can have my room. I could bunk with one of my team."

"That's very generous of you, but I'm sure Vi will come up with something since the governor will be bringing his entourage, I'm sure." They stood just looking at each other. "You doing okay, I mean, after the article?"

She sighed. "I've gotten more attention than I need, if that's what you mean."

"But what you did was so incredible…" He shook his head. "You're a hero."

"Hardly. I'd prefer to just blend into the shadows, thank you."

She could see that there was more and braced herself.

"Vi also mentioned that the governor wants to meet you." He looked as if he hated being the bearer of the news, given how she felt. "I know how you hate this but I think he might be giving you an award at the press conference."

TJ groaned and shook her head. She didn't want any of this.

The marshal quickly added, "I could be there at the press conference, if you wanted. I could make sure whatever he has planned is short and sweet. Get you out of the spotlight as fast as possible. We could do it uptown in front of the general store so there wouldn't be as many people. It would delight Vi."

She couldn't help but smile, touched by his thoughtfulness. "Thank you, I'd appreciate that. Let's just hope he forgets about it." The marshal's look said he wouldn't count on that.

"How about I buy you a bag of those donuts you like so well?" Leroy asked.

The gesture was so caring that she couldn't say no. "Only if you'll share them with me." He nodded and they walked back through the fairgrounds following the deep-fried sweet scent.

They hadn't gone far when she got a call from Vi. She listened to the woman's excited words, said, "I'll be right there," and disconnected.

"Everything all right?" Leroy asked looking concerned.

"That was Vi. The man from the governor's office is down at the store and anxious to talk to me."

"You want me to come with you?"

TJ shook her head. "I'll be fine. I know my attitude about being in the spotlight may seem silly."

The marshal's expression was so serious it almost made her laugh. "I know how you feel because I'm the same way. I just want to do my job. It's reward enough."

She reached over to squeeze his arm, touched by his words and his concern. How could she tell him that one of the best nights of her life had turned into the worst after she'd accepted the Teacher of the Year award in front of a large crowd in Denver?

The night had been so magical. She'd felt like a fairy princess. Later she would blame that euphoria for the mistake she'd made that had changed everything.

JENNIFER MULLEN HAD heard enough of the argument between her aunt and uncle. She mentally added Axel to her list of people she wanted to see before she left town. Being back in Buckhorn had resurrected some painful memories. Especially about her uncle.

As she watched him start to walk slowly away, she remembered one night when she'd first come to her aunt Vi's house. It had been late when she'd awakened to find a large shape framed in the doorway. It wasn't the first man she'd seen framed in her bedroom doorway late at night.

She'd held her breath, terrified that he was going to come into her room and hurt her like the others had done. That's when she'd heard her cousin Tina say, "Dad? Is everything all right?"

Axel had quickly closed the door. Jennifer heard a muffled "I heard a noise. I was just checking on your cousin."

She'd lain in bed trembling, hearing the lie, and knowing he would be back. They always came back like thieves in the night. From that night until she'd moved out, she'd kept a chair pushed against her door. Axel knew that she knew. She'd seen it in his eyes in the weeks that followed. She'd promised herself that when she grew up, she'd take care of everyone who'd ever hurt her.

Catching her reflection in a window of one of the carnival trailers, she stared at herself, suddenly startled. Her face was thinner than she remembered it, her skin lacking color, her eyes... She looked into her eyes surprised how sad she appeared. She'd come here to celebrate and not just Buckhorn's birthday. She'd escaped, fooled them all. She was free to have some fun, to make some mayhem. So why did staring at herself make her feel so lost and alone?

She wanted so badly to be her old self—at least for a while. Even as she thought it though, she questioned how wonderful her old self had been. Maybe not all that great given the way men had treated her. She felt the old anger simmering just below her skin as she thought of her uncle and the other men who'd thought she wasn't good enough. When she felt like this, she wanted to hurt someone.

Unless Dr. Moss could fix that little problem, then he couldn't fix her. But she reminded herself that he was no longer going to get the chance unless she went back. Unless she lived long enough to go back.

She didn't want to think about that now. She could hear music and the roar of voices in competition with the shrieks coming from the carnival rides. She wanted to be a part of this. She refused to think about what would happen when they caught her again.

But before that happened, there were things she had to take care of. She watched her uncle wander away from the fairgrounds toward the creek and disappear into the trees. A strong sense of purpose burned inside her. There had to be a reason that she'd gotten out and come here.

She'd seen into Axel's black heart. She thought about the way he'd abandoned Tina, his own daughter, not to mention his wife. Aunt Vi deserved better. She'd taken Jennifer in, given her a job, seen that she had a place to live and treated her more like a daughter than a niece. She owed her aunt.

Jen adjusted the baseball cap to hide those haunted eyes and most of her face. Then she fingered the steak knife now hidden in her jacket pocket that she'd pinched at a truck stop back up the road. Staying in the shadows behind the fair-grounds, she started to head for the creek and Axel when something stopped her. *Someone.* A ghost from her past.

She felt that old hurt and humiliation catch fire in her belly. She wrapped her fingers around the blade of the knife and changed her plans.

CHAPTER NINE

As TJ WALKED into the front door of the Buckhorn General Store, Vi grabbed her by the arm and ushered her down the hallway to her office.

"Here she is," Vi said, practically shoving her in the small room. "I have to get back to the fairgrounds." With that she closed the door and left.

TJ barely had time to take in the office and the man standing with his back to her. He'd been inspecting the array of photographs on the back wall. She had only a moment to assess him. Tall, broad shouldered, dark hair freshly trimmed, wearing a dark suit, he turned at the closing of the door.

The moment she saw his face, she felt a rush of panic as she recognized him. Her heart thundered in her chest. All her fight-or-flight defenses filled her. Hadn't she dreamed and dreaded this moment? Hadn't she often wondered what she would do if she ever saw him again?

He smiled and took a step toward her. "So you're the hero of the hour."

Adrenaline rushing through her veins, she tried to catch her breath even as she knew she wouldn't flee. This time, she would stay and fight if that's what it came to. She'd spent almost four years changing her life for this moment.

TJ felt his gaze rake over her body before focusing on

her face again. His smile broadened. "That was some stunt you pulled off on the Ferris wheel."

She felt a quickening in her chest. Not fear, not even anger. Just an initial earthshaking shock as it hit her at gut level. "You don't remember me, do you."

He frowned, considering her for a moment. "I'm sorry, have we met before?" He shook his head. "I can't believe I'd ever forget a woman like you." The big smile, the cheesy line, the casual lie, it was all too familiar.

TJ reminded herself that she wasn't the innocent, trusting woman she'd been the night he'd approached her after the awards ceremony. She'd actually still been holding her award when he'd insisted on buying her a drink and had fawned over her before asking if he could buy her a celebratory dinner. He'd pulled out his phone and made reservations at some swanky restaurant he told her about. How could she say no? A handsome, obviously successful man had asked her out on the most exciting night of her life.

They just had to make one stop. His hotel room upstairs.

"Clearly you *have* forgotten," she said, fighting to keep her voice even. "Let me refresh your memory. Denver. I'd just won the Teacher of the Year award," she said shaking her head at how foolish she'd been. "I was so naive, but I suspect that was part of the attraction."

He frowned. "I meet a lot of people with my job. Teacher of the Year? That's great and now you're in security?" He took a step toward her. "That's a big career change. I might not remember the night we met, but I can assure you as far as the attraction part—" he dropped his voice, the smile almost blinding "—nothing has changed. You're gorgeous."

He was flirting with her? She felt sick to her stomach. "You really don't remember talking me into coming up to your hotel room so you could change for dinner. At least that was your excuse. I doubt I really have to tell you what happened after that since I'm pretty sure I wasn't your first date rape."

He took a step back and held up both hands. "I'm sure whatever happened was consensual."

"No. No, it wasn't. But I'm also sure that *no* is a word you hear a lot and ignore."

He licked his lips nervously. "If I were you, I'd be careful about throwing around accusations like that. You do understand that I'm the advisor to the governor of the state."

"That's right, you work for the governor."

"*With* the governor," he corrected. "I'm Prescott Rutherford Hollingsworth, his friend as well as his advisor."

"So that's where the Worth came from," she said. "The name you gave me that night, knowing I would never be able to track you down." He hadn't been lying exactly. He'd just left out some crucial details regarding his name.

He continued over the top of her words as if she hadn't spoken. "The governor sent me here to arrange everything before his speech the last night of the event. He plans to hold a press conference to congratulate you. So I'd strongly suggest…" He closed the distance between them. She could see him gritting his teeth to hold back his fury.

For just an instant, she felt that old fear of being helpless. He was a large, strong man so he'd had no trouble holding her down on the floor of that hotel room. But she wasn't that woman anymore, was she.

He seemed surprised when she didn't take a step back but stood her ground even when he grabbed her arm. He squeezed it just hard enough that she knew he was reminding her how much larger and stronger he was. "That it would be a mistake for you to make trouble."

"Unless you want that arm in a cast, I suggest you let go

of me right now." She said the words clearly, calmly, holding his gaze as she did. "I've changed. I now fight back."

He hesitated only a moment before he let go of her and took a step away, visibly agitated and just worried enough that she suspected he would think twice before he touched her again.

"Everything all right in here?" Vi asked as she popped her head in the door of her office. Neither of them answered, but the woman didn't wait for an answer. "If you need me, I'll be at the fairgrounds." With that she left, leaving the door open.

"Worth," she said with just enough sarcasm to make him narrow his eyes, "you can tell your boss that I appreciate his interest, but I don't want an award. I was just doing my job. I'm sure you can coordinate the rest with Vi. And then you can drop dead." She turned and stepped through the open doorway, not looking back as she left.

She was shaking inside from the encounter, but she felt strong. It was like she could finally breathe after all these years. A man like him would never understand what he'd taken from her and how it had changed her life. She'd dreamed of calling him out to his face.

Now she'd gotten the chance. Telling him off felt better even though he deserved worse. But she'd always known she had no legal recourse. It would have been her word against his.

She told herself that all she had to do was get through the next few days and with luck, she'd never have to see Worth again.

CHAPTER TEN

As TJ reached the fairgrounds, her cell phone vibrated in her pocket. Nearby, one of the carnival rides came to life slowly, noisily. She felt her phone vibrate again. Pulling it out, she checked the screen. She didn't recognize the number, so she hesitated, realizing she was more upset about her encounter with Worth than she'd admitted to herself.

She hoped the call wasn't from another news outlet wanting an interview. She let it continue to ring as she walked to a far corner of the fairgrounds where it was quieter. "Hello." Nothing. She took a breath and tried again. "Hello?"

"Maybe we should meet and talk about this."

Worth. Her stomach roiled at the sound of his voice. "I said everything I had to say."

He chuckled. "The thing is I'm not sure I believe that. I think you may have misunderstood my intentions… I can't have you saying these things to anyone else."

"If you're worried that I'd tell your boss, the governor—"

"It's my word against yours, but I don't think you realize how bad that would be for me."

"Maybe you should have thought about that before you lured me into your hotel room in Denver."

"Look, I don't even remember you, but I'm sure you wanted it as much as I did."

"We both know that's not true otherwise I wouldn't have been begging you to stop. I wouldn't have left your room in a torn, stained dress that cost me a week's wages, blood running down my thighs, sobbing. Your last words to me were 'Don't pretend that you didn't want it.' So don't pretend now that you didn't rape me."

"Stop throwing that word around," he said sounding desperate. "You have no proof that I did anything to you. You can't even prove that we met that night."

"Save it," she snapped. "And don't call me again. You know the kind of man you are and so do I. If that scares you, maybe you'll think twice before you invite another woman to your room."

She disconnected and turned, startled to see Marshal Baggins standing only yards away as if he'd come looking for her and now regretted it—just not as much as she did.

How much of the conversation had he overheard? She didn't want him hearing any of this. She still felt shame and embarrassment for being so naive and foolish four years ago. Even now knowing that she wasn't to blame, she didn't want anyone to know. Especially the marshal.

She turned away quickly, her hands shaking as she tried to get herself under control. Seeing Worth again had shaken her, bringing back that horrible night. But that woman he'd taken advantage of wasn't her anymore.

Taking a deep breath, she let it out and turned around, her mind scrambling for an excuse for what Leroy might have heard, only to find the marshal gone.

Leroy wasn't sure exactly what he'd heard moments ago. But he'd heard enough to know that she'd been on the phone with a man. A man who'd threatened her. A man who'd hurt her. And maybe worse, he'd caught TJ at a weak moment, something he hadn't expected and something she wouldn't have wanted him to witness. Seeing the look of surprise and grief in her eyes, he knew she'd never wanted him to see that kind of vulnerability in her either.

He'd been looking for her to find out how the meeting had gone with the governor's advisor. She wasn't looking forward to the press conference. He'd wanted to reassure her. TJ was so strong, so capable, so confident, it surprised him how badly she hated the attention.

Could it have anything to do with what he'd overheard?

He had hurried away, not wanting to embarrass her and knowing if he'd stayed, he would have. From the moment he'd met her, he'd thought the woman was tough as nails, as his grandmother would have said. Strong, determined, a woman who took no guff off anyone. He'd seen her in action, doing her job, and had felt a renewed respect for her. She was good at her profession, but he'd forgotten that under all that toughness was a woman. A desirable, sexy, vulnerable woman.

So who had she been talking to on the phone? Someone who'd scared her? His first instinct had been to go to her. To comfort her. To demand to know who'd caused her any pain. He'd felt so protective of her seeing that vulnerability in this amazing woman.

But he'd known that sympathy was the last thing she would want. That too surprised him. He knew her even though they'd only just met. Just as he instinctively sensed that the last thing she would want him to do was bring up what he'd heard.

He couldn't help being upset and not just about the man who'd hurt her, but why her reaction had affected him the way it had.

He thought about last night on the dance floor. He'd felt a slight tremble in her body as he'd taken her in his arms. She'd saved that boy by risking her life. She hadn't wanted anyone else to know how scared she'd been that she would fail. That glimpse he'd gotten of her vulnerability had drawn him like metal to magnet. Just like moments ago.

He wanted to slay her dragons. To fight a grizzly bare-handed. To get her justice for what had been done to her. Whoever the man was, he was still threatening her from what Leroy had heard. If only TJ would let him in. Maybe he could help. He had no doubt that she thought she could handle it herself.

He knew that if she had her way, she'd want him to just stay out of it. Leave her alone. Let her face this herself.

To hell with that, he thought. He'd be watching out for her now. Damned if the woman hadn't gotten to him.

WORTH WAS SHAKING he was so angry, so upset, so afraid. What the hell was he going to do? He'd never dreamed he'd run into some woman from his past with an axe to grind. "Sounds like the chickens have come home to roost," his former nanny would have said. The old bag with her keen eyes, she knew him too well. He wondered what had happened to her. She would have enjoyed this—the bitch.

As he tried not to panic, he replayed their meeting in that dingy general store office. TJ Walker had recognized him right away. From what she'd said, she'd never forgotten him, had probably been thinking about him all this time. The thought made him aroused despite his revulsion.

He felt a ray of hope. Maybe there was another way to handle her. He'd give it some thought but if he could talk her into another date… He wouldn't mind having a chance to clear up her confusion about him. If only she could see that women loved him. Then maybe she might cut him some slack.

It was a long shot though, he thought as he was reminded

of the steely glint in her eyes when he'd grabbed her. He wouldn't make that mistake—unless the two of them were alone. She thought she could handle him? He'd see about that.

In the meantime, he couldn't let the governor come to Buckhorn. He couldn't trust that TJ Walker wouldn't change her mind and blow his life out of the water. While it was true it was his word against hers, he didn't need this attention. The woman was considered a hero! Her courage and quick thinking had gone viral.

He couldn't have a woman like that telling stories about him. No, he'd talk Jamie out of coming to Buckhorn and he'd get himself the hell out of this town. The more she saw of him, the more worked up she might become and start blabbing about him and some night in Denver he couldn't remember.

The moment he reached his vehicle, he considered calling the governor. The sooner Jamie canceled, the better. But he was still too shaken. Jamie would sense something had happened.

No, he'd wait until he got back to Helena. They still had time to cancel. On the way, he'd figure out what he was going to say. In the meantime, TJ Walker had better keep her mouth shut.

He made a U-turn in the middle of the town and headed back the way he'd come. "Buckhorn," he said under his breath. He hadn't wanted to come here in the first place. It was little more than a wide spot in the narrow two-lane highway. He wouldn't let it ruin everything by putting the governor and TJ Walker together. Jamie already had more than a passing interest in the woman, not realizing—just as Worth hadn't—that the woman was out for blood when it came to men.

Buckhorn's birthday celebration would be over soon. TJ Walker and her security team would move on, and Worth would never have to see her again. She had been just another conquest in a long line of them. Forgetting her this time would be even easier.

Trying to relax, he glanced at Buckhorn in his rearview mirror. Some meaningless hookup wasn't going to derail his plans for the future.

TJ TOOK A deep breath and let it out slowly, as anger shouldered away some of the pain from what Worth had done to her four years ago—and what he'd said to her when she'd confronted him earlier. She hadn't known how to process the fact that he didn't even remember her or what he'd done to her. It told her she was one of many, which made her sad and sorry for the other women he'd sexually assaulted, angry for them too.

Worth*less*, she thought with disgust. She couldn't imagine anyone that callous, that cold and calculating. He'd known exactly what was going to happen—certainly not a celebratory dinner—when he'd talked her into "stopping" by his room so he could change.

Her phone vibrated in her hand. For a split second, she thought it would be him again and braced herself.

With relief, she saw it was Ash. Trouble. She took off at a run.

Ten minutes later she'd helped Ash with a bunch of teenagers who were giving one of the carnival operators a hard time, and turned the ringleader over to the deputies, who said they knew the kid's parents.

Still she had trouble getting Worth off her mind. What were the chances that she would run into the man here in Montana? She thought of her first night here, riding the

Ferris wheel to see the view of the town. Hadn't she sensed then that something had brought her to Buckhorn for a reason? Some might call it closure since as far as she was concerned it was over. That night in Denver when she'd left the hotel in pain and tears, she'd known that if she went to the cops, it would be her word against Worth's. She was the one who'd gone up to his room.

She knew he wanted her to think that he was right, that in his way of thinking, she'd been asking for it. She knew better, but it had taken her a while to realize the truth. She'd put a name to what he'd done to her, knowing there would be no justice.

At least she'd gotten to look him in the eye and tell him what he'd done to her, she told herself. It was enough. It had to be. Unfortunately, it wouldn't save the next trusting young woman he targeted. But maybe it would make him think twice.

Going public now after all this time would only drag her name through the mud, she told herself. Worth in his lofty job would end up unscathed and probably sue her for defamation of character. No, there was no justice, so the only satisfaction she could take was that she had the overconfident Prescott Rutherford Hollingsworth running scared.

WHAT STOPPED JENNIFER cold was Billy Butler, jock extraordinaire and the bane of her existence in high school. She wasn't sure how it was that she'd even recognized him. It had been years but then again how could she forget him? She used to sit behind him in English class and he'd fart purposely, then turn, hold his nose and announce loudly that she was the one who'd let one rip. Then other boys would hold their noses and laugh. She would kick his chair,

getting dirt from her shoe soles on the back of his jeans—
not that that alone had been enough to make him stop.

Now here he was, holding hands with a woman with long
dark hair. Jennifer fell in behind them. She wasn't worried
about him seeing her. She bet he wouldn't remember her
even without her disguise.

The woman with him said something, stopping in front
of the fortune teller's booth and pulling on his hand in obvious encouragement for him to come inside with her. Jennifer stopped at a jewelry booth and pretended interest in
a pair of silver earrings.

"Come on, it will be fun," the woman said, pouting, but
it was clear that Billy wasn't having any of it.

"Meet me in the beer garden," he said. "You can tell
me all about it." He pulled his hand free and turned away.

For a moment, Jennifer thought the woman would change
her mind about going into the fortune teller's booth and follow him. But sighing, she pushed through the draped door
and Jennifer smiled as she followed Billy.

She watched from a distance as he bought a beer before
he wandered away from the crowd into the darkness behind the beer garden. Jennifer hadn't gotten a really good
look at his face yet. For a moment, she hesitated. What if
she was wrong and it wasn't Billy?

As she stood at the edge of the darkness behind the beer
garden, she watched him pull out a pack of cigarettes and
light up. In the glow of the lighter, she saw that his hair
was still blond but not as long. His face was fatter than she
remembered, but she recognized that smirk as he looked
up and saw her watching him. He quickly turned his back
on her, stepping deeper into the darkness as if to study the
moon as it rose in the black velvet of the night sky.

She'd forgotten how long his eyelashes were until she

was standing next to him. "You don't happen to have another one of those, do you?" she asked.

He turned, clearly surprised to find her standing so close. The glow of his cigarette lit the intimate space between them as he tried to hide the fact that she'd startled him.

Raising her gaze to his, she dared him to recognize her. There was no recognition in those eyes. Instead, all she saw was annoyance as he said a grudging "sure" and shook one out of the pack. He thought she was some stranger bumming him for a smoke?

Jennifer took the cigarette, slipped it between her lips and gave him a pointed look. Billy sighed and took a slug of his beer, before pulling his lighter from his pocket. He lit her cigarette. She felt his gaze on her face. Was he trying to place her?

She took a drag although she'd never liked the taste of tobacco any more than she liked the taste of beer. But she knew that if she kissed Billy right now, he would taste like this and that would be all right.

They were alone, all the noise and activity in the background. They'd never been this close before, their faces inches apart. She could hear his breath when he inhaled before exhaling a cloud of smoke over his right shoulder. Junior year, Billy had moved away with his family. She'd forgotten about him until she'd seen him minutes ago and it had all come back. The humiliation, the hatred and inability to do anything to stop him short of murder.

"You don't remember me," she said as he finished his cigarette, dropped it and ground the butt out in the dirt.

"Should I?" he asked and drained his beer.

She watched him crush the can in his hands and drop

it next to the discarded cigarette butt. "You might wish you had."

He flashed her that smirk. "I don't think so," he said and began to turn away without giving her a second glance.

Jen acted instinctively. All that pent-up anger from all the men who had ignored her, mocked her, used her and thrown her away like trash rushed to the surface with Billy Butler at the top of the list. The steak knife was suddenly in her hand. She'd move so quickly that he wouldn't even realize what was happening until she'd thrust the blade into the soft flesh just beneath his ribs and turned it.

She was on him too quickly for him to stop her. Her cigarette falling from her mouth, she grabbed hold of his still thick hair with her free hand and pulled him down for a kiss.

Before the kiss ended she could have stabbed him four times, she thought. Instead she ended the kiss by shoving him away and holding up the knife in front of his face so he could see how close he'd come to being one of her victims.

"You always were a piece of shit, Billy." His eyes had gone as large as saucers as he finally remembered her. No doubt he'd heard about the men she'd killed. His mouth opened in a silent scream as she kicked him in the groin and he dropped silently to his knees in the dirt.

"I guess the party's over for tonight," she said. She dropped down next to him as he writhed on the ground, felt around for his wallet and removed all the bills from it. She took one last look at him still in pain in the dirt before walking toward the creek, keeping to the shadows beneath the pines as the moon rose higher over the fairgrounds.

She felt confused and upset. *You've been a bad girl*, she thought as she walked, her voice in her head sounding like Dr. Moss's. "But it's not your fault. Someone did something to you when you were young. We will discover what it was together. You will remember and it will free you of this… compulsion you have to hurt people."

By the time she reached the dirt road at the edge of town, she couldn't remember what had happened back at the fairgrounds—except there was an ashtray taste in her mouth that made her feel sick to her stomach.

CHAPTER ELEVEN

TJ WAS SURPRISED how late it was. She could have left hours ago. But she knew why she was still here, she thought as she looked around the fairgrounds. She couldn't face going back to her hotel room.

She'd spent the day being stopped by well-meaning people who wanted to thank her or congratulate her. She didn't feel like a hero. Seeing Prescott Rutherford Hollingsworth III had reminded her of the time she'd been a victim. Victim. Hero. They were just words. She didn't want to be either.

Her cell phone buzzed in her pocket. She pulled it out, afraid it would be Worth again. She wasn't sure how she would react if he threatened her again.

She took a breath and hit Accept. "Hello?" She heard nothing on the other end of the line. Walking away from the noise to a quieter spot, she said again, "Hello? If you don't say something, I'm going to—"

"Sorry, I got interrupted," said a female voice.

TJ didn't catch the woman's name. All she heard was "reporter" and "*Billings Gazette*" before she disconnected and turned off her phone.

Stepping from the dark shadows at the edge of the fairgrounds and back into the lights, she noticed that the crowds had dwindled. Worth had gone back to Helena, hadn't he? Or was he still hanging around? She found herself studying the faces who passed her as her steps took her toward the comforting sound of the band playing at the back of the fairgrounds.

There were fewer people dancing as the clock ticked down to the closing hour. She noted that the beer garden had shut down. Once alcohol service was suspended, the crowd thinned quickly. She realized it wasn't just the music and people who'd drawn her. She'd come this way looking for Leroy, but with more than regret, she didn't see him. She told herself it was just as well, given the mood she was in tonight. She hadn't seen him since earlier when she'd feared he'd overheard her phone call.

She told herself to go to the hotel and try to get some sleep, but she didn't move. She kept remembering last night and being in the marshal's arms on the dance floor, as dangerous as it was. Her fear was that in his arms again she would unburden herself to him. She didn't want the marshal to know. If it was hard for her to have to carry the knowledge with her, it would be even harder for Leroy. He was a man of the law. He'd want justice, something that wasn't going to happen.

She pushed the thought away, remembering instead their dance last night. Once he took hold of her, Leroy was in charge. There was no question about who was leading, she thought now with a smile. He was a man who knew who he was. A man who made no excuses for it. A lawman who would risk his own life to save others. But there was also open compassion and caring in the marshal. She'd seen the look on his face after he'd overheard at least part of her phone conversation with Worth. He'd hurt for her.

Because of that, he was also the kind of man who could steal a woman's heart, she reminded herself. So why hadn't he yet?

"You're still here?" She turned to see Z coming toward her. TJ hadn't heard the young woman approach, which was one of Z's talents. "Seems I caught you daydreaming. About anyone in particular?" Z looked pointedly at the dance floor.

She cringed inwardly, realizing that Z knew her a little too well after the jobs they'd worked on together. She knew that the security personnel who worked for her must speculate on her personal life—or the lack thereof.

"Sorry I took off at breakfast," she said ignoring the obvious reference to the marshal. "That article… I don't like—"

"Being singled out for anything," Z finished for her with a chuckle. "But it was a flattering piece and should be good for business. And the marshal's glowing comments were a positive addition. He seems to be a nice man," she said going back to the original subject. "He has a lot of confidence in you, and he clearly likes you." She cocked her head. "You do realize that, right?"

"Z—"

"I'm going to walk the perimeter unless there's something else you want me to do."

TJ shook her head. "Then you can call it a night. Take the middle shift tomorrow. I'll cover in the morning." Z nodded, but hesitated as if there was more she wanted to say. "He was here earlier, in case you're wondering. The marshal," she said as she took a couple of steps back. "He acted as if he was looking for someone."

"Get some rest," TJ said with a shake of her head and Z laughed and left.

She had a standing rule. No romancing on the job. Not between security personnel and certainly not with the locals. But still it happened and usually ended badly. More than broken hearts, it often meant that the job they were paid to do didn't get done well.

TJ wasn't about to let that happen. Still, she didn't like that Z had picked up on something she hadn't let herself admit. She wasn't just attracted to Leroy. She liked him. Respected him. It wasn't just the article going viral or running into Worth after all this time that had her feeling so vulnerable as she looked up and saw the marshal. Her heart did a little dip.

LEROY HAD BEEN looking for TJ earlier when he'd gone back to the dance floor as the night wound down. Maybe it had been wishful thinking, but he'd kind of expected to find her there. He'd been disappointed when he hadn't. He'd been worried about her after what he'd overheard earlier. Something else he hated to acknowledge—especially to her.

He'd left the dance area, but now he'd found his way back before the last song of the night. He had optimistically— and just as foolishly—found himself procuring two cans of cold beer from his friend Dave at the beer garden before it closed for the evening. He'd gone over to where the band was playing thinking that like him, TJ might want—if not another dance, then at least a cold beer. They'd made it through another day without any major disasters.

"One of those for me or are you planning to drink them both?"

He turned at the sound of her voice, his heart ticking up a beat, more than pleased to see her. She stood at the edge of the darkness, but there was enough moonlight above them that he could see her face clearly. She wasn't a classic beauty. Like her features, she was unique in every way, he thought. "I'd hoped I wouldn't have to drink them both," he said as he joined her.

She smiled as she took one, popped the top and raised it in a toast. She did seem glad to see him and she had a great smile. "To another day down." He watched her take a long drink, admiring her slim throat as she swallowed. She lowered the can, licked foam from her upper lip and grinned. He thought of the donuts she loved, the glisten of sugar at the corner of her mouth earlier. At the time, he'd thought the woman seemed to attack life with no apologies. Also with apparently no fear. He thought he knew better now.

The two of them stepped away as the band finished its last song of the night, the music dying away along with the sound of voices as the dancers as well as the musicians wandered to their vehicles to leave for the night.

TJ moved along the side of the beer garden until she reached the back. She leaned against the makeshift wall in the shadow of the nearly full moon and looked out over the pasture to the trees that lined the creek before turning her gaze on him. He could feel her studying him, the sounds of the late summer night dying around them, making him feel as if they were the only two people left on earth.

He joined her in the darkness and opened his own beer to take a drink. It tasted wonderful and yet he knew he didn't find the same pleasure in it that she obviously did. From here, they had a view of mountains and the valley beyond Buckhorn. He could make out a few lights in the distance. Even with the moon up again tonight, they were in its shade here.

"The beer was a good idea," TJ said, those green eyes on him. "Thanks. I get the feeling that I make you...uncomfortable."

He smiled into the warm darkness. "Something like that."

"You're nothing like I expected, Marshal."

Leroy gave her a side-eye. "I wouldn't be so sure about that." She chuckled and he took another sip of his beer, way too aware of this woman. The night air was now a fusion of scents, TJ's light summer-sweet perfume an integral part of it.

She looked out beyond the fairgrounds, one finger drawing in the condensation on her beer can for a moment. "I think it's the uniform. Once you put it on, you're the marshal you think everyone expects. By the Book Baggins. But when that uniform comes off and you drop it on the floor..." She was staring out toward the mountains. He could see that she was fighting a grin, clearly teasing him.

"You think I would drop my uniform on the floor?"

She let out a soft chuckle and seemed to give in to the grin. Her gaze shifted to his and he felt a start at the directness of it. "Under the right circumstances, I know you would."

He laughed. It felt good. He let his head loll back against the makeshift wall of the beer garden, staring up at the stars, unable not to imagine the right circumstances with this woman. It wasn't the kind of image a man could easily ignore. He felt a wistfulness along with a sharp, hot stab of desire. The night felt more sultry, more intimate with each passing minute. They were alone on one of the last nights of summer in Montana.

"Are you flirting with me, Ms. Walker?"

"You can't tell?" She moved closer. "Maybe it's the moonlight," she said almost contemplatively. "Or maybe you're the first man I've met in a long time who makes me want to throw caution to the wind."

Leroy suspected there was more to it, but right now he didn't care even if her earlier phone call was the cause. He wasn't going to question it. He met those amazing eyes of hers, reached over and took her empty hand and drew her back deeper into the dark shadows. Balancing his beer on the wooden ledge of the structure, he reached to take hers.

He'd never wanted to kiss a woman more than he did this one. Right now. Right here on this moonlit night. He could smell pine and water and the hint of carnival food that still hung on the air—and that soft touch of her perfume that teased him as he drew her to him.

Her gaze locked with his, her lips parting slightly as he cupped the back of her head and drew her to him. Her skin was cool to the touch, her hair silken in his fingers. Even without the direct glow of the moon, he could see the flash of desire in her eyes as he brushed a thumb over those full lips.

She was like the kind of wild carnival ride he would never go on under any circumstances. But tonight, secluded here in the warm darkness all alone, he couldn't resist even as his good sense argued with him not to. She'd started this and now her gaze promised that she was in for the whole ride.

He leaned toward her, his fingers digging deeper into her hair. He'd thought the kiss would be tender, slow, maybe even a little tentative. But the moment his lips touched hers, he knew that she wanted this as much as he did. The smoldering need inside him burst into searing flame. He took her mouth, her lips warm and urgent with the taste of beer. He kissed her with a fervor he'd never known and she returned his kiss with a passion of her own.

Leroy enveloped her slim body in his arms and deepened the kiss. Her tongue met his with the same urgency he felt, making him want more, need more of this woman. Desire ran like a molten river through him. No one had spurred this kind of need in him—until TJ. He didn't just want to protect her. He wanted her.

THE MOMENT SHE saw the marshal standing there with two cans of beer and that smile on his face, TJ had wanted this. She reveled in what felt like dangerous, exhilarating freedom. She had never wanted anyone like this. Her breasts ached, her nipples hardened to pebbles even before he touched her.

She groaned against his mouth as he slid his hand under her T-shirt to stroke her bare skin as his fingers glided up to cup her breast. A moan escaped her lips as he ferreted out her nipple, squeezing the tip and making her legs go weak as she leaned into him. She'd wanted this, needed this, but it surprised her, the emotions the marshal brought to the surface.

What she hadn't expected was the effect his kiss had on her. She'd wanted it and more. When he took her in his arms, she hadn't thrown on the brakes. Instead, she'd yearned for more as a firestorm of desire had rushed over her as he'd drawn her closer.

Opening the snaps on his Western shirt, she'd pulled it apart, flattening her palms against his rock-hard six-pack and surrendering to feelings deeper than she'd expected. It was like opening a floodgate that she'd held in check for too long. There had been other men, decent men unlike Worth, who had wanted to be with her, but she'd kept them all at arm's length.

Marshal Leroy Baggins had pushed aside the protective walls she'd built around her as if they weren't constructed of iron and steel. He'd bulldozed them down with one kiss. She wanted this man come hell or high water, she thought as she reached for the buttons on his jeans not worrying about where they were or what was about to happen—until she heard the deputy's voice come over Leroy's radio.

"I've got a man here who swears he saw Jennifer Mullen at the fairgrounds earlier," Deputy Yarrow said. "I thought you might want to talk to him. His name is William Butler, a former classmate of Jennifer's. He says she had a knife and that if he hadn't gotten away from her, he knows she would have killed him. I have him at the fairgrounds annex office by the parking lot. I saw that your patrol SUV was still here."

CHAPTER TWELVE

FOR A MOMENT, the two of them just stared at each other with the jarring and sudden return to earth. Leroy cleared his voice and said into the radio, "I'll be right there."

TJ felt a flush of embarrassment wash over her. What if the deputy had come looking for them and found them a few minutes from now? She took a breath, fighting to still the surging emotions raging through her. Her skin felt hot and not with just embarrassment at how close they'd come to being caught. What had they been thinking? They hadn't.

Stepping back, she gave him room to pull his clothing as well as himself together. She did the same. She could tell he wanted to say something. She felt the same way, though words escaped her right now.

Strangely, along with unfulfilled yearning, she felt disappointment. She'd never meant for it to go this far and yet now she wished that it had. Maybe then she could get the marshal out of her system.

She felt the marshal's penetrating gaze on her and felt the full force of the intimacy they'd just shared. She told herself that she didn't regret it, but still it scared her. She'd let down her defenses.

"I guess we should be glad that Jennifer didn't kill the man," Leroy said into the thick silence. She nodded. "I've been dreading something like this from the time I heard that Jennifer had escaped."

So this was the way he was going to handle this? Work as usual?

He finished straightening his clothing and looked at her. She couldn't read his expression. "I guess I'd better go see what the story is."

So he was going to pretend it hadn't happened? Or just ignore it?

"I guess you'd better."

LEROY SWORE SILENTLY. Damned if he hadn't almost been caught with his pants down. What the hell had he been thinking? It had felt like they were all alone in the world, but they had been far from it. Just the thought that Deputy Yarrow of all people might have caught them...

He knew he should say something to TJ. But right now he couldn't even give voice to what he was feeling. His heart was still pounding, his blood running hot, his desire making his body throb. He wanted this woman like he'd never wanted anything in his life.

Yet he couldn't believe that he'd almost taken her out behind the fairgrounds beer garden like a rutting teenager. He couldn't have been more embarrassed unless the deputy *had* caught them.

"I'm sorry. I have to go." He didn't want to leave her like this. But he also couldn't take the time to try to tell her everything he was feeling right now. "I'll see you tomorrow?"

She nodded again and he knew he was blowing this, but there wasn't nothing he could do about it right now.

As he moved past her, he tried to brush a kiss across her lips. But she turned her head and it landed on her cheek. He swore under his breath as he walked away, feeling like a heel. He feared that he'd hurt her feelings, something that pained him. She was the last person on earth he wanted to hurt.

Leroy forced himself to shift gears. He had to do his job. Usually, that wasn't a problem. Right now, it took all of his concentration. Where was By the Book Baggins when he needed him? Hadn't he known Jennifer might strike again?

As he reached the small makeshift office at the fairgrounds gate, he saw Deputy Yarrow waiting. The look the older deputy gave him questioned where he'd been and what he'd been doing. Or maybe Leroy was just reading that into the man's expression.

What he found himself wondering as he looked from the deputy to the couple standing nearby was how William Butler had managed to get away alive from Jennifer.

Yarrow introduced Leroy to William Butler and his girlfriend. Butler appeared agitated as he recounted his encounter with Jennifer. He talked fast, using a lot of hand gestures, avoiding eye contact. The man was clearly still scared as if realizing that he'd dodged a bullet. But he was also lying about something, Leroy thought.

"How did you know Jennifer?" the marshal asked.

Butler explained that he used to live in Buckhorn, had some classes with her.

"Isn't she the one you used to tease all the time?" the girlfriend asked, making Butler flush.

"It was just good-natured fun," Butler said and flashed her a warning look.

"Why did you wait so long to notify anyone?" Leroy asked.

"I didn't recognize her at first," the man said. "But once I saw the knife, I didn't care who she was." He shuddered and his girlfriend put a protective hand on his shoulder that he seemed to shrug off.

Leroy could feel the tension between the two of them. Did the girlfriend know he was lying? He suspected it had been her idea to tell the law about Jennifer. William Butler it seemed would have been happy to put the incident behind him.

"How did you manage to get away from her?" Leroy asked.

Butler shook his head. "It all happened so fast. She came at me, I saw the knife, I shoved her away and took off. It wasn't until later that I realized who she was and how dangerous the situation had been. It's a wonder I'm not dead right now." He glanced toward the darkness beyond the fairgrounds. "Isn't she supposed to be locked up somewhere?"

Leroy took down Butler's phone number after taking his statement. "If you see Jennifer again—"

"That won't happen," the man said quickly. "We're getting out of here. I looked into her eyes…" He shuddered again. "There is no way I'd chance running into her again. No way."

As the couple hurried to their vehicle and drove out of town, Leroy looked out across the dark landscape to the river and trees and, beyond, the mountains. "You believe his story?" he asked his deputy.

"Sure, don't you?"

"I believe he saw someone who scared him. If it was Jennifer, then he's lucky to be alive." Why hadn't she killed him? It sounded like there was some old animosity there. "Well, at least now we know that she has a knife." He met the older man's gaze. "Be careful. I believe that he saw Jennifer and that she's still out there," he said and walked to his vehicle.

By the time he slid behind the wheel, he felt bone tired and filled with regret. He should have said something to

TJ. He should have told her how he felt. The thought made him laugh as he started the engine. How the hell did he feel about her and what was he going to do with those feelings?

BY THE TIME she reached the hotel, TJ had done her best to play down what had happened between her and the marshal. She'd reminded herself that in two days, she would be packing up and leaving for her next job. She reminded herself of that fact even as the impact of the kiss still thrummed through her veins. Just the thought of what the kiss might have led to...

She'd even tried to convince herself that she hadn't felt anything earthshaking. It was a lie. If not for the deputy radioing when he did, she knew the kiss would have gone much further. A part of her ached because it hadn't.

And if it had? Then what? She didn't know. A future with Marshal Leroy Baggins? She scoffed at the idea. They hardly knew each other, not to mention how different they were. But even as she tried to convince herself that tonight had meant nothing between them, she knew her heart desperately wanted more. After Worth, she'd questioned if there were any good men left. She'd met a few but none like Leroy Baggins.

What was she going to do? she wondered as she went up to her room. She couldn't have Leroy, but could she ever forget him?

LEROY FELT WORN OUT, but he knew he couldn't sleep even if he tried. Instead, he needed to focus on Jennifer. She was no fool. She'd been spotted. She'd need somewhere to hide. He thought of Shirley Langer. If she was in town, Jennifer might go to her.

He had to check it out. He still couldn't believe what he'd

let happen tonight with TJ against the side of the beer garden. The fact that anyone could have walked up on them had been the last thing on his mind.

He swore under his breath. What was wrong with him? That had been so out of character. Just like the desire still coursing through his bloodstream. He'd never been like this with another woman. Then again, he'd never met anyone like TJ Walker, he reminded himself. He shook his head, remembering how he hadn't wanted to stop. When the deputy had radioed, he'd been startled, TJ still in his arms, him not wanting to let go.

Reminding himself that he had a killer probably still loose in Buckhorn, he tried to put TJ out of his mind. Right now he needed to be By the Book Baggins. Earlier, he thought he'd seen Shirley in the crowd. When she'd spotted him, she seemed to go out of her way to avoid him. He hadn't thought much about it, but looking back he'd gotten the impression she'd been looking for someone. Jennifer. Had the two planned to meet here at the fairgrounds during the celebration?

He wouldn't have been surprised since he'd checked a while back and found out that the only person who'd taken Jennifer's collect calls from the mental facility over the years since her incarceration had been her old friend Shirley.

That had surprised him. He'd wondered about that relationship since he'd gotten the feeling that Jennifer had been the more dominant friend, with Shirley more the follower. After Jennifer's arrest and his interview with Shirley, he'd felt as if she was almost relieved that her best friend was somewhere safe behind bars.

Except now Jennifer wasn't.

He told himself that Shirley could be here for the celebration, but he feared it was more than that as he climbed out of his patrol SUV and walked across the highway to the Sleepy Pine Motel. Shirley used to manage the place before she left town. He was acting on a hunch that it was the one place she might stay on her visit. The new manager was about Shirley's age and was originally from Buckhorn.

His hunch paid off. While it was late, he raised the manager from bed to find that Shirley was staying on the couch in the apartment behind the motel office.

"Could I have a word with you?" he asked Shirley when she came out to the office rubbing her eyes and trying to wake up. She wore a T-shirt and shorts, her feet bare. He suggested she put on something warmer since the late summer night had cooled. He motioned to an old wooden picnic table out back letting her know that he would be waiting for her while she got dressed.

"What's this about?" she asked when she finally came back out wearing the same T-shirt and shorts, having added only a pair of socks. She did however look a little more awake.

He offered her a seat at the table before he said, "I saw you at the fairgrounds earlier. I thought you saw me." She swallowed and said nothing. "I'm wondering why you're in town."

She shot him a look of defiance and what could have been guilt. "I have every right to be here. This was my home." Her voice broke. "I can come here whenever I want."

Leroy raised both hands in surrender. "Of course you can. So you came back for the celebration?" She gave a slight nod that was more like a shrug. "I'm just wondering if your being here has anything to do with Jennifer Mullen."

She looked surprised. "Why would you think that?"

"I know you've been in contact with her." He waited, but

she didn't respond. "Are you aware that she has escaped from the facility where she was being held?"

Eyes wide with shock, Shirley rubbed her bare arms as she hugged herself and looked around as if suddenly scared. "She's here, here in Buckhorn?"

"You haven't seen her then?" Shirley shook her head, her face pale from what could have been more than shock. Was it fear? "You weren't meeting her here?"

A hard shake of her head. "She told me to come because she couldn't. She said she wanted to know what it was like, who I saw…"

He studied her, trying to decide if he believed her. "You didn't suspect that she planned to escape?"

"No," she said emphatically. "I wouldn't have come if I thought that was her plan." She looked around as if she half expected Jennifer to come out of the darkness. The sun would be working its way up the backside of the eastern mountain range before long, lighting the sky to silvery blue. "Does she know that I talked to you after she was arrested?"

"I don't know. I certainly didn't tell her if that's what you're asking." She hugged herself tighter, looking close to tears. Shirley had shared some of the shocking things that her friend had said and done a year or so ago, but denied knowing anything about the killings. She'd also told him that Jennifer kept a diary hidden in her room. That diary had gotten her sent to the mental institution rather than prison.

"I need you to call me if you hear from her." Leroy pulled out one of his cards and reached across the table to hand it to her. She took the card with trembling fingers and closed it in her fist.

She looked like a woman who was about to run. He wondered if she would stay long enough for Jennifer to get in touch as he rose from the picnic table. "One more thing. Did you know someone named William Butler?"

Shirley started to shake her head but stopped. "There was a Billy Butler in our class."

"He said he used to tease Jennifer," Leroy said. He saw her eyes widen in alarm as she realized what he was asking.

"Did she...?"

He shook his head. "Why would she want to kill him?"

"Billy was always farting in English class and pretending it was Jen who'd done it. She hated...him." Shirley shook her head as if in denial. "You're sure she didn't..."

"He said he got away from her before she could." Shirley didn't look any more convinced of that than he did. "If you see Jennifer—"

She stumbled to her feet, his card clutched in one fist as she backed away from him and the picnic table and the news he'd brought her. "I won't see her." She shook her head and looked out into the darkness again. The fear was back in her eyes. "I'm leaving as soon as I can get packed and get out of town."

He couldn't blame her. "But if you see her first, you'll call me."

Shirley Langer nodded, but he could tell she planned to be miles from here soon, with no intention of sticking around to give her old friend a chance to find her.

AFTER A LONG DAY, Vi had headed home wanting only to put her feet up and have a glass of wine. Hell, she might have a whole bottle if she wanted to. She hadn't seen Axel again. That alone lifted her spirits.

Attendance at the celebration had increased each day. The small entry fee would go into the town's general fund. Vi had a number of pet projects she hoped it would pay for.

She figured tomorrow's take would be better. The last day would be the best, she told herself—when the governor of the state would be having a press conference in front of her store and giving the closing speech.

She smiled to herself. The celebration was even better than she'd expected. Her smile turned sour though as she recalled seeing her niece. Surely Jennifer wasn't why she hadn't seen Axel again, was she? She didn't want him dead—just gone. Mostly, she didn't want anything to spoil the birthday celebration.

Ahead, she could see her house sitting against the mountainside with a view of the valley and of course of the town. Vi always felt better once she was inside her home and alone. She'd had the house built after Axel left. Before that, the two of them had lived over the store until Tina was born and then moved into a larger house just a block from the business.

Living in town had made sense back then. But after Axel deserted her, she'd needed a change. Her headlights fell on the wall of glass framed in rock. Just the sight of the place pleased her.

She parked, climbed out and mounted the steps to the first floor to shove open the door. Few people locked their houses in rural Montana. She wasn't one of them. Stepping in, she turned on the lights as she headed for the kitchen and the wine she had waiting. Vi loved this house with its many windows and light open space. Axel would have hated it. Just the thought made her smile.

Even though it was late, she opened the wine, poured a glass and did what she did most nights. She called her daughter. Tina had always been her sounding board whether she'd appreciated it or not.

They might not be blood, but Vi had relied on Tina from

the time her daughter was old enough to talk. It wasn't like she'd been able to bounce anything off Axel, whose usual response was "Doesn't sound like it's any of your business. I wouldn't worry about it if I were you." Fortunately, Tina had always listened and had often helped Vi make a decision even when she didn't always take her daughter's advice.

"Mom?"

She could tell that she'd awakened her, but she did love Tina still calling her mom. "Sorry. I thought you'd be up reading."

"I was, but I finished the book and fell asleep. What's wrong?"

She hadn't realized that she was going to, but she told her about seeing Jennifer at the fairgrounds.

"Have you told the marshal?" Tina asked sounding wide awake and worried now.

"Is Lars home?" Vi asked avoiding the question.

"He's working late tonight trying to get caught up since the celebration has pulled him away from his normal job. Not that he minds," she added as if realizing Vi might take that as a complaint against her and her celebration. "Mom, you need to let Leroy know about Jennifer."

She nodded to herself. She'd taken Jennifer in, given her the Mullen name, treated her like a daughter. How could she call the law on her?

"I heard that several news outlets have asked for the photos you've taken during the celebration so far," Vi said, making another attempt to change the subject. "You're not working too much, are you? I mean, are you feeling all right?" she asked, thinking of Tina's pregnancy. Her daughter had had a shock yesterday. They both had. But some-

how Vi figured Tina wouldn't mind being the daughter of
Earl Ray and Tory Caulfield. She might even be relieved.

"I'm fine. The baby is fine." It's what she always said
when Vi worried. "You have to call the marshal."

She sighed. "You're right."

Vi knew that Tina had anguished over the fact that neither of them had visited Jennifer in the mental institution.
Vi had been dead set against it, saying it wouldn't be good
for her or the baby. Tina and Jen had been so close before
all the ugly stuff happened. She still couldn't believe that
Jen had done what they said she had. But she thought this
was the way Jennifer had wanted it—no communication—
and that's why her niece had never tried calling her. At least
that's what she told herself.

Silence, then, "How did Jen look?"

Vi took a sip of her wine. "Fine, I guess. She dyed her
hair red."

Tina made a sound, a cross between a chuckle and a
sob. "She always wanted my red hair. I hope she doesn't
get into more trouble."

Vi thought of the finger gun Jennifer had pointed at
Axel. "Maybe Leroy has already picked her up and taken
her back to her padded cell." It was wishful thinking. She
doubted her niece would be that easy to catch. It wasn't
like the marshal didn't already know Jennifer was on the
loose and had been for a few days. "I think the celebration
is a success, don't you?"

She heard the smile in Tina's voice. "It is, Mom. You
did a great job."

She felt her eyes burn. "You'll still call me mom?" Her
voice broke.

"You'll always be my mom. You're the only mother I've
known. Nothing has changed."

Vi wished that were true, but she was glad that Tina wasn't going to start calling her by her first name. "I should let you get some rest." And yet she hated to hang up and break this now tenuous connection. She didn't want to let go. She and Tina had seldom seen eye to eye. That's because Tina was a better person than she was and they both knew it. That was one reason Vi needed her daughter so much.

"I am tired," Tina admitted.

"Kiss my granddaughter for me and good night," Vi said and disconnected before she tried to drag out the conversation any longer.

But as she disconnected, she heard a noise. The night had been still, the nearly full moon casting long dark shadows. She heard the sound again and looked up. Something was moving around in the attic.

Or someone.

CHAPTER THIRTEEN

IN THE ATTIC, Jen climbed up on an old chaise lounge and lay listening. Earlier she'd heard her aunt downstairs on the phone. She wondered if her aunt would call the marshal or throw her out. But she didn't really expect Vi to do either—just as she hadn't all those years ago when Jen had shown up at her door crying and homeless and afraid. Vi hadn't hesitated to take her in and make her part of her family.

For a long time, Jen lay listening. The soft chaise lounge felt amazing. She hadn't had any piece of furniture this comfortable to sleep on for a very long time.

Mentally she set her internal alarm for just before sunrise. Her aunt hadn't called the marshal on her, but Jen knew better than to push it. After all, she was a murderer—or so they told her. Most people wouldn't want one in their house, especially in the light of day.

Tomorrow loomed with all kinds of possibilities. She needed to find her best friend, Shirley, who'd promised she would come. She better have. Jen also couldn't leave Buckhorn without seeing her cousin Tina and daughter, Chloe. She'd spotted her cousin earlier, but Tina hadn't seen her. She wanted to surprise her when she showed up at her house. She'd missed her and couldn't wait to meet Chloe. But she didn't want to run into Lars so she would wait until he left before entering the house. She suspected the back door key was where it was always kept. Some things hadn't changed, she hoped.

It felt strange to see all the transformations in Buckhorn that had been made and she realized that life had gone on without her. That made her a little sad. Maybe a little angry. She tried to think of something happy, like seeing her friend Shirley. Or meeting a man who might fall in love with her. She'd never had much luck with guys before her incarceration and was doubtful it might happen now. Maybe she was never meant to find true love. She'd never been as lucky in love as her cousin Tina.

So far, she'd caused little trouble, she told herself. She'd avoided running into the marshal or his deputies, although she'd seen them. She'd stolen some money, but she had to eat.

She ignored the disgusting taste in her mouth and the insistent nagging feeling that she'd done something wrong though as she willed herself to sleep, hoping nothing spoiled her Buckhorn reunion. Closing her eyes, she fell into a deep sleep.

ALL THE WAY HOME, Worth thought about how to get the governor to change his mind. Most of the time, he could influence him. But every once in a while, Jamie would dig in his heels as if to remind Worth who was in authority. As if he forgot. Jamie was his ticket to where he wanted to be in the next five years. It wasn't a pie-in-the-sky dream anymore. He'd heard the talk. Jamie's name was being spread around as the kind of candidate the party needed.

Which made it so much worse that Worth was now being put in this risky position—and by a woman. Maybe he could have handled it better, but she caught him off guard. How was he to know that they'd met before. Not just met, but screwed. Now, after all this time, she wanted to complain about it? He certainly didn't recall any hookup like the one she described. He'd never had any complaints, well, none that he took seriously.

Women. They dressed, flirted and talked a good game. They accepted the drinks and dinners he bought them. Just because one of them had second thoughts and things had gotten a little rough, she had no right to try to ruin his future.

If he could talk Jamie out of going to Buckhorn, then he thought that would be the end of it. But if they returned to congratulate TJ Walker, it might be just enough for her to say something to the governor about his best friend and advisor. He had no idea what Jamie would do because it was critical that he avoided scandal until the next presidential election. He might decide Worth was too much of a liability.

And if TJ went public… Worth shuddered at the thought. It might bring other women he'd bedded out of the woodwork for their fifteen minutes of fame and totally destroy his future.

If he couldn't talk Jamie out of going to Buckhorn and congratulating TJ during a press conference, then he'd have to make sure TJ Walker kept her mouth shut.

CHAPTER FOURTEEN

DAY THREE

TJ HADN'T THOUGHT she would be able to sleep last night. But she'd stripped down and climbed under the covers knowing she needed the rest. It had been an eventful night.

Her thoughts had gone straight as an arrow to the marshal. Her breasts had tingled with the memory of his taking the weight of one in his palm. Her nipples had hardened instantly at the memory. She'd groaned and rolled over onto her side and told herself that she'd never get to sleep at this rate.

She'd steered her thoughts to Jennifer. By now the young woman could already be arrested. Leroy could have been on his way to the mental facility and Jennifer would soon be locked up again. Eyelids growing heavy, she'd snuggled down in the covers and thought of Leroy and wondered what he'd say when they saw each other again. He'd sure seemed at a loss for words last night. But then so had she.

As the sun streamed in through the open curtains of her room, TJ sat up with a start. She'd been having a dream… and definitely not her usual nightmare about that horrible night four years ago.

Her gaze flew over to the other side of her bed. She half expected to find the marshal stretched out naked in the bed next to her. *Now there was an image she wouldn't soon for-*

get. She groaned and lay back down. Her whole body quivered. The dream had been so erotic, and the marshal had been so...damned sexy and a lot more experienced than she'd thought he would be.

Definitely a dream, she said to herself as she swung her legs over the side of the bed and headed for the shower. She couldn't imagine that the sexy, amazing lover in her dream had been Leroy Baggins. Still, she couldn't shake off the fact that it had been him. It had been that real.

Twenty minutes later, dressed and ready for work, she hopped on her motorcycle and raced to the fairgrounds.

"TJ?" The sound of the marshal's voice made her freeze just as she was about to park her bike. She felt heat radiate from her face downward at just the sound of his voice. She felt naked.

Stop acting so ridiculous, she told herself. It was a *dream.*

Turning, she thought she was prepared to face him. "Marshal." Her voice broke. It was his mouth. She remembered it on hers and his big hands on other parts of her body so intimate and real and recent that she could almost taste him on her lips still.

"YOU'RE UP EARLY," Leroy said studying her as she finished parking her motorcycle. He felt as if he'd caught her off guard. She didn't seem to want to face him. Was this about last night? Was she embarrassed and wished it hadn't happened?

She turned. He saw her tug at her lower lip with her teeth. Nervous? He felt uneasy as well. He thought about how they'd been interrupted last night and how far it could have gone if the deputy hadn't called.

If she was upset with him about last night... "Are you okay?" he had to ask.

She shook her head, a nervous laugh escaping as her gaze still avoided his. "Just not quite awake yet."

He knew that wasn't true and couldn't help being curious as to what had caused this change in her. But by the time she lifted her gaze to him again, she smiled and he told himself she was fine. Maybe at some point they would talk about it. Or not.

As he started to relax, assuring himself that things were back to normal between them, he realized that something rattled him more than he wanted to admit. TJ had a glow about her, a softness, almost a vulnerability that he hadn't seen before. She looked like a woman who'd had a lover last night. Apparently a skilled one.

Leroy cleared his voice, feeling more uncomfortable at the path his thoughts had taken. Her love life was none of his business. Still, he couldn't help but think about what they'd shared. There's no way she had a "date" last night after their romantic encounter, was there?

"I think we're in for a long day," he said, desperately needing to rein in his thoughts and fill the silence between them. "I was just about to go up to Vi Mullen's to talk to her about canceling the rest of the celebration. Would you like to come along?" He mentally kicked himself. Couldn't he see that she was trying to get away from him?

Like the kiss last night, the invite had been spur-of-the-moment. But he realized he could use her help if for nothing more than moral support with Vi.

"Sure," she said, not sounding all that convinced.

Leroy saw the slight flush and hated to admit that he was jealous as hell if there was another man who'd put that glow in her cheeks.

"ALL SET?" JAMIE ASKED the moment Worth walked into his office.

He'd had a restless night, not even dropping by his so-called date's house to see if her husband had returned or not.

Now he shook his head, searching for the right words to make this not happen. "Buckhorn is even more of a waste of time than I thought it would be." He stepped in, avoiding Jamie's gaze as he sat down. "Up to you, but I can't see why you'd bother."

At the silence that followed, he looked up to see Jamie studying him.

"What happened?" the governor asked. Damn, he knew him so well.

"*Nothing* happened. That's the point." He could feel his friend's gaze on him.

"Did you meet her?"

"Vi Mullen?" He scoffed. "She's old enough that I doubt she'll even be around for your next election."

"Not *her*. TJ Walker."

Worth hesitated, afraid Jamie wasn't in the least bit fooled. "She isn't interested in more publicity about her heroism."

Jamie frowned. "You told her I wanted to meet her?"

He nodded. "Sorry, she wasn't impressed."

The governor laughed and leaned back in his chair smiling. "What's really going on?"

"Nothing, it's a long drive to the middle of nowhere and I didn't sleep well last night." He sighed. "I'm just tired. Like I said, not worth your time but do whatever you want."

A few minutes passed. Worth pretended interest in his phone as he waited and hoped.

"How did you leave it?" Jamie finally asked.

"I told the Mullen woman that you would get back to

her." A lie. The old bat thought it was all settled. She'd be upset when Jamie canceled.

"Give me her number," the governor said.

Worth pulled the note Jamie had originally given him from his pocket, got up and walked it over to him and waited. The room grew uncomfortably quiet as Jamie studied the name and number written on the note before picking up the landline. Holding his breath, Worth thought he'd talked the governor out of the trip as he watched him dial.

"Mrs. Mullen? I just wanted to let you know that I'm looking forward to speaking at your closing event. Yes, we'll definitely do a press conference prior to that to congratulate the head of your private security team." Jamie looked up at him before he said, "TJ Walker. That shouldn't be a problem, should it?" Silence, then, "Good, I'm glad to hear that. My advisor questioned whether she would be available." A beat, then, "Good. He must have misunderstood. By the way, did you happen to find a place we can stay?"

Swearing under his breath, Worth turned away unable to keep the anger and fear from his face. Behind him he heard the governor say, "Staying on a supporter's ranch would be perfect. Please do thank him. You'll send the directions to the ranch? Wonderful. See you soon." As Jamie hung up, he said, "Get packed. We're going Western so dust off your boots and your Stetson. It's Buckhorn or bust tomorrow unless you can tell me why we shouldn't go."

He turned around slowly and shook his head. "Like I said, if that's what you want…"

"It's what I want. Mullen said she guaranteed that TJ Walker would be at the press conference. You all right with that?"

"Why wouldn't I be?"

The governor considered him for a long moment. "That's what I'm wondering. You didn't get out of line with her, did you?"

Worth shook his head as he headed for the door.

"Where are you going?" his friend demanded.

"Going to dust off my boots," he said over his shoulder, no longer able to hide his growing fear that TJ Walker was going to ruin his life.

Unless he stopped her.

LAST NIGHT AFTER her call to her daughter, Vi had considered calling the marshal. She knew she probably should have. It wouldn't have taken him or one of his deputies any time at all to get to her house since she wasn't even a mile from the fairgrounds and she knew the marshal was staying in the hotel until the celebration was over.

But when she took out her cell phone, she'd turned it off rather than made the call. How foolish she would feel if it was simply a wild animal that had gotten into her attic. She would have gotten the marshal out here for nothing.

Though she did consider what she would have done if she knew for a fact that it had been Jennifer. Would she have made the call? She knew she should have called Leroy to tell him that she'd seen her niece.

Last night, she'd opted to merely go to bed. The celebration was almost over. The governor was coming to Buckhorn, to her celebration. She'd been determined that nothing would spoil this moment for her.

But she had locked her bedroom door just in case the wild animal in the attic came downstairs.

Vi had closed her eyes. She'd tried not to think of Tina and Chloe and the new baby. Not her blood. Hot tears had scalded her cheeks. She hadn't bothered to brush them away. How much more would she have to lose?

It reminded her of her mother's beloved vase that Karla Parson had purposely broken. She'd fallen asleep thinking of ways to get even with Karla. Hadn't she thought that during the celebration would be the perfect time to settle that old score? Her plans to get even with Karla calmed her some, and she'd fallen into a restless, nightmare-filled sleep only to awaken with a start this morning.

Was there really something dangerous in her attic?

JEN HAD AWAKENED this morning with the first light of sunrise, feeling refreshed—and surprised to find herself not locked in a padded room. For a moment she couldn't remember where she was. Or worse, what she'd done.

She had a sudden flash of a man's face. Billy Butler? Had she...? She didn't think so as she looked down at the clothing she was still wearing. No blood, she saw with a strange relief. The jerk had been asking for it, but Jen was glad that she hadn't spoiled her aunt's celebration.

Now though, if Billy told anyone he saw her, even more law enforcement would be looking for her. Which meant she had to be even more careful and she would be smart to change what she'd been wearing.

Creeping down from the attic, she went back through the mudroom, where she'd seen some of her aunt's old clothing on the way inside the house. She told herself she'd be horrified to be caught in any of Vi's old gaudy sweat suit sets. That was until she'd realized that she could hide in plain sight in these old lady clothes.

She chose the tawdriest glittered sweatshirt with a leprechaun jeering from behind a gleaming pot of gold and a pair of green sweats that almost matched. Tucking her hair up under a large sun hat from the closet, she'd looked in the mirror by the back door.

Nearby, she found a pair of sunglasses and a crocheted market bag. She swung the strap of the bag over one shoulder and checked herself out in the mirror. Jen had to choke down a laugh so she didn't wake her aunt. No one would recognize her in this getup. She stuffed what money she had left and the steak knife in the bag and covered the contents with an old towel.

As she did, she thought she heard an approaching vehicle and quickly left through the back door to crouch in the early morning shadows next to the house.

CHAPTER FIFTEEN

"THANKS FOR COMING ALONG," Leroy said as he drove out of town toward Vi's house. After last evening, he felt too aware of TJ even in the large patrol SUV. He hadn't been able to quit thinking about her and was still shocked how close they'd come to making love last night.

"No problem."

He glanced over at her. She was looking out her side window toward the valley. He wondered what she was thinking. So far neither of them had mentioned last night and he sure as hell didn't want to bring it up.

"Vi needs to know about the incident with Jennifer and William Butler," Leroy said. "Apparently she has a knife, her weapon of choice, so there is definitely reason for concern. I can't shut down the entire celebration, but I think it's a mistake having the governor come here. Jennifer is a loose cannon. There's no telling what she might do."

He glanced over at TJ again. She seemed to have something on her mind. She sat chewing on her lower lip as if miles away. He recalled the glow to her this morning. Was she thinking about some man? Not the one who'd hurt her, he hoped. Not the one who'd threatened her on the phone yesterday. Was the man in Buckhorn?

It was a jarring reminder how little he knew about this woman who kept stealing his thoughts and worse. She'd started a fire burning in him. Last night it had burst into flames and look what had almost happened. He couldn't even explain the feelings she evoked in him. He wanted to protect her and at the same time, he wanted to ravage her.

He shook his head since it was the first time he'd admitted it even to himself. "Anyway," he said, clearing his voice. "I'm hoping you can help me convince Vi." When she didn't respond, he asked, "Is everything all right?"

"You sure that's the only reason you invited me along?" TJ asked shooting him a narrow-eyed look. It wasn't the only reason he'd invited her. He'd wanted to see her. He liked her. He enjoyed being around her. He felt something he'd never felt before around her. Not that there weren't things about her that scared him, he reminded himself. Sometimes she was…reckless…as if defying not just gravity but death.

"I'm hoping you will protect me when Vi goes for my throat," he joked, not nearly ready to voice how he felt about TJ.

She nodded. "Vi's pretty wiry. But don't worry. I'm sure I can take her." She didn't smile when she said it. He knew enough about women to know that she wasn't happy with him. Whatever was bothering her though would have to wait.

As he pulled up to the house, he saw that Vi's car was still in the driveway. He'd figured because of the early hour she would still be home. In truth, he wasn't looking forward to butting heads with the woman. To say Vi could be contrary was putting it mildly.

Cutting the engine, he glanced over at TJ. He'd wager her current disposition had something to do with last night. The incident was never far from his mind either as they approached the front door. But this was why no one should have an affair with a coworker, he told himself. Except he and TJ weren't having an affair, were they?

He knocked and they waited.

It was cold in the shade of the home even as the sun topped the mountain behind the house to turn Montana's big sky golden. Leroy knocked again and glanced at TJ. He couldn't keep his eyes off her. She looked beautiful this morning, the breeze ruffling her long hair, her eyes bright and expectant. As he watched her—as if she felt the tension between them as strongly as he did—she pulled her long hair up into a ponytail and tucked it under her hat. As she straightened, she had the look of a woman ready for anything.

But she was also starting to look as concerned as he was. Jennifer had been spotted in Buckhorn with a knife. Would she have come to her aunt Vi for help or a place to stay last night? What if Vi refused?

He knocked again, then tried the door. Unlocked. He turned the knob and pushed as he called, "Vi? It's Marshal Baggins!" The house was cold inside and he could feel a breeze as if a window or door had been left open somewhere. "Vi?" He could feel concern growing as he moved through the entryway and into the kitchen. He had a good view of the living room from there. His gaze went to the hallway that he assumed would lead down to the bedrooms.

The breeze though seemed to be coming from another hallway off to the right toward the back of the house. "Vi?" He felt TJ tense next to him. She too was looking toward the hallway where the breeze was coming from. Catching his eye, she motioned she was going to check it out and disappeared before he could stop her.

Leroy unsnapped the strap over his service revolver and was palming the grip at his side when Vi appeared from the other direction. As she came out of the hallway, she looked as if she hadn't slept well, her hair sticking up in all directions. She wore flannel pajamas that were too large for her thin, petite frame and her feet were bare.

But it was the gun in her hand that had Leroy gripping his own weapon.

"Leroy?" Vi demanded as she lowered the gun. "What in the world? I heard someone…"

TJ appeared again. "Back door was standing open."

"It blows open occasionally," Vi said shaking her head. "The two of you had better have a good explanation for this."

He swore as he holstered his gun again and let out a relieved breath. "We knocked, but when you didn't answer…"

"I was asleep," she shot back and glanced at the clock on the wall. "What are you doing here at this hour?"

"We need to talk," he said. "A former classmate of Jennifer's saw her yesterday afternoon at the fairgrounds. He said she had a knife and pulled it on him. Fortunately, he got away."

Vi seemed to sway a little with the news as she stepped into the kitchen, set the gun down on the counter and moved to the coffeepot. "So nothing happened," she said as she proceeded to make coffee.

"Only because, according to him, he managed to get away," Leroy said. "Vi, I shouldn't have to tell you that your niece is dangerous and now we know for a fact that she's in Buckhorn and *armed*."

Vi shook her head as she turned on the pot, then opened a cabinet to pull down three cups. "He's sure it was Jen?"

The marshal rolled his eyes. "They went to school together. After I talked to him, I talked to Shirley Langer."

Vi made a rude sound. "I wouldn't believe anything that

young woman said. You know she tried to split up Lars and
Tina. My daughter put up with it for a year. What is she
doing back in town?"

"She came for the celebration." He quickly continued
before Vi got off on another old rant. "Shirley swore that
she hadn't seen Jennifer. Vi, even Jennifer's best friend is
frightened of her." He could see that Vi had a willful blind-
ness when it came to her niece. "You can't keep sticking
your head in the sand about this."

Vi spun around to face them, her face rigid with anger.
"What is it you want me to do?" she demanded.

"I'd like to shut down the celebration until Jennifer is
caught," Leroy said. "She's a threat for the entire community."

"Ridiculous. You'd send all these people home?" Vi demanded. "You probably don't mind the bad publicity, but
the governor won't like it."

He groaned, knowing that the logistics were huge to
shut down the celebration. He'd thrown it out there, hoping
that when he made his "compromise" she would go for it.
"Speaking of the governor…it's too dangerous for him to
give a speech closing night if Jennifer isn't caught."

He had noticed that TJ seemed distracted, her gaze going
to the hallway where she'd found the back door open.

"Did you know the stairs to your attic are down?" she
asked and seemed not to realize that she'd interrupted his
argument with Vi—not that he'd been getting anywhere
with the older woman. "Mind if I have a look up there?"

Vi looked surprised. "I was probably looking for something and left it open." She waved away any further discussion about the attic ladder. "You're not canceling the
governor's closing celebration speech, Marshal. So, I sug-

gest you do your job and find Jennifer, although I would bet that she is long gone by now."

Leroy thought his head might explode. He watched Vi reach for the coffeepot. She motioned with it to him and TJ. "Coffee?" They both declined.

"I can't believe Jen," she said with a sigh as she poured herself a cup. "After more than a year of my planning, she isn't going to ruin this celebration for the town."

Leroy took a deep breath and let it out slowly, doing everything in his power not to lose his temper. "Vi, did you ever see the movie *Jaws*? We can't pretend that there's nothing to be afraid of here when we know there is a shark swimming around possibly looking for a victim. It's not safe for anyone to be here."

"You're exaggerating," Vi said with a huff. "You make Jennifer sound like a mastermind criminal. She's just a sick girl. It isn't like she's going around randomly killing people. Jennifer isn't going to kill the governor."

"Please listen to reason, Vi. We don't have the personnel to protect him. If you don't call him, I will."

Vi cradled her coffee cup in her hands. "He won't cancel."

"Darby interviewed Butler in her online paper," Leroy said. "The story is in this morning's paper. People know that Jennifer has escaped, that she was at the fairgrounds yesterday and that she's armed. I would imagine a lot of people will think twice about attending the event today." Vi pursed her lips but said nothing.

"The governor needs to know," TJ said and Leroy was grateful that she'd chimed in, not that it seemed to have any effect on Vi.

"Why don't we just see what the day brings," Vi finally said. "If no one shows up, I'll reconsider. Just think, if you're right and fewer people do attend, then it will be easier to spot Jen."

"We'll see what the situation is at the fairgrounds," Leroy agreed. "But I'm going to call the governor and give him a chance to change his plans."

Vi shook her head. "The solution is simple. Catch Jennifer." With that she put down her coffee cup and turned on her heel. "I have to get dressed. You should get down to the fairgrounds, both of you, because unless I'm wrong, the celebration is continuing whether you like it or not. Just try turning all those people away and see what happens." Once down the hall, she slammed her bedroom door to punctuate her point.

CHAPTER SIXTEEN

"JENNIFER'S NOT GONE," TJ said as they left Vi's house and drove toward Buckhorn. He shot her a look. "I'm pretty sure she spent the night in Vi's attic and left this morning when she heard us arrive. It would explain the open back door and the stairs to the attic being left down."

He swore and slammed his palm against the steering wheel. "I was so preoccupied arguing with her aunt... You think Vi knew?"

"I wouldn't be surprised. She didn't seem all that surprised when I questioned her about the attic stairs, and she made excuses for both. I don't think the back door blew open—unless Jennifer didn't close it properly on her way out."

Leroy shook his head. "It would be just like Vi to help Jennifer rather than call me. Having her niece arrested would put a damper on the celebration."

"If I'm right, it would explain why Vi came out of her bedroom with a gun in her hand. She might not have called because she was afraid of what Jennifer would do."

He shook his head. "Vi always acts so oddly I didn't think anything of it. I'll send a deputy out to check the area around the house, but at this point I doubt it will do much good." TJ agreed.

"I did see some clothing hanging by the back door that I don't think is Vi's," TJ said. "If Jennifer changed into something she found at her aunt's, she might be easier to spot—or not. A lot of women Vi's age dress in gaudy sweatshirts. There were several old ones hanging by the back door."

Leroy smiled over at her as they reached the fairgrounds. "You're good at this." She shrugged, unable not to feel buoyed by the compliment. It meant a lot coming from him. "Good call, TJ."

She noticed that he had been stealing glances at her all morning. Was he really going to ignore what had happened between them last night?

JENNIFER HAD HIDDEN in the pines and waited until both the marshal's and her aunt's vehicles had left before she tried the back door. She wasn't surprised to find it unlocked. Her aunt probably thought that she wouldn't risk coming back. Or Vi had known that if she wanted into the house she would break a window. Not that she wouldn't feel bad about it though.

She wandered around her aunt's new house, admiring it, before she raided the refrigerator. She'd known Vi wouldn't rat her out. She owed her aunt, that's why she would hate to get her into trouble. She'd thought about taking care of Uncle Axel as a favor to her aunt, but it didn't have the same appeal it had yesterday. She didn't want to spoil the celebration.

It bothered her that she was having trouble remembering why she'd thought coming back to Buckhorn had been a good idea. She still wanted to see Shirley and she couldn't leave until she stopped by her cousin's. She was excited about seeing Tina's little girl, Chloe. It worried her that she might get caught and not get the chance.

Stuffed from the food she'd found in the refrigerator, she checked her aunt's cookie jar and smiled at the money her aunt always kept there. She felt as if Aunt Vi had left the wad of bills for her and stuffed them into the market bag that she'd taken.

She was about to leave when she spotted her aunt's gun lying on the kitchen countertop. She picked it up and checked to find out if it was loaded. It was. As she added the weapon to her aunt's bag, she thought about the day Tina had taken her out to the quarry and taught her how to shoot. They'd been twelve.

"Should you ever need a weapon," her cousin had said, "Vi keeps the gun and cartridges next to her bed." It was as if Tina had always known the day would come and Jen would need it, she thought as she left.

Taking a trail along the creek, she headed toward town, promising herself that today she wouldn't get into any trouble. But in case she did, she now had a gun.

LEROY COULDN'T BELIEVE his eyes when they reached the fairgrounds. He had really thought that news of an armed, mentally unbalanced woman who'd recently escaped from the criminally insane ward of an institution would keep people away. Not to mention Butler's story that appeared in the paper about her attacking him.

But Leroy was wrong. The parking lot was filling up fast. There appeared to be more people here than there had been even yesterday. He was wondering how they would ever find Jennifer in this crowd. She was cagey. She knew her way around Buckhorn. He doubted they would see her unless she slipped up.

All he could hope was that they found her before she could hurt anyone. By tomorrow night, Buckhorn's birthday would be over. All they had to do was make it that long. But today's turnout made him realize that tomorrow night's could be even larger with the governor attending. He had to get Jamie Jacobsen to cancel.

"What is the appeal knowing it might be dangerous?" he asked, voicing his wonder out loud at all the people who'd come back today.

"What is the alternative? Never taking a risk?" TJ demanded.

He parked and he and TJ exited the patrol SUV to walk into the fairgrounds.

"I think some situations require cautiousness," he said and looked over at her. Her green eyes shone, not with humor but anger. "So we're finally going to talk about last night?"

"Last night? Oh, did something happen?" she asked sarcastically making him laugh. "You actually remember?"

"Every moment," he said seriously. He had purposely avoided the subject of the kiss and their intimate encounter, he had to admit. He hadn't known how to broach the subject. Or was it because last night he'd thrown caution to the wind? He'd acted on the spur of the moment, knowing it was risky and foolish and unprofessional, and yet he couldn't help himself. He didn't look at her as they continued walking.

"I think I proved last night that I'm not always too cautious, don't you?" he asked. "I'm not adverse to taking risks when there's a good reason."

Her laugh held little humor. "You mean after you've debated the pros and cons and decided it's worth the risk?"

"That is the sensible approach to most things." He stopped, touching her arm to turn her toward him. His gaze locked with hers. He saw challenge there and not for the first time. "I haven't been able to forget anything about last night." It didn't help that her mouth was so damned kissable. "If you're asking if I regret it, I don't." He lowered his voice. They were only a breath apart. "If anything, I want to kiss you right now. I want to more than kiss you even knowing that you could be gone by tomorrow night, and I might never see you again. Is that risky enough for you?"

She held his gaze. "I'm glad we're not pretending last night didn't happen." Before he could react, her mouth was on his. She tasted sweet like the sugared cinnamon donuts she so loved. Her lips were warm and parted, and his mouth responded as if it had a mind of its own.

Just as quickly as she'd initiated the kiss, she pulled back. "Tonight. My room at the hotel. Number 304. Seven?" And then she was stepping away smiling, but that challenging look still in her eyes. "Hope that's not too much of a risk for you."

He couldn't speak. His pulse pounded from the kiss, heat racing through his veins. Just the thought of what she was suggesting…

As she stepped away, she glanced over her shoulder, clearly pleased with herself for taking him by surprise. "See you later. If you dare. But you have plenty of time to evaluate between now and then."

He watched her go, shaking his head and smiling. She was daring him to do the one thing he'd wanted to do desperately? Teasing him? Flirting with him? Determined that last night would not be ignored, she'd upped the stakes. More than that, she was challenging him to take a step that could change everything—at least for him. Had she really invited him to her hotel room knowing what would happen between them? Maybe making love didn't mean that much to her.

But it did to Leroy. It wasn't just a physical act to him. His heart had to be in it. Putting his heart at stake with TJ was more than risky. He already felt as if she'd stolen a huge part of it. Was he willing to take that chance knowing that she would be leaving?

He let out a groan. How could he not go? His pulse thrummed as he bit down on his lower lip. The woman had nudged something awake in him that he realized had been hibernating like a grouchy old bear for way too long.

Leroy swore under his breath. If anyone was going to nudge him awake, why did it have to be TJ Walker? And yet he found himself watching her walk away as if hypnotized by the sway of her hips and his growing need for this woman.

He pulled off his Stetson, raked a hand through his hair and looked around, hoping no one had witnessed their encounter—let alone their kiss. He could still taste her on his lips. He found himself smiling again even as he thought of all the reasons he should stop this before it got completely out of hand. He couldn't go to her room tonight—even as he knew that nothing could keep him from it.

As he turned to go in the opposite direction she had gone, he nearly collided with Vi Mullen.

"Well, now it's clear," Vi said primly. "It's TJ."

For a moment, he had no idea what she was talking about. "I beg your pardon?"

"Why you haven't found my niece," she said impatiently. "You're too busy kissing the hired help." With that she stormed off.

THE MOMENT TJ saw Ash's face, she knew that he'd seen her kiss the marshal. She gave him a look, daring him to say anything.

"Isn't any of my business," Ash said trying to hide a grin. "But I would never have guessed he was your type."

She shot him a more sharp look. "I was trying to make a point."

He chuckled. "I assume he got it?"

TJ thought of the marshal's stunned expression and had to smile. She'd been determined that Leroy wasn't going to keep ignoring what had happened between the two of them last night. But it was more than that. She'd gotten a taste of what it would be like to be with the marshal. She wanted By the Book Baggins. Out of curiosity to see what happened when he let his guard all the way down. Or maybe because she felt something deeper than she ever had before and couldn't just walk away from it without finding out what it was.

Either way, she couldn't explain it to herself so she sure as the devil wasn't going to try to explain it to Ash. It was risky, even for her.

"We need to find Jennifer Mullen." She told him how she thought the woman might be dressed, based on Vi's other clothing that had been hanging by the back door. "She might be wearing a sweat suit with a lot of glitter."

"Got it," Ash said, smart enough to go with the change of conversation. "We'll find her."

She hoped he was right, but as Leroy had said, Jennifer was smart and so far, she had evaded them. "Remember, she's apparently more dangerous than she appears."

"Aren't all women?" he asked grinning and walked away before she could reply. Ash seemed to think that she was playing the marshal. Maybe kissing Leroy had been only to prove a point. But he couldn't kiss her like he had last night, and then not admit it had happened.

As she touched the tip of her tongue to her upper lip, she recalled the rush of heat that had coursed through her. There was some powerful chemistry there that she hadn't expected. Dangerous chemistry in so many ways since all of this would end soon. She was leaving after closing ceremonies tomorrow night or early the next morning. Her job would be over. She'd have no reason to stay.

Wasn't that why she wanted tonight with him? She had known that she would regret it if she didn't see where this went. As cautiously as Leroy moved, she'd had to nudge him. Was it so wrong to want this with a man who made her feel this way? Even if tonight was all they ever had, she had to go for it. Yet it felt more risky than her climb up the Ferris wheel.

Then again, he might not show up.

As THE MARSHAL walked through the fairgrounds looking for Jennifer, he spotted his friend Dave Tanner setting up the beer garden for the day. Leroy had been fighting a variety of different emotions since TJ's kiss and her proposition. The invitation had felt more like that than a date. That he wasn't even debating whether or not he would go told him that he wasn't himself. But then again, he hadn't been the same since this event had started—and he'd met TJ Walker.

He couldn't shake the fact that he might not ever see her again after tomorrow night. Because of that, surely he didn't want to start something with her. But he also knew that nothing could keep him from showing up at her hotel room tonight. He knew it was out of character. Good sense told him not to get involved with this woman for so many reasons. So why was it that all he could think about was getting her in his arms again?

"Got a minute?" the marshal asked his friend. Dave looked up and waved him into the back. Dave Tanner was the most down-to-earth man he knew and one of the nicest. He trusted him. Also, as a bartender, Dave had probably heard every sad story there was to tell.

"I need advice. About a woman." He blurted it out, making Dave laugh.

"You're talking to the wrong man," his friend joked.

"You've been a bartender for years, you recently fell in love and not for the first time, I might remind you," Leroy said. "I figure you're as close to an expert as anyone when it comes to women."

"Oh, please," Dave groaned.

"Come on, you had to have learned something."

His friend chuckled. "Why don't you tell me about this woman."

Leroy started to deny there was any one specific woman but saved his breath. "I can't figure her out. She seems so confident, so strong, so together. She has her own business, she's smart and funny and so capable."

"But?"

"She scares me. She's reckless. Also, I think there might be another man, hell there could be men in every town she's worked in across the country. On top of that, she's leaving after tomorrow night. I don't know if this is just a fling for her—and the way things are going, it could get serious—at least for me." He rubbed the back of his neck. It wasn't like him to lay his problems on anyone else's doorstep, let alone open up like this to his friend. He could see that Dave was surprised.

"Sorry, my friend, but it sounds to me like you've already fallen for her."

He started to deny it, but hell if he hadn't, he thought with a curse. Fast and hard, and while he should be standing on the brakes, he was going for the accelerator and he was already out of control and it was scaring the hell out of him.

Dave nodded as if seeing the answer on his face. "I think you have your answer. Terrifying, huh."

CHAPTER SEVENTEEN

ASSUMING THAT VI wasn't going to do it, Leroy found a quiet spot a good distance away from the fairground noise to call the governor's office. He started by speaking to one of the two state security officers who guarded the governor whenever he traveled. That highway patrol officer routed him to the governor's office.

But not even his badge could get the governor on the line. Instead, he was connected to the governor's assistant, who handled all travel details.

"I need to speak to the governor about his plans to come to Buckhorn," the marshal said after introducing himself.

"Is there a problem?"

Leroy told him about Jennifer Mullen's escape from the mental facility and that it was believed she'd pulled a knife on someone during the event and was still at large. "I think the governor would be wise to cancel."

"In that case, let me put you through to him," the assistant said.

A moment later the governor came on the line. Leroy told him the situation.

"You're looking for her, I assume? I'm not scheduled to speak until tomorrow night. I would think you would have found her before then."

"I can't promise that is going to happen," the marshal told him.

"Well, I have to admit, I'm not all that concerned," the governor said. "This woman, has she made a threat against me? No, that's what I thought. I appreciate you calling, Sheriff, but—"

"Marshal. Marshal Leroy Baggins."

"—I don't see a need to cancel."

"I really wish you would reconsider—" He realized that the man had already disconnected. He stared at his phone for a moment in frustration. Again, Vi was right. Nothing was going to stop this celebration or the governor from giving his speech.

When he saw TJ, he told her the news. "The governor's coming to Buckhorn come hell or high water."

She didn't look happy about the news. "Extra security?" she asked.

"I've called in a couple of game wardens in the county and alerted the highway patrol. That's about all I can do unless something happens and we need them. Jamie Jacobsen's right about one thing. We don't even know that Jennifer will be a problem. Hopefully, we'll catch her before he arrives."

"And if not?" she asked.

"Let's hope she has nothing against our new governor," he said. He'd been worried about this celebration from the start. The governor's appearance here would only raise the odds of trouble tenfold. Add Jennifer to the mix and you had a rodeo, he thought. "It's not like Jamie Jacobsen has any enemies," he grumbled under his breath.

TJ laughed. "I would imagine he's thinking he's coming to rural Montana, where he just assumes everyone here voted for him."

"Yeah." His radio crackled at the same time she reached

for her phone buzzing in her pocket. They glanced at each other, both no doubt expecting more trouble.

TJ QUICKLY CHECKED her phone and was already moving in the same direction as the marshal. Lane was calling for backup near the fortune teller's booth. This would be the fourth fight that had broken out today, TJ thought as she kept pace with the marshal. At once she saw that Ash, wearing his navy T-shirt with SECURITY written boldly across his back, had joined the dustup, taking on one of four men who'd apparently jumped Lane and one of Leroy's deputies.

She saw even before she reached the free-for-all that the combatants were all drunk, which made them more dangerous. Just yards from the ruckus, one of the men pulled a knife and turned to attack Ash from behind.

TJ rushed up behind the man and kicked his right leg out from under him. As he began to fall, wailing in pain, she grabbed his wrist and twisted the knife from his fingers before he hit the ground.

Leroy had jumped in to break up the fight as well. When she looked up, he was staring at her as he handcuffed one of the troublemakers. His other deputy had arrived and was helping cuff the man she had on the ground. "Take them all in," the marshal said. "I want that knife for evidence." Lane and Ash offered to assist in getting the men to the makeshift hoosegow that had been erected until offenders could be transported to a real jail in the next town. Slowly, the crowd dispersed, the excitement over.

"Nice work," Leroy said to her as the men were taken away and everyone went on with their business.

She nodded and said, "You too. We make a pretty good team."

His smile transformed his face, making him more than

just handsome. She felt a pull of attraction even stronger because of her invitation for tonight. "One more day," he said and sighed.

One more day. Then she'd be packing up and gone. The thought filled her with regret of what might have been. But this was her life. She never stayed in any one place longer than the job required.

With a start, she realized that she hadn't had another call from Worth. The governor would be coming to Buckhorn tomorrow, but maybe Worth wouldn't be with him. She took it as good news that she hadn't heard from him as she looked up to see the older woman who'd come out of the fortune teller's booth. The woman wore a bright-colored caftan, her dark hair wrapped in a turban with several long errant strands framing her face. Her face and hands were weathered, her fingers bejeweled. An array of bracelets softly tinkled at her wrists as she moved.

TJ watched her deep-set dark eyes shift from the marshal to her. TJ felt a shudder as the woman suddenly crossed herself. All the color had drained from the woman's face as she stumbled back and disappeared behind the dark, thick drape that hung over the doorway of her booth. Like the woman herself, the outside of the booth was brightly colored. A sign with a large eye read Madam Zorna, All Seeing.

As TJ stared at the spot the woman had disappeared from, wondering at her strange reaction, the braceleted arm reached out to hang a sign on the curtain. CLOSED.

"Something wrong?" Leroy asked.

TJ felt his warm fingers on her arm and shook herself out of the fugue she'd been in only moments before. She told herself that she was being silly. It wasn't like she believed the woman could see the future.

"Fine." But how else could she explain the woman's strange reaction?

TJ turned away, but she kept thinking about her grandmother who would occasionally cross herself like that and mumble, "Someone just walked across my grave."

"Back to work," she said, needing to get moving, needing to get out of her own head. Was she regretting her earlier impulsive invitation to the marshal? Yes and no. She wanted this and yet she knew she was playing with fire. What if after tonight, she didn't want to leave him? Where would that leave her? She had a business to run, a business that required moving her team around the country, around the world if necessary.

She was suddenly distracted by movement. Out of the corner of her eye, she saw the older woman come out of the back of the fortune teller's booth through a side door next to her camper trailer. She was no longer in costume. Dressed in slacks, blouse, sans all the jewelry, her dark hair flying loose around her shoulders, she moved quickly through the crowd toward the parking lot as if on her way to a fire.

For one fleeting instant, TJ almost followed her, more than curious as to why the woman seemed in such a hurry. Whether she wanted to admit it or not, the fortune teller's earlier reaction had disturbed her. Unlike her grandmother, she'd never been superstitious. Yet she remembered her grandmother foreseeing her mother's death. Her grandmother just hadn't called it cancer.

THE FAIRGROUNDS WERE already filled with crowds as Jennifer slipped in. Dressed in her aunt's garb, her hair tucked up under the large straw hat, the large sunglasses hiding not just her eyes but most of her face, she had no trouble blending in. She was thinking about her promise to herself not to get into any trouble when she looked across the main street through town and spotted her friend Shirley.

She watched Shirley load a small bag into her car. Surely, her friend wasn't leaving, was she? Apparently so and Shirley seemed to be in a hurry. Jennifer remembered Dr. Moss mentioning her diary. Jennifer had known at once that Shirley had broken her vow. Instead of destroying her secret diary, her best friend had turned it over to the marshal, who'd given it to the doctor.

Jennifer felt the bitter taste of betrayal rise in her throat as she headed toward where Shirley was frantically loading her car beside the motel. At the sound of someone calling Shirley's name from inside the motel apartment behind the office, her best friend went back inside as if she'd forgotten something.

Moving quickly before Shirley returned, Jennifer climbed into the back of the unlocked car and covered herself with an old blanket lying in the back seat.

TJ WAS MAKING her rounds later when she saw that the fortune teller's booth was open again. She hadn't seen any sign of Jennifer and was beginning to wonder if the woman might have left town.

Curious about the elderly fortune teller, she pushed aside the dark heavy drape surprised to see a young woman sitting behind a small table instead of the older one.

"I was looking for—"

"Madam Zorna? She had to step out, but I can tell your future."

On the table in front of the woman were a deck of tarot cards, a crystal ball, a teapot and a teacup as well as a credit card machine. The sign on the wall read: Your future $20. The young woman pointed to the chair in front of the table.

Through an opening in the draped walls of the room, TJ could see another tented room attached to the small camper trailer. "Will Madam Zorna be back?" she asked.

"Not today." The woman picked up the cards. "Looking for love?"

"Not today," she said and backed out of the booth. As she did, she collided with the marshal.

"Good news?" Leroy asked with a tilt of his head toward the booth she was exiting. His face was in shadow under his Stetson, but she could see the mischief sparking in his blue eyes.

"My future is bright," she said and smiled. "Actually, I was looking for the seer who was in the booth earlier. Did you happen to see her?"

"An older woman," he said and frowned. "I only got a glimpse of her. Is there a problem?"

Was there? She shook her head. "I'm sure it's nothing, but she seemed…upset after the fight. She closed her booth right after that and left."

He was studying her now, still frowning. "I'm sure that's all it was."

She wasn't sure of that at all. "Do you know anything about her?"

He shook his head. "She's part of the carnival crowd, I think. But you could ask Vi Mullen if you're worried about her."

TJ nodded and changed the subject. "It's been fairly quiet today. Only four fights and two arrests." Quiet like before a storm, she thought.

"Let's hope that's the extent of it."

"The day's not over yet," she said, reminding him that they still had tonight. She wondered if he was getting cold feet.

He met her gaze and chuckled. "I haven't forgotten. It is hard to think of anything else." He dragged his gaze away to look toward the mountains. "I wanted to compliment you and your team. You've done a great job. I'm sorry I was... skeptical at first." He turned back to her.

"Thank you," she said, though thrown off guard. He almost sounded like he was saying goodbye. "You're still not sure about me, though, are you?"

"If you're asking if you worry me sometimes..."

"I don't blame you. I worry myself sometimes."

"But at the same time, I like the way you challenge me. This might surprise you, but I've never been a risk taker."

She laughed. "I had no idea."

He shook his head as he got a call from one of his deputies about a problem down at the beer garden. "I better check on this."

Behind her, TJ heard movement and caught a glimpse of the young fortune teller peering out of the booth. Had she been listening to their conversation? The curtained door swung shut and a moment later, TJ heard the woman make a call. She caught only the beginning of the conversation as a nearby carnival ride began, drowning out everything else.

What she heard was, "She came back, just as you said she would."

LEROY WATCHED TJ step away, wondering if she was having second thoughts about asking him to her room. He certainly had. No good would come of letting himself get any more involved with this woman.

He took care of the problem at the beer garden and left to patrol the fairgrounds, always on the outlook for Jennifer. As he passed Madam Zorna's booth, he thought again of the concern TJ had shown for the fortune teller. The booth had the closed sign out and there was no sign of anyone. Maybe the woman had taken ill.

His thoughts quickly circled back to TJ. He questioned whether he could trust his instincts when it came to women. There'd been that cute little redhead in elementary school. They'd moved away. In middle school, it had been a dark-haired girl with big brown eyes. The one time he'd tried to talk to Pixie, she'd punched him in the stomach. She'd later ended up being sent away to reform school.

High school and college hadn't been much better. He'd dated but hadn't fallen in love. Once he joined the marshal's office, he'd been too busy to even date—not that he'd met anyone he wanted to ask out.

Lately, he'd begun to wonder if he'd ever run across a woman who would turn his head, let alone steal his heart—especially since he hadn't been looking. He'd thrown himself into his job as deputy, then found himself in the marshal position with a lot to learn and a whole lot more responsibility. He knew the other deputies called him By the Book Baggins behind his back. The job had become his life.

Then along came TJ. He thought about the first time he saw her. That alone should prove just how wrong she was for him. TJ was a risk taker. Nothing in life seemed to stop her, as if she was fearless with apparently no thought to her safety.

Like when she'd taken down an intoxicated man with a knife. She never hesitated to jump into the fray. She just charged in without hesitation just as she had when she'd climbed the Ferris wheel to save that boy.

TJ took too many risks and yet that was the business she was in, wasn't it? He couldn't help but wonder if she'd always been like that or if something had happened to make her that way. He felt as if he was having trouble separating the woman who risked her life at every turn with the one he'd held in his arms on the dance floor, the one he'd kissed with more passion than he'd ever known, the woman who'd invited him to her hotel room tonight. Who was TJ Walker? Did she even know? Was he falling for a woman with a death wish?

"Leroy?"

He realized that he'd been so lost in thought that he hadn't heard anyone approach. From the look on Earl Ray's face, he'd been trying to get his attention for some time.

"Earl Ray," he said feeling the older man's keen eyes on him. "Sorry, my mind was miles away."

The older man appeared upset. "I was looking for Tina. She was supposed to meet me here. She's always so punctual. I thought you might have seen her."

He heard worry in the man's voice. "You tried to call her?"

"She's not picking up. I'm about to walk down to her house in case I missed her. If you see her, would you be so kind as to give me a call?"

"Of course." Leroy met the man's gaze. Neither of them said Jennifer's name, but it was clear that they'd both been thinking the same thing. If Jennifer had stopped by to see her cousin… "You sure you don't want me to come with you?" the marshal asked as another scuffle broke out down by the donut booth.

"No. Still no sign of Jennifer?" Leroy shook his head. "You have your hands full here. I'll holler if I need you."

Leroy saw TJ stepping between two teenaged boys who'd been about to come to blows. He thought about coming to her aid, but it appeared she didn't need it. Was there no risk she wouldn't take—including asking him to her room? But maybe he was the only one who was taking a risk—with his heart, he thought.

His doubts aside, he couldn't wait to be alone with her tonight.

SHIRLEY TOSSED HER sweater onto the passenger seat of her car and slid behind the wheel. She'd wanted to leave last night but Claire had talked her out of it.

"Too many deer on the highway during a full moon. Not to mention how upset you are. You're in no shape to be driving."

"Jen's in town. The marshal said she threatened someone with a knife!" Shirley was frantic with worry that Jen would come after her next if she didn't get out of Buckhorn.

"Sit down. Drink this." Claire had eased her down on the couch and shoved a glass in her hand.

The smell of alcohol had risen to her nose making her want to throw up, but she'd downed the amber liquid in one gulp and coughed as the whiskey burned all the way to her toes. She'd known Claire was right. She had needed to calm down before she left or she'd get herself killed out on the highway. She'd grimaced at the strong taste of the alcohol, but quickly felt it move through her, soothing and calming her.

"Now I know why Jen was determined that I come here," she'd said. "I had no idea that she would escape. She must have been planning to meet me here." She'd felt a start. "What if she'd been planning on the two of us running away together? It would be just like her to drag me into her troubles or worse."

She'd felt the alcohol making her want to melt into the couch. She hadn't slept well on the couch last night and then finding out this. Claire had refilled her glass. She'd drunk it down and pushed the glass away. She'd felt like a rag doll, her muscles so slackened that even if she still wanted to leave, she didn't think she could get off the couch.

"I really doubt she would hurt you, but not to worry," Claire had said quickly. "The doors are all locked. No one is coming in. My shotgun's by the back door. You're safe. I can tell that you need sleep more than anything."

"I'm leaving once it is full light," Shirley had told her, her words slurring as she lay over on the couch and closed her eyes. That was the last thing she'd remembered before waking up late this morning.

Claire had been in the office with a guest who wanted directions to an area hot springs he'd heard about. A twenty-four-hour news station was on the television, the volume turned down so low that Shirley had caught only a few words, but she recognized the man speaking. Governor Jamie Jacobsen. He said something about visiting Buckhorn.

She'd looked around for the remote, found it and turned off the television. Her head ached with what felt like a hangover. As she'd pushed herself up off the couch, she'd caught a whiff of alcohol from the glass on the end table and had to make a run to the bathroom to throw up. What was in those drinks?

The marshal's visit last night had come back in a flash. She'd thrown up, rinsed out her mouth with a handful of water and hurried back into the living room to pack. She'd been out the door in no time, only to have Claire call her back, saying she'd forgotten her sweater, and to chastise her for not saying goodbye.

"I was going to call once I got home," she'd lied. She'd been so scared that she hadn't given a thought to thanking Claire.

Now as she started her car, she glanced in the direction of the fairgrounds. She realized with both relief and regret that she hadn't gotten to see her former lover Lars or his wife, the pregnant Tina. She told herself it was for the best as she shifted into gear. Seeing either of them would have only made her feel worse and she felt bad enough. She shouldn't have come back to Buckhorn.

Now all she wanted to do was get out of town again. Never in her wildest dreams had she thought Jen would escape—let alone that she might come back here. If what the marshal had told her was true, Jen had maybe almost killed Billy Butler. Hadn't he moved away when they were in high school? Like her, he must have come back for the birthday celebration. This was like a bad dream.

Shirley had been so convinced that her former friend would never get out of the mental facility. Or if she did, that she would be headed for prison. She'd felt guilty about the things she'd told the marshal, including mentioning the diary and breaking her promise to Jennifer to destroy it. But she'd thought that Jen needed help and that a mental facility would be better than prison for her. Shirley had thought that maybe whatever was in that diary might help.

Driving out of town, her hands shaking on the wheel, she told herself that she wouldn't be back. That she couldn't get out of Buckhorn fast enough. She wasn't even that sure that her leaving had that much to with Jennifer. Buckhorn was like a bad dream filled with heartache for her. She'd lost her friend, she'd lost her lover. What was wrong with her?

She slammed the heel of her hand against the steering wheel, furious with herself that she had put herself in danger for *closure*. Like she would have found it in Buckhorn. Jen had always said she was a fool. Well, she'd certainly proved it this time by letting Jen talk her into this.

Here she was again about to see Buckhorn in her rearview mirror. She warned herself not to look back, to not think about Lars or Tina or Jen. Yet she couldn't help herself. She started to look in her rearview mirror when she heard a rustling in the back seat.

She froze, hands gripping the steering wheel, knowing at gut level what she'd find in the back seat. *Who* she'd find hiding back there, waiting to strike. Shirley didn't need to look in the rearview mirror. Just like she didn't need to scream.

But she did both when she glanced in the mirror and saw Jennifer right behind her.

She screamed and hit the brakes. The car rocked furiously. She swung it off the road into the shallow ditch, dirt and tall dried weeds flying over the hood and onto the windshield before she could get the car stopped.

"Shirley, you don't drive any better than you used to," Jen said chuckling. "Worse, you look like you've seen a ghost. We need to talk. Not like those cheery phone calls we've had all these months. I want to talk about my diary and your broken promise."

She couldn't speak, her throat had gone desert dry. Nor could she move. The marshal was afraid Jennifer had come back to Buckhorn to settle some old scores. He hadn't known who exactly Jen would target, but Shirley had known the moment he'd told her that her former best friend had escaped.

Now all she could do was stare at Jen in that straw hat. She'd often wondered what Jen would look like if she ever saw her again. She was shocked at how much she hadn't changed. Not only did she look the same—except for that awful red-colored hair—but she looked almost…normal.

Until Shirley met her eyes.

If she'd had any doubt before as to how this would end, one look in those eyes and she knew. She grabbed for the car handle, flung the door open and threw herself out into the ditch at a run.

Behind her, she heard her once best friend coming after her.

CHAPTER EIGHTEEN

JENNIFER FELT LITTLE satisfaction as she drove back into Buckhorn. She hadn't wanted to believe that her best friend had turned on her, breaking her promise and turning over the diary she was supposed to have destroyed. Worse, that Shirley had been so terrified of her to run off like that.

Shirley was the only one who even knew that Jen kept a small faded pink diary. But not even her best friend knew what was in there. Every evil thought, every evil deed. The only reason Shirley even knew about the diary was because her friend had caught her hiding it. Jennifer hadn't wanted Shirley to know about the worst of it, the man with the shadowed face. From the time she was very young when she heard him outside her bedroom door, she would squeeze her eyes shut tight and not open them again until he was gone.

He only appeared in the middle of the night. She would hear the sound of the door opening, hear him moving toward her bed. Eyes squeezed closed, she'd listen to the jingle of his belt buckle, the *zzzzzz* as he unzipped his pants and the sound of both hitting the floor.

Jen knew not to scream unless she wanted his hand over her mouth. The first few times he'd pushed down so hard that she couldn't breathe. She didn't want that. She also knew not to tell. If she told, the people she loved would die. She never told anyone about the man with the shadowed face.

That's what upset her the most about Shirley not destroying the diary and, worse, handing it over to the authorities and her doctor. After Tina had given her the diary and told her that she could write down anything she wanted, no one ever read it—not even Jen after she'd written down her feelings, opening her heart and pouring out her pain.

She'd never wanted anyone to ever read those entries. She especially didn't want Aunt Vi or her cousin Tina to know. She'd always feared that if anyone she loved knew about the shadow-faced man, he'd come back and kill them all.

"If anything ever happens to me, I need you to destroy the diary," she'd told Shirley. "Swear to me on your life that you will."

Jennifer would have destroyed it herself, except she'd been arrested and hauled away too quickly. She'd depended on Shirley to see to it. Now she felt a deep, aching disappointment in Shirley. Her friend had let her down. If the shadow-faced man found out, he might hurt Vi and Tina and maybe even Chloe.

That she'd loved Shirley as a friend and trusted her made her feel even more betrayed. Shirley just didn't know what she'd done, the harm she'd put people in. Jen had thought her best friend had cared about her. She'd been wrong.

But like the other painful, dark things in her life, Jen pushed this too from her mind. Dr. Moss had wanted her to dig up all the ugly stuff and wade through it like quicksand. That frightened her more than being locked up in the hospital. She was glad that she was never going to see Dr. Moss again, she thought as she saw the small western town appear on the horizon and slowed Shirley's car.

She had to see her cousin Tina and meet Chloe, who was

growing up so fast. She hated that she was missing out on so much and now Tina was going to have another baby.

As she started to pull into the fairgrounds parking lot, she saw her uncle Axel and felt her stomach knot as she parked Shirley's car.

She felt the weight of the gun pulling down the bag on her shoulder as she climbed out of the driver's seat and hesitated. She told herself that lucky for Uncle Axel she didn't have time to deal with him right now. Leaving the car, she cut through the fairgrounds anxious to lose herself among the crowd.

By now Tina would have heard that she was back so it wouldn't be much of a surprise. Still, she was excited to see her cousin and looking forward to borrowing some decent clothes. Tina had always shared her clothes since they were about the same size. Jen didn't doubt that she still would.

AFTER HIS VISIT to her house this morning, the marshal was surprised when he checked his phone and saw that Vi was calling him. "Vi, if you're calling to ask if I've caught your niece yet—"

"I should have told you before this, but someone broke into my house last night."

He stopped walking. "Vi, I know Jennifer stayed at your house last night in the attic. I sent a deputy out there to make sure she wasn't still there. She left some of her clothing in your back entry. Why didn't you tell me that this morning or better yet call me last night?"

"I'm telling you now," she snapped. "She took some of my clothing."

Leroy ground his teeth. TJ had already figured that out. "This would have been handy to know earlier. What clothing? We need a description."

"I'm not completely sure because I keep old clothes for yard work by the back door."

"You must have some idea."

"A sweat suit set. I went home at lunch. The faded green leprechaun one is missing along with a large straw sun hat and a market bag." She described both. "I think she also took a pair of sunglasses too." She sounded scared.

"Why call and tell me now, Vi?"

Silence, then, "That gun I had this morning? I left it in the kitchen in my hurry to get down to the fairgrounds. When I went back at lunchtime, it was gone."

Leroy swore. "What else did she take? Any ammunition?"

"The gun was loaded. I checked. She didn't take extra ammunition. So she only has six bullets."

Just six. He swore again. "Vi, I can't believe you're just telling me this now?"

"Well, she hasn't shot anyone obviously or you'd have already heard about it," Vi retorted. "Don't hurt her," she added, her voice suddenly filling with emotion. "Please tell me you won't hurt her."

"We'll try to take her in peacefully, but ultimately it will be up to Jennifer—especially now that we know she's armed with both a knife and a gun. Vi, if you see her—" He realized that she'd disconnected.

JEN MOVED AT the edge of the shadows, keeping close to the vendor trucks. Her plan was to cut through the fairgrounds, keeping to the crowds, and then head into town by way of the tree-lined creek.

She had just reached the far side of the grounds when she heard a sound directly behind her and spun around. She saw no one. Yet something prickled at the back of her neck. She swallowed, unfamiliar with true fear. There had always been the apprehension of getting caught, going to prison or, if she got lucky, the mental institution.

But this feeling was different. A chill moved over her skin like a bad rash, revving her pulse past the usual throbbing thrum and laying a crushing weight on her chest. She tried to breathe, feeling something very dangerous in the darkness, something...deadly.

Run! Adrenaline pumped through her veins. She instinctively picked flight because fight wasn't an option. She got in one step before he grabbed her, picking her up off her feet and sucking her back into the darkness between two large trucks.

She smelled him, rancid sweat from his brand of excitement and no recent bath or change of clothing. He clamped a hand over her mouth, the other arm looping around her waist. The bag slipped from her shoulder as he swung her around, her feet dangling inches above the ground. He pressed his face into the side of hers reminding her that K. Bob was both strong and as large as a giant compared to her.

"Hey, Jenny girl," he whispered. "Thought you could get away from me, didn't you?"

She bit his filthy-smelling hand and kicked him as hard as she could in the shins. He dropped her to the ground, crying out in pain. She spun on him, spitting out the vile taste in her mouth before demanding, "What are you doing here?" as she reached into the bag hanging from her shoulder. She found the knife first and closed her hand around the handle. "I told you not to follow me."

He quit rubbing his hand and smiled. "I didn't follow you. I've always been one step ahead of you, little girl." Even in the dark shadows between the vehicles, she could see that there was something wrong with K. Bob. At the hospital they weren't allowed to identify that look as "crazy," but she didn't know any other word for it.

"How did you know I would be here?"

He chuckled. "I saw your scrapbook." He smiled as if to say "You think you're so smart, but who's the dummy now?"

K. Bob was right. If he'd figured out where she'd gone then she could be sure everyone else was onto her as well. Putting the article in the scrapbook had been a mistake.

"I'm hungry," he said. "You got any money in that bag?"

This morning she'd taken what cash she could find in her aunt's house and stuffed it into the bag.

She let go of the handle of the knife, realizing she wasn't in danger as long as she gave K. Bob some money. He could take it easy enough. He looked like he might have played professional football. She didn't know his back-story, but she'd heard rumors that he used to be somebody. Hadn't they all before they'd been caught and locked up. All she'd ever seen him doing was writing letters—and hiding them. He too had made friends with one of the guards, who she'd heard had snuck the letters out of the institution to be mailed. She couldn't imagine who he wrote to.

Reaching in, she pulled out the bills and shot K. Bob a warning look. "This is all I have." Like he wanted to hear her problems. "Here, take it. I'll get more. But," she said as she pulled back the money before he could snatch it from her hand. "You have to promise that you'll get something to eat and then leave Buckhorn."

"I promise you won't see me again." He grinned as he took the money.

She shook her head, knowing he would probably get caught after causing a disturbance of some kind. The options for him being picked up were limitless. She was surprised he hadn't been already. Unless Marshal Leroy Baggins hadn't heard about him, which was likely now that she thought about it. Why would the mental institution notify the local law here about K. Bob? He wasn't from Buckhorn. Leroy's only interest would be in her.

Jen thought about telling K. Bob not to mention her when he got caught, but saved her breath. She was planning to cut her visit short after seeing her cousin. She watched him disappear into the shadows, relieved to be rid of him.

It wasn't until she was almost to the creek that she realized the market bag felt lighter. She checked and cursed K. Bob. When he'd grabbed her, he'd taken the gun she'd borrowed from her aunt Vi.

EARL RAY WALKED away from the fairgrounds and headed the few blocks into town. He hadn't driven from his house since he knew parking would be impossible to find. Also he liked walking, especially this time of year before the heat of the day was too warm.

He stretched out his legs, taking long strides, anxious to get to Tina's house that she shared with her husband, Lars, and their daughter, Chloe. He'd seen the marshal's reaction to Tina being late. Jennifer. It was on everyone's mind who knew her—and had heard that she'd escaped from the state mental hospital.

As he neared Tina's house, he felt a cramp in his right calf and had to stop for a few moments. As he did, he studied the street. It was quiet, only the distant sounds of the carnival at the fairgrounds in the background. He could hear birds singing and an occasional vehicle on the main highway through Buckhorn.

After rubbing the pain out of his calf, he walked the rest

of the way down the street, telling himself he was over-reacting. At least he hoped that was the case.

The house was a custom-built cottage style with a wide front porch and large windows. Tina, who was an artist and a budding photographer, loved light. That's why she never closed her front blinds.

Only they were closed now, he noticed, his stomach dropping at the sight.

TJ FELT AS if her thoughts had been on a roller coaster ride since waking up this morning after her erotic dream about the marshal and expecting to find him in her bed. Was it any wonder that when Leroy hadn't acknowledged what had happened between them last night, she'd upped the ante by inviting him to her hotel room tonight? The dream had been so sexy and so real. It was as if she could still feel him on her skin, still taste him, still pick up his scent on her body.

After tonight, it would be real. She shivered with expectation and also a little concern. It was a gamble since she obviously was attracted to the man. She liked him maybe a little too much. She shook her head. He might not even show up. She swallowed, remembering the look she'd seen in his eyes. Oh, he'd show up. He wanted this as much as she did and that also concerned her. She was more reckless than she'd been before the night she'd gone up to Worth's room.

Was she being reckless with her heart and the marshal's?

It was just sex, she told herself. Whether the encounter would live up to the one in the dream, well, that was yet to be seen. She and Leroy were nothing alike. As if that mattered, she reminded herself. They would have had one night together to get this out of their systems. After tomorrow, she would be gone and Marshal Leroy Baggins's world

would go back to normal. Wasn't that what he'd wanted before this birthday celebration? Did he still feel that way?

She'd been looking for Jennifer all morning and so had
her team. So far nothing. Maybe the woman had left town.
Or maybe not, she thought as she saw the older fortune
teller skirting the rear of the booths to get to her own.

TJ followed. She had to know what was up with the
fortune teller. At the booth, she waited for the woman to
remove the closed sign. The moment it disappeared, TJ
pushed the curtain aside and stepped in. Madam Zorna
started to welcome her but stopped midsentence as she
recognized her.

"Is something wrong?" TJ asked as she moved closer to
look into the deep-set dark eyes.

Madam Zorna shook her head. "You just surprised me,
that's all. My booth isn't open yet."

"Really? You just removed your closed sign. I'd like a
reading. Unless you have a problem with me or my money."
TJ pulled a twenty from her pocket and tossed it on the
table. She could see the woman hesitate, but only for a
moment.

With a slight nod, the fortune teller said, "Please have a
seat." She motioned to the chair in front of the small table
as she busied herself straightening the caftan she wore, her
bracelets tinkling softly.

TJ sat down in the folding chair in front of the table covered with a plush purple throw. She noticed the patterned
rug on the floor had tiny stars and the gauzy white fabric
overhead had been tacked up to look like puffy clouds. The
air smelled heavy with incense.

None of this is real, she told herself as she looked around.
"I came to see you before but there was a young woman
here," TJ said.

"A friend who fills in for me when I have to leave." Madam Zorna picked up a worn deck of tarot cards with one bejeweled hand as she made the twenty-dollar bill disappear like magic under the other hand. TJ noticed that the deck of cards wasn't the same one that the younger fortune teller had been using before.

With what appeared as reluctance, Madam Zorna held out the cards for TJ to hold. "You have questions. Select the one utmost on your mind and think about it for a moment."

The cards felt warm in her hands. She ran her thumb pad along the worn deck of cards and tried to center her thoughts. What was it exactly that she wanted from this woman? She met Madam Zorna's dark eyes, heavy with mascara and liner, for a moment before she handed back the cards.

As the fortune teller turned over the first card, TJ saw that the woman's hands were shaking.

"Do you know me from somewhere?"

The question seemed to take the woman by surprise. "Why would I?"

"And yet when you saw me before, you seemed...upset."

The woman shook her head. "You are mistaken."

TJ doubted that as she watched her consider the first card she'd laid down. "You are here on a mission." She turned over another card. "You are worried that you will fail." Easy guess since the woman knew TJ was here to provide security for the celebration.

With the next card, the woman hesitated.

"What is it?" TJ asked watching her. No way did she believe that her fate was in this pack of worn cards any more than she believed this woman did anything more than read people and tell them what they wanted to hear.

"I see a man." She shook her head. "No, two men." Madam Zorna looked up. "There is something unresolved from your past. You have been given a choice." She cocked her head to the side, her voice taking on emotion as she added. "One of them you fear. The other you desire. There is passion, the possibility of love." TJ figured this was the woman's standard reading for any woman of a certain age off the street. Wouldn't it stand to reason most adults would have had at least one bad relationship? Weren't most people looking for the possibility of love? "You don't know if you can trust either of them or yourself because there is the chance of getting hurt."

The woman turned over another card. "There is danger."

Again, the woman hadn't told her anything. She worked in security. There was always danger.

She seemed hesitant to turn over the next card and did it slowly, dropping it on the table. TJ caught a glimpse of it before the woman quickly began picking up all the cards.

"What did you see?" TJ demanded. "The same thing you saw earlier when you looked at me?"

The woman avoided her gaze. "It is unclear."

"Would it be clearer if I gave you another twenty?" TJ demanded.

The woman looked insulted. Her lips pulled into a thin, tight line. "You will believe what you believe. I can only tell you what I see."

"But you haven't told me anything. Why did you react the way you did when you saw me after the fight outside your booth?"

"You're mistaken."

"You took off after that like a shot. I want to know why."

Madam Zorna raised her head to meet TJ's gaze, her

dark eyes hard as diamonds and just as bright with anger. "I told you. I see danger."

"Which doesn't explain why you ran off like you did. I suspect you went to see someone, tell someone something."

The woman shook her head.

"You do realize that I could have the marshal close down your booth on a violation. Who did you go to warn?"

"Who is the fortune teller now?" Madam Zorna demanded. "Why don't you tell me?"

TJ said nothing, merely waited.

The woman finally sighed and said, "I called my daughter. Not everything is easily explained in life, even for me. But should something happen to me, I wanted to tell her that I love her." Those eyes locked with hers again and TJ saw tears. "Unless you plan to call the marshal, your reading is over." She started to rise.

TJ rose quickly, bumping the table and sending the remaining tarot cards scattering across the table and onto the floor. She heard the woman say, "Leave them."

But TJ had already dropped down to pick up the one she'd seen Madam Zorna refuse to turn over. Death. She stared at it for a moment before she retrieved the rest of the deck, which she handed to the woman.

"Which one of us is going to die?" TJ asked as she flashed the death card and tossed it on the table. The fortune teller's eyes widened as she picked up the lone card. "Which one of us? Or is that another mystery you don't know?"

"You won't believe me, but I don't know," the woman said angrily. "It was just a...feeling."

A premonition, her grandmother would have called it, TJ thought. But still she wasn't buying into it. "I thought the death card didn't necessarily mean a person would die. Can't it also mean a change?"

The woman glanced at the card, then settled those eyes on TJ again. "Only you can know the meaning of the cards as they pertain to your life and those around you," the woman said noncommittally. "I merely read what I see."

"If you're afraid of what is going to happen, why don't you leave right now?" TJ asked.

Madam Zorna shook her head almost sadly. "It is too late to change what will happen here. Some things can't be avoided."

"Is that why you're staying?" TJ asked.

The woman smiled. "Isn't that why you're staying?"

LEROY HAD ALREADY texted TJ and his deputies with the description of what Jennifer was likely wearing and the news about the gun, when his radio squawked.

"We just found a couple of kids trying to steal a car in the parking lot," the deputy said. "The keys were in it they said so they decided to take it for a spin but only managed to back into one of the other cars in the lot. I checked the registration. The car belongs to a Shirley Langer."

He felt sick. Shirley had been so scared last night that he'd assumed she would be miles from here by now. So what was her car doing in the lot with the keys in it.

"Any sign of Shirley? Check the trunk." He waited, heart in his throat, until with relief the deputy announced the trunk was empty. "Treat the car like a crime scene for now until Shirley can be found."

"Marshal!" Vi's voice cut through the crowd. "Marshal."

He turned to face her. What now?

As she approached, she seemed to be looking for someone. "Have you seen Tina?" she asked, sounding upset.

Leroy frowned. "Earl Ray was here looking for her just a little while ago. He said they were supposed to meet earlier here at the fairgrounds but that she hadn't shown."

Vi's eyes widened. "I haven't been able to reach her. She could just be avoiding my calls..." Her voice trailed off.

"Give me a minute." He called Earl Ray's number. It went straight to voicemail. Vi had her phone in her hand. She tried Tina again. He waited.

She shook her head. "Voicemail. You don't think—"

"They probably found each other and are busy with the photographs and I just missed them," Leroy told her. "Where is Chloe?"

"She was supposed to be with Bessie. At least Tina had mentioned that Bessie was picking her up this morning while she took some photos at the event in the early light."

Leroy called Bessie's cell. She answered on the fourth ring. He could hear the noise of the café in the background. "Do you have Chloe?"

"Leroy? Is something wrong?"

He didn't want to worry Bessie. "So she's there with you?"

"No, Tina called earlier and said she was running late and would bring her by for lunch."

He glanced at the time and thanked her, assuring her he'd get back to her if there was a problem, and hung up. "Sounds like Tina was running late. Why don't you go down to the café. Tina and Chloe are supposed to meet Bessie there for lunch. Call me if you see Earl Ray and Tina."

"Where are you going?"

"I'll check at Tina's. I would imagine she and Chloe are on their way to the café as we speak," he said to Vi, anxious to get moving. Hearing about Shirley's car had him more worried than he was about to admit.

He saw TJ at a distance as he headed for Tina's house, worry nagging at him. Maybe Tina was just running late. But his instincts warned him otherwise.

TINA HATED TO be late, which is why she was always early—except today. She had Chloe dressed, her bright red hair pulled up in a ponytail with an equally bright pink ribbon to match the pink top and flowered leggings her daughter had picked out for the day. She smiled. At least she would be able to keep an eye on her daughter easily enough with all the people in town.

She herself had showered, fixed her hair much the same as Chloe's sans the ribbon and had gotten dressed. She was getting her photography gear together and was almost ready to head for the fairgrounds when she realized that she couldn't find her phone.

With Chloe's help, they searched the house and, not finding it, returned to the bedroom. "You're sure you weren't playing with it?" she asked her daughter.

"No, Mama."

"Well, we're going to have to go without it," Tina said realizing how late it was only because of the clock she'd seen downstairs on the microwave. She'd become so dependent on her phone for everything, she thought as she heard someone knocking at the door downstairs.

Normally, she didn't lock the doors except at night. "I think until Jennifer is caught, we should keep the doors locked, even during the day," Lars had said.

She'd wanted to argue that her cousin would never hurt her, but she realized she couldn't take that chance. She now had Chloe and the baby growing inside her to protect, so she'd agreed.

"That's probably Earl Ray. I was supposed to meet him

at the fairgrounds an hour ago." She realized that she'd had her phone earlier. She had called Bessie to say she was running late.

Tina started to go down and let him in, when she heard the back door open and close. Her heart dropped like a boot to the floor.

Someone was in the house. Someone who knew where the back door key was hidden. Wasn't this her fear the moment she heard that her cousin had escaped from the mental institution?

She looked at Chloe, then at the partially opened bedroom door that didn't have a lock on it. She desperately wanted to grab her daughter and run, but there was only the one set of stairs and no place to run or hide.

"Help Mommy find her phone," she said trying to keep the panic out of her voice. Lars had a key, her mother was too busy to stop by. That left only one other person who knew about the key to the back door. Why hadn't she thought of that?

She was scrambling around the room, terrified that she wouldn't be able to find her phone in time when she heard the creak of footfalls on the stairs.

"Here it is, Mama," Chloe said, holding up the phone. It had apparently fallen off the bed into a pile of her daughter's stuffed animals that she'd been playing with earlier.

As she hurriedly took it from Chloe, she saw that she must have turned off her phone earlier. She had a bunch of messages. From Earl Ray, her mother. She pulled Chloe close and motioned for her daughter to be quiet. Chloe pressed a finger to her lips, eyes wide, imitating her mother.

The floorboards creaked just outside the bedroom door.

Tina fumbled to punch in 911 as her gaze shot to the

door, which was now swinging open. Too late. Jennifer couldn't catch her calling 911. She canceled the call as her cousin filled the opening.

CHAPTER NINETEEN

TJ HAD SEEN the exchange between the marshal and Vi from a distance. From the body language of both, she could see that something had happened. As she watched Leroy head toward town in his long-legged strides, she hurried to catch up to Vi.

"I need to speak with the marshal," TJ said. "Do you know where he's headed?"

"He's going over to my… Tina's. You haven't seen her, have you? Red hair, pregnant, a camera around her neck and a toddler clinging to her?"

"I know who Tina is," TJ told her. "Maybe I'll try to catch up with him then."

She'd heard the anxiety in Vi's tone and had seen her glancing around as if she hoped to spot Tina in the crowd.

It was the way Leroy took off that worried her. He must have known he could make better time on foot than going to the parking lot for his patrol SUV.

Vi, she noticed, was headed toward the main drag of Buckhorn, while Leroy had disappeared into the residential part of town. TJ had learned to follow her instincts. Something was wrong. She could feel it as she ran after Leroy. He had a head start but she was determined to try to keep him in sight.

She tried not to think about what Madam Zorna had told her—or hadn't. But the woman *had* picked up on something. Two men. Something unresolved from her past. Generic enough for any woman's reading. Yet she didn't have to even speculate on what hers might be. Worth.

TJ had hoped it was over. She was willing to put it behind her—just as he had so easily done. But what Madam Zorna had said made her wonder if it would play out here in Buckhorn. Only if Worth pushed it.

Ahead, she saw the marshal turn down a side street.

TINA PULLED CHLOE more tightly to her, but her cousin didn't seem to notice.

"Oh, you must be Chloe," Jennifer cried as she hurried into the room and dropped to her knees in front of them. "You can't imagine how long I've wanted to meet you." She looked up at Tina. "Hey, cuz. I guess you didn't hear me knocking. When did you start locking your doors?"

Tina's heart was a hammer in her chest. She had to swallow and catch her strangled breath before she could speak. "Hey, Jen." A part of her was screaming still for her to grab Chloe and run, but her brain argued against it. *Be cool. Pretend everything is normal. Don't panic, whatever you do.* "Lars must have locked us in. He worries with so many strangers in town."

Her cousin's gaze went back to Chloe. Tina could see that her daughter was curious and not afraid because she'd been raised in a town where there had been no one to fear. Fortunately, she'd been too young to remember that awful day in the café when three desperate men had come in—a day Tina could never forget since she'd thought for sure she was going to die.

Now here she and Chloe were again with a killer standing in front of them.

"Aren't you going to introduce me?" Jen said, not looking at Tina.

"Chloe, this is my cousin Jennifer." Her voice sounded almost normal to her, but she was quaking inside.

Jen touched a lock of Chloe's long red hair and Tina tried not to cringe even as she told herself that her cousin wouldn't hurt either of them.

"Where'd you get that pretty red hair?" Jen asked Chloe.

"From my mama," her daughter said proudly and glanced back up at Tina. "I'm going to have a brother or a sister. Mama doesn't know yet. Daddy says it's a brother." Chloe mugged a face. "I hope it's a sister."

Jen looked up again, her gaze meeting Tina's. "I can't believe the way she talks and she's how old?"

"Three. She's picked up language like a sponge." Her voice cracked as she hugged her precious, precocious child to her.

"I had to see her," Jen said. "See you too. I'm sorry."

Tina nodded and felt every part of her soften. This was her cousin who she'd loved like a sister. "Me too." She swallowed. "I should have called, come to visit—"

Her cousin waved that away. "I didn't want any of you to do that. Anyway, you've been busy." Jen chuckled, her gaze going to Tina's protruding belly. "Lars has been busy too." She looked to Tina's face again. "You're happy."

It wasn't a question, but she nodded. She realized that Earl Ray would be getting concerned since she was running so late. It would be just like him to come by the house. She couldn't let that happen. She had no way of knowing what Jennifer would do.

"Funny story though," Tina said. "Wait until you hear." She turned to Chloe. "Would you do Mama a favor?" Her daughter quickly pulled away, her eyes bright, eager to do a big-girl thing for her mom. "Go downstairs and get Mama and Jen two colas from out of the fridge. You can get two plastic glasses out of the dishwasher and fill them with ice. We'll be down in a minute." Her daughter brightened. Normally, she wasn't allowed to get into the cabinets for glasses. Nor was she supposed to pull up a chair to get ice. "You're sure you can handle it?" Chloe nodded. "Don't worry, Jen and I will be down soon."

"Okay, Mommy," Chloe said and stepped past Jen, smiling broadly as she went. Jen rose to watch her go. Tina wanted her daughter out of this bedroom, away from Jen. She wanted them all out of this bedroom. There were no weapons in here, but there was a shotgun downstairs on a high shelf in the kitchen pantry. Just in case.

The moment Chloe disappeared Tina was anxious to draw her cousin's attention back to her. "Axel isn't my father," she said and Jen turned back to her with a shocked expression. She repeated the story Earl Ray had told her, knowing that if anyone would appreciate the irony, it was her cousin.

Jen moved restlessly to her closet and was going through her clothes as she had so many times before. It sent a chill through Tina. This woman was a killer and yet Tina still felt a connection to her, felt both love and compassion for her tinged with fear.

"Vi always said that you were nothing like her," Jen said. "She must have had a conniption fit when she heard." She turned from the closet. "She knows, right?"

Tina nodded and rose. "I should go downstairs and see how Chloe is doing."

Jen seemed to hesitate. "Mind if I borrow a few things to wear?" She looked down at the clothing she had on.

Tina registered the sweat suit outfit for the first time

and recognized it. Her mother's? Surely Vi hadn't lent it to Jennifer, in which case, her mother had aided and abetted a known criminal. Just as Tina was about to do.

"Help yourself, then come on down." Tina started for the door, but her cousin reached out and grabbed her arm.

Shaking her head, Jen said, "Let me change and we'll go down together. I'm sure Chloe is doing just fine. She's like you. Very capable."

Hearing what could have been a threat in Jen's words, Tina knew this wasn't negotiable. "Fine, but quickly. Chloe isn't all that capable." She moved to sit on the edge of the bed because her legs had gone weak. It was hard to make idle conversation. She'd loved this woman for too many years, and yet she now knew how dangerous Jen could be. If Earl Ray showed up…

"So Earl Ray is your father," Jennifer said as she pulled a blouse and pants from the closet and proceeded to put them on. "You've always been lucky."

And you've always been jealous of it, she thought. That Jennifer had always felt as if she was the unlucky one made Tina feel more anxious. Jen seemed to be watching her out of the corner of her eye. Which was why Tina was determined not to give her any reason not to trust her—let alone turn against her.

Jen had just finished dressing when there was a loud crash from downstairs. They both looked at each other as Tina shot to her feet and rushed for the door.

LEROY HAD FOUND Earl Ray trying to see in the front window of Tina and Lars's house. Earl Ray had quickly signaled that something was wrong—just as the marshal had worried.

"The curtains are closed and the front door is locked,"

Earl Ray whispered. "She doesn't do either. I can hear someone in there. I was debating how to proceed."

They both suspected that Jennifer was inside. Leroy didn't want this to turn into a hostage situation. Nor did he want a shootout. Either way, according to Vi, her niece now had a loaded gun.

"I'm going around to the back door," the marshal said. "Stay here. If the coast is clear, I'll let you in. If not—"

"If not, I'll find a way in to help," Earl Ray said.

Leroy hurried around to the rear of the house. Just as he suspected, the back door was not only unlocked, but also a single key was still in the lock. Drawing his weapon, he slowly turned the knob and let the door yawn open. He could hear someone rattling around in the kitchen. Cautiously, he stepped in and closed the door quietly behind him. He could hear what sounded like ice cubes being dropped into a glass.

As he neared the corner where he would finally be able to see into the kitchen, he heard a child's voice singing a song with both a tune and words he'd never heard before.

He peered around the corner into the kitchen to see Chloe standing on a chair in front of the refrigerator busy putting ice cubes into one glass then another. Seeing her alone, he quickly holstered his weapon. She glanced up as if sensing she wasn't alone. Leroy quickly winked at her as he covered the distance between them.

Chloe smiled broadly and started to speak in a too-loud voice. He hushed her as he took the glasses from her and picked her up off the chair. "Whisper. Where's your mom?"

The girl lowered her voice as if they were playing a game. "Upstairs with Jen. Mama said I could get the glasses and the ice."

He was relieved that Tina had gotten Chloe out of the

situation. But the two might be coming down the stairs at any time. "Let's surprise your mama." He took her hand and walked her over to the front door. Unlocking it, he said, "Earl Ray is going to take you down to the café so you can see Bessie."

"But the glasses," Chloe cried and tried to pull away.

"I'll tell your mama what a good job you did. I bet Bessie has a treat for you at the café."

The child quit trying to pull away. "What does she have?" she asked Earl Ray.

"Let's go find out," the man said giving Leroy a nod of both concern and good luck as he took Chloe's hand. "So, you met your mom's cousin Jen?" he asked as they started away.

Chloe nodded. "She liked my hair."

The marshal closed the door and turned toward the kitchen. He knew they'd be coming down at any time, but he didn't want to wait. He chose two mismatched glasses from the cupboard, then dropped them on the tile floor. Both shattered as if he'd fired off a shot. Glass went everywhere.

He moved quickly, maneuvering around the shards, as he stepped into a hiding place where he could see the stairs. Then he waited.

JEN STOPPED HER cousin before she could get out the bedroom door. "Let me go first. In case there's a problem." Tina had no choice. She could see Jen trying to figure out all the angles. "Wait, I need to put on some shoes."

But Tina didn't wait, she was too concerned for her daughter. She shouldn't have trusted her with the chore, but it was the first one that came to her mind. Chloe was too young. As Jen turned to grab shoes, she ran, berating herself all the way down the stairs for fear that she'd put her daugher in more harm's way.

"Chloe?" she called as raced for the stairs. "Are you all right?" She took two steps at a time. No answer. "Chloe?" Her voice was high and strained.

She could hear Jen right behind her, the sound of her steps softened by the fact that Jen hadn't taken the time to pull on shoes. A million horrible thoughts flashed through her head as she turned the corner.

To her shock, the marshal grabbed her, covering her mouth with a hand as he dragged her back out of sight to the thunder of bare feet on the stairs. "Chloe's safe with Earl Ray," Leroy whispered in her ear. Tina hadn't realized how terrified she'd been until she felt tears of relief break loose and trail silently down her cheeks.

TJ SAW THE marshal say a few words to Earl Ray before going around to the back of the house. She slowed, not sure exactly what she should do until the front door opened, Earl Ray stepped just inside and came back out with Tina's daughter. The front door closed abruptly.

As Earl Ray and the child hustled away in the direction of town. TJ slipped around to the back of the house. The back door stood open. She'd barely reached the bottom of the porch steps when a figure came flying out.

TJ only had an instant to recognize Jennifer Mullen before the escapee launched herself off the porch at a run directly at her. There was no time to pull the weapon tucked in the holster under her arm. All she could do was tackle the woman in midair. The force took them both to the ground.

The hard ground and Jennifer nailing her with an elbow in the ribs knocked the air from TJ's lungs. Struggling to breathe, she was determined not to let the woman get away.

But Jennifer was strong and fought like it wasn't the first time someone had tried to hold her down.

Wrestling for control, TJ felt the woman unsnap the holster under her arm and pull out the weapon. She felt the sight dig into her side as Jennifer turned it so the first shot would go in just below TJ's ribs. Only God knew where it would come out—if at all.

TJ drew on every ounce of strength she had left to wrench the gun from the woman's incredibly strong grip. All she could think about was the sound of the shot and if she would even feel it as the bullet tore through her body. In those impossible seconds, she thought of the marshal and their night they had planned together.

She grabbed Jennifer's thumb on the hand holding the gun. She knew it might be a mistake, her last. She wrenched it hard, heard the woman cry out in pain, but her grip weakened. TJ tore the weapon away as Leroy came crashing out of the house. With relief, she felt Jennifer, kicking and screaming, as she was being pulled off her.

Lying on the ground on her back still fighting to breathe, TJ holstered her weapon with trembling hands and looked up at Montana's big sky. The sight had never looked so beautiful. She thought about how close she'd come to dying and felt her body shudder.

As she sucked in fresh mountain air, she heard By the Book Baggins cuff Jennifer Mullen. Glancing in his direction, she thought that he'd never looked so good either.

CHAPTER TWENTY

TJ WAS STILL lying in the grass, staring up at the sky, when Tina ran out of the house. She rushed to TJ, dropping to her knees beside her. "Did she hurt you?"

"Only my pride," TJ said as she pushed herself up into a sitting position. Her ribs hurt like the devil with each life-affirming, glorious breath. She saw Tina's gaze lift to where the marshal had Jennifer cuffed.

Tina's face was already tearstained, but at the sight of her cousin in cuffs, the sobbing started. She watched Tina slump down next to her as if relieved and yet filled with heartache for her cousin.

"It's all right, Tina," Jennifer said as if seeing her cousin's distress. "Sorry about your clothes though." Tina shook her head as if the ruined clothing was the least of her worries. "Don't come see me. Promise? Dr. Moss says he's going to make me well."

TJ could see Jennifer's eyes flood with tears. "It could take a while. But I'm so glad I got to see you and Chloe. Maybe I'll be well so I can meet your new baby."

Tina began to weep harder. TJ put her arm around her and closed her eyes to the scene as she heard the marshal on his radio requesting backup and a vehicle. She concentrated on breathing, her whole body quaking from the close call. Jennifer had been fighting for her life and TJ had been forced to do the same. She'd literally dodged a bullet. For so long, she'd felt fearless and within a few seconds she'd come close to losing her life.

She looked at the marshal, felt his worried gaze on her and gave him a thumbs-up. She was all right. Bruised, but not broken. Just as she'd been the night Worth had defiled her.

As several deputies came running around the back, Leroy handed over Jennifer to be locked in the back of one of the patrol cars. Tina stemmed the flow of tears, rose and pulled out her phone, saying she had to call Earl Ray.

Leroy walked over and offered TJ a hand up from the ground. He pulled her to him, holding her carefully as if he could see that she was in pain. She looked into his blue eyes, eyes so like the Montana sky, and wiped at tears she hadn't realized she'd cried. In his arms, she felt a calm come over her and realized she was no longer trembling. What was it about this man? All the good things a man should be, she thought.

After a moment he drew back to look into her face. "You're sure you're all right? Maybe we should have an EMT—"

"No, I'm fine. Just sore, that's all," she told him. His hug had hurt but she hadn't cared. She felt as if she was still waiting for that gunshot, a close call that had made her realize that she'd been pushing the odds for a long time.

Leroy dropped his voice. "I'm taking Jennifer in myself. I'm not sure when I'll get back." He met her gaze. "Maybe it's better if we didn't—"

"I'll be waiting in my room for you." Their gazes locked for a breath-stealing moment.

He nodded. "I'll see you then."

IT WAS LATE by the time Leroy reached TJ's room. He tried the door, not surprised to find it unlocked. But as he stepped in, he felt a start. She was sprawled, facedown on the bed, wearing the same soiled clothing she'd had on earlier. It appeared this was as far as she'd made it before collapsing.

As he closed the door behind him, he called her name softly. She didn't stir. He moved toward the bed, worried that she'd been more injured than she'd admitted earlier. He quickly checked for a pulse and was rewarded with a strong thump—strong, just like her. He couldn't help but smile down at her as he debated leaving her a note and going to his own room.

Leave her alone? He couldn't do that. He'd seen her retrieve her weapon from the ground earlier and knew that she'd had a close call. He'd faced death a few times in his career. He knew the toll it took on the soul.

Also he'd come to know this woman over the past few days. He couldn't leave. Not tonight. Not after the day she'd had. Not after the day they'd both had. When he'd seen TJ and Jennifer grappling for her gun…

In the bathroom, he began to draw her a hot bath. He poured in the soothing salts that he saw on the counter and watched the water foam with tall peaks of bubbles. It smelled like TJ, a scent that made him go weak with longing. Not tonight, he told himself.

Back in the bedroom, he sat down on the edge of the bed and gently touched her back.

She stirred. "Leroy?"

"I'm here," he said. He gently rolled her over, seeing her grimace in pain. He carefully began to remove her clothing. TJ watched him, a faint smile on her lips, her eyes hooded but what he could see of the green was bright. "Are you really all right?"

"I just hurt in a few places," she said. "I'll be fine."

He smiled at that. "I know you will." He finished removing her clothing with a little help from her. Her body was as beautiful and luxurious as he knew it would be naked, but sex was the last thing on his mind as he swept her up and carried her into the steam-filled bathroom. Carefully, he lowered her into the tub.

She sank to her neck in the bubbles and chuckled. "You've thought of everything. Except one thing."

"What's that?" he asked, ready to get her anything she needed.

"You." She pointed to the opposite end of the tub. "There's room for two in here."

"TJ," he said with a shake of his head. "I don't think we should—"

"Let's see how the bath goes," she said and ducked under the water. As she came up, her long hair clung to her skin, dark against light. She laughed and brushed her face free of the soap bubbles. "Strip, Marshal."

Leroy chuckled, then slowly began to remove his boots, then his socks. He could feel her gaze on him like a warm caress as he unbuttoned his uniform shirt, then unbuckled his belt and let his pants and briefs fall to the floor—just as she'd said he would do—before stepping buck naked into the tub with her.

TJ SMILED AS she leaned back in the tub as Leroy straightened out his long legs on each side of her. There was something so comforting about the warm water, the bubbles and Leroy here with her. Only their legs touched in the silky smooth bubble bath and for a while that's all she wanted or needed.

She could feel where the sight on the weapon had dug into her flesh. Her ribs still ached, but fortunately they weren't broken. In the full mirror against the wall, she could see that there was a scratch on her face, another on her arm and shoulder.

But she no longer felt that mind-numbing exhaustion she had earlier. "Jennifer?" she asked.

"She's settled in. She actually seemed relieved to be back with Dr. Moss."

Nodding, she closed her eyes thinking how much she'd enjoyed watching the marshal remove each item of clothing. As he'd taken off his shirt, she'd seen that his chest was smooth and tanned and muscular like his arms. As he'd unbuttoned his pants and let them drop from his slim hips, she'd smiled at the sight of his tighty-whities and what bulged beneath them before those too hit the floor. The man was gorgeous.

Opening her eyes, she touched him with her toes, making him raise a brow at her. "Are you sure about this?" he asked.

She smiled, knowing that she'd never been surer of anything.

"Your ribs look awfully bruised."

She nudged him again in the crotch and his body reacted. Her smile broadened as he grabbed her foot and gently began to massage it, all the time, his gaze remaining locked with hers. What she saw there sent heat rushing to her middle. Bubbles bobbed around them. When she spoke, her voice sounded rough with emotion. "I'm good to go, trust me."

Bending his knees, he slid closer, wrapping her legs around him, until they were almost chest to chest. Desire coursed through her in waves. Earlier she'd been exhausted both mentally and physically. Once she'd lain down on the bed, she'd passed out cold.

But now she felt more alive than she had in a very long

time. She felt like celebrating the fact with this man who'd somehow gotten to her. She'd built a wall around herself after what had happened in that hotel room with Prescott Rutherford Hollingsworth III. While she'd learned how to defend herself, she had kept her heart wrapped up tightly believing she might never trust another man.

But By the Book Baggins had sidled up on her, disarming her defenses and going straight for her heart without trying to enchant her. She hadn't even put up a fight. Instead, she'd fearlessly opened herself up to him, she thought now as he moved closer to kiss each bruised spot on her before dropping his mouth to her lips.

As he deepened the kiss, she reached for one of the mesh bath sponges in the tray by the tub, poured foaming body soap on it and slowly began to wash his broad, muscled chest.

His gaze met hers for a moment before he took another sponge and liberally poured soap on it before he began to gently wash her shoulders, dipping down to circle her breasts. Liquid fire rushed through her veins as bubbles floated around the two of them. She wanted this man desperately. For so long, she hadn't let herself feel anything let alone want a man this much.

With Leroy, she felt as if her body had been waiting for the right man to bring her back to life again. His tender touch ignited her every sense as his wet, slick fingers brushed over her already achingly hard nipples. She let out a moan of pleasure as he gently pulled one nipple, then the other, before his fingers trailed downward.

When he touched her bruised ribs, she winced. "I'm fine," she assured him. If he stopped now, she couldn't bear it. He kept moving across her stomach to find her most sensitive spot between her legs.

She leaned back, arching against the pressure as her pleasure rose and rose until she felt the sweet release come hot and fast. She pushed up into his arms. "I want you inside me," she breathed as she tried to catch her breath.

As if he felt her need as much as his own, he pulled her over onto him until she was straddling him. She hugged him, kissing his neck, his shoulder, his lips, her sore ribs forgotten as he entered her, filling her as he hungrily lathed her hard nipples with his tongue before taking her mouth. She came quickly and ached for him to do the same.

"Not yet," he said and pulled out to reach for a towel.

The rest was a blur of pleasure before they ended up in her bed having safe sex—after all, she thought later, Leroy was By the Book Baggins.

Later, as she lay wrapped in his arms, she realized it was the first time she'd felt safe with a man in four years. She closed her eyes and fell into a deep, restful sleep—until she was awakened by a ringing cell phone and sun streaming in the windows.

At first, TJ thought it was *her* phone. Her heart began to pound immediately.

But it was Leroy's cell that was ringing from his jeans still lying on the bathroom floor. She watched him scramble to answer it.

CHAPTER TWENTY-ONE

DAY FOUR

"GOOD NEWS," THE governor said early the next morning as Worth climbed into the car that would take them to Buckhorn. "That woman who escaped from the mental ward has been caught. I had a feeling she'd be captured before we arrived in Buckhorn and I was right. So it's all good. Nothing to worry about."

Worth could feel his friend's gaze assessing him. He knew he had to quit acting like this trip was a short walk to the gallows. But for him, it could be. He had no idea what TJ would do. The thought that she was enjoying having him over a barrel like this made him furious. If she thought he'd hurt her that night in the hotel, she had no idea how much he wanted to hurt her right now. He swore that if she ruined his career, he would kill her.

"Woman trouble?" Jamie asked, jerking him out of his thoughts.

"What makes you ask that?"

"The scowl you've had on your face. We're getting great coverage on this trip to Buckhorn. Did you happen to catch my comments on the morning news?"

He'd seen it. Jamie all decked out in Western attire, taking off his Stetson to smile into the camera. "I'm looking forward to my visit to Buckhorn," the governor had said.

"I personally want to commend those involved in the capture of a dangerous, recently escaped mental patient. I especially look forward to meeting the woman who saved that young boy on the Ferris wheel. It's that kind of heroism that made this country strong. I want to shake the hands of both Marshal Leroy Baggins and TJ Walker for a job well done.

"It is equally my honor to be speaking at Buckhorn's 125th birthday celebration closing ceremonies this evening. Towns like Buckhorn are the backbone of this state, of this nation. My hat's off to the residents and those who have worked so hard to make it what it is today." With that, Jamie waved his Stetson as he stepped away.

"It was pure Jamie Jacobsen," Worth said.

The governor snorted and seemed to relax. Worth wished *he* could relax. "I'll be congratulating both the sheriff and the woman. What was her name again?"

"TJ Walker."

"Imagine, first she saved the boy on the Ferris wheel and yesterday she helped in the takedown of the escaped killer. My kind of woman." Worth groaned inwardly. Jamie had no idea.

"I would imagine she'll be working all day since she's the head of her security team."

"At the press conference I'll invite her out to the ranch tonight after my speech and the event is over," the governor said as if he hadn't heard him. "How can she say no to the governor of this great state?"

"Hello?" Leroy cleared his voice. "Hello?" He'd slept so soundly that it took him a few moments to wake up.

"Marshal Leroy Baggins?"

"Yes?"

"This is Officer Horace Brown with the Montana State

Highway Patrol. I understand Governor Jacobsen is planning to speak at an event near you in Buckhorn?"

"Yes, what's this about?"

The officer cleared his throat. "It's just come to my attention that you had a female escapee that you captured in Buckhorn yesterday."

"I took her to the hospital myself," Leroy said as he felt his heart begin to pound. "Don't tell me she's escaped again."

"No, as far as I know, she's still incarcerated. I'm calling about another patient at the mental institution. A man named Kyle Robert Archer. Are you aware that he escaped at the same time as the female patient?"

Leroy tried to shake off the remnants of sleep. "No."

The HP officer cleared his throat again. "Governor Jacobsen is still planning on speaking at some closing event in Buckhorn tonight?"

"As far as I know, yes."

"Were you made aware that the governor has been getting death threats from Archer, who signs his letters K. Bob? Archer has been locked up in a state mental facility for some time even though he has found a way to get the threatening letters to the governor. When you caught the other escapee, it came to our attention that the two of them might have been in on this together. With the governor planning to make a speech there tonight and Archer's threats—"

"You think this patient might be in the area," Leroy finished for him as he finally made sense of what the officer was saying. "Have you notified the governor?"

"We have been unable to reach him. His office said he's en route to Buckhorn." Leroy swore under his breath. "Given the threats Archer has made against Governor Jacobsen, I thought you should be warned."

"Surely under the circumstances you can get the governor to change his mind," Leroy said.

"While he hasn't taken the threats seriously, if he knows that this man has escaped and might be in Buckhorn tonight…"

"He has scheduled a press conference early afternoon here."

"We are going to continue trying to reach him, but you might see him before then. He needs to know that the threat could be real if he speaks there tonight."

Leroy sighed. Jacobsen would probably see it as a sign of weakness to cancel. The man wouldn't want to hurt his image as a tough, no-nonsense good old boy to his Montana constituents. "All right. Send me what information you have on Archer. I'll take the governor aside at the press conference in case he hasn't talked to you. I'll try to dissuade him from making an appearance tonight. I hope you're planning to send some men to help us out, in case he goes ahead with his speech."

"We're hoping that won't be necessary, but yes we can send a couple of troopers. I'll send a description of Archer. I'm sorry you didn't have this information sooner."

Leroy disconnected and, turning back to TJ, told her about the call. "I thought we were home free with Jennifer caught. We aren't going to be until this celebration is over," he said coming back to the bed.

"Maybe the governor will have the good sense to cancel," she said.

"Well, at least I'm going to try and convince him of that. It's only a matter of hours before the celebration ends. If we can just get through it." His gaze met hers.

She could see that he didn't want to think about what would happen when the Buckhorn celebration was over any more than she did. After today there was nothing keeping her in Buckhorn, nothing keeping them together. Both could go on with their lives, their jobs driving them apart.

Leroy drew her toward him. As he did, his fingers brushed over the backside of her shoulder. He froze when she flinched at his fingertips on her scar. He drew her forward until he could see what it was that he'd missed last night in the dark. "Are those bite marks?" he asked in shock.

"It's nothing," she said. "Just an old scar."

Someone had bitten her hard enough to leave a scar?

CHAPTER TWENTY-TWO

TJ COULD SEE both his shock and his concern. "I don't want to talk about it, please," she said as his cell phone rang again.

He groaned and moved from the bed to check it. "It's Vi," he said with a curse.

She listened as he took the call and assured the woman that both he and TJ would be at the press conference early this afternoon in front of her store. TJ knew then that they wouldn't be making love again. Not now, probably not ever since this was day four of the celebration and with everything that was going on, they were going to be busy.

If she was smart, she'd leave tonight. She would have to wait until after the governor's speech. She was still employed to provide security and now there was possibly a threat against the governor.

Leaving was the best thing for both of them, she told herself. No reason to prolong the inevitable. What were the chances that what she was feeling with Leroy was going anywhere? She had a security company to run, and she knew from the scuttlebutt about Leroy that he was unavailable. His job would always come first. The man was a confirmed bachelor. Nothing had changed.

She still had to get through a press conference. Worth would no doubt be at the governor's side. Just the thought of seeing the man again—

Leroy returned to sit on the edge of the bed, his back to her. "I wish you'd tell me about him."

Her heart leaped to her throat and began to beat so hard she feared he would hear the panic in her voice. "I don't know what you're—" She didn't finish because he'd turned to look at her. Pinned with those blue eyes, she couldn't lie. She felt tears burn her eyes. She'd already opened herself to this man because she trusted him. She'd let him into her bed, into her heart. *Be honest with him. Tell him.*

"I know there is a man," Leroy said, his voice husky with emotion. "He's been calling you. I suspect he's hurt you in the past, but now he wants to see you again, doesn't he?"

Wow, he pretty much nailed it—even if he did have it all wrong. "You've been talking to Madam Zorna," she said trying to joke it off. His gaze killed any humor from her words. "You're right. There is a man. But it isn't what you think."

As hard as it was, she told him about the night she'd gotten the teacher's award, a night she was still recovering from.

Leroy's eyes widened in alarm. "I hope you went to the police."

"It would have been my word against his. I was the one who went up to his hotel room. I don't think I have to tell you how allegations often go in court. Maybe I would have gone to the police that night. But as much as it embarrasses me, I didn't even know his real name. I later realized why he hadn't told me the truth."

"But if you don't know his name… Isn't he the one who's been calling you?"

She nodded, not surprised since he'd obviously over-heard her end of the conversation that day. "I didn't know his name—until I saw him here in Buckhorn. I got to face him and call him on what he'd done. Of course, he'd made excuses, but ultimately I think I got through to him because he's afraid I'm going to tell his boss and he might lose his job."

"His job? Who is this man?" Leroy asked between gritted teeth.

"He's the governor's right-hand man, his best friend and his advisor. Prescott Rutherford Hollingsworth III or Worth as he'd called himself."

Leroy rose from the bed as if he'd been hit with a cattle prod. "Are you kidding me?" His handsome face registered shock with equal amounts of fury.

"When he saw me, he didn't recognize me, didn't even remember me." She let out a bitter laugh, too close to a sob. Taking a calm breath, she said, "I never thought I'd get the chance to tell him to his face what I thought of him. That night I'd been too frightened, feeling too foolish and ashamed of myself for trusting him, too...hurt."

"I'm so sorry," Leroy said, returning to the bed to pull her into his arms. She could feel the tension in him, the anger, the frustration because she'd felt it herself for too long. As marshal, she knew he would want justice for her.

"You can see why he's worried. Isn't there talk that Jacobsen might be the party's next candidate for president? I would imagine Worth plans to ride his coattails all the way to the White House and that's why he's so upset."

She saw the muscles tightening around his eyes, his jaw, the veins in his throat pulsating. Just as she'd feared, she regretted sharing this because of what it had done to this loving, wonderful man. Leroy was one of the good ones.

"I'm so sorry, TJ," he said, his voice rough with emotion as he got up to pace the room. "That bastard should be behind bars."

"I survived it," she said, lifting her chin, calling on her stubborn determination. "In fact, Worth made me the woman I am today. I'm no longer that starry-eyed young girl he met and took advantage of."

"You are a strong woman despite that piece of garbage," he said turning to look at her. "You need to tell the governor, expose this man for who he is."

She shook her head. "I want to put it behind me now more than ever. Anyway, I suspect his good friend the governor knows exactly what kind of man Worth is. Apparently they've been friends for a long time. The governor probably isn't any better."

Leroy swore. "Now I understand why you wanted to keep a low profile." His eyes widened. "This man will probably be at the governor's press conference." He stepped to the bed and took her hands in his as he looked down at her. "I think you need to tell your story to protect any future victims… Maybe there are other women—"

"I wish it would be that easy. But I have no proof that it hadn't been consensual."

Leroy let go of her to pace the floor again. "How can you stand in front of the cameras and smile when you know what this sick son-of-a-bee is capable of doing?" he demanded.

She mentally kicked herself for telling him. Of course he would want to slay this dragon for her. She could have made up something about the scar, but he was too good a lawman not to put it all together.

"I've said all I need to say to him," TJ assured him. "You can see why I've never told anyone about this, and I especially didn't want you knowing. There is nothing anyone can do."

The marshal's blue eyes blazed. "I'm the marshal of

this county, how can I do nothing knowing what I do?" he demanded.

She rose and moved to him. "Because you're acting like my lover instead of the law. This happened a long time ago. Even if it wasn't my word against his—"

He swore, shaking his head before his gaze settled on her again. His hands balled into fists. "I want to punch his lights out."

TJ cupped his strong jaw and made him look into her eyes. "Trust me, the impulse will be much worse once you meet him. But that is not the kind of thing By the Book Baggins would do."

"I hope you're right about that," he said, his voice rough with anger. "You know I'd fight for your honor."

TJ swallowed, felt the heat of tears fill her eyes as she nodded and smiled. "I know." But causing a scandal with the governor and his advisor and friend would put Leroy's job at risk. It wasn't worth it. Worth wasn't worth it.

He pulled her into his arms. She wrapped her arms around his neck and let him take her back to bed, glad she'd been wrong about their lovemaking being over. For a while they both forgot about Worth and the day ahead of them.

LITTLE SURPRISED LEROY. Even less rattled him. Going into law enforcement had always made sense to him because of the way he handled himself. He remained calm, used his head, figured the angles and did what had to be done. He wasn't impulsive. He was always levelheaded. He operated on facts, not emotion. He wasn't called By the Book Baggins for nothing.

Now he found himself at war with such volatile emotions that he had trouble containing them. He'd had an ordinary childhood, and an even more ordinary adulthood since he'd gone straight into law enforcement from the university. There'd been no trauma other than what he saw in other people's lives first as a deputy and now as marshal.

But hearing TJ's account of her encounter with Worth had thrown him for a loop, as his grandmother used to say. He'd never felt such rage, such pain, such a need to get justice for TJ. He also realized he was running scared because…he'd fallen so hard for this woman. Last night had only made him want her more.

That thought hit him hardest. He couldn't let anything happen to her. She'd admitted after their lovemaking this morning that Worth had threatened her on the phone. He wanted to confront this man and make sure he never bothered TJ or anyone again.

What scared him was how angry he was. A part of him wanted to hurt the man like the man had hurt TJ. That need, not just for justice, shook the very ground he walked on as marshal.

"I'm going to go down to my room to shower and change for work," he said as he pulled on his pants and picked up his uniform shirt. She still lay on the bed where he'd reluctantly left her. He turned to meet her gaze, wanting, needing to say so much more.

"I'm fine," she said as if seeing his turmoil. She rose, naked as a jaybird, to hug him. She gave him a look as if to remind him that she'd been living with this for four years. As if he could forget that.

"I'll be back," he said as she passed him headed for the bathroom.

Prescott Rutherford Hollingsworth III thought he was above the law. He thought he was safe because of who he was and who he worked for. He thought he could do whatever he wanted without consequences. He was clearly some-one in a powerful position with powerful friends.

Leroy realized that Worth would be traveling with the governor to Buckhorn. If he was running scared, then he couldn't let TJ tell the governor or anyone else what he'd done.

That alone froze his blood. Worth had gotten away with what he'd done once. What if he thought he could do it again?

"Let's go to the fairgrounds together today," Leroy called through the partially open bathroom door over the sound of the shower.

"All right," she called back.

He hesitated for a moment, wanting to join her in the shower, wanting to make love one more time, maybe their last. Mostly he wondered how he could live with this knowl-edge, let alone live without TJ if she left after tonight.

But right now, he had to concentrate on keeping her safe, then he would deal with keeping her from disappear-ing from his life after the event closed tonight.

He picked up her cell phone where she'd left it. He knew her password because he'd seen her put it in earlier. Open-ing her phone, he added the tracking device, telling himself he'd never have to use it. But just in case…

AFTER LEROY LEFT, TJ stood under the hot spray, feeling the weight of what she'd done, telling the marshal. Now he was carrying the weight of her burden and she hated that. Worse, she'd seen how much he wanted to protect her. She'd also seen his fury against the man who'd harmed her. She could imagine how hard that must be for a man of the law, ruled by the law.

She finished her shower, wrapped a towel around herself and turned on the television. A commercial came on as she dressed. She thought of their lovemaking. Being in Leroy's arms, she'd felt so safe, so cherished… But she never should have told him about what Worth had done.

At the sound of her name, she turned to stare at the television screen. The local news station had led with the story of the governor's visit to Buckhorn. She heard Leroy's name and then her own mentioned again.

She listened to the governor's statement. Just as Vi had told Leroy, the governor was determined to congratulate the two of them. It was the last thing she wanted since she knew Worth would be there.

TJ felt her stomach roil at the thought of seeing Worth again. Worse, the marshal would be with her knowing what Worth had done to her.

Prescott Rutherford Hollingsworth appeared on the television screen. She reached over and turned off the set. She knew he didn't want to see her any more than she did him. After today she would never have to see him again.

Unless he followed Jacobsen to the White House, she reminded herself. She groaned at the thought of seeing his arrogant face every time she turned on the news.

Her cell phone rang. She didn't recognize the number. She'd blocked Worth's number so it might be something important. This was still her job, which she reminded herself would be over by tonight. Until then… "Hello?"

"Please don't hang up."

She swore under her breath. "I asked you not to call me again." He'd figured out that she'd blocked his number and used another phone.

"I didn't call to argue with you." She could practically hear him grinding his teeth. "I called to apologize. I'm sorry for whatever you think I did."

She groaned. "I've had to live with what you did to me that night for four years so even if an apology would fix it, that wasn't one. We both know what you did. Let's just leave it at that."

"I want to make it up to you," he said before she could hang up. "I'm on my way to Buckhorn for the news conference and the closing event. Let me take you out afterward and prove that I'm not a bad guy. I'll change your mind if you let me."

"No, thanks," she said, trying to keep her tone cordial when she wanted to scream. He wasn't a nice guy and they both knew it. Did he really think she would fall for that line of his a second time? Apparently he did. She disconnected and blocked this number as well, her hands shaking with anger.

WORTH SWORE AS he saw that the governor was waiting for him, standing next to the car at the gas station, looking impatient.

"Everything all right?" Jamie asked.

He could feel his friend's gaze on him as they climbed back into the car. "Just an upset stomach." He'd asked for the gas station stop so he could call TJ—for all the good it had done. The clerk had let him use her phone after he'd flashed her one of his smiles.

"You worry me sometimes," Jamie said, but didn't elaborate as he got busy on his phone, which was fine with Worth.

He hadn't been able to sleep last night. His blood had thrummed so hot in his veins that he had to kick off the covers. All he could think about was what TJ Walker might do at the press conference. Point at him and yell, "That's the man who raped me!" in front of the news crews and their cameras?

She'd told him not to call her again. That alone had made him furious. Like he was going to take orders from this woman? Didn't she realize who he was?

That was just it. She knew *exactly* who he was and now she thought she had him right where she wanted him—running scared. TJ Walker was going to ruin his life—unless he stopped her.

He tried to calm down as he replayed the phone call in his head. What had made him think that she might be reasonable? He would have taken her out for dinner—if there was someplace in Buckhorn to eat late. What did she want from him?

She wanted to destroy him. He told himself that she couldn't even prove that they'd ever met. He could just deny it. But he knew with the Me Too movement he might not be believed. Her accusations would follow him like a bad smell.

Worse, other women might come forward. Wasn't that what really had him worried and unable to sleep? Once she opened her mouth... It wasn't like she'd been the first to lead him on, get him all worked up and then say no like he could just stop. Like he wanted to stop. Screw that. Maybe he'd gotten a little rough. But women had to learn that they couldn't come on to him and then throw on the brakes. As far as he was concerned they had it coming.

While she couldn't prove that he'd been the one to rape her—neither could he prove that he hadn't. The media would turn over every stone. It wouldn't be that hard for them to find out that he was in Denver the night of the alleged attack. If TJ Walker came forward with her allegations, he knew there were women he'd bedded who would jump on the bandwagon just for their fifteen minutes of fame. Look what had happened to other men in power who'd been brought down by a handful of women after one of them had started making allegations.

No, he thought now. He couldn't let this Walker woman come forward. He'd tried to charm her, offering to make it up to her and she'd brushed off his attempt at an apology. She said that all she wanted was to call him on what he'd done.

Yeah, right, although he didn't think she was the kind of woman who wanted the notoriety or the attention. So maybe the answer was to buy her off. It wouldn't be cheap since she had her own business and seemed to be doing well, but it would be worth whatever it cost. He would make her sign a nondisclosure agreement, tying her hands so she couldn't come forward later.

And if she refused? He glanced out the car window. He felt fresh panic rising as his pulse pounded in his ears. Time was running out. He could see Buckhorn coming up on the horizon. He had to do something and fast.

If she refused, she wouldn't give him any choice. She didn't realize who she was messing with. But she would soon—unless she took what he offered her and kept her mouth shut.

CHAPTER TWENTY-THREE

TJ DIDN'T WANT to tell Leroy about the phone call. He was already upset enough. But the moment he returned to her room, he seemed to sense something had happened during the time he'd been gone.

"Tell me what's wrong," he said as he quickly moved to take her in his arms. He was no fool. "You heard from him again."

She swallowed and reluctantly nodded.

Leroy's handsome face became chiseled with anger. "What did he say?"

"He wanted to make it up to me by taking me out to-night," she said.

"You have to be joking." He let go of her to pace the room. "The man is incorrigible." He spun to face her. "What did you tell him?"

"That I wasn't interested, but I get the feeling he isn't going to let it go. I've told him repeatedly that I've had my say and now I'm putting it behind me, but he's afraid I'm going to say something."

"If I were you, I *would* say something," Leroy snapped.

She shook her head. "And have my name attached to his forever, have my life dragged through the mud by the media, get to relive what he did to me over and over when it would still come down to my word against his? No, thank you."

"How can you let him get away with what he did?"

She stepped to him. "You have to understand. Even if I had known his name, I wouldn't have gone to the police four years ago. I certainly wasn't going to put myself through a trial. I was an elementary school teacher. He was already involved in politics and had the name, the money, the lawyers behind him." She sighed. "It still comes down to my word against his. All he had to say is that I wanted it."

Leroy groaned and raked a hand through his hair before he pulled her to him. "I'm sorry, it's just..." He stepped back to cup her cheek in his palm, his blue eyes locking with hers. "I went into this business in the hope of getting justice at least part of the time. It's pure hell knowing he is going to get away with what he did to you."

"I should have left well enough alone, but how could I not face him and call him out on what he'd done to me? I want to put it behind me now and forget I ever crossed paths with Prescott Rutherford Hollingsworth III." Right-hand man to the governor of the state, he couldn't have looked more professional, more respectable, more innocent. "If it's any comfort, he seems terrified by even the thought that I might go public because it would ruin his political career. Let that be enough. Let's hope that after the press conference, he'll realize that he's safe and that he better not think of assaulting another woman and this really will be the end of it."

WHEN LEROY HAD gone to his room, he'd quickly learned as much as he could about Prescott Rutherford Hollingsworth III. Worth was exactly the man TJ had described. He came from a wealthy family, attended a fancy boarding school, elite college and now had money, power, influential friends and what appeared to be a squeaky-clean reputation.

For the first time, Leroy really understood why some people took the law into their own hands. They wanted justice, they wanted it immediately and if they didn't do something, the Worths of the world would go scot-free.

But as much as he wanted to give the man some of his own medicine or worse, he wouldn't because he was By the Book Baggins from his Stetson to his boots. It was who he was down to his soul.

At the same time, he wanted to spare TJ the humiliation of having to pretend at the press conference. The governor was planning to shake her hand and commend her for her bravery in saving the boy. The only way he could keep that from happening was to talk the man out of coming to Buckhorn and bringing his advisor with him.

In good conscience, he had to warn Jacobsen about Kyle Robert Archer. He called the number he had for the governor, but didn't get any further than the state highway patrolman had. He would have to wait until Jacobsen reached Buckhorn.

"Are you sure you're up to this?" he asked TJ and instantly regretted his words. Of course she was. "What am I saying? You're the strongest, most determined woman I've ever met."

She smiled. "I just want it over. My hope is that Worth will think twice before he does this again to another woman."

The marshal swore under his breath. It didn't seem near enough. "He'd just better not come near you."

"I'm sure he wants this over with as much as I do now that he realizes he can't charm or con me."

Leroy wished he was convinced. He'd known men like Worth. He'd had to deal with them as marshal. They believed they were above the law. Often they were.

"This is why I didn't want to tell you," she said touching his arm.

He felt that electric thrill surge through him. He met her gaze and smiled, still in awe that this woman had come into his life. The question was how to keep her safe until he could convince her not to walk out of his life after tonight.

THEY WERE ON the outskirts of Buckhorn when they finally got cell phone coverage. Worth heard the governor's phone chime. He watched Jamie check the message. The governor swore.

"What is it?" he asked, afraid it might have been something from TJ Walker.

"A bunch of messages from the state police and one from my wife." He proceeded to tell him that Pamela would be joining them today and apparently planned to stay the night as well after Jamie's speech.

"That's odd," Worth pointed out unnecessarily and raised an eyebrow in question as he tried to hide his glee. "I thought you said there was no way she'd want to come along?" With Pamela in Buckhorn, there would be no way Jamie could invite TJ back to the ranch for a drink. Not that he thought she would have agreed anyway. But this way, there wouldn't be even the question of Jamie getting close to the woman.

"She's angry that I didn't mention where I was going. Seems she saw the news and thought this would make good optics for us to be here together. I wonder where she got that idea?"

Worth shook his head, lifting his hands in surrender. *Maybe she isn't as naive about your extracurricular activities as you think she is*, he thought, but didn't dare say.

"She knows good press when she sees it. I get the impression that Pamela has some political ambitions of her own."

The governor grunted again. "You're right. She's more than likely thinking that if I can't get into the White House then she can. The hell of it is, she's more qualified than I am."

Worth said nothing, trying to hide his smile. Pamela was coming to Buckhorn. That meant she would keep her husband away from TJ Walker and avert disaster. This couldn't have turned out better if he'd planned it—not that he hadn't had a hand in the outcome. All Worth had had to do was drop a few hints to Pamela. She could be easier to maneuver than her husband sometimes.

"The state police want to talk to me." Jamie pocketed his phone. "Probably about security tonight."

Worth turned his thoughts to how to get TJ Walker alone.

"You still want to congratulate the marshal and the security woman, right?" he asked the governor.

"Of course," Jamie snapped. "Pamela said she'd meet us at the press conference since she's coming from the other direction." He didn't sound excited about meeting TJ anymore. "She's sending her driver and security home and staying with us out at the ranch."

That relieved Worth, but he knew that it didn't solve the problem. He felt his stomach roil and knew he would never be safe until he'd taken care of TJ Walker.

AT THE FAIRGROUNDS, Leroy saw that Buckhorn was gearing up for another big day. With Jennifer caught, he had been breathing a sigh of relief. But Shirley Langer was missing and presumed dead even though there had been no sign of a struggle nor any blood in her car.

And now he had another mental institution escapee, K.

Bob, to worry about. He definitely couldn't let the governor speak tonight at the closing ceremonies although he wasn't sure how to stop him.

Jennifer's fingerprints had been on the steering wheel so they assumed she'd been the one to abandon it in the fairgrounds parking lot. Vi's gardening straw hat had been found in the back seat so they also knew that Jennifer and Shirley had crossed paths. Leroy had deputies looking for Shirley. He'd called the mental institution, but hadn't been able to talk to Jennifer. He just hoped Shirley was found before tonight.

The governor's appearance this evening seemed to be having more of a draw than he'd expected. Jamie Jacobsen portrayed himself as a fellow Montanan—even though his background was that of an entitled rich kid from back East. Throw on a cowboy hat, a pair of scuffed boots and enough voters in the state had bought into his good old boy routine and elected him.

TJ had been quiet on the short drive to the fairgrounds. He still couldn't believe what she'd told him about the man she called Worth. He found himself balling his hands into fists every time he thought about him.

Knowing TJ, she was probably concentrating on work to keep her mind off the press conference and being forced to see the man again. Like him, she wasn't counting on him being able to change the governor's mind about skipping his speech tonight so she would be talking to her team after what they'd learned this morning about Kyle Robert Archer.

Leroy checked the time. They would be meeting with the governor and his advisor soon. He couldn't imagine how TJ could face the man and pretend that she didn't know him given what he'd done to her. Leroy knew it was going to be next to impossible for him to pretend.

The moment he parked, he saw that Vi Mullen was waiting for him. Now what, he wondered.

"I need to see to my crew," TJ had said and quickly escaped as soon as he'd parked. He saw her meet up with Ash and Lane, always impressed by how she handled her team. He'd seen how loyal they were to her. She looked in his direction and he nodded, his gut tightening.

He hadn't wanted to let her out of his sight until this was over. He'd had no choice but to let her go while he dealt with Vi, who was delirious with excitement. The celebration had been a success. Having the governor here for the closing ceremony was the icing on the cake, according to her.

Vi had just wanted to reiterate how important this news conference was and make sure Leroy and TJ were ready. He assured her they were, even though he knew it wasn't true.

Now as he watched TJ approach, she smiled, but he could see tension just below the surface. "Vi seemed in a good mood."

"I'm still going to try and talk the governor out of staying for his speech tonight," Leroy told her.

She met his gaze and appeared to want to say something. He knew that she wanted this to end here, tonight. He figured she couldn't wait to get out of Montana so she never had to see Worth again. But that was the last thing Leroy wanted. He knew he didn't have much time. He needed to tell her how he felt about her. But what if he told her and it didn't make a difference?

"My team is ready," she said. "So am I. We just have to make sure that no one kills the governor on our watch." She dragged her gaze away.

He stared at her profile, completely taken with this woman. "I'm not sure I'm ready." She turned back to him and he saw the shine of her eyes in all that green. He fought the urge to pull her into his arms. He knew this wasn't the time or the place, but that didn't stop him. "TJ, after last night I—"

"It was wonderful," she said quickly as if to cut him off. "So was this morning. But right now, I have to concentrate on getting through this day. Maybe when it's all over…"

He nodded and struggled to change the subject. "No donuts this morning?" he asked.

She shook her head but smiled. "Not this morning." He could hear shrieks of laughter over the clanking and cranking of the carnival machinery among the other sounds of late summer fun.

"Just promise me one thing. Please don't leave without saying goodbye." His words seemed to surprise her.

"I hate goodbyes, but don't worry, I couldn't leave without seeing you again." She bit her lower lip for a moment. "If all goes well, I'll meet you for a dance before the celebration closes down."

"You sure you can do this, because I'm sure as hell not," Leroy told her.

"Have to. What other option do we have?"

He told himself that a man like Worth wouldn't try anything in broad daylight. Still, Leroy couldn't help being afraid for TJ. "If you need me, for *anything*—"

"I still have your number." She grinned and he felt his heart do a loop-de-loop in his chest.

He glanced at the time. "I guess we'd better get uptown to the press conference." She nodded, her jaw set in determination. All he had to do was get through this next thirty minutes or so. Once he talked the governor out of staying for his speech, then Worth would be gone.

Still the future had never felt more uncertain. He reminded himself that he was the law and was good at his job. He dealt with liars, crooks, thugs and even murderers. But right now, he felt helpless. Letting Worth get away with what he'd done—to respect TJ's wishes—would be one of the hardest things he'd ever had to do.

CHAPTER TWENTY-FOUR

TJ WASN'T LOOKING forward to seeing Worth again, but it was time for the press conference. It amazed and rankled her that he'd actually asked her for another date. Was he that obtuse? Clearly, he was. Or was it simple arrogance?

"Ready?" Leroy asked. She could tell that he hated this as much as she did. He wanted to spare her and yet she was going to have to face the man. Just get it over with, she told herself.

"Ready," she said, although all the pep talks in the world couldn't prepare her for this. She tried not to think about the night she'd met Worth, let alone what he'd done to her, and would no doubt do again if he got the chance.

The marshal had insisted that the news conference be held on the main drag of Buckhorn. He'd made the excuse that there would be less congestion than at the fairgrounds and it would be easier to protect the governor. Worth had little option but to go along.

Vi had been delighted to hear that it would be shot in front of her general store. Leroy told her that he and TJ would remain in the store until the governor and his entourage arrived, then they would come out.

"Let's keep this short and sweet, Vi," he'd said. "TJ and I have work to do back at the fairgrounds." He'd told TJ that she could use the store as an escape route. Once it was over, TJ could go into the store and out the back, to keep herself away from Worth. Leroy was trying to think of anything that would make this easier for her, she knew.

He also planned to bring the governor into the store to talk to him about Kyle Robert Archer, he'd said. He would use Vi's office so they could have some privacy.

"Looks like they've arrived." Vi had been watching at the window and now waved frantically for them to hurry out as the governor and his advisor emerged from a large black SUV.

TJ took a breath. She could do this. But she worried about the marshal. He was watching Worth, his jaw set in rage.

LEROY GLANCED OVER at TJ and saw that she had her game face on. He smiled and took her hand, squeezing it quickly before releasing it as the governor and Worth stopped to wave to the cameras and reporters as well as a small crowd that had gathered to see what was going on.

He opened the store's front door letting her go out first. TJ stepped out. As the cameras swung in her direction she smiled, avoiding looking in Worth's or the governor's direction as Leroy came out to join her. They stopped on the sidewalk in front of the general store and let the governor and his aide come to them.

He saw with an inward groan that both the governor and Worth were dressed in Western attire from their new Stetsons on their heads to the fancy boots on their feet. He noticed that TJ was making a point of not looking directly at either man.

The governor moved so he was standing in front of the microphones that had been set up, facing the cameras and the street. Worth was off to his left. Leroy made sure he was between them and TJ.

"I'm delighted to be here in Buckhorn," the governor began to cheers and applause from the small crowd. Buckhorn was just rural enough that probably most of the residents had voted for the man.

And yet he knew there could be at least one person in the crowd who wanted Jamie Jacobsen dead. He found himself studying the faces, looking for Kyle Robert Archer, anxious to convince the governor to pack it in and go back to Helena.

Out of the corner of his eye, he watched TJ. She had a smile plastered on her face for the news cameras and the crowd, but he wasn't fooled. He doubted Worth was either.

TJ WAS AWARE of Worth even though she couldn't see him on the other side of the governor. She'd done her best not to look at him when he and the governor had stopped to preen for the cameras. It made her recall his cockiness. He wanted to believe he was untouchable. Maybe she had convinced him that she wasn't a threat. Still she had to fight back a shudder to be this close to the man.

She realized that she'd missed something, when the governor suddenly turned to her and, reaching across the marshal, extended a hand to her. It was the first time she'd actually looked at Jamie Jacobsen as she took his hand. He seemed to be another version of Worth, cut from the same cloth. But then again, they were good friends, wasn't that what Worth had told her?

"It's an honor to shake your hand," the governor was saying, holding her hand a little too long. "I have something for you." He motioned to Worth, who stepped forward, but still she didn't look his way as the governor took an envelope from Worth and pressed it into her hand. "This kind of heroism makes me proud to be an American." That got another cheer from the growing crowd that was gathering.

She took the envelope, her palm damp, as she mumbled, "Thank you, but I was just doing my job." She stepped back and the governor shook the marshal's hand and commended him.

"I'd like to shake your hand as well," Worth said suddenly standing directly in front of her. He'd taken the opportunity when the governor was shaking hands with Leroy to confront her. She'd looked up and there he was.

He reached for her hand. She still had the envelope pressed in it, so he grasped her other hand, drawing her forward toward him. "We need to talk," he whispered and squeezed her hand hard enough to make her meet his gaze. Those eyes. She hadn't forgotten anything about them. She could hear the governor at the microphone. No one seemed to notice her and Worth—except for Leroy.

The marshal stepped forward. "Excuse me," he said to Worth. "I need to speak to my head of security." He drew her away, forcing Worth to step back as Leroy opened the general store door, and with relief, she stepped inside, the door closing behind her.

The moment the door shut, she swallowed and fought to catch her breath as she wiped the hand that Worth had touched on her jeans. She felt sick at what she'd seen in the man's eyes. He wasn't through with her, she thought as she made a beeline for the back door. But she was through with him.

THE PRESS CONFERENCE OVER, and TJ safe, Leroy stepped back outside. "Governor, a moment of your time."

Worth started toward him, but Leroy held up a hand.

"I need to speak to the governor alone." He was blocking the door. No way was he letting Worth go inside. The man started to protest, but the governor waved him off saying, "I'll see you at the car," and turned his attention to the marshal.

Leroy ushered the governor inside and back to Vi's office. He noticed that TJ was nowhere in sight and figured she'd headed back to the fairgrounds. Of course she'd want to get to work.

"The state police and I have been trying to reach you," Leroy said, anxious to get this over with and find TJ. He'd seen her expression. Worth had whispered something to her. He was worried that he'd had another flimsy proposal for her. "I understand you've been getting death threats from a man named Kyle Robert Archer. K. Bob?"

The governor chuckled. "I appreciate your concern, Sheriff, but this isn't the first time I've been targeted by a political fanatic. I don't take rantings seriously."

Jacobsen went out of his way to prove just how Montana he was even though he hadn't been in the state all that long. Short of wrestling a grizzly bear, Jacobsen had been in the headlines before for his so-called "down-home" behavior.

"Marshal," he corrected, "Marshal Leroy Baggins," and went on to tell him that Archer had escaped from the same mental hospital as Jennifer Mullen. "We suspect he is here in Buckhorn for your speech tonight."

Leroy saw the governor's surprised and worried expression before he said, "I see," and looked toward the front of the store and the street where the camera crews were no doubt still standing around waiting for him to come back out.

"I would strongly advise against you speaking tonight

at the closing ceremonies," the marshal told him. "I have limited officers. Quite frankly, Governor, I'm not sure we can keep you safe."

JAMIE COULDN'T BELIEVE what he was hearing. He nodded, taking in what the marshal was telling him while he tried to hide his concern. Moments before the marshal had asked to talk to him, he'd seen Pamela arrive. She'd missed the news conference, which would upset her enough. If he told her he wasn't giving his speech after all, she'd be furious.

Worse, the news crews were still outside waiting for him. If he announced that he wouldn't be speaking tonight all this would have been for nothing. He'd be lucky to get a short clip on the news with him congratulating the Walker woman. The big news would be that out of fear, he'd canceled his speech.

The marshal was waiting.

All his instincts told him to cancel the speech. It would be the prudent thing to do. But even as he thought it, he knew canceling would make him look weak. Not the image he wanted to portray. This was the Wild West. He had enough voters who thought he was in over his head since he wasn't born and raised here.

"I'm sorry, Marshal, but I didn't come all this way not to speak," Jamie said. "But I promise to keep it short. Don't want to give anyone in the crowd a chance to put their sights on me." His laugh held little humor. He felt as if he already had a gun to his head.

Worse, he was disappointed that he wouldn't get any alone time with the gorgeous heroine who'd saved that boy, so his trip here had been ruined anyway. He knew things weren't going to get any better—unless he could get Pamela to go on home. Little chance of that since he knew she'd want to take the stage with him tonight.

Maybe if he told her there was a killer out there with a bullet with his name on it... Or maybe he'd get lucky and Archer's aim wouldn't be quite true. The sympathy vote might take him all the way to the White House and there were other Pamelas out there, some with even deeper pockets.

TJ HAD GOTTEN only as far as the alley before her cell phone buzzed in her pocket. She knew who would be calling. Worth had said they needed to talk. She groaned, considering letting the call go to voicemail. But would he only track her down to talk to her if she didn't answer?

"What do you want now?" she demanded, wondering whose phone he was using.

"How did you know it was me?" She said nothing, waiting. "Don't hang up. I know I haven't handled this well, all right? I feel bad about that. I want to make it up to you."

"I already told you—"

"You've made it abundantly clear how you feel about me," he said impatiently. "But how can I make this right? How do you feel about some form of compensation for any pain and suffering I might have caused you?"

"*Might* have caused me?"

He rushed on, clearly ignoring her. "In return, I'll need you to do something for me."

She couldn't believe this. "You're offering to buy me off?" Add to that, he wanted her to do something for him? The man was delusional.

"Name your price. I know you want this over and done with as much as I do. I'm in town so let's settle this now."

"How many times do I have to tell you that I don't want

anything from you? I only confronted you so you would understand that what you did was wrong. I'm not even sure you get that. But I had my say and now I'm done with this. All I want is to put you and what happened behind me for good. And I hope you wouldn't take advantage of any other women."

"Please reconsider. Meet me tonight after the governor's speech. Once you sign the NDA then you and I will never have to see each other again."

Was he serious? A nondisclosure agreement? "Wait, the governor's still going through with his speech tonight?"

"You know about Archer? Of course you do," he said with a bitter-sounding laugh. "I saw how close you and that lawman Baggins were at the press conference. Is there something going on between the two of you?" She couldn't have spoken even if she'd wanted to.

Bile rose in her throat. She had to end this once and for all. "Drop dead, Worth." She disconnected.

At the back door opening, she turned to see the marshal, her eyes locking with his as she pocketed her phone. Her breath caught in her throat at the look on his face. She could see how hard that had been on him. It was his empathy for her that brought tears to her eyes. She fought the tears as he stepped to her and drew her close. She breathed in the scent of him, relishing being in his strong arms, and pulled herself together.

"He called you again, didn't he," Leroy said as he stepped back to look at her.

"He offered me money to keep my mouth shut."

The marshal swore and, jerking off his hat, angrily raked a hand through his hair. She recalled her own fingers running through those thick dark strands not all that long ago as the two of them were locked in passion. "What did you tell him?"

"He wants me to sign a nondisclosure agreement and put an end to this."

"You aren't serious."

"I always dreamed of telling him what I thought of him to his face and now I can't get rid of the bastard."

Leroy swore. "You can get a restraining order," he said with a shake of his head. "But I wouldn't trust him."

She let out a laugh tinged with bitterness. "Believe me I don't. But that won't be the end of it. His world is threatened and he is afraid." The marshal didn't look convinced. "He said the governor didn't cancel," she said, changing the subject.

"No." Leroy shook his head.

She'd had to relive the worst experience of her life by confronting Worth. She couldn't imagine what being forced to shake the man's hand had done to the marshal. "Are you all right?"

His laugh held no humor. "You're worried about *me*?" He shook his head and cupped her face in his large, warm hands. "Do you have any idea how I feel about you?"

She felt a lump lodge in her throat. She wanted this Montana lawman more than she'd ever wanted anything. With the marshal, she'd opened herself up, feeling again. He had every cell in her body vibrating. His touch had awakened every emotion in her. Her body was quick to react to the sound of his voice or the mere sight of him.

She wanted this desperately. She wanted to not only feel it all, but also to surrender to him completely. Last night and this morning had only been a taste of what they could have together. She yearned for more and when she looked into his blue eyes, she saw that same yearning burning there.

"TJ." He said it on a breath, the sound sending shivers racing over her. His knuckles grazing her cheek.

She closed her eyes, losing herself in his touch. She hadn't realized that she'd parted her lips until she felt the callused flesh of his thumb as it brushed across her lower lip.

The sound that came out of her was pure and primal. Leroy Baggins had unlocked the closed-off parts of her and now there was no holding back. Her eyes opened to meet his. She saw the desire in his eyes as she cupped the back of his neck and drew him down until his mouth was on hers.

The kiss was all hunger and need. He pressed her to the brick wall next to them, molding his body to hers. She wanted this desperately with no thought to where they were yet again.

Leroy shook his head as he drew back. "Not the time or the place," he said with regret as he touched her cheek, his gaze locking with hers. "TJ Walker, you have to know. I've fallen for you. I've never felt like this before."

All she could do was nod as her eyes went liquid with tears. She'd thought she could never feel anything like this and now that she had… "I know," she whispered. "I'm as surprised as you are. I never thought I would ever feel this way."

The back door was flung open and Vi Mullen was calling his name. He swore under his breath and then called over his shoulder that he'd be with Vi in a minute, before he turned to TJ again. "I don't want you meeting Worth alone."

How could she agree to that? "He already suspects we are an item."

"Doesn't matter. This man hurt you once. I can't bear the thought that he might try again." He took a step back, holding up both hands before she could argue. "I know you're a force to be reckoned with all on your own, but I also know that you take chances with your life."

She looked into his handsome face and felt grounded after four years of feeling untethered. "You know, I might not be doing that as much as I used to." She smiled. "I've met a man who's encouraged me to change my risky ways."

"Really?" he said and returned her smile. "How odd since I've met a woman who's taught me that some risks are worth taking."

"After tonight, I'll be free of Prescott Rutherford Hollingsworth III for good. Right now though, I need to tell my team what's going on," she said.

The marshal looked as if he hated to let her go. "I should have known that Jamie Jacobsen's ego wouldn't let him cancel. His wife is here so I would imagine she intends to take the stage with him. Let's just hope that all three of them will be on that stage tonight. That way we'll know where Worth is—at least until the governor's speech ends. When it does, I'll be waiting for you. I believe you promised me a dance."

Vi called again from the back door, reminding him that she didn't have all day.

"We'll meet up at the fairgrounds," Leroy said. "I contacted the state police and all area personnel including game wardens have been alerted. We're as ready as we can be under the circumstances."

She nodded. "All we can do is hope that Kyle Robert Archer is miles from here."

CHAPTER TWENTY-FIVE

WORTH TRIED TO reassure himself that he would be in the clear soon. Unfortunately, he couldn't trust TJ Walker not to change her mind and blab to anyone who would listen. She was too much of a wild card. Add to that Marshal Leroy Baggins. That hick marshal might talk her into pressing charges. There was something going on between the two of them, he was sure of that. From what he'd seen at the press conference, the lawman was clearly enamored with her.

When they'd returned to the ranch after the press conference, Worth had gone outside and was now pacing the yard, too anxious to sit or stand still. Pamela and Jamie were inside arguing. They'd argued most of the way out of town. He had enough problems without listening to the two of them.

He couldn't help thinking about how wrong he'd been about TJ Walker. While he didn't remember her, he knew she must have seemed like the type he liked. Meek and unassuming, naive and guileless. He must have looked into those big green eyes and seen wide-eyed innocence. So what had changed her into this spitfire who thought she could threaten him?

TJ Walker didn't know who she was dealing with. But did he? He thought of her climbing the Ferris wheel to save that boy. He felt a ripple of fear move through him and regretted that their paths had ever crossed even as he reminded himself that she had no proof that they'd even slept together.

If she didn't sign the NDA and yelled rape instead, he would deny it until his last breath. Not that it would help, he thought as he balled his fist. She had him over a barrel, so to speak, and she knew it. He was so angry that he could—

"Worth?"

He turned and realized Jamie had come outside. How long had the governor been standing there?

"Sorry?" he asked, having missed anything Jamie had said.

"I asked if you've set up everything for this evening." He was frowning as he moved toward him. "Are you all right? You're sweating."

He wiped his forehead, surprised to find that he was. "It's just hot out here." It wasn't. If anything it was cooling down quickly. Soon the sun would dip behind the tall mountains to the west and the temperature would plummet even though it was late summer.

He was sweating and his legs felt shaky. Damn that woman.

"If you're sick maybe you should stay here on the ranch tonight rather than go in for the…"

"No, I'm fine." It would be just like Jamie to leave him miles from town without a vehicle. He had to see TJ Walker. He had to get this settled so he could put it behind him. Too much was at stake tonight to blow this.

Worth couldn't believe that the governor was taking death threats so well. "You're sure about this?"

Jamie shrugged.

"Everything is ready for your speech," he told his boss. "I assume Pamela is joining you onstage?"

Jamie smiled then. "Of course, and you'll be right by my side as well since we're in this together…all the way to the White House, right?"

TJ PREPPED HER team as Leroy and Vi took care of last-minute arrangements for the governor's speech. She knew the marshal was still hoping that the speech would be canceled when the governor came to his senses.

She wasn't counting on that as she finished letting her team know about the latest threat at the celebration. They now had a photo of Kyle Robert Archer. It was an old photograph unfortunately. Even if it had been a good one, finding Archer in the many people attending wasn't going to be easy.

"Our main priority tonight is to make sure the governor is safe," she told them. "If any of you spot Archer, don't try to take him down by yourself. Call for backup."

TJ couldn't bear the thought of any of them getting hurt. This wasn't the job they'd signed up for. But with security, you had to take whatever was thrown at you. She'd enjoyed it. But that was before she'd met Leroy. She felt as if she had a lot more to lose if things went sideways tonight. She could feel the weight of the gun in her holster and knew that it wasn't just the threat against the governor and dealing with Worth that was weighing her down. She was worried about Leroy. Anything could happen tonight.

Back at the fairgrounds, TJ concentrated on looking for Kyle Robert Archer. How were they going to find him in this crowd—if he was even still in the state? The governor's appearance seemed to have brought in everyone from the county and then some. She'd never seen so many ranchers and cowboys among those gathered tonight at the fairgrounds.

As for Worth, she would be handling that herself. She suspected he would be up on the stage later with the governor and his wife. She figured Worth would be looking for her when the governor's speech was over—unless she saw him before that.

She told herself that being the governor's right-hand man could be a disadvantage for Worth tonight. He couldn't very well abandon his boss on a night when a killer might be in the crowd with the governor's name on the bullet.

So signing the NDA should only take a few minutes. It galled her that he wanted her to sign one. She assured herself that if anything, the NDA would prove that Worth had something to hide. If either of them had their way, the agreement would never come to light.

TJ sighed and straightened her back to her full height. She knew the kind of man she would be facing tonight. She hadn't the first time she'd met him. He hadn't looked dangerous. Wasn't that why she hadn't realized what he was? Because he dressed in expensive suits and had an air of confidence and wealth about him, he didn't look like a rapist.

She touched the weapon holstered under her jacket and reached down to make sure the small, flat pocketknife was in her boot. She wasn't taking any chances this time. For all of her training, she knew that she would still be no match for him if he got the jump on her.

He was stronger, heavier, taller and more powerful. That was why she would have to take whatever advantage she had to defend herself—if it came to that.

KARLA PARSON WAS all dolled up and ready to go to the celebration tonight—just as Butch had promised her. But one look at her good-for-nothing boyfriend passed out on the couch and she knew it wasn't happening.

She thought of her mother. "You always pick the losers." It could have been the last thing her mother had said to her, given that the woman had said it so many times.

Admittedly, it appeared to be true of this one. Butch had promised that he would take her. It appeared the only way that was happening was without him since he was in no shape to go anywhere.

She stepped to the couch and moved him just enough to fish his wallet from his hip pocket. There wasn't a lot of cash left, but enough, she told herself as she tossed his wallet on the floor and started for the door. She could always find someone who'd buy her a beer and she was sick of sitting around waiting for her life to begin.

The thought made her laugh. Who was she kidding? At fifty-seven, she often felt as if life had passed her by when she wasn't watching. How else had it ended up so badly?

"Gee, could it have been your rotten taste in men?" her mother would have said. While alive, Nancy Green had never been one to mince words. "Or the fact that you never wanted to work and always thought some man was going to *support* you." At which point, her mother would laugh. "You could have made something of your life, Karla. It's your bad choices that have you where you are. No one else is to blame."

All true, she knew. Not that her mother had been any kind of role model in life or in death. Nancy Green had taken the easy way out. Karla still didn't know why and realized she probably never would know why her mother had killed herself. But all that aside, Karla realized that she actually missed her mother's badgering. How messed up was that?

She hated the route her thoughts had taken as she climbed into her battered sedan. Dressed in her best pair of jeans and a new shirt, she wasn't going to let the past ruin her night. She turned the key. The motor labored but finally started, making her smile. Luck was on her side. She had money in her pocket, and she was headed to town to party. She intended to make the most of it.

If her luck held, Butch wouldn't wake up before she returned. *If* she returned before daylight. Maybe she'd get even luckier and meet someone nice. Anything was possible on a night like this, she thought as she looked up at Montana's big sky and saw the full moon. It was golden against the black velvet explosion of stars. Anything could happen tonight.

Karla thought of slow dancing in the moonlight like Cinderella at the ball. Only she wasn't taking off at midnight and leaving the prince to chase after her. Nope, she had other plans for tonight.

VI FELT PUFFED up like an outdoor cat in winter. She breathed in the excitement in the air. It seemed to buzz in her ears, growing louder as she neared the fairgrounds. The last night of the celebration. The fairgrounds were packed to bursting. She'd done it. She'd pulled off a Buckhorn birthday celebration that people would always remember. She'd made herself proud.

Aside from a few glitches... She ground her teeth at the thought of her niece's appearance and usual bad behavior. But fortunately even having a murderer on the loose hadn't dampened anyone's spirits. Then there was Axel, but she'd handle him tomorrow when he came to pick up his check.

She smiled to herself. Not even the marshal and his gloom and doom concern about some other escaped mental patient ruining things could bring her down. The governor's earlier live interview had only spurred more interest in Buckhorn and its celebration. His speech tonight was being broadcast on several news stations. It would be the grand ending of the event that she'd dreamed of, Vi thought.

But she did wonder what she would do after this. How could she top it? She refused to think about it as she entered the fairgrounds. She did love all the activity, the sights and smells, the shrieks coming from the carnival. It was all too perfect.

That's when she saw Karla Parson. The tramp was sucking on the can of beer in her hand and making eyes at several men who appeared to have stopped to talk to her. Just seeing the woman brought down Vi's good mood as if it had been shot from the sky and had hit the ground hard, practically knocking the air from her lungs.

She would never forget that Karla had purposely broken her mother's vase and let her take the blame for all these years. Even when the truth had come out, Karla hadn't felt the least bit of remorse. It galled Vi as she walked toward the woman.

Karla didn't see her coming. She was too busy flirting.

Vi didn't have to hit her hard, just clip her with a sharp elbow to the ribs and throw her off balance. Karla would have gone down, if one of the men hadn't caught her. But the can of beer flew from her hand, hit the ground and rolled, beer spewing everywhere.

Karla let out a surprised yelp. Until she saw who'd crashed into her. "Oh, you hateful bitch! You did that on purpose!"

"Sorry," Vi said, clearly not meaning it. "I didn't see you standing there."

Not giving Karla a chance to denigrate her further, Vi hurried off, tossing over her shoulder, "Enjoy the celebration!" After that, she felt better. It wasn't as if she'd pushed

Karla off the Ferris wheel, which she'd definitely considered, Vi thought with a laugh and glanced at her phone.

The governor would be here soon. There were already people around the stage, waiting in anticipation. Vi would be introducing him shortly. She smiled. Not even Karla Parson could ruin this night.

THE DRIVE INTO Buckhorn from the ranch seemed interminable. Worth couldn't help feeling anxious. While the car's back seat was wide enough for the three of them, Jamie and Pamela were apparently not speaking to each other. The tension in the car was thick as dense fog. Not that he minded their angry silence. He had enough trouble of his own.

For years, he'd had a plan for his future. He was finally on the brink of seeing it come together. He couldn't let some woman he didn't even remember ruin it for him. He patted the NDA carefully folded into his pocket. She would sign the agreement. One way or the other, he told himself an instant before the right front tire blew.

There was that moment when he thought the driver wouldn't be able to keep the car on the narrow road. That he would die like this seemed inconceivable. He wanted to howl at the unfairness of it.

His heart was pounding as if trying to burst from his chest before the driver got the vehicle stopped. Jamie swore and climbed out to oversee the changing of the tire. Worth stayed in the car, trying to get his heart rate back to normal. He was sweating again, wound tight with worry.

He had to get TJ to sign the NDA, which meant he had to get her to somewhere private if he hoped to keep this under wraps. That would be the hard part, he told himself, but he'd figure something out. He thought best under pressure, he told himself.

Somehow he'd find a way to break away from the governor to get to TJ. And if she didn't sign? She would regret it.

He just wanted this night over, he thought as he reached into his jean jacket pocket for the handkerchief he'd put there earlier. He never perspired this much. Not good optics.

As he pulled out the handkerchief, he glanced up, surprised to find Pamela watching him with obvious annoyance.

"What the hell are you doing?" Pamela demanded, shifting in the seat and brushing against him in her attempt to put distance between them.

He saw the NDA fall out of his pocket. Before he could grab it, she snatched up the agreement and unfolded it to see what it was. Silently, he swore and bit back a retort. The woman thought everything was her business. She would definitely be a high-maintenance First Lady.

Her eyes widened as she recognized the form and looked from Worth to Jamie pacing impatiently outside the car. "Is this for Jamie?" There was an edge to her voice as sharp as a knife's blade. He'd filled in TJ Walker's information so all she had to do was sign. "It's that woman. The hero who saved the boy. I saw the way he was looking at her. But he certainly must have moved quickly."

Worth opened his mouth, but quickly closed it. He didn't want her knowing the truth for obvious reasons. But once she confronted Jamie… "It's mine."

Pamela let out an oath. "Yeah, right. I wasn't born yesterday." She gave him a withering look, shoved the NDA at him and turned in the seat to face outside rather than look at him. He could live with that, he thought.

He carefully refolded the form and put it back into his jacket pocket. Would she tell Jamie? He had no way of knowing. *You see the trouble you've caused, TJ Walker?*

CHAPTER TWENTY-SIX

TJ COULDN'T BELIEVE the crush of people inside the fairgrounds as the time came for Governor Jamie Jacobsen to appear. Were there really that many people who had come to Buckhorn to hear him speak? Or was it just because it was the last day of the celebration and they were hanging on to summer before letting it go?

"Just promise me you'll be careful," Leroy said. "You tell me the minute you see him." He held her gaze. "I mean it, TJ."

She nodded, although she was pretty sure that by the time she saw K. Bob, it would be too late to call for help. She didn't want to take any unnecessary chances, she realized. She had been reckless, but when she looked at Leroy, the last thing she wanted to do was risk her life.

"The governor should be arriving soon," he said.

She didn't need to check her weapon. It was fully loaded. She raised the collar of her jean jacket and patted the pocket holding her cell phone. The night air was getting colder, signaling that summer was drawing to a close here in Buckhorn. "I'm all set."

He nodded, but she could see that he was worried. So far there'd been no sign of the governor or his entourage. She would be watching for Worth, but her main objective was Kyle Robert Archer.

TJ stood at the edge of the crowd gathered around the

stage as Vi Mullen continued to speak about Buckhorn's history and future as she killed time until the governor took the stage. She could tell that the crowd was getting restless. She checked the time. The governor was running late.

Unless he'd changed his mind.

The thought came with both relief and aggravation. She was so ready to be done with Worth. She was tired of letting the past run roughshod over her future. What that future was exactly, she didn't know, but she was looking forward to the possibilities.

Onstage, TJ could tell that those gathered weren't the only ones getting impatient. Vi looked anxious. Surely the governor would let her know if he wasn't going to show up. Then again maybe not.

It surprised her that this event had ever been on the man's radar. But midterm elections were coming up. Maybe there was pressure for him to get out in the rural areas to nail down support. TJ didn't follow politics and knew she would even less after this. If a man like Worth was involved in them, she wanted nothing to do with politics.

She tried to concentrate on her job. Whether or not the governor showed up, there still might be a killer around the fairgrounds waiting for the opportunity to take the man's life. Mentally, she estimated the distance a sharpshooter would have to stand at to get a kill shot as she searched the crowd for Archer. They had no idea what kind of weapon he had in his possession.

Earlier, she'd climbed up on the stage and looked over the fairgrounds toward the town. There were several two-story buildings in town, but she doubted even a sniper could get a clear shot unless the target stood at the very edge of the stage. Archer wasn't a former sniper. He had worked in the tech industry before his breakdown. Nor was there a clear shot from the mountain range behind the stage and the mountain range on the other side of the valley was too far away.

There was only one way to kill the governor once he took the stage—from the audience with a handgun. It would have to be up close and personal. This was Montana. She'd already seen gun-toting cowboys here at the fairgrounds. A live shooter that exposed would have a difficult time getting away.

"Finding the history of Buckhorn captivating?" said a familiar male voice next to her.

She'd been so lost in thought that she hadn't heard Leroy approach. He'd startled her, reminding her not to take her attention off the crowd around her. "You have no idea," she said as she turned to smile at him.

Between the lights from the stage and the full moon, everything was painted in golden light—the marshal as well. He was a handsome devil, no doubt about that. But she'd gotten beyond his good looks and knew what a kind, generous, special man he was. She felt her heart ache. It was all she could do not to cup that strong jaw and kiss those lips. She yearned to be held in his arms right now.

As if feeling her intense gaze on him, he nervously brushed back a lock of his dark hair that had fallen over his forehead. Thick lashes now veiled those blue eyes as if he was thinking the same thing she was.

His cell phone buzzed and he excused himself to step away, but not far. Vi droned on, the crowd growing all the more restless. Where was the governor? Where was Worth?

TJ looked around for both K. Bob and Worth and told herself that both probably wouldn't appear until the governor did.

LEROY COULDN'T HELP the churning in his stomach. A few minutes ago, he'd taken a call from one of the highway patrolmen, who had been called out to an accident. That meant there was one fewer state police officer available. Several of the state highway patrol were already on the grounds as well as numerous other law officers including game wardens from the area. If everything went south tonight, more could be helicoptered in as needed.

He tried to relax a little, but it was impossible. Too much was at stake tonight. He saw TJ moving along the edge of the crowd. He knew she was looking for Archer. With the old photo they'd been given and the fact that they had no idea what he might be wearing or, if he was armed, what weapon he might have managed to acquire, Leroy felt as if they were flying blind in a blizzard. He got another call, this time from one of his deputies who'd been searching for the missing Shirley Langer.

"Found her," said Deputy Kenneth Yarrow. "Alive but scared. She'd been hiding out until she heard that Jennifer was behind bars again." Relieved and surprised, Leroy was glad Shirley had been found alive. "She's wondering where her car is since she's anxious to leave town apparently."

Leroy had inherited the deputy when he'd taken the marshal position. In his fifties, Yarrow felt he'd been passed over for the marshal job and had a chip on his shoulder that Leroy hoped he wasn't going to have to knock off.

"Get a statement from her and then let her take her car," he told the deputy. "Good work." Yarrow said something under his breath he was glad he didn't catch.

He watched TJ disappear into the crowd. Losing sight of her, he cut his call short as he walked in the direction she'd gone. As unrealistic as it was, he didn't want to let her out of his sight. There was so much he wanted to say to her. She needed to know how he felt. That he didn't want her to leave tonight or even tomorrow. He wanted her. Period.

That thought brought him up short as he realized it was more than the growing need that had been building from the first night he'd laid eyes on her. TJ was the first woman he'd wanted for keeps.

That there was any chance that he might lose her tonight… He shook his head, his logical mind arguing that Leroy Baggins couldn't have fallen in love in three days time. But it was true. TJ had changed him. He couldn't let anything happen to her.

That was why he didn't know what he'd do if he saw Prescott Rutherford Hollingsworth first and that scared him. What had happened to By the Book Baggins? He'd fallen in love and tonight, he felt he was a man first, then a marshal.

He moved through the press of people gathered around the stage as Vi droned on. Was the governor even going to show? But if not, would Worth?

As if on cue, Vi announced to a roar of cheers and applause that the governor was about to take the stage for the closing celebration speech. She took her time introducing him. Leroy tuned out her words as he searched the area. He could see uniforms among the crowd. They were as ready as they could be under the circumstances.

He saw two state police escort the governor, his wife and Worth toward the stairs up to the stage and take their positions at the back of the platform. Leroy would have felt better if the governor had brought more security, but then again it was a huge state—over 147,000 square miles—with only just over 250 state troopers.

Other states like California were 20,000 square miles larger, but had more than 79,000 state police. Leroy knew the lack of state police had to do with the fact that Montana had only 6 people per square mile compared to states like California with over 250 people per square mile.

But it made his job damned hard at a time like this, the marshal thought shaking his head. He looked around for TJ, relieved to see her heading back in his direction along the edge of the crowd.

Leroy let out the breath he hadn't realized he'd been holding. He saw that his deputies were in position to the far left and right of the crowd gathered around the stage. He didn't see TJ's team, but he knew they were close by.

He pulled off his Stetson, raked a hand through his hair and tried to calm his apprehension. He told himself that if they could just get through this night without any trouble, he could breathe freely again.

K. BOB HAD spent all of the money Jennifer had given him. He'd looked for her, hoping she'd gotten more, but he hadn't been able to find her. His stomach rumbled loudly. What he wouldn't give for a corn dog. He felt a little sick after all the cotton candy he'd eaten, and his fingers were sticky when he reached into his pocket and touched the gun.

He told himself that he'd get to eat soon. As the sky darkened, he knew it wouldn't be long now. He looked up at the stage where the governor would be standing soon. He'd picked a spot close to the stage but off to the side in the shadows and now he didn't want to move for fear that someone would take his spot. But he wished that he'd taken a piss first. He tried not to think about it as he waited. He'd waited a long time for this opportunity. He licked his fingers, wiped them on his shirt and stuck his hand into his pocket to hold the gun.

He couldn't wait for the governor to take the stage. Wouldn't be long now.

KARLA WORKED HER way toward the sound of Vi Mullen's voice coming over the microphone. She was still angry. That beer the bitch had spilled had cost her almost three dollars! Why did Vi have to be so vengeful?

She sighed as she neared the stage and the people gathered there. Some of them were blocking the entry into the beer garden. She really could use another brew.

As she began to work her way through them, she noticed a large man in the shadows on this side of the stage. He seemed bored by whatever Vi was going on about, shifting from one foot to the other.

Karla pushed her way to the counter and ordered a beer, forking over another three dollars and cursing Vi. As she turned to look back at the stage, Vi was saying she was going to hand over the microphone to the governor.

There was clapping, a roar that filled the night air, as Karla heard the sound of boots climbing the wooden stairs to the stage. A man in a large Stetson appeared first, followed by a woman dressed to kill. But it wasn't until another man in an even larger Stetson took the stage that the crowd began to really cheer and clap. Karla figured he must be the governor.

Bored, she took a sip of her beer and noticed that Vi hadn't left the stage. Instead, she'd moved off to the side at the rear, her back to Karla and that man who'd been waiting impatiently in the shadows. Vi didn't notice that she was blocking anyone's view, not that she would care. She had her hands clasped together, her attention on the governor as he stepped up to the microphone.

Karla pushed her way closer to the stage where Vi was standing. She planned to tell Vi to move the hell out of the way. The crowd shifted as people tried to see the governor better and she was able to cut through to the side of the stage closer to Vi. She could have cared less about being able to see the governor during his speech. She took another drink of her beer. It wasn't her first or her last she hoped. She'd just have to find some nice man to buy her next one.

In the shadow of the stage, she saw that there was a narrow set of stairs tucked back into the stage. Karla made her way toward them, thinking she would sit down on the steps and wait for this to be over and the dance to begin.

She was so close to Vi that she could grab her and trip her up—just as the woman had done her. She imagined Vi falling on her face on the stage and had to take a drink of her beer not to start uncontrollably laughing.

Because of that, she hadn't realized that the governor wasn't speaking. She now saw that there appeared to be a problem with the microphone. "Vi probably broke it," she said under her breath.

She smelled the man before she felt him move closer to her. Like her, he was trying to see around Vi for a view of what was going on. He stepped in front of her, blocking her view as Vi started to move toward the governor and the defunct microphone.

Fuming, Karla pushed to her feet and stepped around the man. Who did he think he was, blocking her view? She was about to unload on him when she saw him pull a handgun from his pocket and aim it at the governor an instant before Vi stepped in the way—blocking his shot.

CHAPTER TWENTY-SEVEN

TJ TURNED AT the shriek of teenaged girls on one of the rides as the first gunshot echoed off the back of the stage. Her gaze went to the Ferris wheel etched black against the colors of the dying sunset. There was one place a killer could get a clear shot of the stage and possibly get away with murder. The same spot where she'd surveyed the fairgrounds that first night.

All Archer needed was a rifle and ammunition.

As she started to turn toward the Ferris wheel, she saw a woman throw herself up onto the stage and take down Vi Mullen. A second shot followed almost immediately. By then, the air was full of screams and shouts and the sound of people in panicked movement. She'd lost sight of everyone onstage including Worth.

"Shots fired! Live shooter!" she heard Leroy shout into his radio. One of the deputies' radios went off next to her as she tried to work her way toward the stage through the bodies shoving past her.

Like the crowd, TJ couldn't tell at first where the shots were coming from. She had started toward the Ferris wheel, but realized the report of the second shot had been much closer.

People were fleeing in confusion. She'd lost sight of Worth, she realized when she heard the third and fourth shots in quick succession. Return fire? She didn't think so.

"The governor is down!" she heard coming from one of the state police radios. "Repeat, the governor is down."

She caught a glimpse of the stage. There was no one still standing. A large Stetson lay next to the edge. She had no idea who'd been hit. For all she knew, Worth was one of the people who'd been shot. She also didn't see the marshal as deputies pushed their way toward the stage through the surging, screaming crowd.

The noise was deafening. Everyone seemed to be falling all over each other to get out of the way, running every which direction, driving her back from the stage. Caught in the crowd, she searched the faces for the shooter. She thought she glimpsed Leroy in the blur of cowboy hats, but she couldn't be sure.

As she was swept up in the stampeding mass of terrified people she spotted a large man in a baseball cap. He appeared to have come out of the shadows along the side of the stage. He had his head down, both hands deep in the pockets of his sweatshirt. Unlike the crowd, he wasn't moving with the haste of those surging around him.

Her pulse jumped. Kyle Robert Archer? She couldn't get a good look at him as her view kept getting blocked. She fought to keep him in sight as she worked her way in his direction against the moving mass of people that swarmed around her.

He turned, seemed to spot her and quickly veered off to duck between two vendor booths and disappear. The fairgrounds had become a roar of screaming people, sirens and the squawk of police radios.

She fought her way through the crowd, needing to get a better look before she called for backup. Pushing past where the man had disappeared, she ducked in between the first two booths. But when she found herself behind the rows of vendors, there was no sign of the man.

Even back here, there were people scrambling to get away. As they pushed and shoved, screaming and shouting in panic, the noise was deafening around her. She searched for the man, not completely sure she was following Kyle Robert Archer. But he'd certainly gotten away quickly for a man who didn't seem in a hurry. Maybe he'd gone into one of the booths to hide.

She glanced back and saw a large man enter the tented back of the jewelry booth next to the small camper trailer of Madam Zorna. Just before the jeweler's tent door flapped closed, he glanced back at her. It was Archer!

Suddenly shoved hard in the back, she stumbled into the man in front of her. He swung an arm back at her as if he thought she was trying to impede his progress. His arm hit the side of her head.

Stars danced before her eyes, darkness pushing in around them. For a moment, she thought she was going to black out from the blow and be crushed by the stampeding crowd.

She blinked, waiting for her vision to clear, as she was pushed along. She couldn't lose Archer.

Still woozy, TJ dug in her pocket for her phone and tried to call Leroy for backup as she was jostled and shoved along. She started to leave a voicemail, but realized he wouldn't be able to hear it in the roar of the terrified crowd around her.

She began to text Following Archer— But that was as far as she'd gotten when her cell phone was knocked out of her hand. It flew through the air and was trampled before she lost sight of it in the crush of people and darkness. She couldn't see it anywhere.

People flew past her, some crashing into her as they ran. She was shoved this way and that. Fighting against the mass of bodies, she tried to keep her eyes on the curtain hanging over the entry into the booth where she'd seen Archer disappear just minutes before.

In the chaos, she'd completely forgotten about Worth—until he grabbed her.

ALL MARSHAL LEROY BAGGINS'S fears came true with the first gunshot. He watched in horror as bodies on the stage began to fall as he and the other law officers frantically tried to see where the shots were coming from.

He would always remember the roar of the panicked screams and yells almost drowning out the gunshots. He watched, feeling helpless as people were being trampled in the frenzy. It all seemed to happen so quickly and yet seemed to go on forever because of the large volume of people who had gathered. The continued gunfire. The screams and cries. The confusion and terror and blood. It was a nightmare.

Leroy snapped out orders. Find the shooter. He called for backup, knowing they couldn't get there fast enough. He called for more ambulances other than the one that had been on hand in the parking lot since the event had begun.

He pushed his way against the fleeing crowd. Reaching the edge of the stage, he was forced to stay down as other gunshots filled the air. His radio was alive with chatter. All he'd heard was that the governor was down. He could see that there were bodies. The governor was down. So was his wife. No Worth.

"Can you see the shooter?" deputies called back and forth on their radios. "Anyone with eyes on the shooter?"

And just as abruptly as the shooting had started, it

stopped. But everywhere he looked he could see bodies. Some had been knocked down in the scramble to flee. Others had been shot.

Leroy waited only a moment after the last shot before he rushed up the stairs to the stage. The first person he saw was Vi Mullen. He could see that she was yelling something at him, but he couldn't hear her. Vi had a bleeding Karla Parson pulled partway into her lap.

His gaze shifted to where the governor, his wife and Worth had been standing before the shooting began. The governor lay on his back staring up at the sky, blood soaking his Western shirt. But as Leroy rushed to him, he saw the governor blink. Next to him, Pamela Jacobsen hadn't been as lucky. She'd taken a bullet to the throat and now lay in a pool of blood, her eyes vacant.

There was no sign of Worth.

Leroy looked around for him, surprised Worth wasn't assisting with the deputies seeing to the governor and his wife. Had Worth panicked and taken off with the rest of the crowd? Leroy wouldn't have been surprised. He already knew what kind of man the governor's advisor was.

"Hold tight, sir. Help is coming," he told the governor.

What worried him was that he'd lost sight of TJ as well. He tried to reach her. Her phone went to voicemail. TJ was out there somewhere. But so was a killer with a gun and possibly more ammunition and a man who was determined that she never told anyone what he'd done to her. Leroy felt a chill work its way up his spine.

There was no text from her. No message.

Earlier at the hotel, when she went to shower, he'd felt guilty putting a tracker on her phone. Now he was grateful he'd done it. He turned on the device and saw that she was still at the fairgrounds. At least her phone was.

"Marshal! We need your help over here!" one of his deputies called.

He hurriedly pocketed his phone and went to help.

WORTH HAD STUMBLED away in shock. He could have been killed on that stage. The first gunshot had barely registered when there'd been another. He couldn't tell where the shots were coming from. What the hell? All he could think was damn Jamie and his huge ego. He should have canceled. He should have listened to him.

All those thoughts had rushed past along with the panic. At the first shot, Jamie had cried out and dropped to the floor. All he'd wanted to do was get off that stage as quickly as possible.

There hadn't been time to run before the second shot. He'd grabbed Pamela, using her as a shield, and felt her take one of the bullets that could have been for him. Dropping to the stage with her body, he'd ditched his silly Stetson, and begun to belly crawl to the edge of the stage, where he rolled off and fell to the ground. He stayed there for a moment as people were screaming and crying and pushing and shoving past him. He realized that his jean jacket was covered with Pamela's blood. He felt for the NDA form. It was still safe in his pocket.

That's when he'd spotted TJ. She didn't see him. She seemed intent on someone she'd spotted in the crowd. He rose, joining the fleeing mass, keeping an eye on her as he tried to blend in. He realized that she was following someone. The shooter? Who in their right mind would do that?

He'd reminded himself that this TJ Walker was nothing like the woman he'd apparently bedded in Denver four years ago. He traveled so much that all the women were nothing more than a blur of blondes, brunettes and redheads. But that was the problem. None of them had come forward. That's why TJ had to be stopped.

TJ had been so intent on watching the man duck into the booth next to the one with a large eye painted on it, that she hadn't even known he was behind her until he grabbed her, lifting her off the ground.

He hadn't had a plan. All he'd wanted was to get her alone and make her sign the NDA. Or at least that's what he'd thought he was going to do with her until she began to kick the crap out of him.

TJ HADN'T KNOWN who had grabbed her, but her first instinct was to fight. As she was lifted off her feet in a bear hug from behind, she drove an elbow into the attacker's side and was rewarded with a gratifying "Uft!"

She'd thought for a moment that Archer had somehow snuck around her to ambush her from behind. Until she heard Worth curse and recognized his voice.

Her blood ran cold for a moment as she recalled the last time he had her at a disadvantage. She kicked with the heels of her boots catching the man in the shins as she reached back with her one free arm to claw at his face. He howled in pain and stumbled. Still he didn't release her as he shifted his hold on her to half drag, half carry her toward the back of the closest booth.

She grabbed his thumb and jerked it back. He dropped her as he screamed in agony. Her feet hit the ground, but before she could get her balance, his fist came down, catching her in the temple. She stumbled, the world around her dimming. Just before the lights blinked out, she saw Archer in the distance, watching from his hiding place.

CHAPTER TWENTY-EIGHT

WORTH CURSED AS he looked at TJ lying at his feet before glancing around to see if anyone was watching. Back here behind the booths, people rushed past, but paid him no mind. He cradled his wounded hand against him as he waited for the pain to ease.

"Bitch," he said and was tempted to kick her while she was down as he tried to catch his breath and lick his wounds, so to speak. He hadn't known what he'd planned to do when he'd followed her back here. Just talk to her, get her to sign the NDA.

But then he'd seen her and, on impulse, had grabbed her. A mistake, clearly, he thought as he looked at her inert body. What if he'd killed her? He couldn't be sure how much she'd told the marshal, but enough that Worth would be the first person the lawman came looking for.

He swore and squatted down to check TJ for a pulse. Relieved, he found one and hurried to pick her up. Glancing over at the closest place to get her out of view, he moved around the small camper trailer with a huge bright blue eye painted on it. A tent had been attached to the trailer. It too had the garish eye painted on the door flap. He shoved on the opening and the sides of the tent spread apart to let him enter.

Once inside, he lay TJ down on the tented floor. It took him a moment for his eyes to adjust to the darkness. Only a faint light came from deeper in the tent, but enough that he could see that TJ was coming around. Still holding his aching thumb, which he suspected was either broken or dislocated, he watched her eyes flutter open.

As she started to sit up, he stepped back out of her reach. "You do realize that this is all your fault," he said.

She scowled at him as she rubbed her temple and grimaced. Those green eyes of hers pinned him as she rose shakily to her feet and backed away from him.

"If you had just left me alone, none of this would have happened."

"My thought exactly," she said narrowing those eyes at him. "Just think, if you hadn't raped me, we wouldn't be having this conversation at all."

He swore, shaking his head. "It wasn't rape."

"You just keep telling yourself that."

"This is the problem," he said with a curse as he stepped toward her. "You can't keep saying that." He stopped short when he saw her go into a fighting stance. He tried to evaluate whether or not she was up to another attack, but realized he'd had enough. "I just need you to sign the NDA," he said with a sigh.

"Strange way of going at it by hitting me like you did."

He wagged his head. This woman was impossible. "I really can't imagine what I ever saw in you."

"Here's a thought," she said. "How about you apologize and promise never to rape anyone else and we'll never have to see each other again."

He considered that. The governor and Worth's ticket to the White House were probably dead. At least Worth figured Jamie was dead. He'd been lying in a pool of blood the last time he'd seen him.

His thumb felt a little better. Maybe she hadn't broken it

after all, but he was still pissed at her. He could hear sirens over the crowd uproar and what sounded like a helicopter. It dawned on him that no one would hear her screams over all the noise outside. The cops were now busy with the injured and dead, along with looking for the shooter in those exiting the celebration.

"Let's say you're right and I tricked you into coming up to my hotel room where I allegedly raped you." He narrowed his eyes at her. Outside he could still hear sirens and people racing around. "What's to keep me from doing it again right now? Because I don't think you have that much fight left in you that I can't take you and there isn't a damned thing you will be able to do about it." He saw her reach for her gun and realize it was no longer there. As her gaze rose, he pulled the weapon from behind him and pointed it at her as he smiled.

SOMETHING WAS DEFINITELY WRONG. Leroy felt a growing panic as he again checked the tracker on TJ's phone. She hadn't moved. He had to find her. Like a lot of people, she could have been knocked down and trampled and be lying somewhere injured.

Or Worth could have her.

That thought chilled him to his soul.

He tried not to worry. But how could he not? He knew TJ. She could be looking for the shooter. Unlike Worth, she wouldn't have taken off. She'd be doing her job because that's who she was.

He texted her team and told them to look for her. He couldn't call off his deputies to search for her. They were all busy helping the wounded while other officers were looking for the shooter and assisting the exit of the crowd.

Some backup had arrived by helicopter, more was on

the way. Leroy felt confident that everything was being handled. He had to find TJ. Worth could already have her, in which case, he had to find her and fast.

She could be anywhere, but the signal assured him that her phone was still here at the fairgrounds. People were still fleeing the area, but the crowd had thinned as he followed the signal.

He hadn't gone far when it grew stronger, TJ's phone had to be close. He searched the ground ahead of him and spotted her phone lying next to one of the booths.

Hurrying over to it, he saw that the screen was shattered. His gut clenched. Maybe she had been injured and had been taken to one of the ambulances now loading the injured nearby. He picked up the phone, his fear growing. As he did, he saw what appeared to be a text she'd started to him. His blood turned to ice.

She'd been following Archer?

Leroy looked one way down the row of booths and then the other. Which way? He had no idea, just a nagging fear that TJ needed him and if he didn't get there quickly…

People were still streaming through the fairgrounds toward the exits. He could see EMTs working on those who had been injured in the stampede.

Move! He looked again down the row of booths. His gaze fell on the fortune teller's booth in the distance. Goose bumps raced over his flesh as he saw movement through the partially opened door. Why would someone still be in there when the rest of the fairgrounds was being evacuated?

Going with his gut, he pocketed TJ's phone and ran toward the booth.

TJ STARED AT her gun now pointed at her, before shifting her gaze to Worth's smiling face. She thought she couldn't hate the man any worse. She'd been wrong. Her pulse was already pounding like a drum in her veins. She felt dizzy from the blow he'd dealt her. Looking at him, she could hear little over her own thundering heart. She was in trouble and Worth knew it.

His smile broadened. "The tables have turned, haven't they? You threaten me. I threaten you. Only now I have the upper hand."

"You aren't going to throw away your career just to get even with me," she said with more confidence than she felt.

He took a step toward her. "With the governor probably dead, my political career is up in the air. Either way, I still can't let you spread lies about me. When they find your body, killed with your own weapon, they'll just assume it was Archer. But first… I'll make it quick."

She looked into his eyes and knew this was going to end badly unless she could get the gun away from him. Unfortunately, the blow to her temple had left her weakened. Worth had her right where he wanted her. Screaming for help was out since no one would hear her with all the noise outside. Not that she had any intention of screaming. She would fight Worth with every ounce of her strength before she'd let him rape her again—let alone kill her.

As she braced herself for his attack, she saw him hesitate— even with her gun in his hand—as if glimpsing the fiery determination burning in her eyes.

Then he seemed to decide to take his chances and took another step toward her. She knew that nothing was going to stop him—just like last time unless she could—

TJ saw Worth stop midstep as if he'd heard something behind him. TJ had heard it too. The scuff of a shoe sole directly behind the tent door.

Worth started to turn, leading with the gun, but too late.

A large bulky shape filled the tent doorway. TJ didn't have a chance to move before Archer grabbed Worth around the neck in a headlock, forcing him to his knees. Leaping forward, she grabbed the gun, wringing it from Worth's hand before he was dragged back through the doorway. The tent entry flapped shut.

TJ stood for a moment in shock before, gun in hand, she eased the tent door fabric aside and looked out. The moon was high, painting the fairgrounds in gold and making the shadows beside the booths even darker.

Worth lay in one of those shadows outside the tent. She couldn't tell if he was unconscious or dead. Past him, she saw the hulking Archer walking away.

Stepping out of the tent, she started after him but had only gone a couple of steps when Worth grabbed her ankle and threw her to the ground. He rolled over on her, one hand going to her throat as the other grappled for the weapon with the other. She managed to get her knee between his legs and went for his groin.

He let out a scream of pain and for a moment she thought she could buck him off her and get the gun free. He was trying to speak, but only harsh rasps were coming from his throat. He licked his lips, his face pinched in pain or was that fury?

Releasing her throat, he doubled up his fist and reared back to hit her as he slammed their hands fighting over the gun to the ground so hard that she feared she'd broken bones. "Bitch," he managed to say before he started to swing his fist at her face.

TJ caught movement behind him, and recognized the figure that came out of the tent. Before Worth could punch her, Madam Zorna raised her crystal ball in both hands and brought it down on the back of his head. The horrible sound seemed to echo around her as shattered glass cascaded down over her.

As he collapsed, TJ shoved him off her and fought to catch her breath.

"I wouldn't have let him rape you," Madam Zorna said standing over her. "Just in case you were wondering."

TJ stumbled to her feet, holstering her weapon as she did. In the moonlight, she could see that Worth's eyes were open and staring blankly up into the starry sky. He wasn't going anywhere. Nor would he be raping any more women.

Still, she knelt to check for a pulse. Nothing. Rising again, she looked down the back row of vendor booths for Archer. No sign of him.

On the highway in the distance, she could see the traffic backed up. Horns honked, engines revved. Everyone wanted to get away from here as quickly as possible because there was a gunman on the loose. TJ couldn't blame them.

She frowned as a figure took shape against the backdrop of car lights and noise. He was slim hipped and broad shouldered and he wore his Stetson shoved back like a man who had work to do.

Leroy.

Her heart leaped to her throat at the sight of him moving through shadow and moonlight toward her. At that moment, she knew to the bottom of her soul that she loved this man and would never be able to leave him.

She lifted her arm to wave to him when a large figure came out of the darkness between two vendors. It happened so fast that TJ couldn't even scream a warning. Leroy hadn't seen Archer until he plowed into him, driving him to the ground.

For just an instant, she couldn't move, couldn't breathe. Then she was running, weapon in hand, racing toward the marshal and a crazed killer.

CHAPTER TWENTY-NINE

FEELING AS IF he'd been hit by a freight train, Leroy didn't have time to react to the attack. Archer drove a shoulder into his chest, driving him to the ground and knocking the air out of him. His head connected with something hard and for a moment, he feared he would black out.

Leroy felt him scramble for the weapon holstered at his hip. He grabbed the man's wrists, but Archer was strong, desperate and had the advantage of surprise on his side. He caught the rank smell of sweat and grease and fear as he and the man rolled around on the ground, fighting for the gun.

Gasping for air, his ears ringing from the attack, his vision unfocused, Leroy tried to fight the big man off while at the same time desperate to keep Archer from taking the weapon. He had no doubt that the man would use it. Archer had already killed at least one person, maybe more.

"Get off him!" Just the sound of TJ's voice made his heart leap. Yet he couldn't be sure he hadn't dreamed it. "Get up now! I don't want to shoot you, K. Bob, but I will."

Out of the corner of his eye, Leroy saw TJ standing in the moonlight, her weapon aimed at the man's head. Unfortunately, the man wasn't listening. He seemed single-mindedly determined to get the gun—and use it—and it was taking all of Leroy's strength to keep that from happening.

"K. Bob!" TJ cried as Archer straightened and for the

first time looked at her. "Don't make me shoot you." There was a pleading in her voice that surprised Leroy.

He felt the man's hands loosen on the weapon as he stared at TJ and the gun in her hand. Then in a burst of strength and purpose, Archer wrenched the gun from Leroy and turned it on TJ.

The marshal grabbed for the man's arm holding the gun even as he heard the loud report. A howl rose in his throat as he thought he'd lost TJ, lost everything as the man started to turn the gun on him again.

The second and third shots sounded even louder than the first. Leroy winced at the weapon's report, at the feel of warm blood splattering on his face, soaking into his shirt, at the sight of Archer as he slowly fell forward.

Leroy shoved the big man over into the dirt as TJ dropped to her knees beside him. He would never forget that swell of relief and thankfulness when he saw the love in her eyes. She clung to him as she bent over him and began to cry. *She was alive.* TJ was alive. He knew it wasn't over and wouldn't be until after the investigation and the news finally died down. But for now, TJ was alive. He hadn't lost her.

She sat up, wiping her eyes, and looked at him as if still not believing he was alive. He knew that feeling too well. "You're bleeding," she said and gently touched the side of his head, her fingers coming away red with blood. His blood, he realized, from whatever he'd struck his head on.

He smiled up at her. "Not as much as I could have been bleeding. Are you…"

"Thanks to you, Archer missed me." She met his gaze in the moonlight. "I didn't want to shoot him. He saved my life." At Leroy's surprised expression, she said, "It's a long story."

Leroy started to sit up, but everything began to spin.

"Stay down—help is on the way," she said. The gunshots, he saw, had brought officers running in their direction.

"Worth?" he asked.

She shook her head. "The governor?"

"He'll survive, but his wife wasn't as lucky."

In the next instant, they were surrounded by uniforms. State police took her weapon and Leroy's. EMTs were called. Leroy had a concussion and was going to need stitches.

"I need to check on my team," TJ said. "Also, I need to see if Madam Zorna is all right. We've all had a rough night."

"Part of that long story?" he asked as he was loaded onto a stretcher for transport. She nodded and reached for his hand, squeezing it. "I can't wait to hear it," he said, his gaze locking with hers.

"Don't worry, you'll hear all about it."

TJ HADN'T WANTED to leave Leroy, but she really did need to check on her team and she was worried about Madam Zorna, who'd killed a man. A bad man and she'd done it to save TJ, but still, once that sank in, the fortune teller might be struggling with what she'd done. Just as TJ was struggling with killing the man who'd saved her life.

She told one of the state police officers about Worth as she watched Leroy being taken away, before she walked back to find Madam Zorna where she'd left her outside the fortune teller's booth standing over Worth as if afraid he might come back to life.

"Are you all right?" she asked the woman.

Madam Zorna met her gaze. "I'm going to need to buy another crystal ball."

TJ smiled. "My treat." She sobered as she looked down at Worth. This was not the way she'd wanted it to end and yet maybe this was always the way it had to.

As law enforcement took over, getting her and Madam Zorna's preliminary statements and information, TJ contacted her team. All three were fine. They'd been busy helping those injured in the chaos and assisting law enforcement. They were glad to hear that Archer had been caught. Maybe someday she'd tell them how the man had saved her from Worth only to later force her to kill him or be killed along with the marshal.

It was almost daylight before she finished with law enforcement at the fairgrounds. She'd planned to go straight to the hospital until she saw how badly her clothing was soiled with dirt and blood. In her hotel room, she showered and changed, unable not to think of her and Leroy in that tub not so long ago.

She called the hospital to check on Leroy and was told she wouldn't be able to see him as doctors were busy stitching him up. She'd been assured he was in stable condition but would be kept overnight for observation.

TJ lay down for a moment out of more emotional exhaustion than physical. She hurt all over.

When she awoke it was afternoon. She was calling the hospital when there was a knock on her door. Opening it, she cried, "Leroy?"

Without a word, he kissed her. "They wanted to keep me in the hospital after they patched me up. But I couldn't spend another minute away from you." He held her at arm's length, those blue eyes of his taking in her face as if he'd never seen it before. "You are so beautiful."

She smiled, shaking her head. He couldn't have been more handsome. "I was just calling the hospital. I was on my way to see you. How's your head?" She took in the bandage peeking out from under his Stetson.

"Turns out I have a pretty hard skull," he said and grinned.

"I could have told you that," she said as he bent to kiss her again.

CHAPTER THIRTY

TJ WOKE IN a panic. Suddenly she couldn't breathe. She had to get to her bike. She had to get out of here. She had to run. She gasped for breath, a weight on her chest so heavy that she thought she would suffocate.

And then she was in Leroy's arms again and he was holding her, telling her to breathe, that she was safe, that he wouldn't let anything happen to her ever again.

Even though she knew that was a promise he couldn't keep, she finally caught her breath. All her bravery had escaped her as she'd gasped for her next breath. She was free of Worth, but not free of the fear that she could acknowledge now that she'd been living with for four years. She knew it was why she'd been reckless with her life.

There had been a point even after it was over that she'd wanted to get on her motorcycle and not look back. She'd wanted to run and not just from what had happened to her four years ago and almost again the last night of Buckhorn's celebration, but from the fear of risking not just her heart but her life to this lawman. By the Book Baggins wasn't a man who would take anything less than all of her. Was she ready to surrender her heart to him?

She could see that she wasn't the only one who'd been afraid of falling in love. Leroy had been hiding behind his star as the youngest marshal in the state. TJ had never wanted to feel vulnerable again.

With Leroy she'd opened herself up to a different kind of hurt—falling in love. She hadn't seen it coming. In the nightmare, she'd been desperate to get on her bike and keep running from her own vulnerability.

But now she was wide awake in Leroy's arms. Drawing back to look into the marshal's blue eyes as the nightmare waned and the panic attack faded, she managed to smile at him. She was through running from her fears.

Vi Mullen sat in the uncomfortable hospital chair having an even more uncomfortable one-sided internal conversation with herself. Her nemesis, the woman she'd assaulted not all that long ago over a broken vase, hadn't just saved her life. Karla Parson had taken a bullet for her.

It was hard to comprehend. Even harder to accept. Vi had held such contempt, such disdain, such hatred toward Karla for so long it was inconceivable that she now had to be indebted to her. Hadn't she thought about getting Karla on the Ferris wheel during the celebration and pushing her off?

What if the woman never regained consciousness? That would take care of having to thank her, she thought and cringed that she'd even let herself think such a thing. The question was what to do when Karla did wake up. *How did you repay someone who had saved your life?*

She had no idea. The waiting was hard since she felt so conflicted. Vi knew she should be filled with gratitude. Karla had saved her life! But she still didn't like the woman and couldn't imagine them ever becoming good friends. What if Karla demanded some kind of payment?

Vi sighed, wishing that she didn't often think the worst of people. So filled with pride in her achievements and knowing what was best for not just Buckhorn but everyone in it, she'd realized sitting here that she didn't have even one friend she could call to wait here with her.

Tina had come by and Earl Ray and even the marshal. They'd tried to get her to go home, to get something to eat, to rest—just as the nurses had encouraged her to do. But if Vi was anything, she was stubborn to the core. She wasn't moving from this chair until Karla opened her eyes. It was her atonement. She refused to entertain even the thought that the woman would never regain consciousness and she would have to sit here until—

"Vi?"

She blinked and realized that she must have dozed off. Stumbling to her feet, she moved to the bed. "How are you?"

"Shocked," Karla said. "What are *you* doing here?"

"I'm ringing for the doctor." Vi pushed the button next to the bed.

"Why aren't you putting a pillow over my face? You must be going soft."

Vi looked down at the woman. "You saved my life. If you hadn't knocked me out of the way—"

"You were blocking my view." But she smiled when she said it.

"Why would you do that? Risk your life for me?" Vi asked, really wanting to know the answer.

"Beats the hell out of me," Karla said. "I haven't understood the things I've done since I was a kid." She tried to shrug, but grimaced in pain. "Some things are just a mystery."

A nurse came into the room, followed by a doctor.

"I'm going to leave, but I'll be back," Vi told Karla, who said, "Whatever."

Vi left, thinking she'd pick up some magazines, maybe

some candy, for Karla. By the end of the week, she figured she'd be sneaking Karla in beer and cigarettes. She shook her head wondering if Karla would even notice if she didn't come back. Probably not.

As Vi left the hospital, her steps seemed to lighten as if a weight had been lifted from her. By the time she reached her car, she'd convinced herself that there was nothing essentially wrong with her attitude, no matter what anyone said. Life had made her the way she was. Everyone could just as well accept it because she couldn't imagine changing at her age.

Jutting out her chin, she straightened her back and began to feel like her old self again. She was alive and she had businesses to run. Winter was coming so there was work to be done to get ready for it, she thought as she slid behind the wheel.

Karla would be fine. No reason for Vi to return to the hospital. One of the woman's no-account boyfriends would come around to pick her up when she was released from the hospital. Vi need not worry about her. Karla'd been taking care of herself all these years. Nothing had changed.

She took a deep breath and let it out. The celebration hadn't gone exactly like she'd hoped and now she felt that the town was slightly tarnished. While waiting for Karla to wake up, Vi had been thinking about starting an online site called something like What I Love About Buckhorn. People could comment. Maybe they could even post announcements for events in town. It would show the world that Buckhorn was a nice community. A destination town even.

Glancing in her rearview mirror, she smiled at herself. She was Vi Mullen and there wasn't anyone else around who could accomplish what she could. Tomorrow was a new day and Buckhorn needed her.

She left the hospital thinking to use the hour's drive back to Buckhorn to plan her online site. There was more traffic than usual with the celebration over and some people just now leaving.

But a half hour out, she glanced in her rearview mirror to see the flashing lights of a patrol SUV. Her gaze went to the speedometer before she braked and pulled over to the side of the highway. She hadn't been speeding.

She started to reach for her license and registration, wondering if she had a taillight out or something else was wrong. At the tap on her driver's-side window, she jumped before she recognized the officer and groaned inwardly.

Deputy Kenneth Yarrow smiled broadly at her as she whirred down her window. She'd gone to school with him since they were close in age. Since her divorce, Ken had been especially friendly.

"Vi," he said now. "Nice day for a drive."

"I'm coming from the hospital."

"I just heard that Karla Parson regained consciousness. You've been over there all that time?"

She nodded. "So I'm anxious to get home. I know I wasn't speeding so—"

"Nope, you weren't. I just wanted to warn you about the road ahead. Wind's been blowing tumbleweeds across it, filling up the barrow pits. Might want to slow down through that stretch."

"Thank you, I'll do that."

"Maybe I'll see you around," he said as she said, "Have a nice day," and whirred up the window. She quickly started the car and pulled back on the highway, leaving Ken looking after her.

It had been so long since any man had paid her any kind of attention at all, that at first she hadn't realized what Ken might be after. Now that she did, she wondered why it had to be Kenneth Yarrow and how she was going to let him down if he ever asked her out. Or maybe, if he got around to asking, she would go out with him.

Didn't she deserve a new beginning?

JAMIE JACOBSEN SLAMMED his laptop, wanting to heave it out the window, but his shoulder hurt too much. The news media had played down his injury calling it a graze. "Graze, my ass," he said with a curse. He was in pain. He had scars from where the bullet had entered and exited.

But his wound was nothing compared to Pamela's, he reminded himself. She always had to outdo him, even in death, he thought grudgingly, and winced at his lack of compassion. His beautiful wife was gone.

So was his career. He was doomed to be a one-term governor. Even the dead wife sympathy card wouldn't win due to the Worth debacle.

"How had Jacobsen not known that his best friend and advisor had been raping women in states where he campaigned?" one reporter had demanded. "This definitely brings into question if this man should be governing any state in the union let alone our country since it's no secret he's had his eye on the presidency."

Had he known about Worth? Or had he been so self-absorbed that he hadn't questioned it when his friend returned from a date sometimes with scratch marks on him?

He'd known that Worth liked it rough, but since no women had ever come forward... Until TJ Walker.

It had all come out when a nondisclosure agreement with TJ Walker's name on it was found in his pocket. Once

Walker had been questioned in Worth's death, it had all come out and other women had come forward.

The media had run wild with the story, calling Worth a serial rapist who'd used his job with a variety of politicians—including Governor Jacobsen—to hide the fact for years. The scandal had hit every tabloid in the country, gone viral on the internet and was doomed to destroy the careers of all those who'd unwittingly assisted Worth in his crimes—himself included.

Jamie kept thinking how glad he was that Worth hadn't been taken alive. The tales his old friend could tell about him. At least he'd dodged that bullet. But he was definitely caught in the overflow. This wasn't going to blow over soon.

He'd never get in the White House as the youngest president. But maybe the presidency wasn't off the table. It would take some powerful memory loss in the political world though. He would need some very influential men behind him. He would also need a wife with both assets and some power of her own.

With the right spin, Jacobsen thought he might make a comeback. At least he hoped so since he had few skills to make it in the real world and his family money was gone. Politics was all he knew.

The bad part was that he missed Worth. He missed his friend more than he missed his wife, if he was being honest. He wondered if he could ever find someone to watch his back the way Worth had. He would need that, he thought even as he told himself there were things about himself he was going to have to change.

If Worth had taught him anything, it was that bad behavior could catch up with you. But even as he thought about dispensing with his bad behavior, he wondered idly if people ever really did change or were they just kidding themselves that they could? He had his doubts when he thought of TJ Walker.

He did wonder if he and Ms. Walker would ever cross paths again. He'd still like to have a drink with her. He reminded himself that probably wasn't going to happen. He wouldn't be staying in Montana after his term was up. He would be hanging up his Stetson and boots, he thought with a chuckle.

He was made for better things than being governor of this backwoods state, he told himself. But he would have to start looking for another Worth. There was that one guy at boarding school. Hadn't he become a lobbyist for a big pharmaceutical company? What was his name?

LEROY FINISHED THE paperwork on the deaths of Pamela Jacobsen, Prescott Rutherford Hollingsworth III and Kyle Robert Archer. The list of those injured was longer, and included Karla Parson, who had saved Vi Mullen's life.

There would be investigations into the deaths. Leroy had known it would all have to come out. Once that nondisclosure agreement for TJ was found in his pocket and TJ gave her statement, other women had started to come forward.

It didn't take long before the governor was under attack for his alleged part in aiding and abetting a serial rapist.

Leroy figured Jacobsen had at least suspected the kind of man he'd hired—if he hadn't already known during their long association. Because of the fallout, Jacobsen would be a one-term governor. Maybe people would forget before he tried to run for the presidency, but Leroy figured enough women would still be around to remind the voting public.

The marshal's concern was for TJ. He knew how much she hadn't wanted to be dragged through this. He had wanted to shield her from what he could, but he hadn't been surprised when she'd faced it all head-on. The woman was a hero, after all.

While the mess made good fodder for the tabloids, Leroy was still struggling with how close TJ had come to dying at Worth's hands. If it hadn't been for Archer and Madam Zorna… He just hated that he hadn't been there for her. Worse, he'd almost gotten her killed when she'd come to his rescue.

Fortunately, they'd ended up saving each other. He supposed that was something. TJ had told him repeatedly that it was her fault. She should have waited for backup. Under the circumstances, she'd done what any of them would have given the same set of facts. She'd gone after a bad guy only to run into a worse one.

Archer had helped save her life only to lose his own. Clearly that's the way he had wanted it.

Pushing back his chair from his desk, Leroy rubbed his eyes as he thought about how ridiculous his fears had been when Vi Mullen had told him about the birthday celebration she was planning for Buckhorn. He shook his head, thinking how that Leroy Baggins couldn't even imagine how bad it was going to get, not in his wildest dreams.

Or that it would bring him a love like he'd never known.

Rising, he reached for his Stetson. Karla was being released today. There was going to be a small ceremony outside the hospital for her. Leroy would be handing her a commendation and a fifty-dollar gift certificate from the general store.

When he'd told Karla about it, she hadn't looked impressed. "What for? I didn't do anything."

"You saved Vi's life," he'd told her. Numerous witnesses had confirmed that if Karla hadn't knocked Vi down, she would have taken the bullet meant for the governor. Instead Karla had saved both of their lives.

"Seriously, do I have to do this?" Karla had complained. "I mean, I don't mind the money, but I don't need some dumb plaque."

"It's actually just a sheet of paper," Leroy had told her, making her laugh and hold her side where she'd been shot.

"Whatever," she'd finally said, and he'd taken it for agreement.

Afterward, he would visit TJ.

EARL RAY COULDN'T help worrying about his daughter. Tina had been through so much. Finding out that he was her father was nothing compared to her harrowing visit by her cousin Jennifer.

He'd spoken to her after the fact and knew that she'd been scared for Chloe—and herself. He could imagine how hard it had been to see her cousin taken away like that.

He knocked at her front door, afraid he might be intruding. Their relationship was just beginning and he wasn't sure of the unwritten rules yet. He might be the last person she'd want to see.

But when she opened the door, she gave him a smile that went straight to his heart. "How are you doing?" he asked as she ushered him inside.

She met his gaze and tears filled her eyes. He held out his arms and she stepped into them as if they'd always been father and daughter.

"I just feel so bad about Jennifer," Tina said as she moved back to wipe her tears. He handed her the clean handkerchief he tucked in his pocket each morning, something his mother had taught him.

She blew her nose, balling it in her fist as she invited

him to sit down. "I just feel like I let her down. She came to me…" Her voice broke. "All she wanted was to see us, to see Chloe and me…" She blew her nose again. He could see that she was fighting tears. "I was afraid of her and I feel so ashamed."

"You shouldn't, but I don't have to tell you that," Earl Ray said. "None of us knew what she was going to do next."

Tina nodded. "My cousin always felt betrayed and cheated. First by her father, then by every other man she crossed paths with. Her mother, Vera, was Vi's twin and they couldn't have been more different. Vi was… Well, you know what Vi is like. Vera was hell on wheels, especially when it came to men. Needless to say Vera wasn't there when Jennifer needed her the most."

"But you and Vi were," he pointed out.

She nodded and smiled in memory as she said, "Jen used to tag after me like she was my little sister, drove me crazy, but I loved her like we were real sisters. Not that it helped. She didn't understand why she didn't look like me. She felt cheated because she didn't get the red hair." Tina shook her head. "Now we know why there is no resemblance. Although she did dye her hair to try to look like me, didn't she." She half laughed and half cried. "It was an awful red."

"You were there for her growing up. I know you used to lend her clothes for dates," he said.

Tina nodded. "But the dates never went like she'd hoped. She was so needy. It was as if men smelled desperation on her. They were often cruel in their rejection of her. Like the rest of us, she just wanted to be loved."

"Most of us don't commit murder when we're rejected though."

"She needed help and we didn't get it for her," Tina said, close to tears again. "Mother always told her to quit picking the wrong men and said she was as bad as Vera. None of that helped. I wanted her to find someone to love, but I'm not sure she would have ever trusted it. You know?"

He did. He thought of his wife who'd given up this beautiful young woman as a baby. He'd trusted Tory and her love for him. Fortunately, he'd been given a second chance at love. Bessie hadn't given up on him. "What happened to Vera?"

Tina shook her head. "Mother always said she was dead. It must have been a long time ago because I never heard about it."

He changed the subject seeing that he'd only upset his daughter more. "I've watched you grow up for years, never knowing we were related," Earl Ray said. He smiled, hoping he got to know her better in the years ahead. His daughter. He was so blessed and so undeserving of all the love he had in his life. But he would continue to work at earning that love as he took care of his family and this small town that had taken him in.

"Would you like to have lunch with me down at the café?" he suggested. "Bessie is making pies today. I believe your favorite is lemon."

Tina smiled. "You do know me, don't you? I would love to have lunch."

"Why don't you call Lars and see if he and Chloe can join us?"

TJ LOOKED AROUND the cottage where she'd been staying in Buckhorn. It had been Earl Ray's idea. He and his wife, Tory, had lived in this house. He'd sold it when he married Bessie, but bought it back when the elderly woman who purchased it had died.

"It's just sitting empty," Earl Ray had told her. "Please stay there as long as you'd like. Give yourself some time."

To her surprise, she'd taken him up on his offer. The rest of her team had gone on to their next job, thanks to the young woman TJ had hired to handle requests from their website and schedule the other security people TJ had picked up from across the country. She'd built Walker Security Inc. from the ground up and now it was able to almost run itself because of the remarkable help she'd hired.

Staying here in Buckhorn had made her realize that she didn't have to always be leading the teams. Zinnia was definitely ready to lead one. So was Ash. She no longer had to carry the load.

But she'd known that wasn't why she'd taken the security jobs in the past. She'd felt she had to keep moving. A week here, a few days there, and then on to another city, another job. She'd been running from what had happened to her. Maybe Leroy was right and she had been tempting death, risking her life because she hadn't really dealt with Worth and what he'd done to her.

It felt strange to stay put with no job scheduled for herself in the near future. But she'd known that Earl Ray was right. She needed some time. Worth was dead, but not forgotten. She often thought about Archer and Madam Zorna and how they'd come to her rescue. She kept thinking of the look on Archer's face when he'd started to turn the gun on the marshal. He'd wanted her to shoot him, the last thing she'd wanted to do.

Leroy was tying up loose ends. He had a lot of them. Pamela's family was threatening to sue the county and Buckhorn and the marshal. Not that she thought Leroy gave much thought to that. He'd been busy making sure everyone else who'd gotten hurt had proper medical attention. Law enforcement officials were covering the county while he was neck-deep in paperwork and investigations into his performance and that of his men.

So she was surprised when he pulled up in front of the house. They'd had little time together, let alone been ready to talk about the future.

TJ opened the front door and walked down the sidewalk to meet him. It was a beautiful Montana fall day. The air smelled of the dried aspen leaves that fluttered in the breeze and the dark pines along the creek. She looked to the mountains, a deep green against the clear blue of the sky. The same blue as Leroy's eyes. Only the tops of the peaks were dusted white from last night's storm with the promise of the approaching winter.

TJ wondered what winter would be like here in Buckhorn. This place—and Marshal Leroy Baggins—made her feel calmer than she had in a very long time.

"I brought you a little something," Leroy said and handed her a bag of donuts.

She laughed as she took them, surprised as she wondered where he'd gotten them. She figured everything would be gone from the fairgrounds by now, though she hadn't gone to look. The thought made her a little sad—even with all the bad things that had happened there. Sometimes she liked to close her eyes and remember being in Leroy's arms on the dance floor.

"I don't know how or where you got donuts, but thank you. You really need to stop bringing me presents."

"Do you have any plans tonight?" he asked.

TJ smiled. She had no plans for the foreseeable future. He'd been going back and forth from his apartment in the next town and his marshal's office to this cottage in Buckhorn with her, spending what nights he could in her bed.

"I thought it was time that we went on a real date." He grinned. "I'll call you with the details." He was walking backward toward his vehicle, smiling, his blue eyes dancing. "Wear something warm."

With that, he climbed into his truck and drove off.

TJ opened the paper bag he'd handed her and took out a warm donut. Bessie at the café, she thought with a smile as she walked toward the house. Leroy probably had her make them, TJ would just bet.

She wondered what he had planned for tonight, hugging herself as she went inside. Who would have guessed that By the Book Baggins was just full of surprises.

JENNIFER SAT AT her regular table. Her scrapbook was open in front of her along with some glue and those dull, pointless scissors lying nearby unused. Several newspapers were piled on the table next to them.

"She's been like that since she returned," the orderly said. "She eats and sleeps and comes in here each day, but it's like she's not here."

The nurse nodded and pursed her thin lips. "Or she's faking it, planning her next escape. If she doesn't respond soon, take her back to her cell. Whatever you do, don't underestimate that one."

The orderly studied the patient for a few more minutes. When Jennifer Mullen still hadn't moved, he put away her scrapbook, the glue and the scissors. She didn't seem to notice. Then he gathered up the newspapers he purposely selected for her because of the articles about her and Buckhorn. He had thought she might like to put them in her scrapbook. Maybe he'd keep them for her when she was feeling better.

He touched her arm, helped her rise from the chair. The

two of them walked out of the lounge and down the hallway. He chatted about the weather and how his lunch wasn't agreeing with him. Jennifer made no response. She walked, shuffling her feet, like a zombie. He'd wondered if she was drugged, but when he'd checked her chart, he hadn't found that to be the case.

They reached her cell. He opened the door, and with only a little persuading, she entered of her own accord, moving to the bed and lying on it. As she closed her eyes, he shut the door, making sure it was locked.

On the way back to the lounge to check the other patients, he couldn't help feeling bad for Jennifer. She'd escaped this place and become a folk legend and from what he could tell, she didn't even know it. Everyone had thought she'd end up killing someone, but she hadn't.

He hated seeing her like this and wondered if anything could bring her back. He would keep collecting any newspapers with articles about her and Buckhorn for her though—just in case.

Vi DIDN'T RETURN to the hospital before Karla was released. Nor was she there when the marshal gave Karla the gift certificate and some commendation for her heroism.

Since she and Karla didn't travel in the same circles, even in a town as small as Buckhorn, Vi knew she would make it a point to avoid her even when she came into the store. She told herself that she was too busy to even think about the past. She'd started the online site she'd come up with, calling it All About Buckhorn. The idea was for residents to post events and ask any questions they had about the town, its history or what was going on.

When no one posted anything at first, she'd put up little tidbits of history about the town and her founding family.

Since then she'd heard that people called the site Just Ask Vi. She'd seen the snide comments. She'd printed them out and posted them on the bulletin board at the back of the store next to the post office boxes hoping to embarrass the people who'd posted them. It was the same place she posted bad checks—those with insufficient funds—and left notes as to who could no longer charge until they paid their bills.

Deputy Yarrow had stopped by a few times. He'd finally asked her out. She'd put him off for now, saying she was too busy, but maybe in the near future. To her surprise, he hadn't taken it well, acting as if he'd only been doing her a favor. The nerve of the man.

The days were getting colder, signaling that winter wasn't far off. Vi had seen some of the businesses in town already boarding up their shops and packing for warmer climes. Snowbirds! She told herself that they wouldn't be missed. She'd grown to love winters in Buckhorn. The tourists were gone. Once the snow began to fall, the town would become a wonderland.

Those who stayed seemed to appreciate that she kept the store open to save them having to drive to a grocery in the next town. Ice fishing season would begin once the ponds froze over, bringing a few fishermen to Buckhorn.

More and more snowmobilers were finding their way to this little town. Vi had heard that the new hotel was going to stay open all winter. That would certainly change things. Tina would be having her baby soon so Vi was excited about the future.

She wondered if she was getting old. Deputy Yarrow had certainly made her feel that way after she'd rejected his advances. What would it have hurt to go out with him? Maybe she was too old because she was pretty content with her life as it was. Her days were full. She checked her online site and gritted her teeth as she began to respond to the nasty comments.

What people didn't realize was that she'd lived in this town long enough that she knew most everyone's secrets. She wasn't one to pass up a good rumor either. If people wanted to play dirty on her online site, she'd let them know what they had in store for them if she were to even hint at the things she knew.

CHAPTER THIRTY-ONE

LEROY LOOKED UP to see the first star of the night shining high above him. The mountains tonight were deep purple, the air chilly but not too cold, he hoped. He couldn't help feeling nervous. He'd been so busy, he hadn't seen TJ as much as he'd wanted. But at the same time, he knew she needed time to deal with everything that had happened. Maybe asking her out tonight was too soon to talk about the future. He didn't know. He was in new territory without a clue.

As he spotted the star, he realized that he'd never wished on a star—not even as a child. His mother said such things were foolish. His grandmother had called it much worse. But right now, he had a wish that he wanted to come true so badly—

"That's my star" came TJ's voice out of the darkness. "I just made a wish on it."

With a tidal wave of relief, he turned to see her standing there and tried to hide his embarrassment. He should have known when he suggested meeting her here that she would come early. She'd probably been watching him—just as she had the first night they'd met.

"Go ahead," she said as she joined him. He could tell by the flush of her cheeks that she'd walked from the cottage. "I don't know of any rule that says two people can't wish on the same star on the same night. If you want your wish to come true, don't let me stop you."

Leroy chuckled. "You know I don't really believe—"

"That if you wish on a star, it will come true?" She raised an eyebrow toward the heavens. "Clearly you won't know unless you make your wish."

He'd been half-afraid that she wouldn't want to meet here tonight after everything that had happened. The fairgrounds had been transformed back into little more than pasture. Gone were the stage, the dance floor, the many makeshift booths. Only one thing remained.

Leroy studied TJ for a moment before he looked up at the bright single star glittering above him. He closed his eyes and made his wish. Then he opened his eyes and looked over at her. She never failed to send his heart over the moon at just the sight of her. "Done."

"I guess now we wait. Or maybe not," she said as he closed the distance between them and, taking her shoulders in his hands, kissed her softly on the mouth. "That takes care of my wish," she whispered as he drew back. Her eyes locked with his. "If yours is what I hope it is…"

"It won't come true if I tell."

She laughed. "I thought you didn't believe in wishes on stars," she reminded him.

"I do now." He took her hand and turned them both to look at the only thing left on the hurriedly constructed fairgrounds. Vi was now working to get locals to vote for a real fairgrounds, promising more celebrations that would bring people to town. She wasn't getting very much support on the idea.

Right now all that remained on the property was the dark skeleton of the Ferris wheel. It looked as if it had been dropped into the field accidently. Leroy wasn't about to tell TJ what it had taken to keep the ride here for a while.

"Shall we?" he asked as he motioned toward the large wheel.

TJ laughed as they walked toward the silent ride. "You did this?"

"To prove to everyone who said Leroy Baggins was too uptight to even ride a Ferris wheel…" He lifted the bar on the chair waiting at the bottom and helped her in. Starting the motor, he put it in gear and quickly hopped on, bringing the bar down as they began to rise into the air.

"I'm guessing you have a plan on how to get us off this," she said and laughed when he shrugged. "Are you sure about this?" she asked as they rose into the night. He watched her lean back to look up at the midnight blue sky filled with stars.

"I'm sure about you," he said as he put his arm around her and they both looked skyward. He thought about the two of them soon to be silhouetted against that wondrous sky.

She leaned into him and he pulled her close. Thrown together they'd shared so much in such a short period of time. The old Leroy Baggins would have been backstepping, afraid of his feelings and telling himself that he needed more time to evaluate everything that had happened before moving forward.

He hardly recognized this Leroy Baggins, a man acting as if he had no fear, his eyes wide-open as he looked to the horizon, ready for whatever the future held as long as TJ was by his side for the ride.

As they rose high into the air, he got his first bird's-eye view of Buckhorn. It looked so small-town homey and peaceful, lights glittering in the darkness. The mountains shouldered in as if trying to protect this place in the middle of nowhere from what might be coming up the highway through the middle of town.

Buckhorn had felt like home with TJ here. He felt a sense of ownership as if he now had a stake in the town's future. "I'm thinking I might let my apartment go and buy a place here in Buckhorn. Think you'd ever want to spend some time here?"

TJ PULLED BACK a little so she could see his face in the starlight. She felt her heart swell and thought about the first time she'd laid eyes on the marshal with his Stetson and boots and his you-are-now-dealing-with-the-law attitude. She smiled. She hadn't known him any better than he had her that first night they met.

"I can see myself here," she said nodding as she looked out at the tiny western town. That alone surprised her. She was a big-city girl—or at least she'd thought she had been. "I'd have to travel sometimes though to continue with my business." He nodded as they made another loop around the wheel and the moon climbed higher.

"Some men would have trouble with that," she said.

He chuckled. "I'm not one of those men." Leroy's gaze locked with hers. "But I think you know that."

As their car began to drop downward, she leaned over to kiss him. "Have you ever made love on a Ferris wheel?" she asked and laughed at his expression. "Can you imagine what some people would have to say about that?"

"I could, but I'm not sure I care." He cupped the back of her head and drew her mouth to his as they began to rise upward once again.

She lost herself in the kiss as he deepened it and the waning moon rose over Buckhorn. The night felt magical as if they were the only two people in the world. Everything that had happened was as gone as the structures that had disappeared from the fairgrounds except for a Ferris wheel that could transport lovers anywhere.

The Ferris wheel motor stopped abruptly. Their car rocked wildly. They held on to each other more tightly, like two people who'd found each other and were never going to ever let go again.

"You get down from there right now!" came the shrieking female voice. "Honestly, Marshal, you have a reputation to uphold in this county," Vi went on. "I heard that this was your fool idea to keep this thing. Now I know why. I hate to think what the two of you might have done if I hadn't come along."

"Actually, Vi, I was hoping you'd stop by." They both laughed as Vi began struggling to get the motor going again so she could make them disembark. "See," he said quietly to TJ. "I did have a plan."

Leroy grew serious as he reached into his pocket and pulled out a small box. He held it out to her. She felt her heart do a loop-de-loop in her chest as she opened it. The ring was beautiful. She looked up at him, wanting to tell him that it was too soon, but even as she formed the words in her head, she knew that there was no perfect amount of time a couple had to spend together to know if it was true love.

"I know this seems quick," Leroy started to say, but she touched a finger to his lips as tears filled her eyes.

"It's beautiful."

He seemed to be at a loss for words for a moment. Clearing his voice, he said, "It was my grandmother's. She wanted me to give it to the woman I loved." His gaze met hers. "I love you, TJ."

She didn't hesitate an instant. "I love you."

"So is that a yes?" he asked.

She laughed. "Yes."

Leroy let out a breath as if he'd been holding it in, worried that she'd say no.

"It's perfect," she said as he slipped it on her finger.

She kissed him as she heard Vi below them still struggling with the motor. The kiss held both passion and promise.

"So did your wish come true?" TJ asked.

"It did actually. I wished that Vi would get the message I left her and show up to turn off the Ferris wheel." He laughed and TJ laughed with him as she saw their future stretched out before them.

There would be other carnivals, other moonlit nights, other adventures and many more nights to make love. There would be children, both boys and girls who looked like them. They would build a good life here, she thought as she looked over at this man she'd fallen so quickly in love with.

"You'd really live here with me in Buckhorn?" he asked as if he still couldn't believe it.

TJ smiled as she looked out over the small town in the middle of nowhere as Vi finally got the motor going and they began to head back to solid ground. "Definitely." She took a deep breath of the night air. She was through running, especially from love and Marshal Leroy Baggins.

As he put his arm around her and she snuggled against him, she realized that she'd come home.

* * * * *

BEFORE MEMORIES FADE

CHAPTER ONE

"WHAT DO WE even know about her?" Vi Mullen demanded of the women gathered at the Buckhorn Café that bright late summer morning.

"Gertrude?" asked Clarice Barber in an appeasing tone, the one she used when she didn't want to hurt anyone's feelings. Gertrude Durham had recently taken over the only garage and gas station in town. "She could be nicer to people. She's a little cranky." That voice was like fingernails on a blackboard for Vi.

Mabel Aldrich quickly agreed in a whisper even though the only people in the café this early in the morning were the women sitting in this large booth. Local women had been meeting there for decades to play cards, gossip over coffee and pie or knit or crochet while they visited.

Vi usually didn't join them, saying she was too busy, which she knew had been fine with everyone. She found their senseless chatter annoying and a waste of time. "The point is, we know *nothing* about her and she's living here in the same town with us."

"I've never seen her in anything but those awful baggy green overalls and a worn-out flannel shirt," Lynette Crest said, as if completely missing the point. "And she should do something with her hair. It's so wiry and wild. That trucker's cap she's never without doesn't help matters. But she is a mechanic who works on cars, so what would you have her wear?"

Exasperated, Vi sighed. "I'm not talking about how she looks or dresses. Who *is* this woman? What do you know about her?"

"What is there to know?" Mabel said, dismissing Vi's concerns, but at least getting back to the point. "Gertrude inherited the gas station from her nephew, Fred, rest his soul. What more do we really need to know?"

It was that kind of blind ignorance that drove Vi wild. "We only have her word that she's even Fred's aunt."

"She was at his funeral and his son Tyrell's," Clarice said as if that proved anything.

Vi wondered why she'd bothered as Bessie Caulfield came out of the kitchen with a fresh pot of coffee and announced the blueberry muffins would need only a few more minutes in the oven.

After Bessie left, Vi resumed her questioning before the women could start talking about baked goods. "Have any of you heard anything at all about Gertrude's past?" There was a general shaking of heads around the table. "Well, don't you think it's odd that she's so secretive about it?"

"Some people just don't like to talk about themselves," Clarice said in that annoying placating voice.

Vi knew for a fact that Gertrude wouldn't even answer the simplest questions like where she'd been living, what she was doing before she took over the garage, if she'd ever been married or had children—and she said as much to the women gathered. "She evaded all of my questions when she came in to buy groceries at the store. Tell me that's not odd."

Everyone grew quiet for a moment. "Some people are just private," Lynette said cautiously.

Vi scoffed at that. Some people just had something to hide. She could tell a lot about a person by the groceries they bought. She hated to think how much she knew about the women sitting at the table this morning. But she kept that to herself.

Gertrude bought only the basics. Eggs, milk, bread, some fruit and only very little meat. But she bought a lot of canned cat food. Did she even *have* a cat?

"She's not on any social media that I can find either." Vi saw that all these old hens were about to say that they wished they'd never gotten on Facebook and that they certainly didn't tweet. She quickly cut them off with "I offered her a box at the post office and she declined, saying she'd use Fred's old one for the garage. Who doesn't get mail? Tell me that isn't strange." As she glanced around the table, all she saw were blank looks.

"I wish I didn't have a post office box," Rose Hanson said. "All I get is junk mail." The others quickly agreed. "No one writes letters anymore. Remember when we used to get long newsy letters?"

"And postcards from friends and relatives when they were traveling," Mabel said wistfully. "Back when a stamp cost a couple of pennies."

The conversation took off from there, covering everything from when conditioner used to be called cream rinse and you could buy a candy bar for a nickel. "A good-sized candy bar too," Lynette added.

Vi told herself she should have walked on by the café this morning. But when she'd seen the neighborhood ladies of a certain age all gathered inside something had made her want to join them. She'd missed female friendship, although it was like missing a limb she'd never had.

As she got to her feet, the conversation veered off to an

air-fryer recipe someone had seen on Pinterest. Vi sighed, feeling like an alien on an uninhabitable planet. No one paid her any mind as she left.

Once outside, she looked down the strip of two-lane blacktop that cut through the middle of Buckhorn, Montana. There were businesses on each side, some of them already getting ready to close. This time of year the tourist season was winding down. By Labor Day it would be over until Memorial Day. Soon businesses would be boarded up with See You in the Spring signs on them as winter swept in.

A gust of wind kicked up dust, whirling it past before disappearing down the highway. Vi blinked as the sky darkened to the west. The weatherperson was calling for a late thunderstorm. Dust motes still danced in the air as she settled her gaze on Durham's Garage and Gas, the only garage and gas station for miles.

The light was on in the small house behind the business. The day after the funeral, Gertrude had moved in and risen early the next morning to begin painting the house a light yellow with white trim. From as far back as Vi could remember the house had been the same dark green as the gas station. The large, gray-haired woman of indiscriminate age had done the painting herself. It had taken her five full days.

Vi thought of that old expression about watching paint dry. Locals had watched with fascination as the job progressed. Sometimes it was downright sad how little happened in Buckhorn.

Pulling up her collar, she started down the street toward her general store. It was about time to open up, although business would be slow. She didn't mind all that much.

With a laugh, she realized that she possibly had too much time to think—and worry. Not that she was wrong about

Gertrude Durham. Vi believed in following her instincts, and right now hers were telling her there was something about the woman that wasn't right.

No matter what anyone thought, she intended to find out what Gertrude was hiding.

AT THE YELLOW HOUSE, Gertrude Durham stood to the side of the window watching Vi Mullen come down the street. Earlier she'd seen a gaggle of local hens headed for the café and to her surprise Vi Mullen not far behind them. Vi usually didn't join the women. It made her wonder what was different this morning.

The woman had been a thorn in her side since she'd arrived in Buckhorn. Always asking about things that were none of her business. The truth was that Vi made her nervous. So much so that Gertrude had gone up to her bedroom earlier, shoved aside the bed and the rug, and opened the trapdoor just to make sure nothing had been disturbed.

It was ridiculous and she cursed herself for letting the busybody make her doubt herself. But better to be safe than sorry. The metal container was just as she'd left it, locked and undisturbed. Her traveling bag with two guns, ammo and several passports in several different names was also where she'd left it. She could leave at a moment's notice if it became necessary. That thought always came as a relief.

She'd closed the trapdoor, replaced the rug and shoved the bed back.

But now, watching Vi Mullen make her way down to the general store, she still didn't feel safe. Across the room, she caught a glimpse of her reflection in the large old mirror on the wall. She avoided mirrors. All but that one had come down the day she'd moved in. She'd tried to remove it, but the screws had been painted over years ago. She was going to have to pry it off the wall and then repair the plaster so she'd put it off. But she had to tackle the job soon. It bothered her seeing a woman she didn't recognize reflected in the glass.

Work. That was what kept her sane. And right now she had to get to the garage. Mabel Aldrich needed a new water pump in her old Lincoln. Gertrude had promised she'd do it today. But first she had to put new spark plugs in Lars Olson's pickup and tune it up for him. The new water pump was supposed to be delivered before nine. She liked Mabel—not that she trusted anyone. Her own fault after years of being on the run.

Dressed in her usual steel-toed work boots, baggy green overalls and one of a half dozen flannel shirts that had belonged to her nephew, Fred, she pushed her trucker's cap down over her head of riotous thick gray hair. She enjoyed the work and often thought how lucky she was that her nephew had left her this place. Just as she was grateful that her father had wanted a son. Because of that, he'd taught her everything she needed to know about fixing just about anything.

Someone else had taught her about being a woman.

The unwanted thought of Ike Shepherd was quickly shoved away as she walked the short distance to the garage and went to work.

CHAPTER TWO

GERTRUDE DURHAM WASN'T the only new face in town, Vi recalled before she reached her general store. Someone was taking over the old hair salon.

Buckhorn had been the same for so long, it seemed strange to see new people in town opening businesses in formerly empty buildings—especially one opening this late in the tourist season. She stopped in front of a building that had been empty for a few years—until now.

Lately Buckhorn had started to grow for no apparent reason that Vi could make out. Her family had settled here back in the 1800s, bought up a lot of the land and opened some of the first businesses. She still owned the general store, the antique barn and a sizable amount of land.

As she peered in the front window, she saw a young woman with short spiky dark hair come out of the back carrying an armful of supplies.

The woman, who looked to be in her late twenties to early thirties, saw her, smiled and nodded toward the front door in invitation. Vi figured it wouldn't hurt to introduce herself and, opening the front door, stepped in.

"Good morning," the young woman said brightly as she began to place the supplies on a shelf behind the salon chair. She wore a sleeveless top, a large elaborate tattoo on one upper arm. Vi doubted it was her only tattoo. A half dozen piercings in her ears suggested that the woman had other piercings in places Vi cringed to even think about.

"Let me guess. Vivian Mullen, right?" the young woman said.

"Apparently my reputation precedes me," she said, getting a laugh.

"I asked around and was told if I had any questions or needed something to ask you."

"I'm the person to talk to," Vi admitted. As post mistress, she provided post office boxes to new residents, distributed advice and knew pretty much everyone in the county.

Finished putting away the supplies, the young woman wiped her hands on her jeans and stepped forward to offer a hand. "Luna Declan."

"Luna?"

"My grandmother's idea. She was an old hippie."

The woman's smile could have melted an iceberg, Vi thought. "Well, it's nice to meet you. What brings you to Buckhorn?"

Luna's cell rang. "Sorry, I have to take this," she said as she dug the phone out of her jeans pocket. "It's my father. If I don't answer, he'll worry. I'll come down to the store to see you later."

Vi nodded and headed for the door. Luna Declan seemed nice enough and she was someone who took her father's calls. Relieved, Vi told herself that maybe she wouldn't have to worry about this one.

Unlike Gertrude Durham.

LUNA WATCHED VI leave as her phone rang again. She'd been expecting the call. She was pretty sure that he'd seen the newspaper article in yesterday's *Billings Gazette*. The jewelry heist had made national news years ago but was now relegated to a back page. She'd torn it out and now had it stuffed in her jeans pocket.

A museum jewelry exhibit heist years ago is about to come to a close as the statute of limitations runs out this week on the getaway driver.

Two armed men entered the museum at closing, tied up the security guard and got away with over ten million dollars in rare jewelry. Both men were arrested but no longer had the jewelry on them. It is believed that they passed the jewelry to their getaway driver as they fled on foot from police. Both later died in prison but never gave up their accomplice.

The driver, a woman according to surveillance cameras, has never been found. The getaway car was discovered torched, any DNA evidence lost. The FBI is still looking for the woman.

In an odd twist, most of the jewels have turned up over the past few years in small churches across the country. One piece though is still missing. Since the heist getaway driver is the only one still alive, it's believed that she has been leaving the jewelry at these out-of-the-way churches.

Once the statute of limitations expires this week on the crime it is unlikely that she would be prosecuted if caught. The museum administrator said he still hopes she will turn in the diamond brooch—if she still has it. The brooch is valued at a half million dollars.

"WELL?" ASKED A GRUFF male voice as she answered the call on the fourth ring.

"I just met the town busybody," Luna said with a laugh as she glanced down the street after Vi.

"Is she going to be a problem?"

"Naw, I can handle her. Don't worry, everything is going as planned."

"I still don't like it," he said.

She sighed. "Trust me, I know what I'm doing."

"Fine. You play it the way you want to. Just be careful. I hope I don't have to remind you how dangerous this is."

"Nope," Luna said as she stepped to the back of the shop where she'd hung up her leather jacket. Her weapon was inside, but in a pinch, she was also deadly with a can of hair spray.

"When do you open?"

"Tomorrow," she said. "I put an ad in the local online weekly newspaper offering specials. I also had some flyers printed. I'll make sure she gets one. With luck, I'll be able to lure her in."

"With the deadline on the statute of limitations, she'll be suspicious and even more dangerous."

"Don't worry. I'm hell with a pair of scissors."

"Don't joke around."

"Dad, I've got this."

He sighed. "I know. But I'm allowed to worry about my daughter if I want to."

She chuckled. "You should be glad that I'm finally using the skills I learned on my gap year before college. I told you beauty college was worth every cent—not to mention all the years I spent at Mom's salon from the time I could crawl. Like she always said, doesn't hurt to learn everything I can so I have options. I rented this place for a song after the last beautician went broke here. It's fate."

"Your mom wouldn't like this," he said, his voice even more gruff with emotion. "She never knew how dangerous retrieval work was. If she had known, let alone that now I've let you…"

"I can do this. And when it's over, who knows, maybe I'll end up staying here and cutting hair the rest of my life."

"Your mother would have liked that. I just worry that you're too much like me." Behind her, she heard the door to the shop open and turned to see a cop filling the doorway. Her heart bumped in her chest at the glint of a star on his shirt. "I'd be happy to make you an appointment... Sure, just let me know what time works for you," she said into the phone, and disconnected.

She smiled at the lawman filling her doorway. He'd removed his Stetson and now held it by the brim in front of him. She recognized the uniform. Deputy marshal. He looked about her age, early thirties.

"Any chance of getting a haircut?" he asked as he released the hat with one hand to rake his fingers through a head full of thick dark hair. He had beautiful sea green eyes with long thick lashes in a classically handsome face. "Vi down at the general store said I should check with you. But I didn't see a sign in the window. Are you open yet?"

Good old Vi. "I was planning to open later today, but now that you're here, come on in. You can be my first client, Deputy. Please have a seat." She took his hat and jacket and put them on hooks along the wall by the door and considered the man. He was a good six-four or -five, towering over her five-foot-five frame. His broad shoulders challenged the fabric of his short-sleeved brown shirt with the county marshal's department patch—identical to the ones on his canvas jacket. His well-fitting jeans cupped a nice behind and slim hips all the way down those long legs to his Western boots.

"I'm Luna Declan," she said as she put a drape around him and caught a whiff of maleness mixed with a light aftershave. It had an intoxicating appeal that she couldn't deny even as she reminded herself what was at stake.

"Jaxson Gray," he said, clearly uneasy as he shifted in the chair. "I usually get my hair cut by the barber over in Lewistown. But he fell and broke his leg. Been closed while he recuperates."

She couldn't help but smile as she turned the chair around and dropped the back to the edge of the sink. He leaned back as she adjusted the water and took in the weapon strapped at his hip. A Smith & Wesson .357 Magnum six-inch barrel, blued finish. She'd been told that Buckhorn was pretty much lawless because the closest officer was a good hour away from either direction. So seeing him had come as a surprise.

"Do you have family around here?" Jaxson asked as she began to wash his hair.

Luna shook her head. "Denver. My father's an insurance agent, my mother was a beautician. She had her own shop. Just your average American family. How about you?"

"My father's a college history professor, my mother's an elementary school teacher. My sister is also an elementary school teacher, and my brother is a school administrator." He grinned and seemed to relax. "I'm the black sheep of the family."

As she massaged his scalp, she asked, "I'm glad you stopped in, Deputy. Do you get to Buckhorn often?"

CHAPTER THREE

EARL RAY CAULFIELD had been known to avoid Vi when he saw her coming. But this time she'd ambushed him.

"Earl Ray?"

He'd stopped by the café to see his wife and have one of Bessie's amazing blueberry muffins that she'd baked just that morning. Both older, he and Bessie had only recently gotten married after years of being best friends. He hadn't even had a bite of his muffin when Vi appeared without warning next to him at the café counter.

"I need to talk to you about Gertrude Durham," she whispered as she slid onto the stool beside him. They were the only two at the counter. The only other customers were in a couple of booths some distance away.

"Coffee, Vi?" Bessie asked from the other side of the counter. She was carrying a full pot and topped off Earl Ray's. Her hair was long and gray, plaited in a braid that fell over one shoulder. Seeing her always made his heart bump in his chest. He'd loved this woman forever but had only recently made her his wife. He hated that it had taken him so long.

Waving Bessie's question away, Vi turned her attention on him again and whispered, "Something's just not right about Gertrude Durham."

"Well, Vi," Earl Ray said as he cut a bite of the muffin

with his fork and watched his wife return to the kitchen. "People say that about you and I always say—"

"I'm in no mood for your so-called sense of down-home humor," she interrupted. "This is *serious*."

He sighed and put down his fork. His hair was more salt than pepper, but he tried to stay in good shape and was for his age. Turning toward her, he settled his dark blue eyes on her and asked, "What seems to be the problem?"

"We need to find out who this woman really is," Vi said adamantly.

"You have reason to believe she isn't Gertrude Durham?"

"Not necessarily."

He picked up his fork, took a bite and chewed, telling himself that Vi was annoying but had a good heart. At least he wanted to believe that. Through the pass-through he could see Bessie watching with amusement. "Why don't I do some checking on her. Would that make you rest more comfortably at night?"

All the steam seemed to leak out of Vi. "Yes, it would." She looked like a woman who'd completed her mission as she rose from the stool and left.

"Are you really going to look into Gertrude Durham?" Bessie asked quietly after Vi was gone.

"I suppose it wouldn't hurt." He was known as the town's military hero. In truth, no one knew exactly what he'd done in the service. But fortunately, he had contacts who often helped him when he needed it. He felt it was his job to look after Buckhorn and its residents.

As he took another bite of muffin, he realized that he hadn't done a check on Gertrude because she'd inherited the garage and house as Fred Durham's aunt. He hadn't questioned it.

But maybe he should have. He hoped he wasn't losing

his edge. Finishing the muffin, he washed it down with coffee and rose. While he was at it, he'd check on that other new resident in town, Luna Declan, the new salon owner.

"So WHAT DO you think?" Luna asked as she offered the deputy marshal a hand mirror so he could check out the back of his hair.

She watched him swivel in his seat. Those eyes of his really were killer. Men should not be allowed to have thick, dark eyelashes like that—let alone eyes that made a girl yearn for the sea. It was so unfair.

He stopped turning this way and that, his expression priceless. "It looks so good. When Bob cuts it…" He stopped as if he didn't want to say anything bad about barber Bob.

"He probably doesn't style it."

Jaxson met her gaze in the mirror. "I guess that's the difference."

"But you like it?" she asked, smiling. She could see that he did.

"I really do." He looked at his haircut a little longer, then handed back the mirror.

"Let me know what your girlfriend thinks," she said, still smiling. She'd already seen that he wasn't wearing a wedding band. Not that the lack of a ring necessarily proved anything. She hadn't been crushing on him or anything as juvenile as that. She just wanted to make a thorough assessment of this lawman so she knew what she might be dealing with.

She'd already sized up Jaxson. He'd be the type to follow the letter of the law, which meant he could be trouble.

"No girlfriend." He dropped his gaze to his boots.

"Well, let's see what your coworkers have to say."

He chuckled. "There aren't many of us. You asked how

often I get to Buckhorn. We're stretched pretty thin and now there's some big celebration planned here in town at the end of summer."

She nodded. "Buckhorn's 125th birthday. It sounds like a wild time." Actually, it sounded anything but. Not that she would be here. She and her shop would be long gone by then if everything went as planned. Strange, but it gave her a little pang of regret. It had been fun playing house here, especially since she had an apartment upstairs that she'd enjoyed decorating even knowing it was temporary.

"Wild time exactly. That's what we're worried about," Deputy Gray said. "We're trying to decide the best way to patrol the area, so you might be seeing more of me over this way." He met her gaze and this time held it longer.

"You stop by anytime, Deputy, and I'll work you into my schedule."

He nodded, smiled and reached for his wallet.

"No, this one's on the house—for luck. My first haircut in Buckhorn."

Jaxson started to argue, but realized she wasn't taking his money. "Well, then you'll have to let me buy you dinner next time I'm passing through."

She pretended to be surprised by the offer. "I'd love that."

He smiled again. He had a great smile, boyish in that very manly handsome face.

"Then it's a date," she said. "I look forward to it."

With that she showed him out and called her father back. "I just met the local law. We're having dinner the next time he comes through town."

"You're playing with fire."

Luna smiled to herself as she disconnected and thought about Deputy Marshal Jaxson Gray. Best to keep him close. Just not too close. She didn't want to get burned.

CHAPTER FOUR

EARL RAY FOUND exactly what he'd expected to find when he dug into Gertrude Durham's background. She'd grown up in Stevensville, Montana—not far from the Idaho border, the daughter of a stay-at-home mother and logger father. She'd graduated from the University of Montana in Missoula in mechanical engineering before returning home to work for her father's logging company. She'd never married and as far as Earl Ray could tell, she owned the logging company that provided her with a decent income. Apparently she'd never had another job until she took over the gas station and garage.

As for what had brought her to Buckhorn, she'd inherited a business and was possibly looking for a change. Seemed pretty open and shut to him.

Though as he closed his laptop, he wondered what it was about Gertrude that had Vi worried. Picking up his cell phone, he called Vi.

"Can't find anything in Gertrude's past to be concerned about," he told her.

"Why is she so secretive then?" Vi demanded, clearly disappointed.

"Maybe she doesn't like being interrogated."

Vi harrumphed. "Mark my words, there's something wrong about her. You'll see."

He hoped Vi was mistaken as he disconnected and typed

the words *Luna Declan* into his computer. Mother, former owner of a beauty shop, deceased. Father, an insurance investigator. Luna attended beauty college, graduated. Also she had a university degree in forensics and criminology.

That raised an eyebrow, but Earl Ray figured that when it came down to choosing a career, she'd followed in her mother's footsteps and opened her own salon here. He closed the file and his laptop. As he did, he brushed off Vi's concerns about Gertrude. At least for the moment.

IKE SHEPHERD COULDN'T believe it. After all these years? He'd flagged the woman's file so that if there were ever any inquiries about her through DNA or fingerprints or any of the aliases she'd used during her life, he'd be alerted. Someone had made just such an inquiry about a woman named Gertrude Durham.

That wasn't the name she'd used when he knew her. Could that be her real name? He felt a shiver move through him as he sat back in his chair. She'd surfaced after all this time? And in Buckhorn, Montana? Was it possible?

Why else would the inquiry have come from there? Why from someone who had top clearance with the military? He typed in the name only to hit a dead end. Earl Ray Caulfield's file was sealed. What the devil?

What kind of trouble had the woman gotten herself into now? Ike ran a hand over his face. In three days, the statute of limitations would run out on the jewelry heist. Gertrude was still wanted for questioning by the FBI. He wasn't the only one who would get flagged with this new information.

Which meant that if he was going to do something, he'd have to do it quickly. He'd actually thought she must be dead since in all this time he hadn't heard anything. So where had she been? Maybe more to the point, what was she now doing? How much had she changed with the years? Or how much hadn't she changed? he wondered with a knowing smile.

"You aren't seriously thinking of going to Montana," he said to himself as he looked around his condo. He hated to admit how bored he'd been since he'd retired from the FBI. "What are you going to do when you find her?" Bring her in? Make a citizen's arrest? In three days, if she'd been involved in the heist, legally she would be free.

He quit kidding himself that this had anything to do with catching her for the crime he knew damned well that she'd been involved in. If she was in Buckhorn, he had to go. He *wanted* to see her. Which was why he shouldn't go. Too much time had passed—not to mention the fact that the woman was dangerous for him in so many ways.

Yet, even as he thought it, he wondered what she would do when she saw him again. He told himself she wouldn't be the woman he'd known. He wasn't the man she'd known either, even though he didn't feel his age—especially when he thought about her.

Even as he tried to talk himself out of it, he knew he was going to Buckhorn, Montana. He was going to see her again no matter how dangerous it could be for both of them. He'd be armed, and knowing her, she would be as well.

He smiled to himself as he remembered one night curled up in bed when she'd finally told him her real first name. "Gertrude?" He'd laughed, shaking his head, not sure he believed her for good reason.

"Don't make me wish I hadn't told you," she'd warned, those dark eyes of hers catching fire in the candlelight.

He'd pulled her to him and kissed her, breathing his new pet name for her against that luscious mouth of hers. "Gert."

"Gert," he whispered to himself now. Even whispering

her name made his heart ache for what had been. For what could have been.

He had no idea what woman he would find when he reached Buckhorn, Montana. Gert had a way of turning into whatever she wanted a person to see. At one point, he'd thought he'd known the real her. But he could have been wrong about that too.

"She's going to break your heart," he told himself as he rose to go pack. It wouldn't be the first time. But it could be the last, he thought as he packed his weapon.

CHAPTER FIVE

IKE FLEW INTO BILLINGS, Montana, the largest city in the state. It was the only commercial airport close to Buckhorn—although it was one of the smallest he'd ever seen. He rented a car right there at the airport and after driving a two-lane highway with few to no towns in between for what seemed like hours, he saw what appeared to be buildings on the horizon.

Mountains soared up on each side of the narrow valley thick with green pines. Now that he was almost here, according to the car's guidance system, he felt his first doubts begin to surface. It had been too long. They were both so much older. Wouldn't it be better just to remember the good times and not chance getting his heart broken again—or worse?

A town began to materialize. He'd suspected Buckhorn was small, but still he was surprised at just how insubstantial it was. He slowed as he passed the Sleepy Pine Motel and the Buckhorn Bakery. He passed a series of businesses. A general store, a café, a beauty shop.

With a start, he realized that he was suddenly past town—and that he'd missed Durham's Garage and Gas on the far edge of Buckhorn.

Braking, he pulled off onto a short dirt road that led to what appeared to be a rather major development coming up. He saw a sign announcing the new Buckhorn Hotel.

As he turned around and headed back into Buckhorn, he couldn't imagine Gert living here. Not after the life she'd had. He felt his heart fall at the thought that this whole trip had been a wild-goose chase. Wasn't there more than a good chance that her real name wasn't Gertrude Durham? That it was just another alias? What if this wasn't the woman who'd stolen more than his heart all those years ago?

Still worried that it was a mistake, he pulled in next to the gas pump closest to the building. In the shadows of the dimly lit garage, he could see someone under the hood of a pickup at the first bay inside.

Getting out, he braced himself for disappointment. He wouldn't find Gert here. He'd never find her. Never see her again—just as he'd thought he'd accepted a long time ago.

"Give me a minute!" called a gruff voice from inside the garage.

He climbed out and, using his credit card, began to fill his tank. He knew he was stalling. The possibility of seeing her again made him anxious, nervous, unsettled. He thought about the first time he'd seen her—the woman he was going to fall completely, hopelessly, heartbreakingly in love with.

He'd been working undercover on a money-laundering case, which was why he'd found himself at a penthouse party in the middle of Las Vegas. He'd just taken a glass of champagne from a waiter when he saw her.

She stood outside on the roof garden silhouetted against the lights of the strip in a red dress that molded to her amazing body, her long blond hair sweeping halfway down her back. He hadn't realized how tall she was until he walked out onto the roof and stood next to her. He had only a few inches on her.

When she turned to look at him, he felt the full impact

of the woman. Her hair framed a perfectly sculpted face he would never forget, from the eyes and high cheekbones to that full mouth. She'd stolen his breath away, but she would end up stealing a whole lot more than that before it ended.

He'd handed her the glass of champagne he hadn't touched yet. She'd captured his gaze and held it as she took a sip.

"I see you've met my lady," Ralph Conrad, the penthouse owner and host, had said as he put an arm around the woman.

"Not officially," Ike had replied, his gaze still on her.

"Irene, meet Ike." Conrad had frowned. "I don't believe I know your last name."

"Jones," he'd said. "Irene…"

"Southerland," she'd said smiling as if she knew they were both lying.

"It's a pleasure," he'd said, wondering how deeply she was involved in Ralph Conrad's crimes. He'd thought how much he'd hate having to cuff her when this finally went down. He'd known then that they would become lovers. It hadn't mattered that he could lose his job, not to mention his life. It had felt as if neither of them had a choice.

There'd been an innocence about her the first time they'd made love. He could laugh about that now. Because other than that, there was nothing innocent about Gert.

By the time the FBI raided the penthouse and arrested Ralph Conrad, she was gone—with a suitcase full of the man's ill-gotten gains.

Ike finished filling up the rental car's tank, took his receipt and finally forced himself to walk toward the open large overhead door into the garage. He didn't want to get his hopes up, but he knew it was too late. His heart was already punching against his ribs in anticipation.

After that first time he saw Gert, he'd found her living in another penthouse, her own in New York City. By then, he'd already been ruined for any other woman.

He heard the clank of a wrench as he approached the figure leaning under the hood. Even as he told himself that this person clad in large green overalls and flannel couldn't possibly be the woman he'd known and loved, he could no more stop himself than not take his next breath.

He was beside the pickup when he said her name. "Gert?"

CHAPTER SIX

GERTRUDE FROZE. That one word spoken in that familiar voice sent her spinning through a whirlwind of emotions and memories even as she told herself she had to be wrong. It couldn't be Ike. Yet that deep, rich voice had her trembling inside.

For a moment, she couldn't speak. Couldn't breathe. Couldn't even think. She'd dreamed of what it might be like to see him again, but that had passed with age. Neither of them was young anymore. They'd had their chance. Now it was gone.

"Gert." This time he said it with such longing, such hope and yet such apprehension that she felt tears burn her eyes. It brought back the memory of her body tangled with his in exquisite pleasure. She'd known that no matter how long they were together, she could never get enough of this man. Wasn't that why she'd left? Because it couldn't last, and she couldn't be there when it was over.

Now he was here in the flesh. This was not the way she'd wanted their story to end. Not in this old dirty garage. Not with her in overalls—all sign of the woman he'd once loved gone. Not with just three days left before the statute of limitations ran out on the jewelry heist.

But she knew Ike. He wouldn't leave until he saw her. Until she faced him.

She'd never felt more like a coward. That was what made

her push away from the front of that pickup to face him. It was the hardest thing she'd ever done—other than walking away from Ike all those years ago.

Straightening to her full height, she wiped her greasy hands with a rag and stepped out to look into the face of the man she'd wanted but could never have.

"Gert." His brown eyes filled even as he smiled. He was the most beautiful man she'd ever known. Age had only made him more handsome, more distinguished. His dark hair was threaded with silver, his dark eyes still filled with sunshine.

Her throat closed at the look in those eyes. It was as if he was seeing her as she'd been all those years ago and not the older woman in her work clothes standing before him.

"Ike, what are you doing here?" she finally managed to say, her voice breaking with emotion.

"Looking for you. Isn't that the story of our lives?"

That voice seemed deeper and richer with age. It sent a pleasurable tremor through her. His handsome face was now etched with lines but his jaw was still carved like granite, his mouth still quirking up on one side when he smiled.

"You always were good with your hands," he said without taking his eyes off her. "So I guess I shouldn't be surprised that you now own a garage."

"I don't know what to say."

"Say you'll have dinner with me."

His words took her by surprise. She looked past him, expecting to see a dozen FBI agents in body armor ready to burst in at any moment.

"I'm alone," he said, as if knowing exactly what she'd been thinking.

She swallowed the lump that rose in her throat before looking down at the garb she wore every day as if doing penitence for the life she'd led. When her nephew, Fred, had died and left her the garage, gas station and house in Buckhorn, Montana, she'd thought it had been a sign. No one would ever find her here. If anyone was still looking for her.

She'd been wrong on both counts.

"Dinner? I—"

"It's just dinner, Gert. Surely for old times' sake. Or have you forgotten the two of us?"

As if she could ever forget. Her eyes burned with unshed tears. "Dinner." She glanced toward the pickup sitting in the bay before looking back at him. "I could meet you at the café later this evening."

"Seven?" He raised a brow as he said it. The last time they'd seen each other she'd agreed to meet him that night at seven. She hadn't shown. Did he really think she would this time?

He didn't move for a few moments. She could feel him studying her. Looking for the woman he'd once loved? Or the criminal he'd spent years trying to find?

CHAPTER SEVEN

IKE. SHE COULDN'T believe that he'd found her. Her heart drummed as she watched him walk to his car. Not an expensive sports car like he used to drive, but something midsize and nondescript. Like a cop might drive. Or an FBI agent.

But he wasn't either anymore. He had to be retired, didn't he? She realized that she was trying to make sense of this. Seeing him again had thrown off her equilibrium. She didn't know what to think—let alone what to do.

He'd found her and asked her to dinner.

She could run. All she had to do was pack up quickly, drive out of this town and start over. It wasn't as if she hadn't done that many times before.

Except that she'd assured herself that all those years of running were over when she'd come to Buckhorn. She'd thought she would stay here until the end. Then again, she had her bag packed under the floorboards upstairs, didn't she? Which meant that she'd known something could happen that would make her run again.

Gertrude took a deep breath and slowly let it out as she watched Ike drive away. He would expect her to run—just as she had before.

She thought about the timing. Three days. She'd been waiting for years for the statute of limitations to run out. It almost had.

Gertrude glanced toward the pickup sitting with its hood up that she'd been working on. She'd promised Lars she'd have his tune-up done by noon. The clock on the wall said it was almost ten.

With a sigh, she walked back to it, picked up the wrench she'd put down earlier and went to work.

But her mind was on Ike and the first time they met at that party in Vegas. He hadn't looked like a cop. Her instincts had warned her that, cop or not, he was a dangerous man. She hadn't been wrong about that.

It was the way he'd looked at her that night. The way he'd looked at her only minutes before. How was that possible? She felt a shiver move through her, the memory so sharp it was almost painful. How could he still look at her that way after all they'd been through? What was wrong with the man?

Gertrude shook her head as she realized that she'd asked herself that same question all those years ago. Ike had known that she was involved with Ralph Conrad and yet that hadn't stopped him. She'd felt his eyes on her all that night at the party.

She'd also seen Ralph watching him, a frown on his face. She knew that Ralph was the kind of man who'd ordered other men killed for much less.

"I want to see you again," Ike had whispered when he'd caught her alone later that evening.

She'd shaken her head. "That would be hazardous to your health, and mine as well."

"I'm willing to chance it," he'd said without hesitation. "What about you?"

She'd met his gaze. She was in a penthouse apartment overlooking Vegas with a man who bought her furs and diamonds. After she'd escaped a life working at a logging company and sawmill, did this man really think she was foolish enough to chance losing what she had for a one-night stand?

She'd laughed. "I'm not that reckless." She'd turned and left him standing there as she'd gone to join Ralph.

But it hadn't stopped Ike. Nor had it stopped her from thinking about him. He'd come to the casino where she danced, hanging around backstage until she got off work—both of them taking a risk since Ralph or one of his men often came by before closing.

But Ike didn't seem to care. She'd thought the man had a death wish. Ralph had to have known. He'd pressured her to move in with him. She'd declined. It was one thing to date a man like him. It was another to become his property.

She knew she was walking a tightrope that was leading to a fall, but she'd finally given in to her feelings. She'd never forget the first time she'd made love with Ike. He was so tender, so loving and yet so sexy. She knew no man would ever satisfy her after him.

It wasn't until the raid when Ralph and his associates were arrested that she realized a part of her had known all along that Ike was the law. FBI.

She'd sensed something was going down and got what she could before it happened. That had been her life. Getting out before trouble closed in on her, taking what she could.

Ike had good reason to be after her. What she hadn't expected was for him to catch her so easily after the raid on Ralph and his associates.

"If you want me to turn state evidence against Ralph—" She was going to tell him that wasn't happening.

But he'd stopped her. "I want you. That's all I want."

She hadn't believed him. "I don't know anything about his operation, and I certainly wasn't involved."

He'd smiled as he'd closed the distance between them. "Isn't it possible that I just want you?" He'd pulled her to him. "I've wanted you from the moment I laid eyes on you." He'd pressed her against the wall, sending her pulse into overdrive as he'd molded his body to hers.

The kiss had been just the beginning. Until the jewelry heist.

LUNA HADN'T BEEN surprised to get Jaxson's call.

"Seems I'm coming back through Buckhorn," the deputy had said. "I was thinking…"

"If it's dinner you're thinking of, that would be great," she'd said, smiling to herself.

He'd seemed to be at a loss for words for a moment. "Seven tonight?"

"Perfect. I'll meet you at the café. It will be good to see you." After she'd hung up, though, she'd warned herself to be careful. Especially with the law. This was a job, nothing more. Keeping an eye on Jaxson was part of it, dating him…well, that was another. Daddy would not approve, she thought and laughed.

She'd been a wild teen growing up. Her father blamed it on Luna losing her mother, but she knew that had only been a part of it. She'd yearned for adventure from as far back as she could remember. Wasn't that why she'd studied criminology? Wasn't that why she was in Buckhorn right now? Wasn't that why she was going to dinner with the local lawman?

She liked taking risks. Anyway, it was just one dinner and Jaxson wasn't her type. Too reserved. But the thought of bringing him out of that did have its appeal, she thought with a grin.

As Gertrude finished with the pickup and slammed the hood, she was startled to find someone standing in the garage doorway. For just an instant, she thought it might be Ike back. Or one of a dozen FBI agents.

But that wasn't Ike's broad shoulders or his long legs. This figure was small and female, which didn't exempt her from being FBI. "Afternoon," the woman said as she approached.

"I was about to close up for the day," Gertrude told her, wondering if she should go for the gun she kept in the garage. It wasn't that far away that she couldn't make an excuse to get it. But she'd gone this long without killing anyone. She liked the idea of ending it that way.

"No problem. I just stopped by to give you one of these." The young woman held out a flyer—the last thing Gertrude wanted, so she made no move to take it. She also thought it might be a ruse.

"It's a special on a haircut. I'm Luna Declan. I just opened a salon in town. This is my first day in business." The woman was eyeing Gertrude's wiry gray hair. "I'd love for you to be my first official customer. With this twenty-five percent off coupon..."

Gertrude took the flyer, her heart rate dropping as she realized that she'd seen the woman working on getting a storefront ready down the street. It had been a false alarm thinking she was FBI. But she knew that if Ike had found her location, even if he hadn't shared her location with his former brothers, others would also be on the way.

"I'm not sure you could do anything with my hair."

Luna Declan laughed. She sounded as young as she looked, her laugh bright as the Montana day outside the garage. "You'd be surprised what I can do."

Gertrude also had no desire to be surprised. Ike finding her was the real surprise. Why he'd come was yet another. Gertrude met the woman's gaze. Why not? She was a woman who'd always taken risks, big ones. Getting her hair cut wasn't one of them.

Her future hung by a thread. Why not let this young woman do something with her feral head of hair? "Okay," she said before she could stop herself. "What time?"

"If you're finished here, I could do it now," Luna said.

She nodded. "Just let me clean up a little and I'll be down."

"Great. See you soon."

Gertrude regretted it almost at once. She'd dressed like this and let her hair go to stay invisible. Not that it made a difference now. She'd been found.

She drove the pickup out of the bay, leaving the keys in it, and pulled out her cell to call Lars and let him know his truck was ready. Mabel had already picked up her Lincoln earlier.

You can still take off, Gertrude told herself as she headed for the house. Running out on a haircut would be the least of her crimes. Her bag was packed. It wouldn't take much to be gone.

But at the house, she showered and changed from her overalls to jeans and a T-shirt. For a moment, she stood in front of that old mirror downstairs, angry with herself on so many levels. Just getting out of the flannel and the baggy overalls made a huge difference in her appearance—even with her hair still an undisciplined mess.

She took off the trucker's cap and chucked it into a nearby chair as she thought of what was hidden under the floorboards upstairs. She could try to hide the last piece of jewelry from the heist somewhere else, but she knew it was too late. If Ike had come here for justice, he wouldn't stop until he found it.

Running was her only recourse—other than facing up to the past. As she stood there she knew she wasn't going anywhere. The past had found her. And she hadn't realized how tired she was of running. Cursing under her breath, she left the mirror and walked down to the salon. If she was going down, at least it would be with a decent hairdo.

Luna was waiting as if she was excited about the challenge. "I have something to relax you," she said as she handed her a glass of wine.

Gertrude took it. "Don't go wild," she grumbled as she climbed into the chair, downed the wine and, handing back the glass, closed her eyes. She couldn't believe she was doing this. There was nothing worse than an old fool.

Except for an old fool headed for prison before the day was over.

"Ready?" Luna asked as she held out the hand mirror to Gertrude. She'd purposely turned the woman's back to the large mirror on the wall. Now she watched Gertrude swallow before reaching for the mirror. Luna waited for her to raise it so she could see herself and the back of her head in the larger mirror behind her. But for a long moment, Gertrude just held it facedown on her lap as if getting up her courage.

Earlier, Luna had breathed a sigh of relief when Gertrude had come through the door. She'd seen the woman's hesitation back in the garage—just as she'd seen the car that had been parked at the pumps earlier.

The man had looked like a cop. But he hadn't stayed long after getting gas and going into the garage for a few minutes. Luna had feared that someone might turn up to make Gertrude run before the deadline was up.

As soon as she'd reached the town, she'd realized that approaching Gertrude Durham was going to be the problem. From what she'd heard, the woman kept to herself, was abrupt and rude and didn't like anyone.

That sounded like someone who'd been hiding out for years. But if Gertrude had the brooch, why was she working on vehicles in an old garage? Was she afraid to fence the piece? It would take a special buyer to sell something that hot. Was that why she'd been giving back a piece at a time? Maybe she wanted this over.

Luna had traced the path of the left-behind jewelry at churches to this county. One piece had been dropped not all that far from here. The person leaving it had been a woman, according to the security camera. She'd pored over the security tape photos of the heist as well. The FBI had gone through a list of the usual suspects. The name Irene Southerland had come up. Irene was wanted for questioning involving a large amount of money that had gone missing from a money-laundering bust in Vegas. The FBI was already looking for the tall blonde.

Right before that last jewelry drop at a church not that far from here, a woman named Gertrude Durham inherited a gas station and garage in Buckhorn, Montana. She was the right age. All Luna had seen was a grainy security photo, but it appeared to her the woman had been tall based on her height in the getaway vehicle she'd been driving. She'd been pretty with what had appeared to be blond hair.

Luna had become convinced Gertrude Durham was Irene Southerland and was now living in Buckhorn. Did she still have the half-million-dollar stolen brooch? Luna certainly hoped so. She wanted her father, who was ready to retire, to end his career on a high note by retrieving the brooch for the insurance company that had insured it.

Even now, Luna couldn't believe that she'd gotten Gertrude in her chair. Now she held her breath as she waited for the woman's reaction to what she'd done with her hair. She couldn't believe how anxious she was that Gertrude would like it.

GERTRUDE HAD REGRETTED doing this the moment the young woman had begun to wash her hair. She might have gotten up and left except she didn't want to be seen walking down the street with her hair dripping wet.

She clenched the handle of the mirror tightly and tried to swallow back her fear. Why had she agreed to this? She should have just met Ike at the café this evening looking like she always did—overalls and trucker's cap over her wild gray hair. It wasn't as if she was trying to impress him. He knew her. Intimately. And she knew herself only too well.

Better yet, why hadn't she gone with her first instinct and run?

Slowly she lifted the hand mirror and felt such a start that she feared she'd made a sound. She blinked and swallowed again. She looked like her old self—though older. The shock brought back memories that flooded her with regret and longing. It amazed her that just doing something with her hair could take years off her face. She stared at herself as if seeing not a stranger—but her real self after all this time.

"The longer bob accentuates your high cheekbones and is becoming, don't you think?" Luna asked as if she couldn't stand the suspense any longer.

All Gertrude could do was nod as Luna swiveled the

chair so she could see the back as well. "You put something on it." The words felt as if she was speaking around a mouthful of pebbles.

"Just a light rinse that took away some of the harshness of the gray," the young beautician said. "Do you like it?" The woman sounded hopeful.

Gertrude nodded again and handed back the mirror. "You did a good…job."

Luna smiled, bringing sunshine into the room. "I'm so glad."

Her enthusiasm, while contagious, also made Gertrude suspicious. The woman had practically roped and dragged her down here to the salon.

"I hope you'll mention it to your friends. You're a walking billboard for my salon."

Luna's words made Gertrude relax. Of course she wanted to start with the worst-looking woman in town to kick off her new business. But surely Luna knew that Gertrude didn't have any friends. Nor was she planning on making any.

That thought came as a sharp reminder of her dinner date with Ike. She likely wouldn't have a future after tonight. Even if Ike didn't have a team of agents waiting for her at the café, how could she stay in Buckhorn? The FBI couldn't be that far behind Ike. Just the thought of where she might go, what she might do, made her ache. She hadn't realized how much she wanted to stay in one place until she'd painted the little house behind the garage yellow and white. She'd actually been thinking about planting some flowers. Maybe even a tree or two. She'd wanted to put down roots for the first time in her life.

CHAPTER EIGHT

JAXSON COULDN'T HELP being nervous. He hadn't dated in more than three years. He wasn't sure exactly how this date had even happened. He told himself it was too soon and yet he couldn't wait to see Luna again. Not that he didn't feel guilty—maybe especially because Luna was nothing like his late wife.

Amy had been blonde, petite and shy. He'd practically robbed the cradle since she'd been six years younger, a mere twenty to his twenty-six. It had been two years since she'd died.

Even after all this time, dating had been the furthest thing from his mind. It was just dinner, he told himself. But that wasn't what really bothered him. It was Luna and the way she made him feel. Just the thought of her stirred a desire in him stronger than any he could remember.

He arrived at the café twenty minutes early and pretended to study the menu. He'd eaten here enough that he had it memorized. Like most small Montana town cafés, the most exciting entree on it was chicken-fried steak. Fortunately, that was his favorite. He wondered what Luna would order. He expected to find out she was a vegetarian. Then again, the woman could surprise him. The thought made him smile and he was just starting to relax when she walked in—ten minutes early.

LUNA HAD SEEN how pleased Gertrude had been. At one point the woman had teared up before she paid and left. It surprised her how much that had touched her. She'd also forgotten how fulfilling it was to make someone happy by simply cutting and fixing their hair. Her mother would have understood why Luna was feeling conflicted.

She'd come here to expose Gertrude and see the woman headed to jail before the statute of limitations ran out. And with luck, get the brooch back. Not that she wasn't going to go through with it. She was doing this for her father, even though he'd fought her for a while, afraid it was too dangerous.

But as she watched Gertrude head down the street toward the gas station and garage, she almost wanted her to get away with all of it.

The townies began to show up all afternoon with the coupon specials she'd handed out, keeping her busy until closing. She barely had enough time to go upstairs to her apartment and dress for her date when her phone rang.

She'd forgotten about taking Gertrude's fingerprints off the wine glass and texting the impressions to her father after the woman left the shop. It amazed her what could be done by computer.

"Is Gertrude Durham also Irene Southerland?" she asked as she answered the phone.

"Your instincts were right on. It's her. But we still don't know that she was the getaway driver or that she has the brooch," he said. "But your part is over. You hear me? Leave it up to the law now."

"I have to go. I have a date." Before he could say more, she disconnected. The clock was ticking. If she wanted to get the brooch and have Gertrude arrested before the statute of limitations ran out, she'd have to do it soon—no matter what her father said. She couldn't chance that Gertrude might suddenly run.

But while she now knew that Gertrude Durham had gone by the alias Irene Southerland and been involved with a man deep in money laundering, she had no proof that Gertrude had been the getaway driver. But the woman in the security photos from the heist and the money-laundering bust, and the woman who'd sat in her salon chair earlier looked alike. Not to mention the fact that a piece of jewelry had been dropped off at a church not that far from Buckhorn by a woman who'd matched Gertrude Durham's description.

Luna checked the time. Jaxson would be waiting for her at the café. Just the thought of him had her going through her closet looking for something fun to wear. She felt sexy tonight. It had been a good day, starting with Gertrude. She'd made quite a lot of money as well and met more of the local women.

Not that she was staying once this was over, she reminded herself. But it was nice to be welcomed to the community anyway.

She chose a yellow sundress with spaghetti straps and a modest neckline. The dress was flirty with a swing skirt that hit her a good six inches above her knees. She chose strappy heels and fluffed her hair instead of spiking it. Standing in front of the mirror, she smiled at her reflection. Tonight she just wanted to enjoy herself since it was probably the only date she would have with Jaxson.

He was already waiting for her in a corner booth when she walked in. She felt his gaze lock on her as she headed toward him.

"Hey," she said as she smiled at him and slid into the opposite side of the booth. Jaxson had dressed up for the date in a button-down pale yellow shirt, which made her smile broaden. The man really was gorgeous.

"You look beautiful," he said and cleared his throat.

Bessie Caulfield, the owner and wife of war hero Earl Ray, came over to say hello to Jaxson and asked how Luna's first day at the salon had gone.

"I might have to do something with this mop of mine," Bessie said, touching the long gray braid hanging off one shoulder.

"I'd love to help you if you decide you want something new," Luna said, realizing how true that was. Bessie was a beauty inside and out from what she could tell. Saying that their waitress would be right with them to get their drink orders, the woman moved on to another table.

Luna smiled over at her date, wondering how this night might end.

JUST AS SHE'D FEARED, Gertrude caused a stir when she walked into the café a good five minutes before seven. Fortunately most people in town this time of year ate early and had already left. But the few that were finishing their meals looked up in surprise. In fact, it took some of them a while to even realize who she was.

Gertrude had spent years avoiding attention, but she had to admit it was rather fun shocking some of the old biddies in town. She saw Luna sitting in a booth with a good-looking young man. He wasn't wearing his deputy marshal uniform, but she still recognized him for the cop he was. She hoped he wasn't here because of her. She'd hate to spoil Luna's date. She felt almost affectionate toward the young woman.

As she took a booth facing the door, she touched her hair and, realizing what she was doing, quickly picked up a menu from behind the sugar container against the wall. It wasn't as if she didn't know what to order, but it had been a long time since she'd eaten anywhere but at home.

It surprised her that he wasn't already waiting for her in the café. He'd always had this thing about being early because his parents had always been late.

It was well after seven and she'd been thinking he wasn't going to show when she heard the door open. She could feel her heart pounding in anticipation of seeing Ike again. Or was it drumming because at any moment the café could fill with armed FBI agents? Had he turned her in? Was this dinner just to throw her off guard so they could take her without a fight?

She looked up, half-afraid it would be the latter. Ike walked in and stopped. She heard the café quiet as the locals took in the stranger in town. Ike, even older, was the kind of man who drew attention. There was an intensity about him as well as a physical presence. He was beautiful and always had been.

His gaze fell on her and he smiled, the smile going to his eyes, as he started toward her. Gertrude thought her thrashing heart might bust from her chest. She felt such a stab of longing. She hadn't realized how much she'd missed this man. Or how good it was to see him. Even if only once more.

CHAPTER NINE

IKE SLID INTO the booth. She'd done something to her hair and changed out of the overalls. Not that it mattered to him, but it made him hopeful. He saw below the surface when it came to her. He'd always liked what he'd seen even when he'd known he should cuff her and take her in to jail.

"You look just like you did the first time I saw you," he said, meaning it.

She shook her head, her eyes shiny with unshed tears. "What are you doing here, Ike?"

"Having dinner with you, Gert."

She gave him an impatient look as she slid his menu over to him.

He wasn't interested in food, but at least they could talk while they ate. It had been a huge relief to see her sitting here waiting for him. "I was afraid you might have run again," he admitted as he opened his menu.

"And yet here you are."

"I'd hoped you wouldn't." He met her gaze over the menu and held it. He hadn't been sure of what he would do if she'd taken off again.

She pulled free of his stare. "I thought about it."

"I'm glad you didn't."

The waitress came to take their order. Gertrude pointed to the Cobb salad and said she'd like a coffee, black. Ike said he'd take the pork chops and coffee with cream and sugar. They closed their menus and the waitress tucked them back against the wall behind the sugar, salt and pepper containers.

"Ike, please, what do you want?" Gert asked the moment the waitress was out of earshot. She sounded close to tears.

He'd never seen her cry and didn't want to now. He leaned across the table toward her. "What have I always wanted, Gert? You."

She shook her head. "I'm not the woman you knew back then."

"You're that woman and so much more."

"What are you saying?" she demanded.

"That we belong together."

She shook her head. "I was happy here."

He saw defiance in her look. He'd never met a more independent woman. He knew she'd grown up dirt poor. He'd seen in her a need to be someone else, which had led them both to this point. But he sensed the reason she hadn't run was because that need no longer burned in her. Maybe, like him, she wanted just to be content and no longer chased by the demons of the past.

"All right. Then I could be happy here as well."

She laughed. "You really don't expect me to believe that you've changed that much, do you?"

He looked past her and frowned. She turned, startled and afraid of what he'd seen. "Do you know them?" he asked quietly.

"That's the deputy marshal and Luna Declan from the new salon," Gert said. "She's the one who fixed my hair."

Ike felt his heart drop as he realized they had less time than he'd hoped.

LUNA HAD SEEN Gertrude come into the café to the surprise of the locals still having their dinners. She was surprised as well. She'd never seen Gertrude in the café in all the time she'd been in town. She liked to think it had been the new hairdo that had made her venture out.

Jaxson asked her a question. She was in the middle of answering when the man walked in the door and headed for Gertrude's booth.

She felt a stab of shock. The man was older but still recognizable as former FBI agent Ike Shepherd. He'd been the lead investigator on the museum jewelry heist. Luna had studied the crime at university. Ike had even come to her class to talk about how the FBI handled the investigation.

The two male thieves had been caught, but they'd never given up the female getaway driver. They'd both gotten killed in a prison break.

She'd been fascinated by the story even before she found out that her father's insurance company had insured the jewelry. Now all but that one piece—the diamond brooch the size of a teacup saucer—had been retrieved. It was a case that had haunted her father for years and intrigued Luna.

It was Ike Shepherd who she'd seen earlier at the gas station, she realized. Had he come to arrest Gertrude before the deadline? Luna couldn't explain the sudden protective feeling she had for the older woman. Luna had never cared about the deadline. All she'd come here to do was get the brooch back to the museum for her father.

Now she feared that Gertrude had gotten rid of it after the former FBI agent had shown up at her gas station. Worse, if he came here to take her to jail—

"Is everything all right?" Jaxson asked, turning his head to glance in the direction of Ike and Gertrude.

"Fine, sorry. I was just admiring Gertrude's hair," she said. "She was my first customer today at my official opening and I have to admit, I love the way her makeover turned out."

He didn't look as if he believed her entirely but seemed satisfied for the moment. He'd had to have seen her shocked expression at seeing Ike join Gertrude in the booth.

"You were telling me how you got into law enforcement," she said.

"That's boring," he said. "I need to apologize to you." He seemed to hesitate. "This is the first date I've had since my wife died."

In surprise, she said, "I'm so sorry."

He shook his head. "It's been two years, but I just haven't felt like…dating." His gaze came up to hers. "Until I met you."

She was taken aback by his admission. "I'm…flattered."

He smiled. "I hope my telling you about Amy doesn't ruin our date."

"No," she said quickly and reached for his hand. "How long were you married?"

"Just a year. She was killed in a car wreck." He swallowed and pulled back his hand as their drinks were brought out by the waitress. She'd ordered iced tea. Jaxson had gone with a cola. They both took a sip, letting the silence stretch between them.

Luna tried not to look in the direction of Ike and Gertrude's booth. But when she did, Ike met her gaze with a surprised look of his own as if he wasn't the only one who'd been recognized.

CHAPTER TEN

GERTRUDE DIDN'T THINK she could eat a bite. Why had she agreed to this? She wanted to believe that the FBI wouldn't be raiding the café at any moment. That everything Ike was saying was the truth. Maybe she'd lived a lie for so long that she no longer recognized the truth.

"You can't be serious about wanting to live in Buckhorn," she said, fiddling with the silverware the waitress had brought with their coffees.

"Why not?"

She chuckled and shook her head. "I can't see you here."

He met her gaze. "*I* can see myself here. As long as I'm with you, Gert."

Gertrude warned herself not to get her hopes up that he wasn't just stalling for time before the rest of the troops arrived and took her into custody. "Are you still with the FBI?"

"I retired about four years ago."

She studied him. "You must be going wild with all that time on your hands." Had he been looking for her ever since he left the FBI?

"I keep busy. Believe it or not," he said, leaning toward her, "I took up gardening."

She laughed. "I don't believe it."

He cocked a brow at her. "I did and I love it. You should see the vegetables I've grown." He leaned back to pull out his phone, and the dark mistrustful side of her figured he was sending a message to the armed men waiting for his signal. She watched him thumb through what turned out to be photos until he found one of a cabbage bigger than her head. He thumbed again, coming up with a bunch of perfectly straight, bright orange carrots. "Admit it, you've never seen such beautiful vegetables. Wait until you see the tomatoes I can grow." He put his phone away.

"What do you do with all of these vegetables you grow?"

"Harvest them, can and freeze them."

"You do that? Not your wife?"

He smiled. "I never married, if that's what you're asking. You?"

She shook her head. The waitress brought their meals. She tried to eat, thinking this could be her last meal as a free woman. But then again, she hadn't really been free for most of her life. Her father had warned her about going out on her own. He'd wanted her to stay and run the logging company and sawmill, but she'd wanted more. Now the logging and sawmill operation made a whole lot more than the garage and gas station she'd inherited. She didn't miss the irony in it since her bad decisions had led to this moment.

"Our growing season here isn't half as long as you have down south," she said, still sure he wasn't serious, but part of her wishing with all her heart that he was.

He shrugged, as if seeing that she was having trouble believing any of this. "I never told you, but I was a fairly good art student at one time. I've gotten back into painting. It's just a hobby, but it keeps me busy."

Gertrude didn't know what to believe. She was still in shock at seeing him after all these years. She'd held most of the memories at bay, afraid to let them in for fear they would drown her.

"How did you find me?" she asked.

"I'd flagged your file, hoping you would turn up," Ike said. "There was so much that didn't get said before you disappeared. In case you don't remember, I told you I was in love with you and that I wanted to marry you. You promised to give me an answer that night at dinner." His gaze probed hers and she felt his pain and her own. "I should have known you wouldn't show up."

She had to look away, heart aching. She'd desperately wanted to stay, to marry this man, to make a new life. But she'd known that she would only drag him down. He was career FBI. He'd already jeopardized that just being with her. He should have arrested her after he found her, following the Ralph Conrad bust.

Instead he'd tracked her down only to take her in his arms and teach her about not just lovemaking, but love itself.

"It wouldn't have worked," she said, unable to look at him. "You knew who I was, what I was capable of. It would have cost you your career."

"It was a choice I was willing to make, or I wouldn't have asked you to marry me."

She shook her head. "I couldn't let you do that."

"Well, that's all water under the bridge in less than three days now, isn't it?" he said. "Do you know who that woman is sitting in the corner booth with the young man?"

The question surprised her. She frowned and turned to glance at Luna and the deputy marshal. "I told you. She's the new hairstylist in town. The man is a deputy sheriff."

Ike nodded. "She's also Luna Declan. I remember her because her father was the insurance investigator whose company insured the museum jewelry."

IKE SAW HER shock and sudden fear. "I doubt it's a coincidence that she just happened to open a salon here in Buckhorn now." Gert appeared dumbstruck. He lowered his voice as he leaned toward her. "Add to that, she's here with the law. My car's just down the street. Let's get out of here. The statute of limitations will be up by the time we get to Vegas. I've already returned the brooch..."

She put down her fork and looked at him in surprise. Her gaze went to the door. He saw what she was thinking. She knew him, knew that he was compulsive about being on time. He'd been late because he'd been to her house. He'd found the brooch and her getaway bag. "Are you really offering me a way out?"

He nodded and smiled. "I have a plan."

Gertrude pushed her salad away only partially eaten. He hadn't done much better on his meal, he thought as he, too, pushed it away and looked around for the waitress. He spotted her in the kitchen at the back.

Reaching for his wallet, he said, "Go on out. I'll pay the bill and meet you outside."

She didn't move. He glanced up at her as he tossed more than enough money for their dinner and a healthy tip. He saw it in her face and felt his heart break for her.

"There's no one waiting outside, Gert. I promise."

She nodded and slowly got to her feet. He watched her go to the door, before he rose and walked over to the booth where Luna Declan and the young cop sat.

"Excuse me," he said. "I need to have a moment with Ms. Declan."

The cop started to question what was going on, but Luna stopped him, saying she would only be a minute. She rose and followed Ike far enough from the table that the cop wouldn't be able to hear.

"I know what you're doing here in town," Ike said without preamble. "You'll find what you've come to Buckhorn for." He remembered her as being very sharp when he'd lectured at her class that day.

He knew he was right when she said, "When?"

"When you get back to your shop. Not now. Later. See that your dad gets it. Because this is over."

For a moment, she held his gaze before she looked toward the door that Gertrude had disappeared through. "You're sure about that?"

He nodded, hoping like the devil it was true. Or would be in a matter of days.

With that he turned and walked out while Luna went back to her date. As he left the café, he wasn't even that sure that Gert would be waiting for him.

"WHAT WAS THAT ABOUT?" Jaxson asked as she slid into the booth across from him.

"That's a former FBI agent who lectured in one of my criminology classes back at university," she said, and gave him what she hoped was a reassuring smile. "He just wanted to say hello. Small world, huh?"

"What's he doing in Buckhorn?" the lawman in Jaxson asked.

She shrugged. "I didn't ask. I assume he's just passing through since he's retired." She thought just the opposite. There was one obvious explanation for why he was with Gertrude. He was taking her in, still FBI or not.

But there might be another explanation, she thought. She'd gotten the impression when he'd talked about the heist to her class and she'd brought up the money-laundering bust in Vegas that he knew Irene Southerland rather well. She had suspected there was more to the story.

Wasn't it possible that he'd come to save Gertrude? What a love story that would be, if true. She wondered what would happen now. If what he'd told her was true, she'd find the brooch in her apartment. Her father would be pleased. Wasn't that what she'd hoped for?

She changed the subject, asking about Jaxson. He'd been reserved at first, but she could see him loosening up. As he told her a story about being the youngest in his family of overachievers, she realized that she liked him. She could relate.

"You like your job?" he asked when he'd finished.

Luna thought about what she'd done with Gertrude's hair earlier today and the other cuts and blowouts she'd done. That wasn't her real job though, was it? "I do," she said even as she glanced toward the window. It was too dark to see where Ike and Gertrude had gone, but at least there weren't a half dozen cop cars with flashing lights outside right now.

By now her father would have made the call. The FBI would have Gertrude Durham picked up before the deadline unless they knew that Ike had already done it. She realized that her father had never planned to let her take it any further than that.

Whatever happened now was out of her hands. She'd done her part. She'd proved her theory that Gertrude Durham was Irene Southerland and the getaway driver in the jewelry heist.

"I've enjoyed this," Jaxson said as they finished their meals. "Maybe we could do this again?"

"I would love that," she said, meaning it. But that would mean staying in Buckhorn. Was she really considering making this her life? She smiled, thinking how her mother would have approved.

GERTRUDE STOOD IN the darkness, heart pounding. It was too late to run. Ike had found the brooch, found her bag. It was over. She watched the dark two-lane highway. A set of headlights appeared. She stood frozen, back to the wall of the building next door to the café as a semi shifted down before driving too fast through town.

She jumped when Ike touched her shoulder. "What now?" she asked on a trembling breath. There were still a couple of days before the statute of limitations ran out. She knew the lawman in Ike would see that the brooch was returned, but did that really mean it was over?

He drew her to him. "I thought we'd go to Vegas, just as I said. Feeling lucky?"

Was he serious? Vegas? She'd thought she'd put that city behind her. "Am I lucky?"

He smiled. "I hope so. It will take a while driving there, but I'm hoping by the time we hit the city limits you'll finally give me an answer." She frowned and he laughed. "You never said whether or not you'd marry me."

She looked into his handsome face. Was this really happening? He bent to kiss her. His mouth took hers, the kiss transporting her back as if the years had never happened. She melted into his arms, feeling as if she'd finally come home.

When he drew back, his gaze met hers. "I love you," he said, his voice rough with emotion.

"I love you." No truer words had ever come from her mouth.

He smiled as he put his arm around her shoulders and they walked to his car. They had a long drive ahead of them and a lot of time to catch up on.

If they reached Las Vegas without any trouble, Gert already knew what her answer would be.

LIKE EVERYONE ELSE in Buckhorn, Luna hadn't missed the bust down at the gas station and garage. It was the most excitement anyone had seen for a while with the town brimming with armed-to-the-teeth FBI agents. But by then she knew they weren't going to find anything incriminating.

She'd just come back after driving straight through to Denver to leave her father the present Ike had left in her apartment. Once she reached the house, she put it on his desk, knowing he would find it when he returned from the case he was working on. She didn't leave a note. He'd know where it had come from, but he'd also be able to honestly say that he had no idea how it had gotten on his desk.

Then she'd turned around and driven back to Buckhorn in time to see the town stormed by FBI agents. Jaxson had called. He thought she might want to spend his day off this week horseback riding in the mountains. She'd loved the idea.

She thought about their first kiss. It hadn't happened yet, but she could imagine it nonetheless. She was staying in Buckhorn. Her father might be surprised by that. Or not, especially after he found out about Jaxson.

But the deputy marshal wasn't the only reason she was staying. She'd fallen for Buckhorn and its residents. She figured Gertrude would be back for another cut and color, especially once Luna heard about the Vegas wedding. It seemed Ike and Gertrude were planning to stay in Buckhorn when they returned.

Most everyone just assumed the FBI raid on Durham's Garage and Gas had been a mistake since no one had gotten arrested. With the statute of limitations having run out and the brooch returned, Luna hoped that would be the end of it.

She smiled to herself, realizing that she made a better

beautician than she had an insurance investigator. And she loved happy endings. She was pretty sure she would get one in Buckhorn.

"I TOLD YOU something was wrong," Vi Mullen said when she cornered Earl Ray at the café a few days after the FBI raid.

"Sorry, what was wrong?" he asked innocently.

"You know darned well," she snapped as she slid onto the stool next to him. "The FBI weren't fooled by her. Or are you going to try to tell me different?"

"Well, since they didn't find anything, I'd say you both got it wrong," Earl Ray said and took a bite of his cinnamon roll. Bessie made the best he'd ever tasted. He'd fallen in love with her the first time he'd bitten into one.

"They thought they would find something, so that means there was something to find," Vi said.

"Innocent until proven guilty, I believe is the way it actually goes."

"Ha!" she exclaimed. "You don't think it's odd that this man shows up in town and whisks her away to Las Vegas for a quickie marriage right before the FBI bust down her door and search her place?"

"No, I think it's romantic," Earl Ray said. "Vi, even the FBI makes mistakes."

"Nothing suspicious about him being a former FBI agent either," she said under her breath.

"Let it go, Vi," he said. "By the way, that new beautician in town sure did a great job on Gertrude's hair before she and Ike eloped. Everyone in town is talking about it and the marriage. I was thinking that you might want to visit Luna and see what she can do with yours." He finished by giving her hair a critical eye. "Everyone is saying it knocked twenty years off Gertrude. Might do the same for you."

Vi opened her mouth, but no words came out, a miracle in itself. She shoved to her feet and stood beside him at the counter for a few moments as if wanting to say more, but fortunately didn't before storming out.

Bessie came out of the kitchen chuckling. "She's never going to forgive you for that," she warned her husband.

"Maybe she'll never speak to me again." He grinned at his wife. "This cinnamon roll is the best you've ever made."

"You say that every time," she said, giving him a playful swat on the arm before returning to the kitchen.

Earl Ray watched her go, thinking how lucky he was. Gertrude too. Everyone was saying that she was a changed woman. He liked the idea that people could change. He was also a sucker for a happy ending.

* * * * *